J. R. Ward lives in the South with her incredibly supportive husband and her beloved golden retriever. After graduating from law school, she began working in health care in Boston and spent many years as chief of staff for one of the premier academic medical centres in the nation.

Visit her online:
www.jrward.com
www.facebook.com/JRWardBooks

J.R. Ward lives in the South with her incredibly supportive husband and her beloved golden retriever. After graduating from law school, she began working in health care in Boston and spent many years as chief of staff for one of the premier academic medical centres in the nation.

Visit J. R. Ward online:
www.jrward.com
www.facebook.com/JRWardBooks
@jrward1

By J. R. Ward

The Black Dagger Brotherhood series:

Dark Lover
Lover Eternal
Lover Revealed
Lover Awakened
Lover Unbound
Lover Enshrined
Lover Avenged
Lover Mine
Lover Unleashed
Lover Reborn
Lover at Last
The King
The Shadows
The Beast
The Chosen

The Black Dagger Brotherhood:
An Insider's Guide

Black Dagger Legacy series:

Blood Kiss
Blood Vow

Fallen Angels series:

Covet
Crave
Envy
Rapture
Possession
Immortal

The Bourbon Kings series:

The Bourbon Kings
The Angels' Share
Devil's Cut

Standalone:

An Irresistible Bachelor
An Unforgettable Lady

J.R.WARD

IMMORTAL

PIATKUS

PIATKUS

First published in the United States in 2014 by New American Library,
A Division of Penguin Group (USA) Inc., New York
First published in Great Britain in 2014 by Piatkus
This paperback edition published in 2015 by Piatkus

A CIP catalogue record for this book
is available from the British Library.

ISBN 978-0-7499-5725-4

Printed and bound by CPI Group (UK) Ltd, Croydon, CR0 4YY

Papers used by Piatkus are from well-managed forests
and other responsible sources.

MIX
Paper from
responsible sources
FSC® C104740

Piatkus
An imprint of
Little, Brown Book Group
Carmelite House
50 Victoria Embankment
London EC4Y 0DZ

An Hachette UK Company
www.hachette.co.uk

www.piatkus.co.uk

To Gary Edlin, D.V.M.,
who gave me ten extra, wonderful weeks with someone I loved.
If that isn't an angel, I don't know what is.

⊢———⊣

Acknowledgments

With immense gratitude to the readers of the Fallen Angels! Thank you so very much for all the support and guidance: Steven Axelrod, Kara Welsh, Claire Zion, and Leslie Gelbman. Thank you also to everyone at New American Library—these books are truly a team effort.

With love to Team Waud—you know who you are. This simply could not happen without you.

None of this would be possible without: my loving husband, who is my adviser and caretaker and visionary; my wonderful mother, who has given me so much love I couldn't possibly ever repay her; my family (both those of blood and those by adoption); and my dearest friends.

Oh, and to my WriterAssistant, Naamah. Book number two in the bag!

IMMORTAL

Chapter One

Sometimes a girl just needed a new pair of kicks.

As the demon Devina strode through the Freidmont Hotel's lobby, she was all about the good feels, strutting it large, hinging those hips. In her mind, her thoughts were locked on last-night action. On her body, she wore skintight leather from her double-Ds to her size nines and all the acreage in between. And talk about pheromones—if she put out any more of them, her fuck-me aura would burn holes through the paneled walls.

Eyes followed her. Men's and women's. But why wouldn't they? Caldwell, New York, wasn't that far from NYC, and famous people came up all the time from the Big Apple. Besides, even though they didn't recognize her from movies or TV, she was still a world-class beauty.

At least in this current suit of flesh.

Back to the shoes.

She was heading to the revolving doors, crossing that smooth stretch of shiny, creamy marble, when she saw the stilettos—and stopped dead. Under a Plexiglas case, as if they were jewels, the pair of golden Louboutins was spotlit from above, and oh, the loveliness: The entire skin of each of them was covered in a million micro Swarovski crystals, until their surface looked liquid.

And the style? Razor-thin heels that were high enough to put you *en pointe*. Tiny toe box to show off the cleav. Hidden platforms to provide support on the ball of the foot.

And the capper was, of course, the red sole, the underside of the heels flashing the color of a candied apple.

It was love at first sight.

"Madam, would you like to try these on?"

She didn't even look at the man who'd materialized beside her. OCD was a disease of capture, and its hooks were once again nailing her in the heart. Even though she had nearly a thousand pairs in her wardrobe, the idea that she couldn't have this particular twosome, that someone or something might get in the way of her possessing them and keeping them, made her chest tight, her palms sweaty, and her blood flutter through her veins.

"Madam?"

"Yes," she breathed. "Size nine."

"Come with me."

She followed like a lamb, looking over her shoulder to double-check that the shoes were still where she'd seen them. Worse came to worst, she could always just steal them—

In the back of her mind, a whoaaaaaaaaaaa-Nelly rang out. For the past year, she'd been going to therapy to try to stop these kinds of tailspins.

Calm the fuck down, Devina. It's just a shoe. It's only . . .

It is not going to solve your problems with Jim.

Okay, now she felt like throwing up.

FFS, what was she supposed to say to herself? She tried to remember the combination of words that was supposed to put this out-of-control need into a healthier perspective, but there was a traffic jam in her system of neuro-highways. All she could think of was, Get it, keep it, count it.

Get it, keep it, count it. . . .

Get it, keep it, count it. . . .

Damn it, this was a big step back. Thanks to that fully actual-ized, post-menopausal woman with the PhD on her wall and the couch-cushion body, Devina had been making headway with the compulsions. But this . . . this was old-school, and not in a good way.

And yeah, she knew why this was happening.

It was easier to think about the shoes.

The boutique was in the rear of the lobby, and as she walked through the glass-and-marble entrance, the scented air did noth-ing to ease the burn. The only thing that was going to help was—

"Was that a nine?" the salesman asked.

Devina shot a glare over. Mr. Can't Remmy a Damn Shoe Size had a good suit on and a silk tie, and his salt-and-pepper hair was sculpted back from his Botox'd forehead. Turned out the sophis-ticated fragrance in the place was his cologne, and as he fiddled with his handkerchief, his nails were buffed to a high shine.

He was too put-together to kill. And besides, how would she get her shoes then?

"Nine," she said sharply. "I'm a nine."

"Very good, madam. Would you care for a mimosa?"

No, I want my fucking shoes. "Thank you, no."

"Very good."

Left to her own devices, she paced around the fake Aubusson and checked out the other high-ends you could buy. Judith Leiber minaudières. More shoes, but nothing she was panting to have. Akris jackets. St. John knits. Armani dresses.

Catching sight of herself in one of the many mirrors, she checked out her own ass . . . and thought back to how she'd spent the night.

Her one true love had banged the shit out of her. They'd had about eight hours of epic sex up in her suite, just like she'd wanted.

And the fact that the entire time he'd hated himself for it? Icing on the cake.

Jim Heron was a hell of a lover.

Tragically, that wasn't the only thing he was—and therein lay the problem. He was a cheater. He was a liar. And he didn't understand the concept of monogamy: Even after their incredible night? He'd gone back home to someone else.

And God, the idea that that virgin Sissy was the competition? Now that shit made her want to buy everything in this store. Even the crap that didn't fit her.

As she started to estimate the cost, item by item, she stopped herself and tried to placate her OCD with the reality that she was leading three rounds to two in the war over humanity—so if she won the battle for this current soul? By the rules the Creator had set up, she got everything: Not only did she keep her precious collections and her children down in Hell, but she gained dominion over the earth as well as Heaven above.

For someone hardwired like her, it was a wet dream unparalleled, a winning Powerball lottery ticket with a jackpot in the hundreds of billions.

You wanna talk about shoe collections? She could enslave Manolo, Stuie, Christian—and get them to make nothing but footwear for her for time immemorial.

But even better, she'd get Jim—

"Madam, I am so sorry."

Devina turned around. Mr. Manicure had come out from the back . . . but didn't have a box in his hand. "Excuse me?"

"We have only the size eight. I can order—"

The man cleared his throat. Twice. Then he opened his mouth to try to breathe. Brought his carefully tended hands up to his carefully knotted tie. Went walleyed.

"You were saying?" Devina drawled.

A little clicking sound came out of him as he tried to remain composed while failing to bring air into his lungs.

But damn it, if she killed him, how would she find the shoes in the back?

Devina released the invisible pressure. "Bring me the eights."

The man wheezed and threw a hand out to catch himself on the Leiber display, knocking a couple of the hard sparklies off their posts.

"Now," she barked, flashing her eyes at him.

Cue the shuffling across that rug. And the instant he was behind the silk curtain, the round of coughing and wheezing was like an asthmatic in a greenhouse. But he did emerge with a beige-colored box about two minutes and thirty-nine seconds later. Not that she was counting.

She didn't hear a word he said as he approached, her eyes locked on what was in his hands. There was a temptation to snatch the shit out of his grip, but she wanted to see the shoes on her feet, even if they didn't go with her outfit.

Although, dayum, Swarovski and black leather was classic.

Devina hit the row of three damask-covered chairs and kicked off her black Guccis. "Give them to me now."

The box came to her on command and her hands shook as she popped the top and sighed. The pair of red bags with Louboutin's black signature on them were a sight to behold and her hands shook as she took one out and pulled open the drawstring. Then . . . oh, what a beauty.

The gem-like twinkling was better than those little purses. Better than what she'd seen out in the lobby through the display case. And the color was that of Caucasian flesh.

Jim's flesh.

She closed her eyes reverently and sent up a prayer for the salesman to keep quiet—if he said one thing about her feet being too big, she was going to take his head off, and not verbally.

With care, she un-bagged the other one and lined up both shoes side by side on the floor. Then she released the structure of her feet so that as she slid her tootsies into the works of art, her bones and skin were like water filling a vase, nothing but accommodation.

The salesman seemed a little surprised as she stood up and walked around all comfy-comfy, but he wasn't going to say boo, and how lucky for him. Plus, come on, the Loubous were what, like nearly five grand? And he had to be on commission.

Devina smiled as she stared down at her feet, a flush of giddy relief wiping away all the angst about Jim and the war and that fucking Sissy. All at once she was glowing from the inside out, as if she'd had a rip-roaring orgasm, a hot-fudge sundae, and a deep tissue massage all at once.

These were the most perfect shoes in the entire world, and they were hers and nobody else's, and she was taking them to her wardrobe right now—

That bell in the back of her head rang again, the one that told her when she was backsliding. But screw that.

The stillies were epic, and she couldn't wait for Jim to see her in 'em. Preferably while the rest of her was nakey.

Yup, these she would save for him.

Popping them off her feet, she put them back into the box just as they'd been presented to her and double-checked to make sure the little red bag with the extra heel tips was in there. Then she glanced over at the salesman—who was taking a discreet puff from an inhaler.

"Put them on my tab," she said triumphantly. "I'm in the penthouse."

When your man went home to another, retail therapy was the only way to go.

Chapter Two

Standing over a white-and-blue bowl, Sissy Barten cracked an egg so hard, the shell didn't just shatter but vaporized. "Oh, come *on*."

Turning to the sink, she cranked on the water and cleaned off her hand. Which was shaking. Actually, her whole body was shaking, like her spine was a fault line and everything else was in danger of going the way of that egg.

As she cranked off the faucet, the old mansion got way too quiet, and with a jerk, she looked over her shoulder. Hairs prickled across the back of her neck, warning her of . . . what? There were no footfalls, no screams, nobody with a knife or a gun stalking her.

Great. Guess immortals could lose their minds. And wasn't that a happy future to look forward to.

You couldn't kill yourself if you were already dead.

"Damn it," she whispered.

Drying her hands, she grabbed the bowl and washed the thing out. Then she went back to the carton and . . .

Stalled completely. She didn't want to make scrambled eggs for herself. She didn't want to be stuck in this house. She didn't want to be dead and separated from her family. . . .

And while she was at it? She really, totally, absolutely did *not* want to have that image of Jim Heron half-naked in her head. The sight of him coming out of that bathroom in the wee hours of the night, a towel around his waist, a wasted expression on his face, was like a billboard in front of her brain. She saw every nuance of his body, those huge shoulders, the tight abs, the tops of his hip bones, and that little line of hair beneath his belly button.

Mostly, though, she saw the scratches in his smooth skin. There had been three sets of them, and there was only one thing that could have made—

Abruptly, her shaking got worse, and she tried to do something about it by cracking each one of her knuckles.

Okay, this was ridiculous. You'd think, given her current résumé of being a sacrificial dead-ass virgin resurrected from Hell into a war between a pair of fallen angels and a real, live, honest-to-God demon, that the main thing on her mind would not be some guy. Then again, reality had gone wonky on her weeks ago, so could she really be surprised—

She wheeled around.

No one was there. Again. No one was moving in the house or outside on the scruffy grounds. Adrian, the other fallen angel, had gone up to sleep in the attic where he stayed. And Jim? Jim was on the second floor, doing REM recovery from his night of pneumatic sex.

"Damn it . . ."

Bracing her hands on either side of the bowl, she leaned into her arms. In spite of her rising paranoia, fear wasn't responsible for her case of the paint mixers.

The urge to kill was.

And that was only a liiiiittle hyperbole. Because her half-naked, towel-wrapped savior had gotten those scratches on his body from a woman's fingernails. And his mouth had been swollen not from getting coldcocked in a fight, but because he'd been kissing someone. A lot. And his walk-of-shame expression?

Well, that was on account of his clearly having banged someone for hours instead of doing his job. Which just made her furious. Angels responsible for making sure good prevailed over evil? In a war like this? Generally speaking, keeping their eye on the ball was a better idea than being with some whore for hours.

Or, God, maybe she was a nice woman. Who, like, cooked for him as well as gave him great blow jobs.

The more she thought about it, the angrier she got.

Did he have a girlfriend? Well, obviously . . . although maybe that was naive of her. Did men have girlfriends? College students did—but Jim was faaaaaar from one of those—

She glanced over her shoulder for a third time. But nope, Jim was not coming through the doorway. Nobody was.

Hell, for all she knew, he'd already left to have coffee with his—

"Stop it. Just . . . *stop* it."

As her rage level went up another decibel, it felt like an eternity since she'd been a college student taking her mom's car out to the local Hannaford for some ice cream . . . aeons since she'd been approached there by . . .

She couldn't remember that part. Couldn't re-create exactly what series of events had brought her to her mortal end, but she recalled everything that came after that: the viscous walls of Hell, the tortured damned twisting around her, her own pain turning her ancient.

Jim Heron had ended up down there, too—for a time. And Sissy had seen what the demon did to him. Had watched those shadowy minions do . . . horrible things to his body.

"Shit."

All things considered, she should cut him some slack, right? He was a victim in all this, too, wasn't he? So if, in the midst of this war, the man wanted to get a little grind, lose himself in someone, have a break from the horror and the pressure . . . what business was it of hers?

The guy had gotten her out of Hell, and for that solid, she owed him. But that didn't give her the right to get all hot and bothered about him having gotten all hot and bothered with someone else.

Although granted, there was a lot at stake—if he lost, her own parents, her sister, her friends . . . herself and Jim and Adrian, all would go where she had just been. Now that was too horrific to think about. She had been down there for only a few weeks and it had felt like centuries; she had *aged* centuries. If it was going to be an eternity? She couldn't even fathom the experience.

Refocusing, she decided to have another go at the cracking routine. And what do you know, egg number two split in the wrong place, half of the shell ended up in the bowl, and she had to go back to the sink and wash her hands again.

Turning off the water, she stared out the window. The backyard was downright ugly, the landscaping version of a man who hadn't shaved for a week and didn't have a good beard pattern working for him: Even though spring was gaining a firm toehold in Caldwell, New York, with buds forming on the tips of tree branches and the snow gone even from where it had been piled up high by the plows, a coat of green leaves wasn't going to help back there.

In her previous life, she'd be getting excited for summer— even though all that entailed was her sharing an apartment in Lake George Village and serving ice cream at Martha's for two months. But hello, summer was *awesome*. You got to wear shorts and hang out with your friends from high school, and maybe, just maybe . . . meet someone.

Instead, here, she was. An immortal with no life—

"You making scrambled—"

Sissy spun around so fast, her hip slammed into the counter—and her only thought was, Where was the nearest knife?

Except she wasn't going to need a weapon.

Adrian, Jim's wingman, was standing in the doorway from the hall, and the instant she saw him, she calmed down. The guy, fallen angel, whatever, was well over six feet tall, and in spite of that bad leg of his, he was built big and hard. He was also handsome in the way of a military man, with that strong jaw and the stare that followed everything, although the piercings gave him an anti-authority edge.

As did the fact that he was blind in one eye, the pupil having gone milky white from some kind of injury.

He frowned. "You all right?"

Nope. She was rip-shit pissed and absolutely terrified—both for no good reason. "Yup—I was just going to make breakfast."

Like he hadn't already figured that out?

Adrian limped over to the square table in the center of the kitchen, and when he sat down, his body was like a sack of loose bones, landing in the chair with the grace of Twiddlywinks falling. But that didn't mean he was a lightweight.

"What's going on," he demanded.

Yup. For what she'd learned about him, this was pretty typical: straight shooter, no bullshit.

"You want four eggs?" She turned away from him. "Or three."

"Talk to me." There was another groan and she imagined he'd leaned his heavy arms on the table. Or tried to cross his legs. "You might as well. We're the only ones up."

"I guess Jim had a hard night."

"He told you about the loss?"

"Yes." Way to go, Jim. Fantastic. Hope those orgasms were worth it. "So how many eggs you want."

"Seven."

She glanced at what was left in the carton. "I can offer you four. I broke two and I want two myself."

"Deal."

And Jim could fend for himself. Or go ask his girlfriend to make some breakfast for him—

"Girlfriend?" Adrian asked.

"I didn't say that."

"Yeah, you did."

She threw up her hands and pivoted back to face him. "Look, no wonder Jim is losing. He's too busy with some woman to pay attention to what he's doing."

Adrian just stared at her. "You mind if I ask where this is coming from?"

"Let's just say I caught him coming home at four in the morning."

Adrian cursed under his breath—and didn't go any further than that.

Sissy shook her head. "So you know about his girlfriend, or fuck buddy, or whatever she is. You know what he was doing last night."

"Look, it's complicated."

"That is a Facebook status. Not an excuse for screwing around on your job. Especially given the biblical stakes he's playing for."

On that note, she got cracking, so to speak. And made it through the rest of the carton fine. Poured a splash of milk in. Whisked her little heart out as she got the pan warmed up and the butter melted.

"My mom always told me to wait," she muttered.

"For what?"

Okay, either her mouth needed to stop working or he needed to lose some hearing. Like she was going to talk about sex with the guy?

Then again, it'd just be a short convo, at least on her side.

Sissy shot his big, hard body a glance—and decided the topic would probably not be a quickie on his part. "Till the butter was right. Before you put the eggs in, you know."

Ironically, the whole virginity thing was the reason the demon had taken her, the very thing that had set the wheels in motion and landed her here: just a couple of miles away from her family but separated by a divide so great she might as well have been on another planet.

"Something's burning."

"Shoot!" Sissy lunged for the smoking pan and picked the thing up without a pot holder, burning her palm— "Goddamn it!"

From out of nowhere, that murderous rage made her want to destroy something: The stove. The kitchen. The whole house. Blinded by anger, she wanted to splash gasoline around the base of the wooden mansion and light everything on fire. She wanted to stand so close to the blaze her pores got tight and her eyelashes curled.

And maybe, just maybe, she wanted Jim to have to claw his way out to safety.

Big hands came to rest on her shoulders. "Sissy."

She was so not up for some kind of parental pep talk. "I don't need—"

"Jim is not your problem. Do you hear me?"

With a yank and a shove, she stepped away. "It doesn't bother you that he's distracted?"

Adrian stared down at her, that eye on the right positively opaque. "Oh, it does. Trust me."

"So why don't you do something about it! Talk to him or something—you're close, right? Tell him to stop . . . doing what he's doing. Maybe if he refocused, he'd start winning." When there was no reaction, she cursed. "Don't you care about what happens? Your best friend is up in that attic, dead because of—"

Adrian shoved his face into hers. "Stop right there."

The tone in his voice shut her up.

"You and I?" he said. "We get along. We're cool. But that doesn't mean you get to talk about shit you don't know about. You have problems with Jim? I get that more than you realize. You don't appreciate him getting wound in the head about some chick? Join the fucking club. You're worried about what happens next? Head to the end of a very, *very* long line. But watch your mouth about Eddie, 'cause that was before your time and it's none of your damn business."

For some reason, the fact that he was partially agreeing with her just pissed her off even more. "I gotta get out of here. I just . . . I gotta get some air. Make your own eggs—you can eat my share."

Back in her real life, Sissy had never been much of a stomp-and-slammer. She'd been a good girl, the kind who had besties instead of boyfriends, was always the designated driver, and never, ever made a fuss about anything.

But death had cured her of all that.

She marched over to the door, ripped that thing open like she wanted to tear it off its hinges, and pounded her way outside. As she kick-shut those wood panels behind her, it occurred to her that she didn't have anywhere to go. But that problem was solved as a glint of metal caught her eye.

The Harleys were parked inside the detached ancient garage, and she went for the one she'd used before. The keys were in the ignition—which would have been stupid except for the fact that this was an otherwise good neighborhood, and say what you wanted about Jim and Adrian, they were the kind of men who could get a bike back if it was stolen.

And not by calling the police.

Throwing a leg over the seat, she pumped the engine, tilted the weight so she could free the kickstand . . . and a second later she hit the gas and roared off, screaming down the drive past the old mansion's flank, screeching out into the street and powering off.

With no helmet on her head, the wind roared past her ears and mixed with the engine's din. Her sweatshirt offered little buffer between her skin and the cool morning, and would offer even less protection if she wiped out and hit the pavement.

But she was already dead.

So it wasn't like she had to worry about pneumonia or dermabrasion.

Besides, who the hell cared?

Jim Heron came awake like he was shot out of a cannon, palming his forty, jacking upright, ready to pull the trig.

No targets. Just faded flowered wallpaper, the bed he was lying in, and two piles of laundry on the floor in the corner, one clean, one dirty.

For a split second, time spaghetti'd on him, no longer a function that was linear, but a fucked-up mess where the past twisted around the present. Was he looking for a rogue operative? A soldier who was in the wrong place at the wrong time? An assassin who'd come for him?

Or was this a morning from the second chapter in his life? Where a demon's minions were after him? Maybe Devina, herself?

Or was that bitch assuming another mask where she looked like—

The roar of a Harley engine igniting outside his window snapped his head around. Up on his feet, he went over to the window and parted the thin curtains.

Down below, Sissy Barten was on Eddie's bike, cranking gas into the engine, making that Harley talk. With quick efficiency, she freed up the kickstand and took off, blond hair streaming behind her in the spring sunlight.

His immediate instinct was to go after her, either on one of the other Harleys or by ghosting out and traveling on the wind. And he gave in to the impulse, yanking some jeans on, dragging a Hanes T-shirt over his head. He was shoving his socked feet into his combat boots when he stopped.

And pictured his enemy.

Devina was six feet of brunette sexpot—at least when she slip-covered herself in all that appealing flesh. Underneath the lie? She was a pinup only by *Walking Dead* standards. But in either garb, she had the focus of a laser sight, the smile of a cobra, and the sexual appetite of a frat boy on Molly.

In the last round of this war, he'd spent so much time worrying about Sissy that he'd made the wrong call about which soul was on deck. And lost a crucial win as a result.

He couldn't afford to do that again.

The Creator had set up the conflict with very clear parameters: seven souls, seven shots for Jim to influence someone at a crossroads. If the person in play picked the righteous path? Angels won. If not, score one for Devina. Winner got all the souls of the quick and dead, and dominion over Heaven and Hell. The loser was game-over'd.

Pretty clear, right? Bullshit. In reality, the war wasn't playing out along any neat and tidy rules, and the biggest deviation that screwed him where it hurt was that Devina wasn't supposed to be down on the field. Technically, only he was allowed to interact with the souls—but when your enemy was a liar down to her black and evil core? All bets were off. Throughout the entire game, the demon had totally refused to color within the lines—

easy to do when you had no sense of morality, and "fair play" was not in your vocabulary.

Shit . . . Sissy.

Jim scrubbed his face, and felt like a rope being pulled in two different directions.

As a former black ops soldier for the U.S. government, he was hardly the nurturing type. And yet, from the second he'd found that girl hanging upside down in the demon's tub, her life ended so she could function as ADT for Devina's precious mirror? He'd been strung up on her.

The truth was, she was the reason that he was on the verge of losing this whole goddamn war. He'd traded one of his wins to the demon to get her out of Hell. And then he'd been so distracted trying to make sure Sissy didn't lose her mind in the transition, he'd tanked the last round.

If not for Sissy Barten, he'd be up by two and on the verge of shutting things down in a good way.

Instead, all it was going to take was one more fuck-up and Devina was the HBIC—and the aftermath was going to make any concept of doomsday look like an infomercial for luxury time-shares.

He thought of his dead mother, up in the Manse of Souls, spending the eternity she deserved with the rest of the righteous. He cocked this up? Poof! Sorry, Mom, pack your bags, you're retiring down south. Waaaaay down south.

All because I got my head scrambled by long blond hair and a pair of blue eyes.

And yet he still wanted to go after Sissy. Just to make sure . . .

From out of nowhere, he pictured her sitting up in his bed, nothing but a white T-shirt on, her eyes wide as she stared at him.

Her voice had been soft, but strong. *Just kiss me and I'll go. It's the only thing I'll ever ask of you. . . .*

He'd fought the seduction and then lied to himself as he'd given in, his brain insisting it was only going to be a kiss when his erection had known otherwise. Clear as day, he saw himself leaning into her, her lips parting for him. . . .

And then everything coming to a screeching halt as Sissy's voice had said his name—from outside in the hall. Instantly, Devina had emerged from the lie he'd fallen for, the demon replacing the illusion that was in front of him, her black eyes sparkling, her smile pure evil.

The bitch had been out of there a second later: *Well, you can't blame a girl for trying.*

Talk about your crossroads. He was at one now. Either he went after Sissy again . . . or he got with the program and did his job.

Jim finished tying up his boots and headed for the door. Indecisiveness had never been a problem with him before—any more than plastic explosives would take a moment to introspect before going off. And yet, when he walked into the kitchen and saw his remaining wingman cracking eggs over a bowl at the counter, he had no fucking clue what he was going to do.

Adrian put his palm out to cut any questioning. "No, I don't know where she went."

"It's all right."

Ad's eyes narrowed. "Lemme guess—you're going after her."

Jim felt a pull toward that damn door that was nearly irresistible. The idea that Sissy was out in the world by herself, hurting and confused—it was enough to make his heart go snare drum on him.

Curling his hands into a pair of fists, he turned to the table. Went over. Sat his ass down. "We need to talk."

Adrian looked up to the ceiling as if searching for strength. "You mind if I have breakfast first? I hate hearing bad news on an empty stomach."

Chapter Three

Rage was the octane in her veins as Sissy shot through the streets of suburban Caldwell, jerking the Harley into lefts and rights, blowing through stoplights and intersections, flying past a hospital, some strip malls, a school. . . .

Nothing really registered. Not the SUV she cut off or the delivery truck she nearly crashed into. Not the pedestrians that jumped back or the stray black cat that skipped across her lane.

All she could think about were flames . . . the ones she had started days ago in the mansion's parlor. Red, orange, yellow, licking out of the fireplace, fueled by the dusty sheets she had ripped off the furniture and shoved into the oven she'd created. Heat on her face, singeing her eyebrows and lashes, making her pores sting, echoes of the flickering light spotting up her vision. Hunger in her gut for more, more, more. . . .

Jim had been the one to stop her before things had gotten completely out of control—

In the corner of her eye, a pattern registered, one that was part of the real world, not the stuff in her mind.

It was a fence. A ten-foot-high, glossy black wrought-iron fence.

Beyond which were graves.

The Pine Grove Cemetery.

How had she ended up in this part of town? Then again, if you didn't have a destination, a tank of gas and a machine could take you somewhere. Didn't mean you had to go inside, however.

And she really meant to continue on by the place—it just was not the way the Harley happened to go. The gates were open because it was after eight, and as she zoomed through them, her stomach went on the grind.

The landscape of blocky gray markers, and tombs that looked like banks, and white marble statues of angels and crosses made her think of that tattoo on Jim's back, the one of the Grim Reaper.

And this, naturally, took her right back to the fingernail scratches on his chest.

She was still cursing as she rounded a fat turn, ascended a brief hill . . . and found herself at her own grave site. Hitting the brakes, she was surprised that she'd managed to make it to the right place. The cemetery was a maze of all-the-same and she had been here only once before.

When her remains had been sunk beneath the surface.

Funny, she'd always had a fear of being buried alive, those Edgar Allan Poe–era stories of people scratching at the insides of their coffins scaring the crap out of her. Now? Turned out that hadn't been worth worrying about. She'd have done herself more of a favor not to have made that ice cream run to Hannaford's.

Killing the engine, she dismounted and walked across the asphalt strip. The scratchy spring grass was a bright fresh green, and crocuses and tulips were pushing up to the sun, their pale shoots searching and finding warmth, their flowers about to come out and see the world.

She was careful not to step on them as she made her way over to the grave marker that had her name and dates on it.

The groundskeeping staff had done a pretty crappy job with

the rolls of grass over all that loose dirt, the lengths a little cock-
eyed, one of them trimmed too short.

She pictured her funeral mass at St. Patrick's Cathedral. Her
mother crying. Her sister. Her father. She saw her artwork arranged in the narthex . . . and that groundskeeper who had been
so kind to her . . . and all the people, young and old, who had
come to pay their respects.

Abruptly, it was hard to breathe.

None of them deserved this destiny of hers.

And the longer she stood over her own grave, the more she became convinced that virtue was so overrated. If she hadn't been a
virgin, none of this would have happened. Instead, she'd be gear-
ing up for finals right now and in the studio with her favorite art
teacher, Ms. Douglass. She probably should have just given it up
to Bobby Carne when she'd been a junior in high school. Even
though he'd had octopus arms and a tongue like a dripping
sponge. . . .

From out of nowhere, another image of Jim popped up, this
time from when she'd knocked on his door the morning before
and he'd scrambled to open it. His hair had been a mess and he'd
been half-dressed, nothing but loose sweats hanging off the curves
of those pelvic bones. He'd looked at her . . . in a way he hadn't
before.

If she didn't know better, she'd swear it was the way a man
looked at a woman when he—

"Okay, you need to stop," she said out loud.

God, she really couldn't believe he had a girlfriend in the middle of all this. Or that she cared one way or the other.

What she needed to get focused on was freeing the others who
were like her, those who didn't belong down below, the poor fools
who had been sacrificed and claimed because of their virtue.

On this fine spring morning, she needed to put the crazy anger aside, go back to that house, and sit down with that ancient book Adrian had given her. She had to find a way, a loophole, some wiggle room where she could right the wrong that had ruined her own life as best she could for the others like her . . .

It was hard to say how long she had been standing there when she realized she wasn't alone: Just as the iron fencing had gradually gotten through to her, so too did the presence that was in the shadows under the cedar trees over on the left.

A woman. With long brunette hair and tight black clothes. And she was looking right at Sissy as if waiting to get noticed.

Talk about out of place. She was like some model at a fashion shoot, and as she started to come over, she somehow managed to walk across the grass without her stillies sinking into the earth and tripping her up. In fact, it was as if she were floating . . . ?

Sissy's instincts started to roar, her mind making connections and conclusions that were horrific—this was no stranger, and the female, or whatever she actually was, was definitely not out of place in a cemetery.

Run! an inner voice screamed. *Run—get out of here now!*

Except no. She wasn't turning away; she wasn't giving in. She was standing her ground over the symbol of why she needed to fight.

"So you know who I am," the demon said as she got within earshot.

"You look different. But yes."

The demon stopped on the other side of the grave marker, her black eyes glinting. "You look just the same."

The dry tone indicated that that was not a compliment. Then again, you didn't get to be the biggest source of evil in the world because you were a stand-up gal.

"Annnnnd?" Sissy kicked up her chin. "You have something to say to me?"

"Don't kick a hornet's nest, little girl."

"What are you going to do? Kill me? Been there, done that."

The demon leaned forward, her shadow darkening the top of the smooth granite marker. "As if that's the only thing I can do to you."

Sissy shrugged. "Threats don't scare me. *You* don't scare me."

And this was true even though she was alone in the cemetery with the specter of all evil: Her inner anger was a kind of power in and of its own.

The demon settled back on her high heels and crossed her arms. Then she smiled—which was somehow more dangerous. "Do you want to know how I spent last night?"

"No."

"I don't blame you." The demon flexed her hands, her long, red painted nails flashing in the sunlight. "I think it would upset you."

That image of Jim's scratched chest barged into the front of Sissy's mind like it had been planted there deliberately.

Oh . . . God. No—

"Jim's a fantastic lover." The demon reached up and rubbed the back of her neck, arching as if stiff. "Very aggressive. I don't think he'd be for you, honestly. Not that you have anything to compare it to, of course. It's just, you really need to have a certain . . . stamina . . . to keep up with a man like him."

Sissy could feel the blood leaving her head, the world tilting on its axis, the sky spinning around her. "I don't believe you."

"No? Ask him. And go into it knowing that he's in love with me."

"Bullshit. He's fighting against you."

"You want to know how he got his job? I picked him. Me and that simp archangel Nigel put our heads together and made the choice—and the reason Jim was right by my standards? He's got plenty of me in him, Sissy. He's got evil inside, deep under that surface of his. And that's going to win out over the stuff you're no doubt fantasizing about. At the end of this, however and whenever it finishes, he's going to be with me."

In a flash, Sissy's fury boiled up hard and fast once more, taking over her body, her heart, her soul. And the sight of that sly smile made her positively violent.

The demon's voice got lower, so low it seemed to warp. "That's right, Sissy. You got it right, everything you're thinking, the hatred that you feel. Go with it. Be with it. . . . Jim was calling my name all night long, Devina, Deeeevina . . . and that pisses you off. I can give him things you can't, and that eats you alive. Go with the anger, little girl . . . don't be a pussy like you were in life. In death"—the demon leaned forward again—"be strong."

At that point, Sissy's hearing conked out, and yet even though her ears stopped working, somehow she was still able to hear what the demon was saying as images of bloodshed flickered through her mind—

For a third time, something intruded upon her consciousness. A rhythmic sound, repeating over and over, getting louder.

The demon's head snapped around. "Oh, for fuck's sake."

Sissy glanced over and did a double take. It was Jim's dog, and the scruffy, limping mutt was coming across the grass at a clip, ears pricked, short snout angled up like he was giving a lecture.

The demon took a step back. "Listen to me, girl. Jim is not for you." That smile came back. "I can feel your anger from over here, and it's a beautiful thing. Better than a man you can't have, that's for sure. Breathe in and embrace it—let it take you. Be strong. Let it take you, girl . . . be strong and fight back."

Just like that the demon was gone, no poof of smoke lingering where she'd been, no spark of light extinguishing or anything— there was simply air left in her wake, as if she had never been.

But that wasn't true, was it. Deep in the recesses of Sissy's brain, those words were repeating, the demon's voice like a seed planted in earth that was fertile. *Let it take you, girl . . . be strong.*

Where was the dog? Sissy wondered, looking around.

It was only her, however. Her and her grave site. And that anger.

Jim Heron was sleeping with the enemy. And not as in the old Julia Roberts movie.

That bastard.

———

"I'm sorry, what the fuck did you just say?"

As Adrian's forkful of eggs went back down to his plate and the other angel did some more swearing, Jim lit up a Marlboro and took a nice long drag. "Quitting."

"Lemme get this straight. Devina comes to you and says, 'How 'bout we hang it up.'" Ad jacked forward over the table. "And you fricking took her seriously. Was that before or after she won this round?"

"I'm just telling you what she said."

"So what, the two of you just *no más* it and then what? You think the Creator's not going to have an opinion?"

"Relax. I'm not saying I buy it."

"Good. Because then you'd be a fool as well as an asshole."

"I'll take that as a compliment." Jim exhaled a steady stream of smoke. "And she had another happy little update. She says now that Nigel's gone, I'm due for a promotion."

"Excuse me?"

"That's all I know." Jim leaned back and looked at the ceiling, which had had all kinds of flaking paint about a week ago. Now? It was like it had been sanded, sealed, and rolled out with a fresh coat. "Is it me or is this house, like . . . rejuvenating itself?"

At first he'd assumed things were looking better because they had a woman around and Sissy was cleaning. But in the last two days, the changes that had emerged were structural, not anything explained by one hell of a Swiffer job.

"Wait, wait, promotion like what?"

Jim shrugged. "With Nigel gone, I'm supposed to take his place up there."

He pictured the archangel with his three dandy backups, having a proper English tea up in Heaven. Then tried to imagine himself sitting there, passing scones and the sugar bowl around with his pinkie extended and his legs crossed at the knees.

Yup. Right.

Adrian moved around in his wooden chair, his weight causing the thing to groan. "I didn't know that was in the rules."

"What a fucking surprise." Jim took another drag. "We need to verify the information. Any idea where we can go?"

"Yeah." Ad resumed eating. "And he's dead up in the attic."

There was a period of silence during which Ad became a member of the Clean-plate Club. When he was finished, he pushed himself away from the table, cupped the back of his neck with both hands and sprawled.

"Maybe we should just take a trip to Purgatory."

"Excuse me?" Jim asked.

Ad shrugged. "That shit about not making it into Heaven if you commit suicide is no bullshit. Trust me."

As the guy cleared his throat like he'd gone too far, Jim's wheels got turning. "You're saying Purgatory is real."

"Been there, got the T-shirt. Blah, blah, blah."

"So how'd you get out?"

"Eddie."

Jim sat up straight. "You're telling me Eddie went in there and came back out? With you?"

"Hold up." The guy extended his hands in classic stop-it-right-thur style. "I was just being a smart ass—don't even *think* about that. You're our special golden boy, whatever—and Eddie condemned himself to do it. Besides, no offense, but you're still getting up to speed, this is a clutch round, and we both know how well things go when you're 'distracted.'"

The air quotes would have made Jim violent . . . except for the fact that he had come to the same conclusion, which was why he was here and not going after Sissy. As much as it pained him, he needed to win and he needed to somehow keep his job even with Nigel being dead. If he could prevail, and avoid turning into an archangel, then after the great victory or whatever he'd have an eternity to help Sissy. Now was the crisis time for the war, though.

Besides, the rounds had been coming faster and faster. Forty-eight hours. Maybe seventy-two—and he could refocus on her.

"I've got to go over and bring him back."

"Jim, you're fucking crazy—"

"What's my other option?" Jim narrowed his eyes. "If Devina's right, and I'm supposed to succeed Nigel? I can't let that happen. I don't trust anyone else to do this job—I can win this, Ad. I can goddamn win this."

All he had to do was think back to the way he'd spent the night. Devina had a critical weakness . . . and it was him. She wasn't suggesting they both throw in the towel because she was scared of losing—it was because she didn't want to lose contact with him: Unless he quit, he was apparently going to have to step into Nigel's spats and she didn't want to fight with anyone other than him. Fuck the rules, fuck the archangels, fuck the Creator—Devina was a parasite addicted to acquisition and he was her number one target.

And she was going to take that weakness to her grave.

Because he was going to personally escort her there with it.

Adrian's one functioning pupil roamed around Jim's face, and Jim held himself perfectly still. He was prepared to take any scrutiny, because he knew, down to his soul, what he needed to do . . . and how he was going to do it.

"Ad," he said in a low voice, "I can do this."

The other angel almost hid the tremors that crept into his hands. But the fine tic that teased his bad eye was nothing he could camo. "No, you can't."

"What put you in there, Ad. How'd you get over." Not questions, because he knew the answer. "Devina got into you, didn't she. She got to you somehow, and you couldn't take it—so you ate a bullet. You slit your wrists. You hanged yourself—"

"A cliff." The voice that interrupted was so hoarse, it was made of ninety percent air. "I, ah . . . I had made a deal with her to save someone."

Jim waited for the story to roll out. When it didn't, he said, "What happened."

Ad cleared his throat and covered his face with those shaking hands. "I made an arrangement to save someone and I turned myself over to that demon. I was down on that table of hers for . . . it felt like years. Eddie told me later it was two nights of earth time. When I came back, after she released me, I wasn't the same."

Like bats out of Hell itself, memories of Jim's own time down there swarmed and descended, clouding his brain. He knew exactly what Ad was talking about. He'd been on that table, too.

That was how his path had first crossed Sissy's.

After he'd found her body, that was.

"I thought I was okay." Ad shook his head. "I wasn't. I lasted about a week, made some excuse to Eddie about going somewhere. I was going to shoot myself, but I'm an angel, right? I wanted to die flying. So I jumped and did nothing about it . . . the canyon was about seventy feet deep. I hit hard and that was all it took. Split second later—shit, I thought I'd survived. I woke up in Purgatory—I thought it was gray because of moonlight or some shit."

Finally, Ad dropped his arms. His eyes, both of them, were red ringed from tears he refused to let fall.

"Eddie went there because of me, but he was also the reason we got out. The Creator has a thing for love." Ad stared at his own hands, watching them shake. "I mean, Eddie sacrificed himself for me, and that's love, right? Not the dumb-ass romantic kind . . . but the real shit. So yeah, when Nigel went to the Creator and argued for us—that was what worked. Nigel was able to strike an arrangement that freed us about a month before you came along. If we see you through this war? We're free. It's our penance."

"So you can help me find that archangel and get him back."

"Maybe Devina is talking out of her ass, though. Not like that bitch has a problem lying—"

"So you can help me," he repeated.

Ad shook his head again. "Jim, this is a really bad idea."

"But you can get me there, can't you."

"No, that's on you."

As their eyes met, Jim knew exactly what the guy was talking about. "But you can help me out of there."

"No, I can't. Didn't you listen to me? It's not up to us, buddy." Ad looked up at the ceiling. "Your exit visa can only be issued by the Creator."

Jim could sense the guy retreating—and that couldn't happen. "Listen, this is an extraction. Nothing more, nothing less. You think I haven't done one of these before? I'll go in, get him, bring him out—"

"You don't know what the fuck you're talking about."

"There has to be a way." Jim curled up a fist and banged it on the table, making the plate and fork dance. "Even if Devina is wrong? Heaven is stronger with Nigel back up there. Colin's head is completely fucked with the bastard gone, and right now, Bert and Ernie—"

"That would be Albert and Byron."

"Fine, whatever. Call 'em Mozart and Beethoven for all I care. The two of them are holed up in the Manse of Souls, stuck there, while Colin is disintegrating. And this is not a hypothetical. I went up there after I got home last night. All it's going to take is for Devina to get a hard-on to hit the place, and then we got another set of problems we don't need. Hell, the Creator can't even control her, and she sure as shit doesn't follow the rules. What do you think is gonna happen."

"But what if I can't get you back? Then what? Or haven't you thought it through that far."

"Then you take over."

"Not in the rules."

"Fuck the rules. You'll handle things because that's what men like you and me do."

"On that logic, you could just go up and be Nigel now, and let me take care of the next schlub who fills your shoes. Save the trip to the other side and skip the risk that you're going to get stuck there."

"But I'm the reason Nigel's gone." Jim jabbed his thumb into his own chest. "I did it. It's my fault. If I had done shit different . . . except that doesn't matter anymore. I want to make amends for the death, and the only way to do it is to bring him back. I settle my debts, Ad. You hear me?"

Adrian scrubbed his face. "I don't know. I guess there might be a way to get you out."

"See, I knew this was going to work."

"I did *not* say that."

"Whatever, I'm not a quitter. Even if Devina wasn't a liar, I'm not quitting this. I'm marshaling my weapons and moving forward. First, we get Nigel back. Then we're going to hunt down Devina's lair, we're going to take that mirror of hers, and we're going to win these final two rounds. That is our plan. We are going to execute it."

"What about the next soul?"

Jim opened his mouth to reply—but didn't get that far. The back door to the mansion blew wide open like it had been hit by a gale-force wind.

"You're *fucking* her?!" Sissy spat.

Chapter Four

Sissy was breathing hard even though she'd run only the fifteen feet between where she'd parked the Harley and the back door to the old house. Then again, she'd had to hang onto the bike's handlebars with a death grip on the ride back. It was either that or lose total control.

Or had that already happened, even though she'd made it here in one piece?

"Well?" Like Jim hadn't heard her. "You've got nothing to say?"

Jim reached forward and calmly stamped out his lit cigarette. "Sissy—"

"She had you raped!" As Jim's face went ashen, she slammed the door behind herself, shutting them all in. "Did you think I don't know what she had done to you? We all saw it from the walls! I watched when they . . . hurt you. How do you—" Her voice cracked. "How can you be with her after something like that?"

At that moment, she wanted to weep, but she didn't give in. How could she? This wasn't a safe place for her, even though the two "men" who were at the table, both so silent and still, were supposedly angels.

"Whose side are you really on?" she demanded.

Jim put his palms on the table and braced his arms. As he

stood up, it was clear he had an iron lock on his temper, and for a split second, she felt a flash of fear.

But she'd already faced off with the devil herself. So she wasn't about to be frightened by him.

"Fine, forget about what she did to you—she murdered me!" Sissy barked. "That bitch took my life away from me. She ruined my family's lives. Nothing will be the same and nothing will ever be right—and you're *sleeping* with her?"

Jim's voice was deep and low. "Adrian, you need to leave this room now."

The other angel was up and out of his chair before the sentence was finished. And as he limped out, Sissy was glad for the privacy. Shit was going down, and this did not need an audience.

When they were alone, Jim locked eyes with her. "I didn't want you to see that."

"What they did to you, or the scratches she left on your chest last night?"

"Either."

"Too late."

He closed his lids, but she wasn't sure whether that was because he had serious regrets . . . or because he was trying to figure out what to say.

"I just don't get you." She shook her head. "And maybe that makes me naive—"

"This is war," he cut in.

"And that is just sick!" she yelled back. "You're disgusting!"

With an explosive lunge, he flipped the table over, sending a plate flying, scattering chairs. "Do you think I'll stop at using anything it takes to win! Even if it's myself!"

Sissy took a step back, and hit the counter by the stove. Something about seeing his anger got hers under some control.

After a long moment of standoff, she said grimly, "I don't expect you to enjoy it, how 'bout that. Or are you going to tell me men can get it up even though they're grossed out by someone? Didn't think the anatomy worked like that—then again, I'm a virgin, right. So what do I know."

Jim was breathing hard now, his blue eyes glowing, and not in a good way. But he wasn't going to hurt her—in spite of what he'd just done to that poor table, she knew deep down in her soul he would never, ever hurt her.

At least not physically.

He'd already torn her apart on the inside, however. Although she wasn't sure exactly how he'd gotten the power to do that.

"I hate it," he said raggedly. "But I will use any weapon in this war, even my own body. Are we clear?"

"So now you're a martyr as well as a savior? I don't know, like I said, I think men have to enjoy it, don't they."

"I can't do this with you." He started shaking his head. "I'm not going to do this with you."

"As if it's none of my business? Like the outcome of all this doesn't affect me?"

"No, as in you aren't entitled to this airtime." As she gasped, the anger flushed from his face and he stared at her with no emotion at all. "You're the reason I lost the last round. Not Devina. It was you. I was so goddamn worried about you that I couldn't concentrate—and the results were disastrous on too many levels. So I'm not going to do this with you. I can't. I just . . . fucking can't."

She recoiled. "It was . . . me you were distracted by?"

"It sure as shit wasn't Devina."

Jim cursed his way over to the table and righted the thing like it weighed no more than a dime. Then he picked up the plate, located the fork over by the ancient refrigerator, and took them both over to the sink.

"I've got work to do," he said on his way out.

And that was that.

At least on his side.

Sissy went after him, catching him by the arm before he hit the stairs in the front hall. She had to throw her anchor out big time to get him to turn around.

"I don't need you to worry about me," she gritted out.

"Okay, I won't."

She hid her wince. "And as for you and Devina, that's your business."

"Damn straight it is."

"But I need you to let me help."

"Oh, hell no. There's no place for you in this—"

"I earned the right to fight by dying in her bathtub. By being in her wall. I earned the right to be in this, Jim."

"No fucking way—"

"I have to fight for the others like me." That shut him up enough for her to get a word in. "There are more like me down there. And they deserve to be free just like me. So you either let me help you win this, or I'll go after her on my own. Your choice."

"You don't know what you're saying."

"The hell I don't."

"She can read the book."

At the sound of Adrian's voice, both of them turned to the front door. It was wide-open, and the other angel was parked on the front steps of the house, facing the sunshine.

Like he knew he'd gotten their attention, Ad twisted around. "If you want to get in and out of Purgatory in one piece, we're going to need her. Unless you want to spend the next twenty years on Google Translate—and we don't have that kind of time."

"What book?" Jim demanded.

"The one that might be able to tell you what you need to know."

"Purgatory?" Sissy interrupted. "What the hell are you talking about?"

The archangel Colin sat on the river's shore up in Heaven, staring at the rushing water. In his dirty right hand, a crystal dagger rested against his palm, and in his filthy left, a bottle of gin. He'd gotten both from Nigel's tent across the lawn.

The mess upon his flesh had been from his recent endeavors.

He took a deep swig of the Beefeater and squeezed the hilt of the dagger even tighter. In spite of his being an immortal, his body could function in the manner of a human if he assumed the flesh he was in the now.

And that meant he could feel the liquor taking effect, the exhaustion in his bones . . . and the madness in his mind.

Of all the ends he had considered in this war, him sitting alone and Nigel gone had not been among them.

Back at the time of Creation, the archangels had been brought into being as guardians of Heaven and the Manse of Souls. The five of them had been a deliberate balance of qualities, all fingers aboard a single palm, each with a part to play in the balance of function: Byron, who was the soul; Bertie, who was the heart; Colin, the mind; Lassiter, the body.

And Nigel, the rule-abiding leader of them all.

Lassiter had been the wild card, and he had not lasted. Distracted by physical yearnings, he had gotten into epic trouble and been banished, lost to a destiny and destination of which Colin was only vaguely aware. On the other hand, Bertie and Byron had been steadfast and true since the beginning, and now, in this moment of crisis with Nigel gone, they were behind the walls of the Manse, protecting what needed tending to.

Nigel hadn't lasted, either—and the fact that he had quit was a fall from grace Colin struggled with as much as he did all the rest of this tragedy.

Had there been signs he'd missed? he wondered. Some tip-off that Nigel had reached a turn in the journey he could not navigate?

It was impossible not to blame oneself . . . not to feel as if his own hand had been on that dagger when the silver blood of his beloved had been shed.

More than half of him was gone now. The very best part of him was gone.

And the Creator was not prepared to intervene. God had been the first place Colin had gone in desperation. The second had been Nigel's French marble-topped bombé table with its silver tray of fine liquors upon it.

Colin took another deep draft from the bottle, the razor-sharp taste slicing down the back of his throat and fanning the flames in his gut.

His eyes went to the vicious tip of the dagger. Heaven's ambient light entered the clear blade and refracted off its facets in a rainbow of glorious flashes.

He had wiped the silver blood off in Nigel's tent. God knew, in that silk-strewn palace of an abode, there had been plenty of stray cloth from which to choose.

And then he had stripped a bolt of crêpe de Chine from the wall and wrapped the body up.

Fortifying himself with another pull from the neck of the bottle, he twisted 'round and felt tears come to his eyes.

The funeral pyre was a meter and a half off the ground and constructed of an ancient oak that Colin had chopped down in the woods. A ragged trail had developed between where the tree had been felled and where he'd done the building, the path gouged by his dragging the massive limbs and trunk over. To cleave the wood, he'd used the dagger in his hand and the strength of his upper body, and the nails had been harvested from a shed behind the Manse of Souls, old-fashioned, square-shanked strips of metal that he'd banged into place with a rock.

The pyre was not a work of art, especially not when compared to the fine antiques that Nigel had surrounded himself with. Indeed, the archangel had had a preference for things of beauty, a reason, he had often said, for his attraction to Colin.

This was no fitting end for the archangel. No fitting end a'tall.

Colin sat for a time, drinking and thinking. And then he roused himself and went over to his lover. The silk he'd chosen to wrap Nigel up in was a soft French blue—and he'd picked it mostly because he'd hoped the silvery stains from the blood wouldn't show overmuch.

He'd covered Nigel's face. He simply couldn't look at it, because the features and the coloring were too close to health for comfort. It was too tempting to think that if he just waited long enough, and said some combination of words, his other half would sit up and reply to him.

Folly. And that ridiculous impotent optimism had to be put aside.

First, the disposition of the remains. And then he had work to do.

Colin reached over and tucked a fold of the silk in tighter under the body. The concept of prayer, for an angel, was foreign. For one thing, he could make entreaties directly to the Maker, so sending up wishes or hopes upon the air was not necessary. For another, prayer was typically rooted in helplessness or despair, and historically neither was something he'd ever felt.

Tipping the bottle over the body, he poured the clear liquor Nigel had favored out in a steady stream from head to toe; then he took a long drink, put up his palm, and summoned heat. As he cast the energy forth, the super-charged molecules combusted in a burst of white flame, the silver blood and the gin creating an ignition platform.

He stepped back. Kept drinking.

Smoke the color of snow wafted up as Nigel was cremated, and as Colin watched, he thought that the billowing white waves were a kind of prayer—or at least the closest he would ever get to one.

He ended up on the ground, sitting with his legs crossed. The consumption was taking longer than he had thought, and he would not leave until there was nothing left but ashes.

And then he was going to settle this score with Jim Heron.

With the very dagger Nigel had used upon himself.

Chapter
Five

"We need her. What do you want from me?"

As Adrian waited for Jim to respond, he shifted his weight on his feet, trying to find some distribution of tonnage where his bad leg didn't feel like it was in a meat grinder. No luck.

Jim glared up at the stairs Sissy had just put to use. "I don't want her involved in this."

"Yeah. You've said that." Adrian glanced around at the total absence of chairs and sofas in the front foyer. "No offense, but I gotta take a load off."

Limping across the shallow space, he headed for the parlor over on the left side of the house. When they'd first moved in—how long ago was that? A week? Fifteen years?—the house had been entering the final throes of age-onset molting: Wallpaper had been curling up in the corners of rooms, ceilings had been stained and flaking, old Victorian Orientals had been threadbare and unraveling.

Now? As he entered the sitting room, the velvets on the sofas, the silk of the drapes, the molding around the bookcases and the tops of the varnished tables were all pristine—as if he'd walked into a carefully preserved museum piece of life in the late eighteen hundreds. The same was true of that kitchen they hung out in, the forties-era appliances suddenly working like a collection of brand-new GEs, the Formica gleaming showroom-fresh. Upstairs was the same deal, too, all the lace in the privacy curtains and the girlie bedspreads magically filling their own holes and fixing their frays. Creepy shit—at first he'd assumed it was because someone, not him, was cleaning stuff. But no Dyson job could restitch a rug, repair the hem of a chair, replaster a wall.

There was so much else to worry about, though.

As he breathed in, the lingering stench of smoke sharpened the air, and he looked to the hearth. The charred detritus in and around the burned logs looked like paper, as if someone had tried to burn up an old set of encyclopedias. But nah, it wasn't that. The shit was the remains of all the sheeting that had been draped over the old furniture. Sissy had been the one who dragged everything over to the fireplace and lit the match.

Can you say *Phhhhhu-mp!*

The smoke damage had charred the walls around the hearth, and that forty-by-twenty-foot rug, even though it was doing the Oriental carpet version of Botox with the anti-aging, had been toasted but good in a semi-circle.

They'd probably lost their security deposit, thanks to her.

And hell, maybe Jim had a point. If Sissy was already lighting things up . . . this recon trip Jim was about to head off into wasn't going to help her mellow out.

"And why did you tell her?" Jim demanded from the doorway. "What the fuck is that all about?"

"Tell her about what?"

"About Devina and me."

Ad turned around. "I didn't—"

"Bullshit."

Ad leaned forward even though his hips let out a holler. "Let me make this perfectly clear—I didn't say one goddamn thing about you and Devina. You think I want to make this situation worse than it already is?"

Jim stalked into the room, going all caged-animal as he paced around. "Then how did she know—"

"Here it is."

As Sissy came in with the book, Jim froze and just stared at her—and in the strained silence, the only thing that came to Ad's mind was . . . why the fuck couldn't the bunch of them, at least once, have something go their way. Because the math was looking really bad at the moment: Jim had clearly not said anything about his demon lover. And Ad might be an asshole, but he knew every word that had come out of his own mouth, and he sure as shit hadn't spilled.

There was only one other source of that knowledge.

"Now, are you going to tell me about Purgatory," Sissy said. "Or are you two going to try to get through these stereo instructions on your own?"

Jim let off a fantastic string of curses that did nothing to share any information, but did suggest that inanimate objects were in imminent danger of getting thrown.

When the savior finally went quiet, Ad found himself wanting to rub his face with a piece of sandpaper. 'Cause that would be less painful than all this bullshit.

Clearly, the pulpit was his and no one else's. "Okay, so we have a boss—"

"God," Sissy cut in.

"No. Although the Creator is a huge part of everything." Well, duh on that one. "And Jim's bright idea is to go and bring him back."

"He's dead? I thought we were all immortal."

Hadn't he come in here to sit down? He picked a sofa and sank into it with all the grace of a knapsack falling off a counter. "Our boss is no longer in existence, how about that."

"So there is a way out of here? Like, this life—or whatever it is."

"No." He thought of Eddie, but decided, given Sissy's too-intense expression, he was going to keep quiet on that one. 'Nuff to worry about already. "Our boss is in Purgatory, and that's just a different kind of immortal hell."

"There has to be a way of doing this without her," Jim growled in the corner.

Sissy leveled a stare at the guy that could have blown a hole through a bank safe. "You wanna ask your girlfriend? Maybe she can help."

Jim's eyes burned across the room. But he didn't say anything else, the whole by-the-short-hairs thing shutting him up.

Ad shook his head. Man, now he knew how Eddie had felt back in the beginning when Jim and he had gone at each other.

"That book"—Ad pointed to the damn thing—"does it have anything in there about Purgatory? That's what we need to know. I can't read it—Jim can't, either. Eddie could, but he forgot his reading glasses in Heaven."

Sissy came over and sat down on the opposite couch, putting the ancient tome on the short-legged coffee table. The book creaked as she opened it, and a subtle glow seemed to be released by the parchment pages, like it was its own reading light.

Okay, that was one book that was never making it onto the *New York Times* list. There was one and only one copy, and it was not supposed to be in the hands of the angels. Made from the skin of sinners, its "ink" supposedly came from the ejaculate of Devina's minions. Who knew who had composed it. The thing was pure evil, inside and out.

If Devina knew they had the thing? Big fun.

"There's no table of contents," Sissy muttered as she idly flipped through. The writing was so dense, it was as if each page had been brushstroked in black, and it made his head hurt just trying to focus that tight. "And there's no internal organization, either. I've spent hours going through it . . . and I'm not sure how helpful it's going to be about anything."

"Frankly, I'm impressed you can read even a word of it," Ad muttered.

"Well, I took Latin in high school."

"Is that what it is?"

"Or a derivative of it. The good news is, the longer I stick with it, the easier the going gets." Sissy looked over at Jim. "So tell me what you want to do, and I'll see if I can find something on it."

Jim stopped by one of the floor-to-ceiling windows and stared outside. With the morning sun hitting his face, he looked worn-out, instead of refreshed. And that did not bode well for them.

Ad cleared his throat. "I got out only because I was freed by the Creator—thanks to Nigel going to Him."

"You mean Purgatory?" Sissy asked.

"Yeah."

"Holy . . . wait, you've *been* there?" Sissy shook her head. "Boy, all these things I thought were made up . . . I should have listened more in Sunday school, huh."

"Like I said, I was freed at the Creator's will, and I don't know of anyone who's gone there and gotten out on their own." Ad shifted his eyes to the savior. "I will say this—you won't have a lot of time, Jim. Once you're over there, you start to get into trouble almost immediately. The true wearing down takes a while, but you begin to lose yourself directly upon entry. By the time Eddie came in, I was nearly a goner. And I later found out I had been there only a short time."

"Hell was like that for me," Sissy said quietly. "It was . . . forever."

Jim's eyebrow began to twitch and he brushed at the thing.

"So you're going there to bring this guy back—why?" she asked.

"I don't have a choice," Jim muttered as he patted his pockets. Taking out a pack of Marlboros, he lit up. "Either we get Nigel back or I end up taking his place—and after all this shit? I want to be the one who takes down Devina. Plus it's the right thing to do."

"Why do you say that?"

"I killed him. Not directly, but his death is my fault, and even though I'm a professional soldier, it's one I can't live with."

Sissy stared at the man for the longest time. Then she ducked her head into the book and went back to the first page. "Anyone got a pad of paper around here—and a pen?"

Hours later, as Sissy flipped through the pages of the ancient book, she was relieved to find that the words scribbled on the thick parchment were as easy to read as something between the covers of a Nancy Drew. What was not so hot was that, even with the increase in comprehension, she wasn't finding anything on Purgatory.

Most of the passages seemed to be the ramblings of a twisted mind, the commentary loosely integrated and focusing on the nature and composition of souls, the origins of physical life, the layout of Heaven, the balance between sin and virtue.

And the statistics were just plain weird. Why would anyone care to number the stones of some castle up in the sky? The Manse of Souls, it was called?

So, yeah, the pad of yellow paper remained blank beside the book, the blue Bic pen unused. But still, all the getting-nowhere was kind of useful: She hadn't thought of lighting anything on fire for however long she'd had her nose in the book.

Letting out a groan, she stretched her back and eyed the fire-place. When a soft snore percolated up next to her, she glanced at Ad. He was out like a light, his head back on the cushions of the velvet sofa, his bad leg extended at a strange angle with its boot kicked to the side—as if the bones of his calf had healed to-gether wrong.

Jim had left about ten minutes ago, stomping out and taking the black cloud over his head with him.

Sissy pushed the book away, got to her feet, and cracked her right shoulder. Then she walked out of the parlor, intending to go to the kitchen and grab a quick bite—but her plan changed as she caught a flash of red through the windows on either side of the front door.

"What the . . ." In fact, there was a red glow . . . emanating through seemingly every piece of glass around the house.

Rushing for the door, she yanked the heavy panels open.

It was as if someone had dropped an ink bomb on the prop-erty—only it had frozen in place on the free fall, forming a blan-ket around everything: On the far side of the transparent curtain of red, she could see the ugly lawn, the noontime sun, the side-walk and the street . . . as well as Jim standing off to the left, his palm raised and glowing even brighter, as if it were the source of the illumination.

"Jim?" she said.

His head lifted and his eyes opened. After a moment, he dropped his arm and came through the stain in the air, stepping right past the barrier he'd created.

"What is this?" she asked in wonder.

"More protection."

"From what." But like she really needed to ask that?

"Devina. She's already gotten in here at least once."

A chill went through her. "When?"

"The other night."

As he walked up onto the front porch, she put her hand on his arm. "In the house? How?"

Jim pointedly moved himself out of range and laughed with a bitter edge. "She turned herself into you. How 'bout that."

"What?"

"You heard me. She was you, everything from your hair to your eyes to your . . ." His blue stare went to her mouth and stayed put until he seemed to shake himself out of something. Then he leaned in, his heft dwarfing her, his tired eyes nonetheless sharp as knives. "Look, when I say I don't want you in the middle of all this, it's for a good goddamn reason, okay? I don't want to lose you again—and I sure as shit don't want to be thrown off my game by worrying about you."

Sissy frowned, thinking back to—

"When I came and knocked on your door," she said, thoroughly creeped out. "And you were shocked to see me. That's when she did it. Didn't she. That's when she became me."

He turned away and started walking back into the house.

She grabbed his arm again. "What did she do?"

In the tense silence that followed, she remembered when he'd opened up that door of his. He'd looked at her strangely, as if he'd never seen her before. And he was doing the same thing now.

Sissy refused to back down. "What did she—"

"You want to know? Fine." He leaned in again, the air between them growing charged. "She tried to seduce me. She was half-naked in my bed, with your body, your skin, your scent. And it almost fucking worked—how about that."

Sissy blinked as her body registered heat—but not from anger. No, this was something else entirely.

Sexual desire. The kind she'd read about, heard about, seen on the big screen, but never, ever felt. Not even close. And she knew damn well what he was doing here—he was trying to scare her off. Except what he failed to realize was . . . that was a hell of an admission on his part.

She thought back to Bobby Carne and his Bud-in-a-can-fueled come-on. Jim was the farthest thing from that sad production—he was a man, not some high school senior with delusions of being Ryan Reynolds. And the idea that Jim might have been attracted to her, even if it was a lie . . .

Then again, the demon had been driving that bus, so to speak.

Jim broke the eye contact first. "Don't look at me like that."

"Like what," she said in a husky voice.

"Oh, Jesus," he muttered. "You don't even know."

"Jim—"

"No, nope, I gotta go. . . . I really fucking gotta go."

With heavy feet, he stalked through the open door and marched up the stairs, his big body moving fast and with power. A moment after he was out of view, she heard a door slam on the second floor.

There was a temptation to follow him up there. Open that door. Find out . . . what was on the far side of that heat in his eyes. But she had a feeling all she was going to get was a fight.

Or maybe something she wasn't sure she could handle.

She thought of that demon in the cemetery, so sure of herself, so confident. Now, *that* was a woman—entity, whatever—who'd take care of a man like Jim . . .

Great, now she felt like finding a Zippo lighter and putting it to good use.

Instead of taking off after the guy, or going Stephen King and giving in to her inner Firestarter, she went over to the protection spell and put her hand out. As if the glow was a living thing, it came forward to her palm, stretching out to lick at her, and staying connected until she pulled her arm way back.

After playing with the connection for a little bit, she went back inside and closed that reinforced front door. Under normal circumstances, she would have been impressed by the size and heft of all that oak—but nothing was normal anymore, and she had a feeling she could trust whatever Jim had done out there in the yard more than anything built by a human.

Pausing at the bottom of the stairs, she wondered what he was doing in that bedroom of his. The only way she was going to get an answer was by finding out for herself—and how embarrassing would it be to barge in on him changing his clothes . . . making his bed . . . folding his laundry.

Yeah, 'cause he had time to worry about those last two.

Besides, like they'd do anything other than rehash the convo they'd just had?

As she stayed where she was, an inner part of her pointed out that there were, in fact, other things they could do—things that were tied to that light in his eye. Hell, maybe it was time to lose her virginity. And assuming that was true . . . she could not think of a single man, living or dead, who she'd rather give it to than Jim.

"Shit," she whispered.

Chapter Six

Jim was hard as he shut himself in his room.

And not as in hard-headed. Hard of hearing. Hard backed.

Slamming the door, he leaned back against the damn thing. *Bam . . . bam . . . bam . . .* The sound of his head hitting the wood was like the heartbeat in his cock.

As he looked down at his hips and measured the tent his erection had made in his sweatpants, he thought, Man, this was too fucking true about him. Back in his old life, when he'd been deep into black ops and working as an assassin overseas, this would happen to him. Keyed-up, going into crunch time, his blood would be running high, his aggression spiked—and he'd inevitably need to burn some of the energy off.

And not on a treadmill.

But FFS, you'd think with the way he'd spent the night with Devina, this wouldn't be a problem.

Shutting his eyes, he cursed as another round of images assaulted him, pictures of him fucking that demon twelve different ways to Sunday all but blinding him. And then he saw Sissy . . . standing on that porch . . . staring up at him like . . .

Like maybe she knew he wanted her.

The very male-est part of him was totally prepared to test that theory out on the horizontal. Yeah . . . in spite of the fact that he needed to stay the fuck away from her, his conscience and his higher reasoning were more than ready to take a quick vacay just so his small head could get the job done.

Great. Good thinking, right there.

Abruptly, he remembered that picture he'd seen of her at her parents' house, the one where she'd been on the sidelines of some game, her eyes narrowed, her body curled and tensed like she'd wanted to spring forward into the action. Her long blond hair had been pulled back, her face had been clear of makeup, and the other people in the background had been student athletes just like her.

She'd looked her age there.

Downstairs on that porch? That had been a woman. Not a girl.

Frankly, he wished the grown-up divide hadn't been crossed— because retaining it would have been enough to keep him in check. He'd always been into full-on women; he liked sex hard and raw, and that required someone with backbone and passion. Some little chippie with strawberry lip gloss and Hello, Kitty sneakers really, totally wasn't going to fucking do it for him.

He would really have preferred Sissy stay on that side of the line. Trouble was, courtesy of her trip into Hell, her eyes were now devoid of any semblance of youth, her soul having aged in Devina's wall, tempered into steel by the torture and the pain. She was no longer that field hockey player with her friends, hyped up on a game played on high school grounds.

She was a woman.

And this was a problem.

Damn it, he'd had such good intentions. Ever since he'd found her bled out in that bathroom, his only goal had been to get her safe—and he'd checked that off his bucket list by making that po-tentially devastating bargain with Devina. Except what exactly had it gotten Sissy? Out of the demon's wall, sure. But now, all she had was a job combing through an impossible book, looking for a way to get him to and from Purgatory.

Meanwhile, he was upstairs with an issue that, all things considered, he was going to have to cure with his left hand.

"Goddamn it," he breathed.

Shifting his eyes over to the messy bed, he remembered Devina lying on it, clothing herself in Sissy's flesh, hitting him up for sex. That had been his fault. He should have put up multiple protection spells back when they'd moved in.

Then again, if the demon had been able to make it through one, maybe the whole more-is-better thing wouldn't have worked, either.

Shit, how had she pulled that infiltration off? he wondered.

Sliding down until his ass met the floor, Jim propped his elbows on his knees and thought about the many and varied ways a guy could get himself into trouble when he thought with his little head instead of his big one.

And what do you know, the stretch of the sweatpants across his hard-on made him roll his hips—and not because the shit hurt.

I guess I don't expect you to enjoy it, how 'bout that. Or are you going to tell me men can get it up even though they're disgusted by someone? Didn't think the anatomy worked like that—then again, I'm a virgin, right. So what do I know.

"Fuck me . . ."

And that was the problem, wasn't it. Sissy was right: Men couldn't get it up if they weren't into the sex. Unfortunately for him, he didn't necessarily have to like what was happening to get aroused—it was kind of like stabbing your enemy. You were juiced going into the deed, and satisfied when it was over. But that wasn't the same as "enjoying" something.

Somehow, he doubted these subtleties were the kind of thing

Sissy needed to hear about. And he was equally certain that his cock didn't give two shits about them.

It knew what it wanted.

He shifted around again, that rasp across his dumb-handle making him grit his teeth and hiss. And for a split second, he couldn't help but go back to that moment when Sissy had been begging him to kiss her—

All it took to reel shit back in was remembering that it hadn't actually been her.

Annnnd all it took to crank things up again was remembering how she had looked at him down on that front porch.

Another hip roll to relieve pressure just ramped him even more. And before he knew it, instead of heading downstairs and seeing what he could do to help with that forty-pound book, his palm was in fact getting into the swing of things.

Or the stroke, as it were.

What the hell else could he do? The damn erection showed no interest in deflating—and even if he did a tuck-up, he had Jon Hamm proportions, so it wasn't like that was a good enough camo job.

He deliberately kept any thoughts of Sissy out of it. Instead, he concentrated on his tight grip going up and down, and the squeeze on the head, and the twist going around the shaft. He had to drop his knees to get room to work, and as the waistband cut into his ass, he ripped off the damn pants. Pretty quickly, a savage edge took over. Biting down on his lower lip until he drew blood, he let his anger out along with his lust, his hatred of Devina driving him higher, hotter.

It was a sick thing to dwell on, but safer and more gentlemanly than what he felt for Sissy.

The orgasm hit like a lightning strike, stopping his heart, freezing his hand, jerking his legs. Then came the thunder—rolling though his mind, his body, his soul . . . and all he saw was

Sissy, turning in slow motion to face him, her eyes staring up at him with a woman's speculation.

As the release kicked out of his body, he milked it only because he wanted the sex out of him . . . so he could concentrate, get back to work, do the right thing.

In the wake of the orgasm, exhaustion dogged him, pulling at the corners of his eyes, drooping his shoulders. It had been so long since he had slept well.

Nearly three decades, as a matter of fact.

Not since his momma had died.

And as he snagged hold of those sweatpants and used them to wipe up, he thought any true rest was going to be a long, long time coming.

For now, though, maybe he'd just shut his eyes and let the post-climax floats recharge his batteries a little. He didn't have tons of time at his disposal, but then again, he never crashed for long, either.

The last thing he thought of as he drifted off while still propped against the door wasn't a thing at all.

It was the woman downstairs who was searching through that book. He wasn't sure whether he hoped she found anything . . . or not.

Maybe Ad was right and he shouldn't tempt the Fates by giving Purgatory a try.

But as always, he was in between a rock and a hard place.

The shadows were growing long out on the lawn when Sissy got to the last page of the book from Hell. Putting her hands on the small of her back, she stretched for the one hundredth time and looked over at Adrian. The angel had shifted positions around three in the afternoon and now he was lying length-wise on the sofa, one of the velvet accent pillows stuffed under his head. He hadn't moved since then, except for crossing and uncrossing his feet. She knew he wasn't sleeping, though.

Where was Jim? she wondered.

"Upstairs," Ad answered like she'd spoken out loud. "You want me to get him for you?"

She closed the book and stared down at the pitted, stained cover. "I don't know."

A split second later, she heard footfalls coming down the stairs, hitting the front foyer, zeroing in on the parlor.

"Is that your doing?" she asked softly.

"Walkie-talkies are so damn cumbersome. Fuckers require batteries, too."

"Nice trick," she said, straightening her shirt, pushing her hair back.

Right before Jim came into the room, she wondered what she looked like, and wished she had a hairbrush, a mirror . . . maybe some toothpaste.

Dumb, dumb, dumb, she thought. One, there was no competing with the likes of that demon. And two, like she wanted Devina's leftovers?

Jim entered the parlor in blue jeans and a white T-shirt that pulled across his pecs and stretched around the heft of his biceps. His face was remote, and his eyes did not meet hers, but his sheer presence sure got through to her. He was, as always, magnetic, the kind of man anybody would look over at. Was it the height? That build? The perma-frown? That beautiful, shimmering halo around his dark blond head . . .

Okay, fine. Maybe she did want to compete with the damn demon.

Even though that made no sense, and was self-destructive in the extreme.

"I didn't find anything," she announced. "Not one thing."

Unbelievable, really. Considering the tome had how many words in it? Two trillion?

Jim frowned even more deeply. "You're kidding me."

"Nope." She wasn't sure what she had read, actually. The writing had a funny way of going in one eye and out the other. But she was very clear that there had been nothing about Purgatory.

"Are you sure you're reading it right?"

Sissy turned the book around and pushed it across the coffee table to him. "Give it a try yourself."

"I don't know Latin."

"Guess you're out of luck."

"Goddamn it."

"Well, what do you want me to say? It's not in there. I mean, the place exists, because you two tell me it does—so maybe, I don't know, is it possible there's another name for it? Or is there another source of information we can use? Like, have you got an Internet for the afterlife?"

They both looked at Adrian, who was sitting up and rubbing at his dark hair until the stuff stood up like he'd licked a light socket. "Not that I know of." The angel shook his head. "You know, maybe this is something we need to back off from. I've been thinking about it all afternoon, Jim. If by some miracle you manage to get yourself over there, I'm really not sure we can get you back in one piece—even without Nigel. And before you ask, no, I don't think the Creator's gonna be all about helping your ass, especially 'cause you're doing this to get around one of His rules."

Jim cursed. "No, we're going to find a way. I'm not giving up—"

The attack came out of nowhere. One second Jim was standing just inside the room, looking pissed off. The next, a bare-chested man was rushing at him from behind, flashing through the doorway soundlessly, some kind of glinting weapon over his head.

Sissy screamed and pointed—and that was what got Jim ripping around just before he got stabbed in the back. His response was instantaneous, his body bracing against the onslaught, his hands latching onto that raised arm and twisting the blade out of range. But he couldn't throw off the aggressor, the other man as powerful as he was.

It was Colin, the guy from Jim's hospital visit, she realized. The dark-haired one—

Bang! They slammed into the mantel. *Crash!* They knocked over a side table and shattered a lamp. *Screech!* Their combined, thrashing weight pushed one of the sofas off the rug and onto the bare floor. And as the two of them twirled in a deadly waltz, Adrian jumped up, drawing a knife she hadn't been aware of being on him.

But the angel didn't get far.

With a quick surge, the attacker extended his free hand and sent a blast of white light at Ad, blowing him off his feet with such force, the couch he landed on shot across the room and splintered into the wall.

With the angel slumping down to the floor, Jim and the aggressor ping-ponged around the parlor, ricocheting off the walls as they fought for control of that crystal weapon—and Sissy was not about to sit around and wait to see who got tired first. Lunging out of their way, she looked around for something, anything, to help fight Colin off.

She grabbed the first thing she came to, a brass candlestick that weighed as much as a crowbar. The beeswax wick stick went airborne as she picked the thing up, lifted it over her head, and ran across—

Talk about tap dancing. The two men were spinning around with such force, she had to track them, waiting for the one without the shirt to come into range—and not move out of the way before she could nail him. If she guessed wrong? She was going to knock Jim out.

Bingo. Just as Colin came around, she planted her feet, and with every ounce of strength she had, she brought the metal mass across the back of his dark head.

Light exploded everywhere, blinding her and throwing her back just like Adrian—except her trajectory was going to take her right into one of the double-hung windows. With a messy trip-and-fall, she managed to redirect herself off that course—but even as she was cushioned by a swath of heavy velvet draping, the impact stopped her heart and drove the breath out of her lungs.

She didn't lose consciousness, though—so as she went into her own slump, she got to watch the man with the crystal knife lose his footing and go into a stumble of his own, the injury to his head knocking him waaaaay off his game. It was all Jim needed. With a vicious yank, he tore the dagger out of the other man's hand and kicked that hard torso, separating the two with force.

Later, Sissy would endlessly replay the sequence of what happened next, running the reel backward and forward as if there were some other outcome lurking in between the nanoseconds, some other path that could be chosen if only she could find the way to make a splice and insert new film.

But of course, that was a no-go.

As Colin hit the floor, the man looked up at Jim with pure hatred in his red-rimmed eyes. "You killed him!"

"What the fuck—"

"Your hand was on that dagger!"

"—is wrong with you!"

The two of them went back and forth at a scream, their male

voices thundering throughout the house, Jim's accent American, the other man's British.

"I lost him because of you!"

"I know!" Jim yelled.

That shut Colin up. And the man stayed quiet as Jim continued to roar, "And I'm going to get him back!"

A nasty laugh cracked like a whip. "Oh, you are, mate? Precisely how do you intend to do that."

Jim looked across at her. Glanced at Adrian. "You're going to have to help me out. Somehow—"

Ad threw out his arms as if trying to stop a car crash. "Jim! No, don't—"

Jim stared back at Sissy. Opened his mouth like he was going to say something . . . but instead of speaking, he turned the crystal dagger on himself, pointing the sharp tip at his stomach and extending his arms as far away from himself as they could get.

"No!" Sissy screamed as she jumped up.

At the last second, he changed his mind. But not to stop. Instead, he changed angles, dropping his left arm, bringing up the right . . .

. . . and with a vicious slash, sliced his own throat open.

"Nooooooooooo!" Sissy lunged across the carpet as the knife fell in slow motion from his lax hand.

Jim fell, too, as blood poured out of his neck—at least, she assumed it was blood, as it was silver, not red.

Oh, God, it had to be blood soaking the front of that plain white T-shirt he wore.

The sound of his knees hitting the floor was like a clap of thunder, and she reached him just as he sat back on his heels. His mouth was open, gaping, clicking as he tried to breathe through the geyser.

"Jim! *Jim!*" She reached up to press her hands to the self-created wound, but what a waste of time. Even if she'd had yards and yards of surgical gauze, there was no stemming this.

No saving him.

His blue stare locked on hers as he began to list to the side, his massive torso giving in to gravity, his immortal life slipping away right before her very eyes.

Tears speared into her vision as a frantic *not now! not ever!* clogged up her brain: As much as she had been livid at him this morning, she was now terrified of the thought that she had lost him forever.

A chance not taken.

A door unopened.

A destiny unrealized.

And that loss felt worse than everything that had happened to her. Even Hell itself.

"Don't leave me, just stay with me, don't leave me. . . ."

His mouth kept moving, and she realized he wasn't trying to breathe—he was trying to say something to her.

"What?" she croaked. "What are you . . ."

Those lips, stained with silver, moved more and more slowly, the pupils in those eyes expanding as if they were trying to compensate for a lack of light.

Sissy knew the instant he died. It wasn't when his mouth stopped or when the eyes rolled back. It was when the scent of a bouquet of flowers filled the air, choking the inside of her nose and thickening the back of her throat.

It was just as they had told her in Sunday school when she'd been young: When a saint died, you smelled flowers.

Jim . . . the savior . . . was gone.

Chapter Seven

Collections were a good thing.

Of course, hers was probably a little out of control, Devina thought as she stepped free of her office building's elevator.

And how fucking great was that.

Stretching out before her, in a basement that was nearly the size of a football field, rows and rows of antique bureaus filled with a millennium of taking souls were hidden and safe. It was the kind of sight that made her take a deep breath for two reasons: one, they were still where she'd left them; and two, they were hers, all hers.

Her high heels made a clipping noise as she strode over the bare concrete floor. From time to time she paused, put her little bag with the box of new Loubous in it down, and pulled out a drawer. Whether it was a cluster of pocket watches with their gold chains, or a tangle of nineteenth-century spectacles, or a jangle of keys, every single object was cataloged in her mind—she could remember who had owned it, how she'd gotten it from them, and the exact circumstance when she had taken over their soul and put them into her wall. But this wasn't just a happy trip down memory lane. Anytime she touched a metal button or an earring or a keepsake coin, she could feel the person's very essence.

These inanimates were her connection with her children down below, her way of communing with her captives, her tangible tie to her immortal life's work. Millions of objects—and yet, it so wasn't enough. Her hunger was a worm that never stopped turning, and didn't that make the war so much more real to her.

Shit, to think of the fun she and Jim could have.

He could also help her protect all this. Anytime she went away, there was always an undercurrent of fear that something would happen, that she'd get in that elevator, hit the *down* button, and find those doors opening a moment later to a whole lot of nothing. And this was even though she had the best security system in the world: At the moment, it was thanks to a twenty-two-year-old computer programmer from Neuvo-Tec, a company she had "hired" to come here to her "human resources firm" to configure "banks of servers" to properly support her "intranet."

Or some shit.

In reality, she'd created all that fiction just to get the poor virginal sonofabitch and his pathetic pocket protector on her premises. Whereupon she'd metaphorically knocked his socks off with a gold Prada pantsuit and a mile-high pair of Manolos—and then literally knocked his block off by coming at him from behind and overpowering him as he'd checked out the illusion of a computer system. After that, there had been the bloodletting, the ritual, the symbols in the flesh . . . and way-to-go, she had her early-warning system.

If anyone came in on that first floor above, or tried to get into the elevators? Wherever she was, up here on earth or down there in her Well of Souls, she'd know about it.

And she could protect her precious possessions.

Man, it'd be really fucking nice to have a partner in all this. Yeah, sure, her minions were fine when she felt like ordering something around, but they couldn't think for themselves, and

that got boring quick. Jim Heron was the opposite of compliant—
she fought constantly with him, and that was just the hot sauce
she was looking for.

Resuming her promenade, she headed for the back to her bed-
room-ish area. Above her, banks of fluorescent lights glowed like
fake suns, and soon enough, her rolling stands of hangered clothes
overtook the lineup of bureaus. Past her showroom of a wardrobe
came her shoes in their floor-to-ceiling cases; her accessory area,
where she kept her handbags, scarves, and jewelry; and finally her
makeup table, with its mirrors and all her Chanel compacts, YSL
liners, and Estée Lauder foundations.

And then there was her bed, of course. Oh, her bed, with its
acres of Porthault and its down comforters and pillows. She'd actually never had sex in the thing before, but how cool was it going
to be when she broke the mattress in with Jim?

A sudden image of Sissy Barten made her clench her teeth.

Goddamn it, if it was the last thing she did, Jim was going to
lie in that bed with his legs spread and his cock hard and ready,
and he was going to tell her he loved her and beg her to have sex
with him. And when they did get it on? It was going to be total
hotness, because she'd know that she had won and he was with
her forevermore.

That was just the way it had to be.

"Right?" she said to her new shoes.

The good news was that the prospect of putting the twin sparklies in with the rest of her collection was a great de-stresser—
except she had to check one more thing first.

Of all her objects . . . it was the nastiest-looking. Also the
most valuable—in spite of the amount of pilfered jewelry she had
down here.

Her real mirror was in the far corner of the basement. And it
was tucked away in the darkness not just to keep it safe, but be-

cause it was fugly and a half: The thing was at least five feet high and three feet wide—maybe it was even bigger. There was scroll-work around all four sides, and from a distance you might have assumed it was a flowery motif or some kind of French fanciness. Up close, though, it was clear that the undulating pattern was a series of tortured bodies, their limbs mangled or missing, their faces distorted in pain. And fuck the gold leaf—there was a glim-mer to the thing, but it was not from any precious metal.

It was like the glow of a cobra's eyes.

As for the surface of it, the flat plane was pockmarked, pitted, and spotty, more like the skin of an old person than anything re-flective. Then again, she didn't use it to see herself. The mirror was a portal, the conduit for her to travel back and forth from her Well of Souls—and the only way she could get there. Once down in her lair, she could welcome new souls or minions or Jim and Adrian, but she had to be in Hell to do that; otherwise the place was locked up, even to her.

If she lost or broke the mirror? Then *poof!* went the access to her collection of souls.

The horror was too much to think about—

At first she didn't know what got her attention. Twisting around, she searched her private space, eyes narrowing, claws pre-pared to come out. But there was nothing behind her, and no warning from up above that someone had crossed the barrier she'd created.

Walking back into the light, she put the stiff bag with the ho-tel's gold logo on it down on the duvet. Then she stayed perfectly still.

The only one who could get in would be the Creator Himself.

"Jim?" She frowned, wondering how that would be possible. Unless . . .

No, this was definitely about Jim.

Her eyes shot over to her vanity table. In between a Clarins clarifying mask and some Chanel Précision Sublimage, there was something that didn't have jack-all to do with makeup—and ordinarily she wouldn't have been able to tolerate the discordance of objects.

But this one got special dispensation.

It was the hood ornament of her own Mercedes S550 4Matic— and for once, she wasn't rushing to get the thing put back in its proper place. In fact, she'd broken the neck off herself . . . because that trademarked circle with its intersecting lines had a very special accessory of its own: When she'd hit Jim with her car the other night, he'd been clipped by the front hood, and a little part of him had been left behind in the ornament's metal.

That residue in the very molecular fiber of the steel was how she'd managed to get into his house, into his bed, and oh so close to seducing him while pretending to be Sissy.

It was a one-way connection, though. So there was no way he could use it to get to her—

From out of nowhere, a wave of pain rang her chest like a bell, as if she'd been shot or stabbed. But there was nobody around. Nobody up above.

And yet something was wrong, something . . .

"Jim . . . ?" She walked forward. "Jim?"

Suffocation followed. The kind that made her feel like someone had their hands around her throat. Or maybe a rope. Abruptly, she reached up to grab at that which wasn't there, opening her mouth so she could breathe.

Fucking hell, she was now the salesguy from the hotel, her access to air cut off by an unseen force.

Except it wasn't suffocation in the true sense. This was . . . an emotional pain so great it literally robbed her of the ability to inflate the lungs she pretended to have.

"*Jim!*" she screamed, the dots connecting to a terrifying conclusion.

Vaporizing her physical form, she entered the HVAC system ductwork and shot through the innards of the building, expelling herself into the open air through a vent and shooting off in the direction of that old house he stayed in.

Faster, faster, faster . . .

She knew the very moment he left the coil of the earth: A lancing agony overtook her soul, sure as if she had been cleaved in half.

Storm clouds gathered in her wake as she landed on the front lawn of the property he rented, and she rushed for the front door—

The barrier she hit was a brick wall that didn't exist, an invisible, impenetrable force field that repelled her so hard, she fell back on her ass. Looking up in panic, her frantic mind couldn't figure out what the fuck it was—but then she caught sight of a subtle red glimmer. The bastard had locked her out with an additional, stronger spell.

Except it didn't last.

With Jim's life-force having been extinguished, his protection spell lost its source and gradually peeled free of the house, retreating from the roof and freeing up from the walls.

The inevitable recession was like watching him die in front of her, seeing his life slip away.

"Jim . . ." she groaned as the last of it disappeared.

Scrambling to her feet, she ran forward and went to the windows of the parlor. With shaking hands, she leaned into the bubbly old glass and cupped her palms, peering through. . . .

The moan that rippled up through her tight throat was a release of agony. Across the parlor, Jim lay in a shambled sprawl on the floor, his arms and legs helter-skelter, as if he had fallen back without trying to stop himself or protect against the impact. Silver blood was everywhere down his chest, a gaping slash in his throat the cause of the tidal wave.

There was a crystal dagger in his right hand—that was stained with more of that mercury-like substance that filled his veins.

Clearly, he'd taken someone with him.

Such a hero, she thought as she teared up.

And yes, opposite him, Colin the archangel was a shadow of his powerful self, his face drawn in horror, his body straining as if he were in physical conflict—except there was no one coming at him. There had been, though—his face was bruising up and there was silver blood on his hands. The room was also trashed, lamps knocked over, tables overturned, sofas out of place.

Jim had been in the process of fighting with the archangel. Maybe over her honor? That was so like her Jim . . . but it shouldn't have ended like it had.

And she wasn't the only one who felt that way. That dumb whore Sissy Barten was screaming at the top of her lungs as she went over and took Jim's head into her lap, and across the way, Adrian the angel was looking like he'd seen a ghost. Or maybe the Grim Reaper.

The only bright spot was the obvious agony of that girl, and Devina took a moment to absorb the incandescent pain. It was the only balm she was going to have for a long, long while. The shit was going to be useful, too.

But not now. Now, it was all she could do to keep from breaking down.

Splaying her fingers out, Devina leaned in until her forehead touched the cool glass. "My love . . ."

Some animal was loose and going crazy in the parlor.

Oh, wait—it was her, Sissy thought.

With her mouth wide-open and her lungs working with a seemingly endless supply of air, she was making a noise that was part lioness, part atomic bomb detonation. Staring at Jim's lifeless body, cradling him against her, getting stained by his silver blood, she unhinged—

And lunged at his attacker.

Without conscious thought, she scrambled over the floor like a crab, launching herself at Colin, who remained stunned stupid either by her having smashed him on the head or because of what Jim had just done to himself.

She went for the eyes.

She didn't get close. He grabbed her wrists and flipped her onto her back on the floor, straddling her and pinning her arms over her head.

"Fuck you!" she spat at him, fighting against the hold, kicking with her legs, thrashing around. When she tried to bite him, he somehow kept her down while freeing one of his hands—which he clapped on her jaw to hold her head in place.

He didn't hurt her. Just let her wear herself out.

It felt like a year until all she could do was heave for breath underneath him, and still he sat over her calmly, as if he'd put no effort into any of it at all.

As water hit her face, she couldn't figure out where it was coming from—

The man was . . . crying. From out of the strangest-colored eyes she had ever seen, tears were falling drop by drop and landing on her cheeks. And before she knew it, her own were mixing with his, a great wellspring of emotion bursting out and taking over where the anger had been raw as the wound Jim had given himself.

"I have lost, too," he said in a proper English accent. "I am without as well."

"Why did you kill him," she moaned, even though that was not what happened. "Why—"

"I am sorry for your loss." His voice cracked. "I am so sorry. . . ."

She turned her head and looked at Jim's body through waves of tears. His face happened to be tilted in her direction, and for a moment, it was as if the two of them were staring at each other—except there was no life behind his eyes.

Colin loosened his hold. Backed off a little. Backed off a lot.

As the man, angel, whatever he was moved away from her, his legs flopped around like he meant to stand up, but didn't have the strength or coordination. Then he rubbed his face . . . as if maybe that would change what was across the floor from him.

"You wanted to kill him," Sissy said grimly. "I don't know why you're so fucking surprised at this."

"Whate'er has he done to himself," the angel whispered.

From over on the sofa that had been thrown against the wall, Adrian cursed. "He went there to get Nigel back."

Colin's head shot around. "I beg your pardon?"

"He killed himself to go get your boy."

Colin frowned, his black brows locking together. "That is not possible."

"Which was what I tried to tell him, but you know Jim. He makes his own mind up."

Sissy was conscious of Ad glancing her way, but she didn't pay any attention to him. She was too busy searching for that other outcome, wondering why, considering all the levels of magic in this new world she was stuck in, she couldn't hit some metaphysical rewind and make this mess go away.

"No one has come back from there without the Creator's permission," the Englishman said. "You should know that."

"Yup. Brought that up."

"Why ever did you let him—"

"Let him? What the fuck, Colin."

As Sissy pushed herself upright, the back of her neck started to tingle. Reaching up, she rubbed her nape—

Creeeeeeeeeeak.

The sound of the front door opening got everyone's attention. And it was followed by a strange set of footfalls, a repeating shuffle and a punch that sounded like something out of a Wes Craven movie. Then the temperature dropped forty degrees, making the walls crackle and her breath condense in puffs in front of her face.

Sissy screamed at what appeared in the doorway: It was a corpse, an upright, rotting corpse with gray flesh hanging off its bones and stringy hair vining down its pitted shoulders.

Colin and Adrian both jumped up as the corpse held out its hand, the sinew connecting the white bone offering little in the way of a palm. "Jim," it said in a hollow rasp. "You will let me see him."

"The fuck I will," Adrian growled.

"Now is not the time for this."

"Fuck you, Devina."

"Fine, we'll do it the hard way."

The light drained not just out of the room they were in, but the sky itself, blackness arriving like a stain upon the earth. And then an eerie buzzing, like bees were coalescing and beginning to swarm, filled the air.

Someone grabbed her around the waist—not Adrian, the other one. "Adrian!" the Englishman yelled.

"Take Sissy!" Ad barked.

"Have her! Get over here, mate!"

A split second later, Sissy was thrown against the far corner of the room, and the big bodies of the two men walled in front of her. A flash of lightning from outside gave her a quick visual of the corpse crumpling to her knees in front of Jim's body . . . and then all hell broke loose. With the next lightning strike, black, oily forms pulled themselves free of jagged shadows around the room, becoming three-dimensional instead of two, coming alive.

And then all went pitch-black again.

Until the next lightning strike.

This time those black nightmares were closing in on the three of them, prepared for attack.

There was no way the Englishman and Adrian were going to hold them off.

No way.

Chapter Eight

"I love you. . . . I love you. . . . I love you. . . ."

Jim was still saying his last words over and over again as he opened his eyes. Gray. That was his first impression. Gray sky, gray ground. His second was that the suffocation and sense of being smothered from the outside in was gone. So too was the firebrand across the front of his throat and the coppery taste in his mouth.

But his Sissy was also gone. Along with Adrian and the parlor. And Colin.

A vast gray landscape had replaced it all, the flat plane stretching farther than he could see in all directions. The only breaks in the endless horizon were boulders that rose up from the powdery ground, rock formations that were spaced intermittently and at random.

From out of the north—or was it the west? the south? the east?—a coiling wind traveled to him, hitting him in the face, making his eyes sting and his throat go dry from the dust it carried.

Sitting up, he did a full three-sixty with the checkouts. No buildings. Nothing moving. And there was no sunlight, no moonlight, no shadows, just a strange glow that had no source and yet was like the ground cover: endless.

"Shit," he breathed.

Hard to know what he thought he'd find—then again, as of just a couple of weeks ago, he hadn't believed in angels, demons, or that Purgatory existed. So it wasn't like he'd come over here with a layout in mind, or a game plan. But, man, he hadn't pictured this.

Talk about your needle-in-a-haystack routine. So much distance to cover in search of Nigel—and he wasn't sure how much time he had. Devina was back on earth working the war while he was over here, and the best he could hope for was that, as with Hell, time didn't work the same way in this wasteland as it did up where the sun was in charge.

Was this place below the earth? Off to the side in the Milky Way? In the depths of a worm hole? As his mind went into an unsustainable bend, he dropped that line of thinking and went to stand up.

Tried to stand up was more like it.

Getting to his feet required a crapload of effort, as if gravity on this side of the divide were so much more powerful. And when he finally was on the vertical, the ground sank down under his weight, his footprints going deep into the packed dust.

He walked forward because . . . what else was he going to do—

More with the wind, pushing up against his chest as he ambulated, creating a drag he had to fight against. And the dust. Christ, it was like being back in the Middle East—every breath irritated the inside of his nose, and his eyes started to feel like he'd been on an all-night bender, each blink scratching over his pupils and itching his tear ducts.

Abruptly, he thought of Sissy's expression . . . and then none of the physical shit mattered. The horror on her face as he'd sliced his own throat wide-open had been the stuff of nightmares, and the knowledge that he'd put that panic and pain in her eyes was unbearable.

Guessed he'd proven he could put the war ahead of his concern for her, but, man, what a shitty decision. In a shitty situation.

Forcing himself to keep moving, he put one foot in front of the other and thought how much it would help if he knew whether Nigel was here. Was this just his own version of the place? Ad and Eddie had met, but maybe their rules were different? Although, hell, even if the archangel had ended up on this precise plane of existence, Jim had to wonder how to find him. At this rate? He could spend eternity wandering around between the boulders—

Okay, they were not, in fact, rocks.

Statues.

As he came up to one of the mounds, subtle contours that were not visible from afar revealed the figure of a man sitting cross-legged, his arms wrapped around a scrawny chest, his head lowered as if in prayer . . . or sorrow. The clothing was from an older time period, like maybe the Revolutionary War—but with all the disintegration, it was hard to tell. The relentless wind had worn down the edges of the knees, the collar of the heavy coat, the features of the face. The sculpture was degrading into that perennial dust—

"Fuck!"

Jim jumped back and went into a defensive crouch. The "statue" was moving: The arm on the left shifted upward as if there were someone trapped in there or . . . that actually *was* someone.

Gray particles filigreed off the elbow as that limb rose up, as if the person were trying to reach him for help.

It wasn't Nigel, but come on, like he wasn't going to do something here?

Jim crouched down and put his own hand out.

The instant contact was made the entity dissolved into a loose pile of that powdery ground cover, the wind rushing in and blowing it away as if that were the task of the gust.

Within moments, there was no sign that anything had been there at all, the slate wiped clean.

Warning bells went off in his head, and he took a gander at his fingers, his palms, his forearms, his body. He had on what he'd been wearing when he'd crossed over, just a white Hanes T-shirt and a pair of jeans. Things had changed—or were changing—though. The white was not as bright as it had been, like the shirt was in a Tide detergent ad showing what not to do with your laundry. And the blue was fading, too.

He stared down at where the man had been.

Then he resumed his stride, cupping his hands and yelling into the wind, "Nigel! Niiiiiigel, yo, buddy!"

His voice didn't carry far, as if the dust in the air were consuming the volume, eating it alive.

"This was a great plan, asshole," he muttered as he came up to another "boulder."

This one was too worn-down to see any identifying anything. The head was nothing but a bump on top of the mound, the body beneath it arranged in the same fashion as the one before. Or at least that was what it seemed.

He was about to turn away when the structure collapsed, the head falling inward into the triangulation of the body, the wind whipping up and claiming the ash, sweeping it away once more.

Jim coughed to relieve his dry throat, and wondered if the laws of food and water applied in this landscape.

Trudging along, he began to feel a chill in the air. "Nigel! Nigel . . . !"

Think, Jim. Fucking think. What could he leverage to keep himself "alive." And where the fuck was that Englishman?

Serious concerns about the timing of everything dogged him.

Chronologically speaking, Nigel had killed himself two and a half days ago, max. But that was in earth hours. So how long did the guy have before he turned into one of those mounds? Before Jim himself did? The style of clothing of that first man suggested two hundred years or more had passed, and that was good news on one level, because it meant they had some time. Unless everyone's experience here was different?

Man, he could have used some stereo instructions on this place—and of course, that thought brought up all kinds of images of Sissy bent over that beat-up old book, her straight blond hair falling forward, her frown of concentration suggesting she was milking every nuance of meaning out of the words.

As he trudged along, calling out the archangel's name, he tried to tell himself that the reason he was lingering on the Sissy shit was because, like any road left untraveled, it was easy to build up a scenario of perfection. Without having actually been with her, his brain was free to dream up all kinds of utopia—and it was illogical to torture himself with could've-beens that were, in fact, weren'ts.

Besides, it wasn't like he had any track record with grand romances. His sex life was built on a solid foundation of anonymous fucking. Not only had he never been in love; finding a wife or a mother for some children had been so far down his bucket list, it hadn't even made it on the page—

Okay, clearly the war had done his nut in, and his version of crazy was this illusion of having some kind of destiny with Sissy.

"Niiiiiiiigel," he belted out. "Where are you, you sonofabitch . . ."

Looking out over the vast barren landscape, he was struck by the reality that having all directional options open was a unique form of being trapped. And then there was the other happy ass-slapper that Nigel was the anti–Bear Grylls. That scone-fancying,

Gatsby-wearing Englishman wasn't going to have a clue how to survive in any environment that didn't include a croquet set, plenty of sherry, and a quartet playing Bach.

Man, he should have thought this through better.

"Niiiiiiigel!"

Chapter Nine

As lightning flashed and showed off all kinds of minions on the attack, Adrian wished like hell he hadn't lost vision in one of his eyes. Depth perception was a bitch for him now, and he needed it more than ever as he faced off against the demon's collection of oily, formless fighters.

The fucking things had always given him the creeps, and that was when he'd just been by his little lonesome with no one else to worry about but himself. With Sissy behind him and Colin the Crackpot as backup?

Happy Monday—

Feeling a tug on his waist, he twisted around—and discovered that Sissy had just unsheathed his backup dagger. "What the hell are you doing?" he yelled over the thunder.

"I'm going to defend us, too." She palmed the hilt as if there were a possibility, however remote, that she might have a clue how to use the thing. And not for making a salad.

But they didn't need a hero in this situation.

Ad rolled his eyes. "Look, just stay behind us—"

The impact hit him in the face, the sweeping punch ringing the shit out of his bell. Which was the thing with minions: They had Rubber Man's stretch and Tyson's follow-through—and with his bad leg, he couldn't take a hit like he used to. As his weight transferred to the bad side of things, he listed and the world tilted. Throwing out a hand—

Sissy was there to catch him, jacking her body against his like she was trying to keep a tree from falling. And Colin stepped up in front, throwing out a buffering spell that bounced the minion off in the opposite direction.

More lightning strobe lit the room. Another two minions stepped right up where the first had been.

"Not good," Ad muttered. "Really not good."

With a curse, Colin braced his body and put both palms forward, sending out shock wave after shock wave, holding off the attack as still more minions pushed in.

Within moments, they were blocked into the corner completely, an army of Devina's shadows pressing in so tightly together that they became a wall of dense, oily blackness.

Sissy groaned against him, pushing her face into his pecs, but she didn't let go of him, and she didn't drop the dagger. Shit, she was probably remembering them from her time down below.

Colin began to shake, his expression twisting into a grimace. "I can't . . . hold . . . them . . . much longer. . . ."

Great time to go Scotty from *Star Trek*.

And then the chaos only ramped higher. On the far side of the teeming mass of demon servants, a wailing sound rose up. It was Devina, saying Jim's name over and over again as her rotting skeleton mourned over his body.

"Devina!" Adrian hollered. "Devina! Help us get him back!"

More minions continued to layer the protection spell, pushing Colin back even farther. And then a limb broke through, clawing inside—

"No!" Sissy yelled, slashing at it with the dagger. *"No!"*

There was an ear-ringing squeal as the minion retreated. But almost immediately, another took its place. Sissy was on it, scooting around Ad to go up close and personal with that sharp blade. And Adrian followed suit, careful not to throw off his balance or clip Sissy with his own weapon.

"Devina!" he barked. "You stupid bitch! Help us get Jim back!"

Colin glanced over his shoulder, his face straining from the effort. From between gritted teeth, he said, "She can?"

"I don't fucking know." Adrian locked a hand on Sissy's shoulder and yanked her out of range as an entire head came through from the side. "You got a better fucking idea?"

There was an unholy scream as he stabbed that minion right in the temple. And Sissy didn't miss a beat, spinning around and going after one that was trying to get in from behind.

"Devina! Help us get him home!"

Jesus, he hoped she could hear him—and prayed that she fell for it—

From out of nowhere, one of the minions infiltrated the protective field and Ad had no choice but to throw Sissy back and face the thing head-on. Between one breath and the next, he was consumed by a shitload of nasty, the oily body tendriling around him, trapping him as the—

"Devina!" he yelled. "Fucking Devina . . . !"

Nigel, the archangel, hadn't been in unfamiliar territory in . . . how long? Aeons and aeons. Since the moment he had been crafted of the Creator's will and given a form with which to ambulate by air or by foot.

Surveying the vast gray wasteland before him, he wondered if his considered plan to reengage Jim had, in fact, been ill conceived. More than that, he had been unprepared for the pain—

and not in regard to the throes of an immortal dying, but rather that of the heart.

The separation from Colin was nearly unbearable.

This may have been a terrible mistake.

Indeed, Nigel's was not a character of impulse, and at the time he had made his decision and put a dagger to his chest, he had believed down to his angelic marrow that what actions he sought to take were in the best interests of Heaven and their prevailing in the war against Devina. But now, surrounded by this gray barrenness, the solitude and isolation suggested he had, in fact, been rash.

Or mayhap he was simply deep in a suffering that eclipsed all of the good reasons for doing what he had done.

After all, what choice had he had? Jim Heron, the savior, had turned into Jim Heron, the distracted and unreliable: As important as these rounds against the demon were, it would not be the first time that the course of human history was diverted into disaster because some female tempted a man with dire consequences ensuing. Further, to have failed against Devina was untenable even with his love at his side.

Not only would he and Colin lose everything, but Heaven and Earth would become the demon's playground.

There was *so* much more at stake than just himself and whom he loved. And the reality was that the human he had chosen as savior, and in whom he had put his faith, had failed, the losses that had been ever mounting the result of Jim's poor performances, poor choices, and poor allegiance. The sodding bastard had even *given* a win away.

By killing himself, Nigel had created a vacuum up in Heaven that was to be filled by Jim by mandate and Sissy would not be able to follow. Her soul was of the rare nether variety—having been freed of Hell, she could nonetheless not enter unto the Manse of Souls up above regardless of any virtue she possessed, as she was unclean. And whether that contamination was of her doing or was the result of maleficence on Devina's part did not matter.

The castle that protected the souls of the righteous could not be risked.

So Nigel had done what he did, and now he suffered, and Colin no doubt suffered, but there was a chance, assuming their backup savior filled those combat boots . . .

Mayhap all had not been lost.

Adrian, after all, had his own reasons for trying to win. With Eddie in stasis, there was a strong possibility that that wild card of an angel would be tempered enough to be effective.

Although for truth, the very fact that Adrian Vogel was the best option humanity had was a terrible commentary on the gravity of the situation.

With his brain cannibalizing itself with such thoughts, Nigel pivoted in place and regarded all the directions of his current reality. There was no real reason to bother with the turning about, however, as all remained the same: just a flat, dusty plain the color of a dove's long feather with nothing but rock formations scattered here and there.

From out of all compass points, wind began to blow, as if it were a living thing that had just noticed his presence. With dust kicking up into his eyes, he coughed into his fisted hand. His vestments were the ones that had been upon his body when he had done the deed, nothing but a loose dressing robe and silk slippers.

He wished now that he'd brought more clothes.

Suicide was hardly something to pack for, however. At least as far as he'd known it.

Taking a step forward, he found the ground spongy, but not in a damp way. In fact, what was under his feet was a loosely packed bed of fine particles—undoubtedly where that wind got its grit.

As he moved for no other reason than that standing still was antithetical to his nature, he had a further realization.

There had been another justification to do what he had. As head of the archangels, as the tip of the spear for goodness, he had recognized that he could not expect a subordinate to do something he himself would not. The savior Jim Heron may not have perhaps come to know his truth yet, but he was in love with the girl he had saved from the bowels of Hell. It was the only explanation for how he had acted, for those unforgivable lapses in judgment.

The role the savior had taken on required him to put aside his own emotions and interests for the sake of winning the war.

So Nigel had left Colin behind to show that that was not only possible, but imperative.

Would it work? He wasn't sure if he'd even know over here. If Devina took over all of the quick and the dead . . . did that include the lost souls of Purgatory?

If Jim prevailed, nothing would change.

If the demon did, perhaps this horrible, dusty void would seem like paradise.

Trudging on, he became aware of a chill in the air and wrapped his loose, flagging robe closer about.

It was not long before structured thought deserted him and he was left with only emotional despair.

He missed Colin with every inhale of the dusty air. And as his eyes began to water, he thought at first it was but the particles carried upon the wind. Alas, no. It was from mourning his love.

Sweeping his fingers across his cheek, he looked down at the wetness. Within moments, the crystalline tear was covered with dust—or . . . had it become dust?

The wind strengthened abruptly and seemed to concentrate

its efforts upon that which he regarded with a frown. And then his fingertip was cleaned, the tear claimed.

Alarmed, he looked up to the sky that was the same color as the ground. Then peered behind himself.

Nothing but those boulders . . . which he feared were not made of rock after all.

Heart pounding, teeth beginning to chatter, he continued onward with no direction. He had a companion, however. His grief was as another person traveling with him, an entity so tremendous and painful, it was separate from him and yet grafted to his very being.

He could only pray that his noble sacrifice had been worth all this.

If not, he was going to be consumed with a bitterness that might well turn him evil.

Chapter Ten

The hard floor bit into Devina's bony knees as she fell before her beloved and bowed over him.

Even in his immortal death, Jim was looking away from her, his head lolled to the opposite side, his open, sightless eyes trained across the old-fashioned Victorian parlor.

"Jim . . ." she rasped.

As heartbreaking as it was to see him from outside, up close it was even harder. His face still had all its color and his cheek was still warm as she brushed it. He appeared to be merely sleeping—and he was going to stay this way, the sweet bouquet fragrance that wafted around him the only evidence of the passing.

Well, that and all the no-moving.

As her tears began to flow in earnest, clear drops changed to blood-red and fell down her cratered cheeks onto the backs of her hideous hands.

She was so full of grief, not only had she lost the ability to keep her mask of flesh in place, she didn't give a shit that she was without it.

"Jim, don't leave me," she moaned. But it was too late for that. The law of unintended consequences had come home to roost:

Nigel had killed himself because of Jim. And Colin, in a fit of rage, killed Jim. . . .

She was *so* going to slaughter that fucking archangel. As soon as she had the strength to stand up, she was going to unleash the wrath of ages upon him, flaying his skin from his body, digging his eyes out with her own claws, castrating him with her teeth. And then she was going to get really serious.

"My darling love—"

"Devina!"

The sound of her name above the din of her minions barely registered as she rearranged Jim into a better position, pulling his upper body into her lap, turning his head to face her. Ah, there. Now he was staring at her.

The crystal dagger that had been gripped in his right hand fell to the floor with a clatter and she glanced at the thing. As its silver-covered blade caught a burst of lightning, she heard from over in the corner:

"Devina, we can get him back with your help!"

It was Adrian's voice—and she was more than prepared to ignore it when the scene she'd witnessed from the window flashed before her sunken eyes: Jim sprawled on the floor, the idiot bitch Sissy cradling him like she was in a Nicholas Sparks movie, Adrian across the room making like a throw pillow on the sofa . . . and Colin, the archangel, on his ass, staring at Jim like something unthinkable had just happened.

"Devina! We need to get him back!"

She was beyond uninterested in whatever Ad was screaming at her . . . except that expression on the archangel's face nagged at her. Colin's war-minded nature had long commanded her respect, kind of in the way anyone would get careful when a loaded gun was cocked at their head: You either moved carefully around the damn thing or vital shit started to leak.

That archangel was never one to hesitate in conflict, and never the kind who was surprised when he prevailed in an attack.

So why had he been staring at Jim like that?

"Devina! You stupid cunt!"

Reaching across Jim's heavy chest, she picked the crystal blade up off the carpet and brought it to her nose. One deep breath through the Swiss cheese of her rotted sinuses and she knew a horrific truth.

Colin might have come here to kill Jim, but that was not what had gone down.

Jim's own blood was on the weapon.

He'd taken his own—

"No!" Devina's heart pounded. "You fucking didn't!"

If he'd committed suicide, he'd gone to Purgatory . . . which was the one place, win or lose, she couldn't get to. Jim was gone to her forever if he—

Devina twisted around, her exposed spinal cord cracking like popcorn. "Be gone!" she commanded her servants. "Be gone!"

The swarm of oily black minions disappeared faster than a gasp. And in the wake of their departure, Colin's bracing spell had nothing to push against, so his energy exploded into the room, rattling the windows and creating a gust that blew her Gollum hair back. The archangel's own body was affected, too, his weight tipping forward so that he had to catch himself in a tucked roll that brought him right to her. Naturally, he was on his feet in a defensive stance a split second later.

Across the way, Adrian went into a slump, his body landing badly on the rug, all arms and legs going everywhere. Sissy was the only one of the three who remained exactly where she was, a crystal dagger in her hand, her arm up and ready to stab. The girl's eyes were wide as headlights, though—no doubt from her first fight, and maybe, probably, because of what Devina looked like.

But again, the demon didn't care about appearances. No more than somebody who, having been in a motorcycle accident, gave a shit that ambulance people had to strip them naked to save their leg.

"What did he do?" Devina heard herself ask. Gone was the voice of the seductress, the luscious, affected American pronunciation lost in favor of a sandpaper rasp that had the accent of the ancient.

The three of them were heaving to get breath into their lungs, and just as she was about to scream for one of them to quit the panting-dog bullshit, Adrian cleared his throat.

"He went over to get Nigel back."

Devina felt her own lid-less eyes get large in their sockets. She'd been hoping there was another explanation. "Not . . . possible."

"Has happened," Colin said. "Purgatory."

"That's not . . ." She didn't bother with the "possible" again. She was holding the evidence in her own hand. "But why . . ."

Adrian said something. Then Colin. But none of that registered against a flush of warmth and love that spread throughout her whole body. "Oh, Jim . . . you're so romantic."

Of course he'd go over there and risk his eternal existence. It was the only way the pair of them could be reunited: If he could find Nigel and bring him back, then Jim didn't have to go up to Heaven—and the two of them could be together regardless of the war. They could either quit and start enjoying their eternity side by side now. Or they could know the exquisite pain of battle for one last round, have Devina win, and rule Hell as one.

Win-win-win-win.

Instantly, her hideous true self disappeared and the plump young flesh of that model she'd killed back in the eighties sprouted from every atom of her disgusting form, her biddable-beddable-beautiful mask back in place again.

"Oh, Jim," she whispered. Tears were still flowing, the red

drops falling onto his cheeks, but now she knew nothing but joy. "My love . . . you're doing it for us."

God, this was such a poignant moment, she thought, bending down and sealing his warm lips with her own. And how fucking great that it was happening in front of Sissy.

She glanced up and smiled at the virgin. "To think he would risk so much just to be with me. Love is so inspiring." Then she focused on Colin and ditched the Barbara Cartland moment. "So you're saying he needs help getting back with Nigel in tow?"

"No." The archangel's oddly colored eyes narrowed. "I do not believe he can get back a'tall."

"Excuse me?"

"No one passes from Purgatory without the permission of the Creator. You know that. Whether or not he can find Nigel is the least of his concerns."

Cue a dose of cold, hard panic. Which was absolutely, totally not relieved by the silence that followed.

After a long moment, she glanced at Adrian. "You have something of mine."

"Do I."

"A book," she muttered grimly. "Your friend Eddie took it from me—by the way, how *is* he doing? Still hoping for some kind of an Easter miracle? A risen-from-the-dead deal for him?"

The goddamn angel gave her nothing. Not even a facial tic. "Easter's long over. And what book are you talking about? *Our Bodies, Ourselves*, maybe? No . . . in your case, probably a *Walking Dead* comic, right."

"Fuck you, Adrian."

"We tried that a couple of days ago, and it didn't work for me, did it."

The memory of her on her knees, trying to suck off his limp dick, made her snarl. "Maybe you've just lost your edge."

"More likely your appeal is up in smoke. But we digress. What book are you talking about."

The way he arched a brow was such disrespect. And she almost went at him with her bare hands, but she didn't want to disturb her lover—

"I have the book."

As Sissy spoke up, everyone looked at her. And Adrian started cursing. "Sissy, shut the fuck up—"

The demon smiled. "Yes, you know the one. Don't you."

As the demon and Sissy locked eyes, Adrian dragged himself off the floor, his body aching like he'd gotten a hot-stone massage using a tire iron. "Sissy," he hissed. "Do not—"

But he couldn't get across to her fast enough.

Sissy went over and picked up the ancient tome from where it had fallen, righting its pages and reclosing its cover from having been blown open.

"So this is yours," she said.

Devina's black eyes sparkled as she stared up from her Mary Magdalene-with-the-dead-Christ routine on the floor: With Jim's head in her lap and his body splayed out, she had arranged herself with portrait-like precision—but he could give a shit about her Agnolo Bronzino moment.

"Sit down here," Devina purred, indicating the floor beside her.

"Sissy," he snapped. "Don't go over there."

"There's nothing in here about Purgatory." Sissy didn't look in Devina's direction and didn't make a move toward her. Thank fuck. "Nothing."

"You've been reading my work?" the demon asked.

"No one else knows Latin."

"It's not written in Latin."

Sissy shot a glare over. "Fine, whatever, I've been able to make it out, okay."

"Interesting." Devina leaned down and whispered something in Jim's ear. Then laughed as if she and the dead guy had shared a private joke. "And as for Purgatory, I haven't been there, so of course I didn't write anything about the place."

Man, Adrian was thinking seriously of throwing himself out the nearest window. And he got sick at the reminder that Sissy had had that thing in her hands for how long today?

"You wrote all that," he muttered.

"Yes." The demon frowned. "And I seriously did not appreciate Eddie stealing it from me. He thought he could use it to get you back. Didn't work then, did it."

But Eddie had ended up saving him in the end. Still, "If that's true," he said, "why do you need it now?"

Colin spoke up, his English accent clipped. "Because she's going to try to create a portal. Aren't you."

Devina shrugged. "You were the ones suggesting we work together. Do you have another solution in mind?"

"Shit," Adrian breathed.

"What's a portal?" Sissy looked over at Ad. Stared at Colin. "Well?"

When no one spoke up, Adrian did his best to pace around the parlor. It was like trying to motivate a Model T with a broken axle, but staying still wasn't an option. And he wasn't the only one getting serious, either. Colin had braced his head in his hands, and even Devina had dropped the petting act with Jim; the demon was as motionless as a statue, staring off into space like she was doing long division in her head.

Or maybe calculating the very good odds that this was going to fuck all of them in the ass.

As nobody else was going to answer the question, Adrian figured, What the hell. "There are two portals that we are allowed to use—and both were brought into existence by the Creator. One leads to Heaven, the other to Hell. They're how we go back and forth—how she gets down and back." He stopped and faced the fireplace even though there was no flame in it. No logs to watch as they were consumed. No heat to warm his cold hands and feet. "For us to try to make one? For our own purposes? It's a violation of the laws of the universe."

Devina shrugged. "What's the Creator going to do to us?"

"Not sure I want to find out," Ad bit out. "Not sure we got a choice."

"This could indeed get us into serious trouble," Colin tacked on. Then he looked at Ad. "It's on a magnitude of the stunt you pulled that got you punished."

"Which one." Adrian shrugged. "And I don't know why you're giving me the hairy eyeball. I don't have that kind of power—that shit is going to need to be between you and her."

Colin glanced at the demon and muttered something unintelligible under his breath. And yup, she looked equally disenchanted.

At least they were taking the risks seriously.

Devina nodded over at Sissy. "Open to page three hundred forty-one and a half."

Sissy flipped pages back and forth. "Okay."

"What does it say?"

"Which passage?"

"Start from the top."

Sissy opened her mouth and started reading . . . but fuck all if Ad could understand what she was saying. The words were gibberish—and not any kind of Latin he recognized. Hell, he'd even been around when the guys in togas and sandals had been doing their jam, and whatever was coming from between her lips? Not it.

When she finally stopped, Devina nodded. "So I'm correct."

"Yes," Sissy said. "I think you are."

In the silence that followed, Colin looked over pointedly, but Ad had to prioritize panic buttons at that moment—he couldn't worry about whatever connection the two females in the room might be forging. "Look," he cut in, "I don't have a clue what you just read. But the portal idea, while batshit crazy, is probably our only option. If we can create a portal and keep it open long enough . . . maybe Jim can jump back."

"But wait," Sissy said. "If he killed himself to get over there, doesn't one already exist?"

"It's not one that is open to free use," Colin said. "That particular portal is regulated by the Creator, and He has been very clear about its purpose and its restrictions."

Ad glanced at Sissy. "Yeah, the Big Guy ain't too happy with the idea that someone would disrespect the gift of life. You take your own? You're going to get a proverbial slap on the wrist. Purgatory's also where righteous souls who can't let go of something or someone they left behind end up because their sorrow won't let them transition upstairs. Not a pleasant place. It's like Hell."

"Fuck that," Devina bit out. "Hell is *much* worse."

"True. You're there—"

Sissy interrupted. "So how do you make a portal?"

There was another long silence, and again, Adrian was surprised Devina didn't jump in with a whole lot of chatter—and he wasn't sure whether the fact that she didn't was a good or a bad thing.

"Well," he prompted the demon. "What do you think?"

Devina's black eyes ceased to glitter, and her expression, for once, grew remote. "We'd need a tremendous amount of focused energy. Colin and I could face off and each cast an attack spell. In theory, assuming we are of equal strength, the opposing forces will become so great, this plane of existence will not be able to support them, and a tear will be created in the veil between here and there."

Sissy frowned. "How can you be sure the door it opens will be into Purgatory?"

Man, she was no dummy, Ad thought. "We give it a tracer." He glanced over at Jim's motionless remains. "Yeah, maybe if we give it a direction . . ."

Devina bared her teeth like a dog growling. "You're not throwing his body in there. It'll be destroyed and he'll have nothing to return to."

Right, right, right. And if this didn't work, she wouldn't have a new toy to play with.

Ad shuddered at the thought of how she'd use those remains. "Blood, then. His blood."

Colin nodded. "That is logical. The death, such as it was, was very recent. As a soul passes unto another plane, it is never a completely clean transition. Tracers remain in the flesh. In the blood."

There was another long silence as the magnitude of what they were all thinking hit home.

"How can we trust you?" Sissy said to the demon.

"You can't." Devina shrugged. "But Colin would jump at the chance to destroy me—isn't that right, archangel?"

"Oh, aye." Colin's eyes narrowed. "The satisfaction would almost make up for my loss."

Devina's mouth lifted in something close to affection. "And I will never let myself get hurt. So when he hits me, I'll hit him back. Likewise, he won't fail to defend himself either. Satisfied, little girl?"

To Sissy's credit, she didn't take the bait. She just nodded.

After which there was still more silence, which Devina filled by murmuring to "Jim." Shit, considering how well the demon was getting along with the corpse, you had to wonder why she wanted him to come back.

"There's only one remaining problem," Ad said. "Aside from the whole what-if-this-doesn't-work."

"Agreed." Colin scrubbed his face. "In fact, I shall be more concerned if this does function according to plan. It is precisely how the Dead Sea was created."

Sissy glanced over at the archangel. "I thought that was from tectonic plates shifting or something."

"Lassiter," Ad and Colin said together.

At the sound of the name, even Devina rolled her eyes. "Oh, Christ. Him again."

"So at least this has been tried before?" Sissy asked.

"Yeah, and look at how well it turned out." Ad shook his head. "A three-hundred-mile, one-thousand-foot-deep hole in the earth."

"And that still did not stop him," Colin said.

Devina glowered. "I seriously thought the bubonic plague was going to take him out."

"That was you?" Ad asked.

"I had to do something."

"Okay, okay, so what's our problem?" Sissy demanded, like she was trying to refocus the group.

Adrian looked up at the ceiling and could only imagine the Creator's reaction. "The Big Guy's going to be pissed if we do this. There's gonna be repercussions. Fuck the plague for real—He'll come after us, and shit is gonna get ugly."

With Eddie gone and a cock that no longer worked, it wasn't like he had much to "live" for, but that didn't mean he was happy to volunteer for suffering.

"You ready for that?" he asked Colin. "I've already been through the whole wrath-of-God a couple of times, and I'm way down the totem pole compared to you."

Before the archangel could respond, Devina spoke up. "It's going to be fine."

Ad laughed. "You don't have that much power, demon."

"I'll tell Him it's my idea." She stared across at Ad, then Colin. "The Creator begot me on purpose to provide chaos to His universe—otherwise utopia would exist and there would be no need for Heaven. I am His balance, the darkness to the sunshine, the bitter cold to warmth, the scorching heat to temperance. I am the disease to health and the poverty to wealth. I am the cheater who stands side by side with the honorable. This is my nature, His gift to me and the world. He cannot and will not punish what He Himself has conjured up with deliberation. If He does? Then He has failed."

In a quick series of calculations, Ad tested the theory, looking for holes, searching for ways in which Devina's "helpful suggestion" could come back and bite him and Colin hard. He could find nothing: Devina was a lying, cheating slut, but you could always, *always* put your money on her self-interest.

And out of everything in this world and the next, she wanted Jim Heron. She was clearly willing to do anything required to get him back, and she was smart enough to know that she wasn't going to be able to shift blame at the last minute. The Creator knew her too well to buy that shit.

The Creator would, however, believe it was her idea, and Devina might just have a point. And if she didn't? What the fuck did he care. It wasn't his ass on the line.

"You're prepared to go to Him," Ad said, "after it's through. Assuming it works."

"I am. As soon as it's over—and I know what He's going to say. As if He and I haven't been through these conversations before?"

Good point. She'd been fucking shit up on the earth for how long?

"Okay, I'm in," Ad announced.

"Aye," Colin said. "Myself as well."

Sissy spoke up. "Anything I can do, I'll help, too."

Devina's black eyes flashed. "Then let's get my man back."

Chapter
Eleven

"EeeeeeeeeeeeeEEEE-eeeeeeeeEEEEEEEeeeeEEEEEEEEumumum—away—"

As nobody else was around to rock out of tune with him, Jim leaned his head back and kept yelling at the top of his lungs, "Uh-weema-way, uh-weema-way, uh-weema-way . . ." Left foot. Right foot. Left foot. Right foot. "In the jungle . . . the mighty jungle . . ."

He was a really fucking bad singer. Worse even than Adrian had been back in the beginning—before the angel had come clean about the fact that far from being tone-deaf, the bastard could actually give a choirboy a run for his money on the Halle-lujah Chorus. Jim, on the other hand, was the real deal when it came to being the anti-*American Idol*.

His repertoire also sucked ass. He'd been drafted into the XOps system shortly after he'd murdered the rapists who had killed his mother—so it wasn't like he'd had a typical late-eighties high school experience steeped in Van Halen dances and AC/DC delivered into the ears by a Sony Walkman. He did know the words to "Jingle Bells," but that reminded him of his mother, so it was a no-go. He'd already run through "Happy Birthday" a couple of times. Next up after this one? He was weighing the pros and cons of either that thing you were supposed to sing on New Year's Eve or the Twix commercial.

Talk about needing a break.

"EeeeeeeeeeeeeeeeeeeEEEEEEeeeeEEEEEEEeeeeeeeee-uh-umum-away . . ."

He'd tried flat-out yelling Nigel's name for how long? But he'd had to give that up—not that his vocal stylings were fixing the sand problem, but the songs kept him going better than just the name.

". . . darling, don't fear"—a spasm of coughing cut the verse off—"my darling . . ."

Shit, his voice was drying up.

Gray, powdery ground. Relentless dusty wind. A never-ending horizon where the sky was one with everything else. Jesus Christ, this brought new meaning to the word *hell*, but as long as he didn't sit down, as long as he didn't let the cold whip his legs out from under him, as long as he kept going . . .

Yeah, what, he thought. What then.

It was impossible not to wonder how many of the souls before him had motivated themselves into exactly this kind of aimless amble. And in all the distance he'd covered, he hadn't seen one goddamn sign of life . . . or Nigel.

To keep himself from going completely insane, he pictured the only thing that could bring him back from the brink: his Sissy. Her long blond hair. Her eyes that reminded him of the blue snapdragons his mother had grown around their farmhouse. Her voice that had this freaky way of grounding him and sending him flying at the same time. Her clean scent and the mole on the side of her neck and the fact that she had a wonky fingernail on the pinkie of her left hand.

He pictured the way she tended to fiddle with the collar of whatever shirt she was wearing, as if maybe she'd forced herself to stop chewing her lip or the quick of her nails and needed to burn off the twitch.

He remembered how straight her two front teeth were, and how crooked her bottom six were.

When he thought about her, it was as if he recalled every breath she had ever drawn and expelled, even before he'd known she existed.

Great. After all these years, he finally grew a romantic bone in his body . . . and his girl was on the far side of the moon for all he could get to her—

Oh, come *on*, what was he going on about? Even if she were walking side by side with him? It wasn't like that was the way things were going to go for them.

The saddest thing about ending up here, apart from the fact that he'd fucked up the war, potentially lost his mother's place in Heaven, and was going to spend eternity blowing around a *Star Trek* set like some red shirt left behind by the *Enterprise*, was that he'd never told Sissy he loved her.

Then again, maybe he'd done her a favor. Like she needed his bullcrap?

He stared up at the gray sky as his boots sank into the ground one after the other, as his legs strained to keep the stride up, as his body yearned for a sit-down. The isolation made him feel everything so much more deeply . . . until the loneliness and the regrets were as though the sun itself had settled in the center of his chest.

Burning him. Singeing him.

Keeping him both warm against the cold and in utter agony.

For the love of God, was there nothing here, he thought—

At first he ignored the sound, but eventually, the persistence of it registered more than its volume. He stopped and clapped his mouth shut.

Instead of looking at whatever it was, he turned so that his better ear, the left one, was pointing in that direction.

Rhythmic. That was all he got, but it was enough to get him motivated: Even if it was an enemy, at least fighting would give him the sense of getting somewhere, doing something. Dear God, the monotony was almost as bad as the sense that time was running out.

And the memory of everything he'd left behind . . .

Man, if he had the chance to do it all over again, he'd tell her he loved her. He wouldn't make the same mistake again. He wouldn't . . . not tell her.

That was all.

Well, shit, he thought. Guess he wasn't making it out of here, was he. Because a man like him made a vow like that only when he knew he'd never have to live up to it.

In the meantime, he needed to get moving again.

When he went to take a step forward, his heels seemed to have become nailed to the fluffy ground cover. Gritting his teeth, he leaned into his legs and yanked so hard that when shit came free, he actually looked behind to make sure his foot and the stub of his ankle hadn't been left behind.

Nope, he was walking. But there wasn't going to be any stopping again.

Following the only noise other than the wind, he made as much time as he could toward that rhythmic sound, passing by statues of the dead that crumbled as he strode by, holding the bottom of his shirt up to his mouth so he could breathe without having his larynx sandblasted.

"Nigel, where the hell are you . . ."

He asked the question out of habit. Not because he thought he was going to find the guy.

As Sissy watched the demon fawn over Jim's remains, that explosive anger came back, clawing into her chest and giving her heartburn along with the urge to kill. But who was she going to go after? They needed Devina for this miracle idea.

Which might not in fact work. And might end up with the four of them in trouble with God Himself.

Plus, based on what they'd said? If things did go as planned, the parlor, if not the whole house, might be incinerated in the process. Maybe they'd create another Grand Canyon.

The Dead Sea being the starter set, as it were.

As the demon bent down again to whisper something in Jim's ear, Sissy turned away. It was either that or go *Real Housewives* on the bitch. And with the heavy book still in her hands, she opened things up just to give her eyes somewhere to go other than all the really-frickin'-creepy across the way.

The words were so easy to read now, the sentences flowing together, the logic behind the topics making more sense than it had. She was in what she thought of as the inventory section—it was page after page of objects arranged by date and type of metal. After the inventory came a list of places all over the world. There were dates for the locations as well as precise coordinates—

"Yo, Sis."

Startled, she twisted around toward Adrian. "Yes?"

"You might as well stand over here with me by the window. If shit gets critical, we can Hollywood-stuntman it out of the line of fire."

"Maybe that should be 'when,' huh?"

As she followed Ad's lead and settled in beside the angel's heft, she closed the book and put it against her chest. There was comfort in having the weight against her heart, like the thing might act as a shield or something—and then Devina finally got up on her ridiculous high heels and stepped away from Jim. Not exactly something to jump up and down with joy about, but better than the show the demon had been putting on.

And when Colin got to his feet as well, Sissy was reminded that he actually was a good-looking man—not that he was a man. He was slightly leaner than Adrian, but he had the quick eyes of a fighter who was comfortable playing dirty, and the confidence of someone who was rarely, if ever, surprised.

Jim had been able to get a rise out of him, though. All it had taken was that blade across his throat.

The memory was enough to make her nauseous, and every time she blinked, she saw Jim just before he did it, staring at her, his eyes fixated like he was taking her image over the divide and into eternity with him.

"I just want to go back," she whispered.

"To where?" Ad asked.

"Normal." She shook her head and wanted to cry. But refused to let herself. "I just want to worry about school again. And whether my mom will give me her car. I want to get excited about my birthday. Goddamn it . . . I should have enjoyed all of that more."

As the inside of her chest struggled to keep up with the waves of her emotions, she thought, Jesus, this was like she had the worst case of PMS in the world. Infuriated. In mourning. Out of her mind. All in the space of minutes.

Then again, it was hard to believe any of this was really happening. The horror was too much, the new rules of existence too many, the fear and the anger spiking in such rapid rotation now, she couldn't label them anymore.

"Do you think this is going to work?" she asked hoarsely as Colin took one side of the parlor and Devina the other.

"I don't know. I really . . . don't fucking know." Then Adrian spoke up loudly. "Wait, the blood! We need the blood."

Sissy had to turn away and stare out the window as that little detail was arranged. Leaning her forehead into the bubbly old glass, she watched a lone car go down the lane, its headlights two beacons that disappeared all too soon in the dimness: The crush of midnight dark that had arrived with Devina and those gruesome creatures had lifted only slightly, the residual gloaming outside as if the demon's presence continued to strip sunlight from the air.

Or maybe it was just later than she thought? God, that was another thing to mourn: the days when fifteen minutes had actually felt like fifteen minutes. Now time was either going like the wind or not moving at all.

Adrian shuffled back over to her. "It's done."

As she turned around again, he was keeping something out of sight. "Let's do this," the angel called out to the two . . . well, combatants. Devina had braced herself, which was ridiculous in those heels—although somehow she managed to look like Wonder Woman, capable of withstanding all assault even in fuck-me pumps and that black leather jumpsuit thing. Colin, likewise, was in a defensive crouch, looking as grim as death.

Maybe this will all be over, Sissy thought, holding her book right against her chest. And man, having died once, she was not looking forward to a repeat—especially as she didn't know if she had any destination left.

Wasn't going to be Hell this time. At least, that's what Jim had told—

"Shall we?" Colin said, raising his palms.

"I'm ready to dance." The demon put her hands facing outward. "Are we going on one, two, three—"

"No," Colin drawled.

The archangel let loose something out of a Batman movie, the rays of brilliant light shooting from his palms and training on Devina. As her brunette hair was stripped back from her face, she cursed and threw out her version of the same, twin black blasts powering across the parlor.

It was either that or she was clearly going up in smoke.

And talk about atmospheric change: Sissy could feel the warmth and the bitter cold, as well as the powerful electric charge that sparked where the positive and negative met. Hair lifted off the top of her head and all down her forearms—and then things got even more intense. Brilliant flashes of light began to pop free as if from friction, and she felt a strange sensation underneath her skin—like her blood was threatening to boil.

We gotta get out of here, she thought as she glanced at the window. And yet the forces were so great, she wasn't sure even a trip out of Caldwell would be enough.

Maybe this time they were going to create another Atlantic Ocean.

As the ionizing charge increased still further, a hum began to weave through the room, subtle at first, then growing louder and louder until it became like a jet engine, until her ears registered it not as sound, but as pain. Beside her, Adrian took a step back, but it wasn't to jump through the glass. He was bracing himself against the wall of the old house.

"You're going to want to hold on to something," he yelled. "It's going to start rotating."

As Sissy looked around for a good place to lock onto, Ad just reached out and grabbed her, dragging her against him.

"I can give us some extra coverage," he barked. At least, she assumed that was what he'd said—she couldn't hear a thing.

Trapping the book between them, she wound her arms around his hard torso. "How are you going to—"

All at once a shimmering came down over the both of them, the glittering shower cutting the noise and leaving a pattern in the air that she had to look through—like you'd move your eyes into one of the diamonds in a chain-link fence to see out of it.

"Nice trick," she muttered.

"I can also crochet."

Just when she was sure Colin and Devina couldn't throw out any more energy, when she was certain that one or maybe both of them were going to be knocked off their feet—and likely blast the roof off the damn house—a subtle shift occurred.

Instead of hitting straight on, the two opposing forces began to slide past each other. Except there was no reason to duck and cover. Just before the two beams were going to end up breaking free, some kind of elemental force kept them tied—and with no other place to go, they began to bend around and start to circle. But it wasn't easy. The sound was like a huge piece of metal being twisted, a great high-pitched grind that made her wince even with Ad's spell in place.

Transfixed by the magic and the power, all she could think of was the show *Storm Chasers*. Reed Timmer and his Dominator had spent a number of seasons hunting down spring tornadoes and getting right in the middle of them—and to help the viewers understand what was going on, there had been illustrations on how twisters formed thanks to countervailing cool/dry and warm/humid fronts colliding out over the flat Midwest.

Same thing here. The first rotation appeared to be the hardest, Colin's warm force curving around Devina's cold one until the light and the dark doubled back and hooked into their original source. And . . . again. A second trip around. And . . . again. A third.

By the fourth time, she could see how a groove in space-time—or whatever—was being created. Nothing spilled upward or downward, as if the gathering energy were too attracted to itself to pare off willy-nilly. Instead, the circling started to happen with ease.

And then that rotation took on a life all its own.

Through the invisible lockdown Ad had put up around them, she watched as Colin's and Devina's poses changed, shifting from braced to direct their beams to leaning back like they were trying to keep from getting pulled in. And then the two of them were shouting at each other over the whirring noise.

They broke off at exactly the same second: Colin hitting the wall behind him with such force he went Bugs Bunny, his body embedding in the lath and plaster, and Devina going airborne and ending up in the far upper corner of the ceiling. Right before she hit with enough impact to shatter, the demon caught herself with a feline twist and stick, her body adhering itself high above and staying there like she was ready to pounce down.

Except Devina's gravity-defying trick was nothing compared to the storm in the center of the parlor.

The forces were beginning to spin so fast that the alternation of light and dark ceased to exist and all became a resonant thundercloud gray. And that was when the objects in the room started to vibrate . . . then move. The sofas gravitated toward the energy, wadding up the tremendous rug in great bunches, bringing the Oriental along with them. Mirrors and paintings smacked against the walls before breaking free, flying toward the vortex and disappearing into it with unholy flares of blood-red light.

"Stay here," Adrian gritted.

"Wait, no!" she screamed, trying to catch him before he left the protective spell. "You're gonna get lost!"

There was no stopping him, though. And no great footing for him, either. He dropped down, as if trying to avoid the vacuum, and then fought for purchase as his body began to skid over the now-bare floor.

Up on the ceiling, like some great housefly, Devina was yelling. As her brunette hair ripped around, it flashed images of her red lips, parted, bright white teeth gleaming as she tried to communicate. But it wasn't Ad who responded. It was Colin. With obvious effort, he dug himself out of his archangel imprint in the wall—and headed for Jim's remains. When he outed a crystal dagger, Sissy wondered what in the hell he was going to do.

Raising his arm high over his shoulder, he buried that brilliant dagger right into the meat of Jim's shoulder—and then he wasted no time going back to what little shelter he had.

Of course, Sissy thought. If Jim's body were lost in there, he'd have nothing to come back to.

"Adrian! Watch out!" In spite of the fact that he probably couldn't hear her, she pointed wildly at the coffee table. "Ad!"

Whether he heard her or had eyes in the back of his skull, she didn't know—but the angel ducked out of the path of the marble-topped table as it flipped end over end and then went airborne, the gaping maw of that energy sucking it in with another blast of red light. Then it was the green velvet sofa's turn.

Meanwhile, Adrian stayed braced against the suck zone, trying to open something.

Old books vibrated in the shelves and then broke free of their orderly rows, flying through the air like crows, their covers flapping, their pale pages beating against one another until they were consumed. And Ad had to duck and cover again, especially as the heavy candlesticks hit the road for the center of the room.

The angel yelled something back at Devina.

It was a water bottle. That was what was in his hand. And as he freed the cap, the little disk flipped out of his hand.

Jim's silver blood took flight just like the books, but its path was not the same at all. Instead of a quick, messy trip, it congealed, becoming a kind of mercury, and its progression was in slow-mo, whereas everything else was on fast-forward: The distinct silver droplets tripped lazily over one another as they fell into a line and headed for the maelstrom, kept aloft by the energy in the room, attracted to the mouth of the energy swirl.

Adrian didn't wait to watch what happened when the blood reached the destination. He wrenched his poor broken body around and tried to make it back to where he'd been. Just as she'd feared, though, the current had caught hold of him—his shirt being pulled so tightly across his chest that it began to rip in half, his loose pants flapping like sails in a bad wind.

He wasn't going to make it, she thought with panic.

Throwing the book down, she reached through the force field, straining to stay inside at the same time she tried to cover as much distance as she could. Adrian reached out as well, the skin on his face getting pulled taut over his sharp features as he fought against the draw.

"Adrian!" She stretched out as far as she could, some instinct warning her that if she went too far, she was going to fall into the vacuum along with him. "Adrian!"

She knew he was going to trip right before it happened—that bad leg of his could not possibly support the work being demanded of it, and the knee buckled right out from under him.

Fuck it, she thought as she threw herself against the metaphysical links.

Sissy snapped free of the safe haven and was nearly knocked unconscious by the roaring noise. And that wasn't the only thing. The air pressure was so low, her eardrums popped with such violence she was convinced she'd lost all her hearing.

"Adrian . . . !"

She hit the floor herself, thinking a lower profile would give the vacuum less to get hold of. And as she grabbed onto the angel's hand, he glared at her like he was pissed she'd left the spell—

but what the hell? Like losing him was an option? She was *not* going to get stuck here alone with Devina.

The suction on her body was so great, she was surprised her skin didn't peel free—and there was no question: She knew she was going into the vortex, too.

They both were.

This was how it was going to end.

Chapter Twelve

Nigel lost the fight in the most unceremonious of ways. Instead of some great death throe followed by a wheezy Shakespearean monologue, he simply took one last step . . . and landed on his knees.

He had every intention of getting back up. Of keeping going. Of finding something, anything to sustain him in this wasteland.

But there was no where-one-has-a-will-one-has-a-way thing here. Alas, as much as he commanded, demanded, cajoled his body to return upright, it didn't resist so much as ignore his every entreaty.

The cold, which had been ramping up for quite some time, now took over, and to keep some warmth within his flesh he drew his knees up to his chest and tucked his lower face into the folds of his robe. Perhaps just a second of rest. Yes, that was it. And then he would resume. . . .

An image of Colin appeared in his mind's eye. It was a memory from a precious moment of privacy, the archangel standing beside his camping ground up in Heaven. Ah, yes, that dinky campground—no luxurious tent for Colin. God forbid he make any concession to comfort and ease. That hard-headed fighter had naught but a tarp supported at four corners off the ground, and yet whenever Nigel had gone there to find the archangel, the modest quarters had seemed like a mansion by virtue of Colin's presence: The male's bracing body had created walls of precious marble out of thin air, and floors of priceless mosaic from the sand and grass. His resounding intelligence had been the sturdy roof overhead, and his piercing eyes the magnificent front entrance.

In this memory, one that had been common to his moments of repose up in Heaven, Colin had just emerged from a bath in the river, droplets of water running down his pectorals. Except . . . had Colin had a towel around his waist? Or had Nigel given one to him as he'd approached . . . ?

With sudden panic, Nigel couldn't recall exactly the series of events that took place next or the words and gestures that had been shared, the nuances of connection growing murky for the first time.

Indeed, his memories were being stolen from him, diminished by the physical discomforts of being chilled to the bone and choked by the infernal gray sand. In desperation, he tried to reach past the suffering and connect with the very best part of his past. But he could not . . . no, he could not find enough details to re-assure himself that yes, he had been there with that angel. He had known love and shared it with someone who mattered. He had . . . lived in a way humans took for granted if they were very lucky and immortals rarely got anywhere close to.

Wrapping his arms around his knees, he shivered and tried to breathe.

When he went to lift his head sometime later, he discovered he could not. Nor could he release his hands.

Moaning, he attempted to rock from side to side and was de-nied the latitude.

Frozen in position, even as his heart pounded in his chest, he—

"—gel!"

The shock of hearing another voice made him jerk. It didn't lift his head, however.

"Jesus fucking Christ!" The voice was off in the distance, the syllables carried upon the cold wind. "Nigel! Is that you?"

"Jim?" he breathed. "Jim . . . ?"

"What the fuck!"

Yes, it was in fact the savior.

With the last scrap of energy he had, Nigel ripped his head up, and the pain caused his vision to go watery on him. Blinking away the blindness, he saw . . . yes, it was the savior, trudging across the dusty ground cover, his body pitched forward as if he were dragging a sleigh or mayhap a castle's weight behind him.

He was holding the bottom of his thin shirt up over his face, but he dropped it to yell once more. "Nigel! I'm here!"

Nigel reached out, cleaving his arm off his legs, extending it stiffly. "Jim . . ."

His voice carried no farther than the inside of the robe that covered his nose and mouth, but there was no strength to spare to bring the fabric down.

Was this a mirage?

All he could do was wait to find out, and yet even still, he knew this was real—and the sight before him brought true tears to his eyes. Against common sense and self-preservation, Jim Heron had arrived in the desolate landscape, looking as if he were single-handedly capable of reversing the domino effect Nigel had put into motion with a crystal dagger and been questioning ever since.

It was possible, he thought, that he had in fact chosen well.

———◄——————►———

"Nigel!"

As Jim hollered that name again, the yelling was wasted energy—it wasn't like the guy was going to get up and run away. Hell, it looked like the archangel could barely move. And yet Jim was afraid this was a lie . . . or part of the torture.

If the latter was true? Well, at least the shit wasn't monotonous and gray.

As he came up to the colored silk robing, that rhythmic beacon quieted as if its job were done, and for a moment, all he could do was stand there and try to get his breath back.

But it was the archangel. Although, damn, the guy was a shadow of his former self, a pathetically small bundle in this endless wasteland, weakened and cowed. And staring down, Jim found that this was yet another outcome he would never have predicted.

Why couldn't they be surprised by good news?

"Ah, shit, Nigel." There was a temptation to fall to his knees with the guy, but he couldn't afford to risk getting trapped in that position. "How you doing?"

Dumb-ass question if there ever was one.

"Why ever have you come," the archangel whispered hoarsely. The English accent remained, but the hauteur was gone—and Jim found that he missed it.

"I gotta get you back, my man. You don't belong here."

He braced himself for an argument. Something along the lines of the-rules-are-this-and-that, or I-am-my-own-destiny.

"Thank you, blessed savior."

Jim closed his eyes briefly. This was bad, very bad, if Nigel was going the gratitude route.

Snapping into action, he looked around—and then wondered why he bothered. Just the landscape and nothing else—no structure for shelter, no relief from the monotony. The only thing he could do was get Nigel moving, and he feared that was simply masturbation for their feet.

Clearly, the archangel didn't have a bright idea for getting out of here, or he wouldn't have ended up on the ground like this. Or accepted the help. Such as it was.

"Come on." Jim bent over and grabbed hold of the archangel. "Let's get you up."

With a burst of strength, he pulled Nigel off his ass, and had to groan—which was what you did when you tried to lift a piano: The archangel wasn't a fatty, but he offered worse than no help: His bones were snapping as his position was forcibly altered, the breaks like the cracks of twigs under feet while, against his chest, Jim felt Nigel jerk and gasp in pain . . . but the hard-headed bastard didn't put up any kind of protest.

When they were finally on the vertical, Nigel clung to him, and for an instant, Jim just held on to the guy. But he couldn't waste much time with the softie shit.

"Come on, walk with me."

Okay, that was not going to happen. Nigel couldn't even keep himself upright, his legs a disjointed tangle that flopped in the wrong places. Fucking hell—

The first clue that something was wrong was that the wind abruptly stopped blowing around them. Then the cold began to dissipate.

Jim shifted Nigel's deadweight to his left side, freeing up his right hand to fight if he had to. After however long in this gray landscape of WTF, he knew better than to think any change was going to work to his advantage.

And that was before the swirl in the sky appeared directly over his godforsaken head: High above the ground a circle formed, the pattern demarcated by movement, slow at first, then gathering in speed.

"We gotta get the fuck out of here," he muttered.

But there was no running to be had. The fluffy, dusty ground didn't offer good traction, and keeping Nigel from becoming a flower bed in the shit was requiring all the strength he had.

A crack of thunder was so loud it made him wince, and he did the best he could to protect the archangel. Fucking A, he'd asked for a break in the monotony and what did he get? A tornadic supercell. Great improvement. Thanks, Mother Nature—

There was another momentous clap overhead and then the utterly inexplicable happened.

From out of the center of the storm, a large object was birthed from the sky, falling free from up above and landing with a great mushroom cloud of that ash.

"What the . . ." Jim rubbed his eyes in case he'd lost his mind or his vision.

Nope. It was, in fact, the Victorian couch from the parlor. And right after it? The huge rug. Books. The velvet sofa and the coffee table and the candlestick Sissy had brained Colin with . . .

"It's our fucking ride home!" he yelled. "Jesus Christ, they did it!"

He offered a quick prayer of thanks to the Creator—after all, it was kind of hard not to believe in the guy, considering Jim had met Him and this was, or at least had the potential to be, a frickin' miracle.

Except how were they going to—

A sense of lift grabbed him by the hair and shoulders, and he could feel a sudden buoyancy in his body, that super-heavy gravitational hold easing up its drag coefficient on his bones. And abruptly, Nigel's weight wasn't so heavy either.

As the levitation began to take serious hold, Jim looked into the center of the hurricane and wondered how this was going to work. But then the suck zone kicked up big-time, the inward flow becoming undeniable. Dust came with him as he was lifted from the insufferable ground, and he held Nigel in a death grip—literally.

He wasn't going to lose the guy, especially as they started to spin.

Jim kept his eye on where they were headed until the particles in the air stung so badly he couldn't keep his lids open. Then it was a case of faster and faster with the turning until his hair peeled back from his face and the silk robing Nigel had on slapped at them both.

Jim began to lose his grip. "Hold me!"

The archangel dropped his hands instead. Like he'd passed out.

Closer to the vortex they rose, faster and faster they spun, until Jim's empty stomach revolted and he thought seriously of hurling.

And then he didn't think of anything at all, because, like Nigel, he lost consciousness.

Chapter Thirteen

In the suck zone of the parlor, Sissy went horror-movie, clawing at the floorboards as she was pulled on her belly feet-first toward the energy swirl. Bracing herself for being ripped apart, she knew that whatever had happened to all those pieces of furniture, wherever they had gone, was going to—

Except then everything went haywire. Okay, more haywire.

The explosion was so great, her body went into a tumble, arms and legs flying through air or space or wherever the hell she was. Pain lit up over every inch of her skin, like she was being flayed alive, and when she went to scream, something entered her mouth and stung like bees.

Except she wasn't getting sucked in.

She was being thrown free. Violently.

The impact of her hitting the wall was so great she went loose and cascaded to the floor. Her shoulder hurt so badly it had to be dislocated, and God only knew how much other damage had been done. For a moment, all she could do was lie there, but the sudden quiet in the room seemed as dangerous as all the noise had been.

With a groan, she rolled over onto her back and coughed. Her nose and throat were irritated, and as she blinked her vision clear, her eyes felt like they had sandpaper for lids. Gradually, she became aware that there was the strangest sound in the parlor, and it took her a moment to figure out what it reminded her of: sleet. It was just like a subtle chorus of sleet falling inside the house, a hundred million tiny particles hitting the floor.

Sissy pushed herself over onto her side and forced her vision to get with the program. Unbelievable, she thought. The maelstrom Colin and Devina had created was gone as if it had never been, and—bonus!—there was no new national landmark or body of water in its place. The parlor's windows had all been blown out, however . . . and there was, right in the center of the room, a boulder-like mass that was covered with some kind of volcanic ash.

As if maybe all of the furniture and objects that had been sucked into the vortex had been chewed like gum and spit out.

Considering God only knew what it really was, she checked for the others in case there was more fighting to do: Colin was slumped where he had been originally thrown against the wall. Devina was crumpled in the corner on the floor, her anti-gravity thing not having outlasted the explosion. And Adrian was actually upside down on his head, his legs propped up against a stretch of molding like a drunk trying to do a yoga pose.

Nobody was moving—

No, wait . . . that mass in the center of the room was. And as it turned around itself she realized . . . it wasn't solid at all—and it wasn't made of rock. It was an orb of light that was covered in ash. And as it writhed, the gray dust fell from it, revealing something close to a three-dimensional shadow.

Two shadows. Twisted around each other.

Like two people who had had to hold on to each other.

All at once, Sissy's brain came back online. Her body was slower to get with it, but she had enough coordination to crawl across the now-bare and dusty floor.

"Jim . . ." The tears that sprang to her eyes helped get rid of some of the grit. "Jim!"

At the sound of his name, half of the light separated, pulling free of the undifferentiated mass—and then with a sizzle of electricity, it beelined for Jim's remains . . . and found home.

The animation was immediate. Jim's body jumped, arms and legs flopping, that chest expanding as a great breath was taken—

Jim tried to sit up so fast it was like he had jumper cables hooked to his feet—but the dagger Colin had stabbed through his shoulder kept him down.

"Fuck!" he barked, grabbing that side of his pecs with his free hand like he couldn't figure out why things hurt or were stuck. "*Fuck!*"

His curse was so loud, it woke up the other people in the room, but he didn't look around. Those eyes of his went to hers and stayed there.

"Oh . . . God . . ." he whispered. "You're back."

"No," she croaked as her strength gave out from relief. "You are."

Gritting his teeth, he palmed the hilt of the weapon that impaled him and had kept his body from disappearing. Then he yanked the blade free not only of the floor, but his own flesh.

In spite of all he'd been through, and a now bleeding wound, he scrambled to her and grabbed her so hard, she had to groan—but she didn't care. He could crush her as much as he wanted.

She crushed him back.

It seemed impossible that she was holding him. That he had returned.

Jim pulled back and cupped her face between his palms. "Sissy . . ."

Her heart was hammering so much, there was no opportunity for it to beat faster—even though she had the sense that he was going to kiss her. Hell, considering everything that had just happened, the fact that his stare shifted down to her lips and his strong arms maneuvered her into position seemed . . . like a pretty damned good idea.

Because she wanted it, too. She needed to feel him up close and all over—like that was the only way her mind could grapple with the fact that he was actually here.

"Sissy." His voice was almost too deep to register. "I've gotta tell you something—"

"Get the *fuck* away from him," the demon bit out.

In spite of the fact that the parlor was powdered with gray dust, Purgatory's existence and any experience over there disappeared completely as Jim stared into Sissy's eyes.

The vow he had made, the realizations that had come to him, stuck around, however.

Cupping her face, he got choked up not because he didn't know what to say, but because there was too much to get out—and he said her name a couple of times while he tried to direct traffic in his brain.

In the end, he decided to lead with the big one . . . even though the only woman he'd said those three words to had been his mother—so he was beyond rusty.

Except he didn't get that far. Just as he started speaking, the one person he never wanted to see or hear from again piped up.

"Get the *fuck* away from him."

As he looked across the parlor, the extent of the damage they'd done registered dimly—the place was trashed, great holes in the lineups of the bookshelves, windows broken, drapes shredded. Plus ninety percent of the furniture was somewhere else, natch. But none of that mattered as he watched Devina get to her feet.

The fact that the demon was in the house at all was a surprise, given the additional protection spell he'd put up—then again, maybe the thing hadn't survived his second "death." Oh, wait, make that third. And yet, even though her presence wasn't a good thing, it was amusing to see her look so disheveled, her brunette hair a ratty mess, her leather pantsuit smudged with ash, streaks of oozing black on her face and shoulders from where she'd been cut.

What was not a shocker or funny at all was how pissed off she was. Those shark-like eyes of hers were glowing in an unholy way, and her talon hands were curled into claws. She wasn't looking at him, though.

She was focused on Sissy.

And what do you know, that was a match to his ignition, lighting him up from the inside. Shuffling his woman behind him, he got to his feet and faced off with his enemy.

"What the fuck are you doing here, demon."

Her eyes swung over to his. "I'm the reason you're out, asshole." She pounded on her chest. "So show some respect."

"Actually, it was a group effort, bitch."

At the sound of Ad's hoarse voice, Jim became aware that there were two other people in the room: the other angel, who was trying to unpretzel himself over by the windows, and Colin, who was still pretty out of it.

"Jesus," Jim breathed. "You didn't use her to—"

"Get away from him!" Devina lurched forward. "Get away from my man."

Yeah, screw that, Jim thought. In spite of the fact that his body felt like it had been through a meat grinder, he was more than ready to hit her. Just haul off and clock Devina so hard she—

A rhythmic sound broke into the room, strident and loud enough to get even the demon's attention. And it was as Jim twisted around to look behind himself that he realized who and what it was . . . and how he'd managed to find Nigel in that dusty, torturous place.

Dog, who was not actually a dog, was parked between the doorjambs of the parlor, his scruffy little body braced, his muzzle working as he barked at the demon.

It was that noise he'd heard in Purgatory, Jim thought. That beacon that he'd followed in a place with no compass points and no destinations.

Holy shit, the Creator Himself had been the one to lead him to the archangel.

Snapping back to attention, Jim found Devina frozen in place, clearly caught between a jealous urge to rip Sissy limb from limb and a serious sense of self-preservation.

"But it's not fair," the demon bitched. "It's not fucking fair."

Dog kept up with the barking, like he was talking at her. And then Devina looked at Jim, her expression changing into something that seemed a lot like hurt.

With four deliberate steps across the bare, dusty floor, she came up to him, raised her hand over her shoulder, and slapped him so hard both of his ears rang.

"You are too cruel," she said numbly. "And you do *not* deserve me."

One more nasty glare at Sissy and the demon was gone, poofing it out of the room.

"Well, that could have been worse," Ad muttered. "Although, man, we've so lost our security deposit on this place."

Chapter Fourteen

Nigel regained consciousness in the opposite way from the manner in which he'd lost it: slowly and in stages. First came a hazy awareness of being, then a rudimentary thought that he was drawing breath. Next was discomfort . . . that expeditiously ramped up to full-on pain.

Amongst the many aspects of life that were straddled by an entity such as himself, the duality of his nature, both corporeal and ethereal, meant that he was not entirely free of contending with the physical travails of possessing flesh. And such was the case now.

Especially as the shell he had left behind in Heaven reestablished itself over his core, sprouting from the essence of his energetic being.

Naturally, this made the suffering even more acute, and he parted his lips to release a moan.

"His arms are broken," someone said from above him.

"His legs, too."

And then that voice, that special, sacred voice that had both kept him sane and made him crazy, spoke up: "How unfortunate. I shall have to wait until they heal first so that I may break them anew."

Nigel opened his eyes and sought the male who had uttered the words. And there he was, Colin, the archangel, standing off to the side, his arms crossed as if in disapproval, his brows down, as was usual. That stare of his, however, was the very antithesis of the male's typical dispassion: It glittered with a sheen of tears.

It was a death anew to see the hurt he had caused. The betrayal and the injury.

Nigel lifted his hand, as he could not speak—the gesture the only way he could beg. Colin tracked the movement . . . and shook his head.

The rejection was then completed as he addressed Jim and Adrian, speaking some combination of words that Nigel was incapable of understanding. Indeed, he would have withstood the pain he was in ten thousand times over to have a chance of his apology being accepted. But he knew his lover too well to be surprised.

Colin did not spare him another look as he disappeared, leaving nothing in his wake but a pair of footprints in the fallen ash upon the floor.

Nigel closed his eyes and found himself wishing for a permanent death.

"Nigel," Jim said. "Nigel, you still there?"

No, he was not. "Aye, savior," he rasped.

"Listen, we gotta . . . we gotta do something about the shape you're in. We can't leave you like this."

"Aye."

There was a long pause, like the two angels and the transient soul Sissy Barten were waiting for some instruction. He had none to give them. His direction had just left him for a very rational reason as Colin was not the type to make mistakes more than once.

Nor give his heart in that fashion.

"Nigel, can you fix yourself?" Jim asked. "Can you take care of this?"

When Nigel shook his head, Sissy spoke up. "I don't suppose we could take him to the ER."

"Yeah, not sure how that would work." Jim cursed. "But I was trained to be a field medic. I've set a bone or two—although nothing like this."

Nigel cleared his throat and shut his eyes. "I am in your care, savior."

"Okay. All right. We need something to put between his teeth—oh, great, thanks, Ad." A rustling sound. "Nigel? Open up and bite down on this, boss. It's part of a drape."

Doing as he was instructed, he didn't brace himself for new agony. He was in a sufficiency of that already. It was not going to become worse.

"I'm going to start on your right leg, okay?" Pause. "Boss? You with me?"

"But of course, savior," he mumbled around the gag.

Abruptly, Jim's voice became very distinct, as if he'd moved up to Nigel's ear. "You sure there isn't another way to do this? I'm pretty sure you got magic tricks I don't know about."

Oh, there was. But he did not have the strength for it, and more to the point, he was in the mood for a lancing.

"Nigel? Hello? Nothing to say, huh. Okay, get ready."

There were some orders given by the savior to the two others, and Nigel felt a pressure on his hips, as if someone had straddled him and was sitting down. Then his leg was laid out flat, the pieces of bone grinding one upon the other at the repositioning.

The gag was rather useful, as it turned out, his molars sinking into it as if it were flesh.

"On three," Jim said. "One, two . . ."

When "three" arrived, Nigel's lids popped wide-open and he screamed around the fabric in his mouth, the pain so great it appeared as if he had been wrong about being unable to feel worse.

Tears speared into his eyes and fell down the sides of his face, getting into his ears and his hair, and if he could have, he would have rolled over to vomit. Instead, he began to sob, his chest jumping with every jagged inhale, his dry throat racked with his heaving.

Through the great release of sorrow, Jim's voice cut in as if he had once again come up to Nigel's ear. "Do you want me to stop?"

Nigel shook his head and stared at the ceiling through his wailing. He needed to pay for the hurt he had caused and for his lack of courage and faith and for the fact that he had hurt the one entity in the universe who had always stood by him.

"You sure," Jim said grimly.

All Nigel did was nod again.

Sissy watched from three feet away as Adrian sat on Nigel to keep him as steady as possible and Jim reset the leg bones. On the left side, the archangel had two breaks, one of the calf and one of the thigh, and Adrian had to lean down and stabilize the knee after the upper problem was fixed. The arms were just as bad.

She'd had to sit out a couple of field hockey games her senior year thanks to a sprained ankle—and that had been no walk in the park. She couldn't fathom what this must be like. She wasn't going to turn away, however. If there was a chance for her to help, she was going to be there.

That face, though. As long as she lived—or, jeez, "lived," she supposed—she was never going to forget the way the archangel's lips pulled off his teeth and his jaw gritted and his eyes disappeared in folds of agony as he grimaced. And the tears.

They made her want to weep. Not just for him, but for each of them.

When it was all over, Jim was panting from the effort. Coughing, too—which, given the amount of sediment that had come across with him from Purgatory, suggested the place was like a desert. As Adrian unhinged himself from the archangel's torso, Jim sat back and wiped his face on his shirt.

"Without X-rays," he said, "I don't know whether I did more harm than good."

"He'll take care of it." Adrian fell back on his butt. "He could have fixed all of this had he wanted to. Ain't that right, Nigel."

Sissy shook her head. "But why would he—"

The archangel sat up and took the gag out of his mouth with a hand that trembled. He was as pale as a cloud, and as a shimmer fell down the front of his robing, she realized that something like diamonds were cascading to the floor.

No, they actually were diamonds. As if his tears had hardened into the precious stones.

"You good?" Jim demanded gruffly. "Anything else you need?"

"You h-h-h-have p-p-provided a s-s-sufficiency."

"I'll be right back," Sissy said, bolting for the door.

Rushing through the foyer and going into the kitchen, she headed for the cabinets. Popping them open, she found empty shelf after empty shelf. She was looking for some bourbon or gin or something that could warm the guy up and calm him down—

She found the remnants of a liquor stash on the lower level next to the sink. Pulling the bottles out, she had to wipe off the labels of a couple to read them. Most appeared to have been long opened, though, so God only knew what was going on with the insides of them.

One of them still had a seal, however, and when she looked at the label, she muttered, "Gotcha."

On the way out, she grabbed one squat glass from the counter—then thought, What the hell, everyone needed a drink.

When she reentered the parlor, she hesitated, the extent of the damage dawning on her. The place was a bomb zone, but in the words of her father, they had bigger fish to fry at the moment.

Going over to the Englishman, she sat down cross-legged, arranged the glasses, cracked the paper seal, and poured out a healthy serving of the sherry.

She handed the first one to the guy who'd had his arms and legs worked on. Seemed only fair.

As Nigel's strange-colored eyes swung in her direction, he gave her a tired smile. "You are a saint, my dear."

She had to help him keep hold of the glass. "Isn't that your job?"

"Alas, I am no saint." He raised the sherry to her and bowed his head before drinking it all down.

Sissy was ready with the bottle, refilling him before pouring out glasses for herself, Jim, and Ad. And what do you know, the men murmured thanks and accepted the offering in spite of the fact that they probably considered it a little girlie.

Better than hundred-year-old gin, she'd imagine.

The four of them finished the whole damn bottle—Sissy included, even though she'd never been a big drinker even in college. And she had to admit the stuff worked. By the time the sherry was gone, there was color in Nigel's face and his hands had stopped shaking, and he wasn't the only one relaxing a little.

It was like having a Bunsen burner in your stomach, she thought as she put her glass down.

Jim tossed back the last of his and stared at Nigel. "I'm going to assume you're fully returned. As in, I'm going to stay down here and keep doing what I'm doing."

"That is my intention."

"Intention?"

"The Creator is going to be displeased in all likelihood. But I shall take full responsibility. If there is to be a punishment, I shall accept it in your stead."

"Devina says she's going to tell Him it was her idea."

"And you trust her?"

"Good point."

Nigel looked up at the ceiling. "I shall be off then."

"I'm not going to ask you who the next soul is."

"Indeed? After your good deed, I am in the mood to grant you a favor."

"No." Jim's expression grew hard. "I'm going to win this the right way. The way He set it up. I'll find the soul, and she's not getting them this time."

"Fair enough. Let me know if you change your mind." Nigel glanced at Adrian and gave him a nod. Then he looked over at Sissy. "My gratitude for the restorative."

And on that note, the archangel up and disappeared, leaving nothing behind. Just like Colin had.

Sissy reached out and picked up one of the flashing white stones that had fallen to the floor. "Is this really what I think it is?"

"Yeah," Ad said. "The tears of archangels are pretty damn fancy, huh." The guy grunted and stood up. "I'm fucking starved. Between the drama and no lunch, I'm ready to eat the door-knobs." He glanced around. "Lucky for me, 'cause that's about all that's left in here. I'm gonna hit the Seven Eleven and then make a McDonald's run—no reason for the likes of us to eat healthy. Whaddaya want."

Sissy put in an order for two cheeseburgers, a large fries, a high-test Coke, and a chocolate sundae. Jim wanted four Quarter Pounders with cheese and three Cokes.

"Hold down the fort," Ad said as he limped off. "And try to do something about the windows. I think we're supposed to get rain tonight."

Left alone with Jim, Sissy sat and played with the little diamond she'd picked up, moving it around the center of her palm. A minute later, the sound of the Explorer backing down the driveway was louder than it usually was on account of the lack of glass.

"Are you all right?" she asked.

"I don't know."

"That's honest." She looked up. "I'm glad . . . you came back."

Jim rubbed his jaw, and for some reason that made her focus on his lips. Which made her wonder—what they would feel like . . . against her mouth, her throat, her breasts.

"I've got to find the next soul. I've got to—shit, who the hell is it gonna be? And where are they . . ."

She had a feeling he was talking to himself, and that was okay. The rambling gave her an excuse to look at him some more, measure his broad shoulders, his veined forearms, his—

"You're bleeding," she said, pointing to his shoulder.

He glanced at himself. "Who stabbed me? And why?"

"Colin. They were worried your body would . . . God, are we really talking like this?" She scrubbed her eyes. "Sometimes this is just too much. It really is."

"I'm sorry."

Sissy glanced over at the blown-out windows. The darkness outdoors was because of the sun having set, not that demon, but it was hard to feel safe with all the open frames. Then again, why did she think a couple of panes of glass were going to help.

"Are we okay here?" she said.

"I'll put the spell back up. I guess it failed or Devina wouldn't have gotten in here."

"Yes."

There was a long, awkward silence. Probably because his head was tied up in war, and hers was somewhere else entirely.

"What were you going to say to me?" she blurted.

"Huh? Sorry, I got game brain."

As he glanced over at her, she felt foolish. "Oh, it's okay. It's nothing, really. Well, actually—what can I do to help? You know, with what you're doing about Devina."

He opened his mouth. Then clapped it shut. "I'd really prefer you stay out of this. Not because I think you're weak, but because I am."

"You're weak?" She laughed harshly and eyed the way his biceps stretched the sleeves of his T-shirt. "Don't think so."

A strange look came into his eyes. "When it comes to you, I am."

Sissy's heart stopped. "Really?"

"Yeah." He cracked his knuckles one by one. "Listen, I don't want things to get weird, okay."

"Oh, yeah, no, weird is bad."

"But just so you and I are clear, I really fucking want to kiss you right now."

Chapter Fifteen

What the hell, Jim thought. He might as well lay it all out there.

And as Sissy didn't run for one of the very, very open windows, he took it as a good sign. Or . . . actually, a really bad one.

"So kiss me," she said.

Jim actually recoiled. Which proved that the right woman could turn any full-grown man back into a fourteen-year-old with the right combination of words. Although that quick-fire regression was only the first part of his response. The second half?

Pure. Sex.

Fuck the kissing. He wanted to shove her back onto the hard-wood floor, yank her pants down, and get inside of her. In spite of the fact that she was hardly that kind of girl and Adrian would be coming back with twelve thousand calories of fast food at any given minute.

"Or are you going to make me do it?" she asked.

"Do what," he blurted. Christ, like he had amnesia?

"Kiss you."

God love her, she didn't wait for a response. She leaned in, grabbed the front of his shirt, and pulled him to her.

"Oh, fuck," he groaned as he tilted his head. "Fuck me . . ."

Please, oh, shit, fuck me, he thought as their lips met in the middle.

She was soft. She was sweet. She tasted like sherry.

And he took over from there.

Dragging her into his lap, he kissed her hard and held her harder. He'd wanted this for too long and for all the wrong reasons, and in the back of his head, he told himself that was why he was instant hot-'n'-heavy. Then again, maybe it was because she was just so good, so right.

He pushed himself back from her. "Shit."

"What?" she mumbled, leaning into his arms. "What's wrong?"

"I don't know how far you want this to go." Damn it, the way she was pushing her breasts up to him, her body seemed as ready as his was. "You don't have to do this—"

"What makes you think I want to stop."

She put her mouth to his again, and oh, man, wrong call, but sooooo fucking right. And this time he let his tongue do what it wanted to, licking its way in, taking her. That was when she moaned his name.

He almost came in his dusty pants.

Abruptly, she pushed against him, nailing his bad shoulder with her palm. With a hiss, he broke the contact.

"Oh, I'm sorry," she said, wincing. "I didn't mean to—"

"No, no, it's cool. I'm going too fast—"

She settled that score by reaching down for the bottom of her shirt and whipping the whole thing over her head.

Jim's exhale was part curse, part prayer of thanks. Until he realized she wasn't wearing a bra.

"Sweet Mary," he breathed as he looked at her pink-tipped breasts. "You're going to kill me."

"I'm done wasting time," she said, staring into his eyes. "And

I'm done wondering what it's like. And I'm totally finished with fighting the fact that I want you."

Boom. Boom. Boom.

His heart was beating so hard, he had to give his sternum props for keeping the muscle inside of his immortal body.

Staring at her breasts, Jim dipped his head and led with tongue, at the same time he lifted her up to his mouth. As he latched onto her nipple, her head fell all the way back, and she said his name in a rough voice that was sexier than anything he'd ever heard in his life. Worshiping her with his lips, he let his hands start roaming. She was so much smaller than he was, but she seemed just as strong, jacking up against his hold, trying to get closer.

Ninety-nine-point-nine percent of him was ready to take her right here, right now. But the decimal point of decency forced him to be reasonable.

She was, after all, a virgin. And although there were a lot of rules that were off, given the fucked-up kind of existence they both had, she deserved better than a wham-bam for her first time.

Besides, it was entirely possible that she was going to come to her senses and regret this.

He slowed himself down, forced his hands to stay on the outside of her hips, told his cock to pipe-down-big-guy.

She sensed the change in him immediately. "Don't stop."

"Sissy—"

"Don't you fucking dare." She pegged him right in the eye. "Don't."

Well, considering the way she was looking at him? He was incapable of not giving her whatever she wanted: car, house, orgasm after orgasm after—

"How 'bout we compromise," he drawled, dropping back down to her mouth and running his tongue across her lower lip. As she shuddered in his arms, he had to smile. "Yeah, how 'bout we just focus on you."

"Jim, I want—"

"I know what you want. And I'm going to give it to you."

There was nothing like this in the world.

That was the only thing Sissy could think of as she lay in Jim's arms, half-naked and fully turned on. The rest of it was all instinct and heat, a need for something that she'd previously been lukewarm on, a drive to get closer to him than her own skin.

As she arched against him, he didn't leave her hanging, coming back to her mouth and kissing her more. She had the clear sense he was holding everything back on his side, and that just plain sucked. If only she could—

That big hand of his, the one on her hip, shifted down to her thigh . . . and moved inside, inching its way up to the source of her heat.

Everything went heavy and sluggish—in the best way. Moving her leg up and to the side, she gave him all the access he needed as she hung onto the bulk of his shoulders and waited for him to get where she wanted him to be. He went slowly, oh, so slowly, but that was good too, because it meant she could feel everything—from the way his tongue penetrated her mouth, to the hard contours of his arms, to the straining at the tips of her bare breasts and the coiling urgency inside of her.

When he cupped her sex, she cried out and dug her nails into his shoulders—except he just stayed there and kissed her, as if he were giving her a moment to adjust. After a time, though, he began rubbing at her, the pressure and rasp of her panties and the sweatpants exactly what she needed. He wasn't rough, but she wanted him to be. He wasn't fast, but she wanted him to be.

He got the job done, and she wanted him to.

The urgency got raw quick, and Jim didn't tease her. As if he knew this was the first orgasm she was going to have, he took her up steadily and let her body do the rest: That coil deep inside wound tighter and tighter and tighter—and when it snapped free, she felt like her blood had turned into gold, and her bones into fireworks.

His thumb continued to circle as he helped her ride the pulses out, and when it was over, she went completely limp. All she could do was stare up at him through heavy lids.

Well, now she knew why romance novels sold so well. Holy crap.

"Onv gokd tbaj okdrwa."

Sissy frowned and mumbled, "What did you say?"

He repeated whatever it was twice before she heard him right: "We've got to get you dressed."

Jim stretched an arm out, snagged her shirt, and pulled it back over her head. And then he arranged her in his lap, holding her close in his strong arms. The peace between them was as powerful as all the pleasure had been, especially as he stroked her hair back from her face. It was a surprise that a man like him could be so gentle—she felt precious, important, invaluable as he stared down at her like he didn't want to ever leave her.

"What were you going to say to me," she whispered, reaching up and running her fingertips down his hard cheek. The stubble that had grown in was rough, but the skin underneath was warm.

"It was—"

A set of headlights washed across the devastated front of the parlor, and Jim cursed. "Goddamn fast food. He should have gone somewhere fancier."

Sissy had to smile. "I agree."

"Hold on," he grunted, shifting her and then gritting his teeth. As he rearranged what was no doubt an erection and a half, she went right back to where they had just been, hot and hungry. Except now she wanted to pay him back.

Not that she had a clue how to do that. But given his talents? She was willing to bet he could show her.

"We're not finished." She turned his face to hers. "You and me . . . we're not finished."

There was the distant sound of a door slamming and then Ad called out from the back, "Hi, honey, I'm home."

It was painful to watch the warmth leave Jim's face, especially as he set her apart from him and put his clothes back in order.

"Jim," she said. "We are not done."

When all he did was rub his face, she told herself it was sexual frustration and a battle with the good side of his nature. But she wasn't sure—

"I'll come to you," he said in a dark voice. "Tonight."

His eyes slid over to her and they burned like bonfires. "And this time I won't stop."

Sissy's lips parted so she could breathe properly. And the suffocation kept up even as Adrian came in with five stuffed Mickey D bags and started passing around the goods.

All she could think of was how fast they could eat the stuff . . . and get to bed.

Chapter
Sixteen

Devina's hands were bleeding.

As she sat on the foot of her bed, she noticed the blood when she went to pull down the ripped sleeve of her leather pantsuit.

There was also something in her eye. Wiping her fingers off on the bedspread, she discovered that one of her false lashes had come unglued and was hanging off the corner of her lid. She pulled the fuzzy caterpillar-thing free and let it drop to the floor.

It landed in a pile of flesh-colored powder . . . next to a shattered Estée Lauder compact, the mirror of which was cracked down the middle.

Taking a deep breath, her nose tingled at the choking scent in the basement: part Ysatis by Givenchy, Paris by YSL, and Chanel's Coco and Chance Eau Tendre. She wondered idly how long the HVAC system was going to take to air everything out.

Long time.

Especially given that those were not the only perfume bottles she had shattered. The battered remnants of her makeup table were surrounded by broken glass and mangled spray mechanisms. She must have destroyed fifteen different scent containers.

It was nothing compared to what she'd done to her collection.

Looking past the immediate carnage of makeup, handbags,

shoes, and clothes, she could not believe what she had done. In the aftermath of her explosion, she was in awe of herself.

Not a new experience, except this was not something to be proud of.

She had laid ruination to that which was most precious to her—when what she should have been fucking up was Jim's arrogant ass. Worse? She couldn't even remember what it had been like to let it all out. Her rage had been white-hot and blinding—and it wasn't until she'd sat down here and realized that her hands were cut up that what she'd done dawned on her.

At least the Creator had bought her story about the portal, and let that part of things go. Hell, their confrontation after she'd left Jim's had been kind of a letdown—almost as if He had expected it all.

And then she'd come here and . . .

God, how was she going to clean all this up? There were a hundred dressers and bureaus with their drawers pulled out, their contents spilling onto the concrete floor like intestines seeping from a gut wound. Her complex cataloging system, with its internal logic that made sense only to her, was a distant memory as her precious objects intermingled, time periods and geographic locations fucked to high heaven.

There were things that had gotten crushed underfoot, too.

Glasses trampled. Watches smashed. Brass buttons and metal clasps bent out of shape.

Devina flexed her hands and assessed the injuries on her palms. Evidently she'd done a lot of the carnage herself as opposed to working magic.

Getting to her feet, she went to take a step forward and fell to the side, throwing out one of her sliced-up hands to catch herself on a now-empty six-foot-tall shoe rack that was twisted out of shape.

Ah, yes, there was a problem with the shoes she had on. Her right one had lost its sky-high heel, so there was nothing to support her weight on that side.

She went to take both of them off . . . but there was going to be no finding any matched pairs in the mess she'd made. So she snapped the other heel from its base and made a pair of flats out of them.

Purse. She was looking for her purse, the saddlebag Dior she'd worn with the outfit before Jim had gotten lost over in Purgatory, she'd gotten him back, and he'd made some big show out of being reunited with that fucking virgin.

The fact that the bag was metallic silver was going to help with the locating. Should help.

Might help.

For God's sake, she had way too much of the animal-print shit, she thought as she began to wade through the wreckage. Zebra. Tiger. Cheetah. Funny, when all of her handbags had been organized in color lots, she hadn't really seen the rut she'd gotten in.

More lizard, she decided. Croc skin. Maybe some old-school patent leather, and Hermès . . .

"Like Grace Kelly."

God, her voice sounded forlorn even to her own ears.

But damn it, someone like Grace Kelly wouldn't have had her lover get wrapped up in some pencil-stick bitch.

She could dye her hair blond. Yeah, that might work.

"Why, why . . ."

Pushing a sky-blue Birkin out of the way, she kicked an older LV Manhattan onto a pile of Chanel quilted stuff.

It was not going to be enough to just win this round and get Sissy back. She was going to have to . . .

Devina looked around at her things.

. . . do *this* to that fucking virgin.

"Pony" by Ginuwine started playing softly and she wheeled around. Following the sound, she pawed her way through about fifteen thousand dollars of Prada before she found what she was looking for—although by the time she dug out her phone, whoever it was had gone into voice mail.

At least they helped her locate what she'd been looking for.

Wiping her still-oozing hand off on the ass of her trashed leather pantsuit, she called up her therapist's contact info from the address book and hit *send*.

One ring. Two rings. And then came, in the woman's irritatingly calm and sensible voice, "Hello, you've reached the offices of . . ."

Blah, blah, blah. Beep! "This is Devina." She had to switch hands and rewipe. "I've had . . ." As she choked up, she thought about ending the call and starting over, but what the hell. The chick was used to hearing people who'd lost their shit. "I've had a setback. A serious setback. I'm not going to be able to wait until . . ." When was their next appointment? She couldn't remember. "I need to come see you as soon as possible. Please . . . call me."

As she ended the connection, she prayed that the woman had something open in the morning. Afternoon, at the latest.

Because she didn't know how she was going to go on from here.

Like some pathetic loser, she let herself fall to the ground and just sat there, surrounded by the evidence of how fucked her immortal life was. She was too spent to get in touch with her anger and her hatred, too betrayed to marshal some kind of revenge, too heartbroken to even think about Jim.

Devina ducked her head and wondered if maybe this was the Creator's punishment. She wouldn't put it past Him to engineer this torture.

He said He had brought her into being to offer balance to His world and its various humans and creatures. He had always reassured her that she served an important purpose. But she knew better than to believe He was impartial. The truth was . . . He preferred the good.

Always had.

And that did not typically bother her. In fact, she liked being the fly in the ointment—most of the time.

Not at the moment, however. Not in this moment when she was more alone than she had ever been.

Chapter
Seventeen

"Sooooo, I guess I'm going to head upstairs and take a shower before bed."

As Sissy spoke casually, Jim was impressed with the subterfuge: Like she had no agenda and all the time in the world, she crumpled up the wrapper of the hamburger she'd eaten, put it into the closest bag and crammed an empty red French fry carton in there with it. Then she stretched her arms overhead and gave a yawn.

But Jim knew better—especially as she shot him a glance that could have melted paint off a car door. Fortunately, Adrian was all about his Filet-o'-whatever. Or had he started in on his Big Macs?

Like Jim cared.

"Night, Ad." As Sissy went over to the guy, the other angel glanced up and offered his cheek. "Sleep well."

"You, too, Sis."

The kiss she planted on the bastard lasted about a nanosecond and was on an entirely innocent part of Adrian Vogel's body— and Jim still had to call off his inner dogs so he didn't rip his wingman's throat open.

Possessive much? he thought to himself.

Sissy bent over and picked up her trash, and to keep himself from going full-tilt ogle, he made work out of unwrapping his next Quarter Pounder.

"Wait," he said to her. Then he looked at Ad. "You got your phone?"

The angel eased onto one butt cheek and took the thing out of his pocket. "Yeah. You lose yours over in Ash Land?"

"No. Ah . . . would you mind taking a picture?"

"You want a mug shot? I thought you already had a driver's license with a shitty close-up on it."

"No, of me and—" Jim coughed into his fist to cut himself off. What the fuck was he saying here?

"Of the damage to the room," he finished.

"Like you're going to make an insurance claim or something?"

"Just so that we don't screw over the owner."

Ad eyed the destruction. "No offense, but I think that's already happened."

Except the angel started to oblige, putting up his iPhone and clicking away as he kept eating. And after a moment, Sissy floated a wave and took off.

God, he could hear every one of her footfalls as she went up and walked around overhead. He pictured her going down the hall to her room, walking into her bathroom, brushing her teeth—maybe taking a shower. He saw her . . .

Well, shit, he saw her naked. Really, very, totally naked.

Back to the burger. Which now tasted like cardboard and not because it was from the golden arches.

He glanced over at Ad as the angel finished up with the photos. And imagined where things might be if the guy hadn't helped him get back from Purgatory.

"So . . . thank you," Jim muttered.

Ad tucked his phone away, and shoved another load of fries

into his piehole. "You haven't seen how awful these are. Plus I'm thinking I've got grease on the viewer thing."

"You know what I'm talking about."

There was a long pause. "You don't have to say that."

"I do."

"Well, whatever. I had no intention of letting Devina take another one of you. Already lost Eddie—kinda done with the whole immortal-except-not-really bullshit." The other angel looked over. "Besides, you'd have done the same for me."

"Glad you know that. And it is the truth."

"Yeah, I figure if you'd be willing to go to Purgatory for that tight-ass Nigel, you'd have my back, too."

They ate in silence for a while. Then Jim had to ask, "How're we gonna know if the Creator's going to do anything?"

Ad laughed. "In my experience—and I've got some when it comes to pissing the big guy off—it happens quick."

"So you're saying I should save part of this"—he held up his burger—"for Dog."

"I think that would be a good call."

Jim nodded at the drapes they'd pulled across the broken windows. "My protection spell's only going to go so far. We still need to do a better job keeping out the elements."

"It's called Home Depot, buddy. I'll go there tomorrow. Get some plywood and a hammer and nails. I used to be in construction, remember."

Jim thought back to when he'd met the guy . . . and Eddie. Man, the pair of them had been grafted at the hip, a real salt-and-pepper, PB&J-type combo. Death was so damned cruel, he thought.

"Do you know where Eddie is?" he asked.

"Yeah, upstairs in the attic."

"No, I mean . . . where he ended up."

"You thinking about being a hero again?" Ad shook his head. "I'm pretty sure that trying our luck with one portal is more than enough."

"I could go to the Creator, you know."

"You think I haven't already?"

He thought of how hard it must be on the guy. "I'm sorry. About—"

"Hey, let's change the subject, okay?"

"Yeah. Okay." Jim finished his dinner and took a long draw on his Coke. "So we've got to find the next soul. That is mission critical. You got any ideas?"

"They always just seem to come to you." Ad shrugged and stayed focused on his second serving of fries. Or was it his third? "I almost think it's better that way than to put us through some kind of wild-goose chase."

Jim thought back to the first round . . . to Vin diPietro, and the subtle clues that had brought them together. That had been the only time he'd been given any direction. The rest of the rounds had been "luck": Matthias. DelVecchio. Then Matthias again. And finally the twins. Adrian probably had a point, come to think of it.

Maybe he should have trusted the system more from the beginning.

"So, ah, I'm going to crash if it's okay," he said, getting to his feet. "Unless you need help cleaning this up?"

Ad laughed. "I'm tackling the paper bags from dinner, not the room. I think I can handle it."

"Cool. G'night."

He was almost through the doorway when Ad drawled, "Keep Sissy warm, buddy."

Jim froze and looked over his shoulder. Before he could say anything, the other angel shrugged.

"Come on, she didn't say good night to you. You think I'm stupid?"

"It's not like that."

"Don't worry about it." Ad shook his head. "You were ready to leave her to get Nigel back. You put it all on the line for the war. I know your game head's back, and going to stay that way. And listen, if I had a harbor in this storm . . . I'd take it, too. So enjoy it while you can—but keep the sex noise down, 'kay? It's fucking tacky."

Jim frowned. "I feel like I gotta say this. I'm not going to get distracted by anything or anybody."

Again, if he played this right? He and Sissy could work shit out afterward.

In the meantime, however, he had no intention of keeping his hands to himself.

"Roger that," Adrian said from his picnic of one on the floor of the trashed parlor. "But I'm eating your sundae. It's the only kind of enjoyment I got left."

A good half hour later, and Sissy wasn't the only one who'd taken a shower before "bed."

Although she probably hadn't wasted twenty minutes shaving her face, Jim thought as he leaned into the mirror over the bathroom sink.

Double-checking his jaw, he was going for baby's-ass smooth, and he had to give his five-bladed Gillette whatever-the-fuck props. No risk of razor burning her—at least for the next couple of hours.

There was so much steam in the loo that he had to wipe his forearm across the glass again as he inspected the other side. He couldn't remember the last time he'd done this for a woman . . . and then realized that, like the ILY thing, it was a first.

Stepping back, he decided he looked about as good as he was going to. The stab wound in the meat of his shoulder was already on the fast track to healing up, and the bags under his eyes didn't show much as long as he wasn't standing directly under a light. Did she like cologne?

"Not like I have any," he muttered as he picked up his clothes and opened the door.

The cooler, drier air of the landing rushed in like a cleaning crew after a party, draining out the humidity, defogging everything. It did the same to his head—and the dose of reality that followed, the hard shot of crystal-clear on what he was about to do, made him hesitate.

Okay, fine. He was nervous.

Up overhead, footsteps in the attic made creaking sounds: Adrian was settling in beside Eddie again, probably on some makeshift bed that involved old Victorian clothes and a shoe box for a pillow. Not that the angel was going to care. He was made of tougher shit than that.

That SOB had sacrificed so much to win. What had he gotten in return?

Loss of a good friend. And fast food tonight.

Hell of a compensation rate.

With a curse, Jim went into his own room, dumped the clothes he'd been wearing in the dirty pile, and picked out a laundered version of precisely what he'd had on from the clean one: white Hanes undershirt that he wore like it was a T-shirt, blue jeans. He left his feet bare. With any luck, he was going to be naked in a matter of moments so who needed socks and shoes.

He couldn't resist one last look-see in the mirror and actually smoothed his hair down. His buzz cut was growing out, and the fact that the fade wasn't regulation tight made him itchy.

Old habits of being a military man died hard.

Just as he was about to turn away, he narrowed his eyes and thought of Devina. Over dinner, Sissy and Ad had filled him in on the particulars of how they'd created the portal to Purgatory, and that made him think of the two vortexes that the Creator Himself had made.

One was that mirror of Devina's.

He'd seen the hump-ugly thing once before, when they'd found her loft in the meatpacking district. Ad—or had it been Eddie? Probably Eddie—had said that taking possession of it was the way to hit Devina in the nuts the hardest. Steal its transportive powers from her, and she was trapped either in Hell or on this side. But you had to be careful how you did it. You shattered the reflective surface in the conventional way and, assuming he remembered right, you yourself were destroyed, busted into a million Humpty Dumpty pieces.

With no hope of a Super Glue save.

The temptation to eliminate the bitch was nearly all-consuming, but he had to wonder what was on the other side of that. Something worse? The safest bet was to just win the war and let the Creator's rules take care of her.

Except fuck safety. To him, there was a law of equity that demanded she lose the thing that was dearest to her—in light of her fucking with his Sissy and taking Eddie away from Ad.

And PS, he was done apologizing for referring to Sissy like that.

She sure as hell felt like his.

On that note, he left his room and shut the door quietly, even though there was no reason to pretend he was sleeping in his own bed.

Guess he wanted to protect her virtue even in the hypothetical.

Even as he was about to take it.

As he started down the hall, behind him on the main staircase, that fucking grandfather clock started chiming, the gonging noises timed perfectly with each footfall he planted.

Like the damn thing was following him.

Stopping, he turned around, put his palm out, and before he knew what he was doing, created a wall of molecules. Worked perfectly. Whatever that clock was up to, he couldn't hear it anymore.

The door to Sissy's bedroom was the same as all the others on the second floor: seven and a half feet tall, four feet wide, with two sets of raised panels that were larger on the top, smaller on the bottom. The knob was crystal and cut in a sunburst pattern, and as he watched his hand reach out for it, he thought of that old movie *The Sixth Sense*—the knobs that had mattered had all been red.

On that theory, this one should have been made out of a big, fat Burmese ruby.

He didn't knock. Just opened the way in and slipped inside, and in the darkness, the first thing he smelled was shampoo. It was different from the stuff he and Adrian shared, and he was willing to bet it had come from that Target trip.

"Sissy?"

When she didn't immediately answer, an injection of pure panic went right into his cerebral cortex, but then he heard rustling from in between the sheets. Going across to where she lay, he put out his palm for a second time.

Willing a soft glow to emanate from his hand, he found her curled on her side facing him, her blond hair splayed out across her pillow, her eyelids down, her lips parted slightly.

For the longest time he stood there, watching her sleep. Funny, seeing her at rest, being there to protect her . . . turned out to be just as good as the prospect of sex. Felt more right, actually.

After all, people had a way of making bad decisions after life-and-death drama. It didn't mean they were weak—quite the contrary. It meant they had survived and were glad to be alive.

He'd done a lot of that kind of thinking in the past himself.

And hell, if she wanted to use him? He was more than willing to do whatever she needed, be whoever she wanted him to.

Except in the light of the morning, she might well have a different take on shit. And who could blame her if she did.

So, yeah, a little breather to recharge and realign was probably a good thing . . . but he didn't go back to his own room. He walked around the foot of the bed, lifted up the sheets and the blankets, and slid in beside her. He intended to just lie there and listen to her even breathing, but almost immediately, she turned to him like she knew he was there, and snuggled up close.

Holy shit, she was extremely naked.

But that didn't change his plan.

Arranging her in his arms, he tucked her head under his newly shaved chin and closed his own eyes.

He was asleep on the next heartbeat.

Chapter
Eighteen

Sissy woke up to one hell of an alarm clock: warm, broad male hands were caressing her hip, her waist . . . moving up and around to her—

She moaned as her bare breast was captured, and the arch that she pulled next put her up against something hard and hot.

Jim's erection.

Popping open her eyes, she stared out at a bright spring morning. Jim was behind her, and pressing in, and yeah, that was a great eclipser. She suddenly didn't see anything, hear anything, feel anything but him.

Turning to face him, she went to say something, but he was clearly asleep. His eyes were closed, and he started to mumble something that she couldn't understand.

". . . Sissy . . ."

The sound of her name made her smile. "I'm right here—"

Talk about wide awake on a oner. Instantly, Jim was fully conscious, his blue eyes alert, his muscles tensing—like maybe he'd had some wake-ups in the past that hadn't been of the benign beeping variety.

"Hi," she said.

"Hi." He moved his hips back a little. "Ah . . . good morning."

"You should have woken me up last night."

"I liked watching you sleep."

The blush that hit her cheeks ran all the way down her body. "It was the sherry. I'm not a big drinker."

"I got no regrets." He moved a strand of her hair out of the way. "How you feeling?"

"Horny."

As Jim coughed like someone had goosed him in the ass, she had to laugh. "Sorry. I'm into being honest."

"It's good." His eyes went to her lips. "Very good."

His face became super-clear to her, everything about his eyes and his mouth and the intense way he stared at her burning into her brain. Reaching up, she stroked his jaw, then his hair.

That halo of his, that nearly unnoticeable circle of golden light, shimmered around his head.

"You sure you want this?" he asked in a deep voice.

She had to smile. "You're such a gentleman."

"No. Not at all."

Sissy wound her arms around his neck. "Well, I think you are, and yes, I'm sure. Everyone should be with an angel for their first time."

"I'll make it good for you," he murmured as he lowered his head. "I promise."

His kiss was soft and slow as he plied her mouth, and she let the sensations of heat and a drugging intoxication run through her body. He took his own sweet time, his tongue licking over her lower lip before dipping inside . . . and then he was back to just kissing her.

For, like, ever. Until, as much as she was into it, frustration started to war with the enjoyment.

But he was onto her. Just as she was about to say something, one of those hands of his slipped around and caressed her back, her shoulders . . . her arm. . . .

When he found her breast, she was starved for the contact he gave her and she arched against him once more, rustling the sheets—and finding his erection. Greedy to know him, she did some exploring of her own, moving her touch down to his hips.

He took her hand away from his body, planting a kiss in the center of her palm and rolling her over.

"But I—"

Jim covered her mouth with his own and cupped her breast. Then he licked down her neck to her collarbone. "Feel good?"

"God . . . yes . . ."

He sucked her nipple in, and the lust that shot through her jerked her chest up, forcing her breast further into his mouth. With an erotic shift, he rode the wave of her body with his big palms, finding his way down to her thighs. Spreading her legs, she wanted him back where he'd been the night before—and he didn't disappoint her.

His fingers swept up to her core, and the instant he touched her there, another release, even bigger than the first one he'd given her, threatened to take her over.

"Please," she breathed. "Please . . ."

The rubbing down there, the sucking at her breasts, the sense of his own need brought her to the brink. But instead of sending her flying, he held her in place, backing off when she got close, inching her forward so she didn't lose the cut of the desire.

She dug her nails into his heavy shoulders. "Jim . . . I can't hold on. . . ."

His mouth covered hers once more and he kissed her—again with the long and the slow. "Shh, baby, I got you."

That was when he finally shifted over her. She was so dazed she wasn't sure what he was doing when there was a pause. But then she realized he was pushing his jeans down.

"You sure about this?"

"*God, yes.*"

Given how crazy she was as she writhed underneath him, she couldn't believe how in control he kept himself—but it came with a cost. His jaw was clenched and his voice was rough and fine tremors wracked his powerful body as he settled in between her legs.

She still couldn't feel him against her sex, though—except for where his thighs pressed into her core.

"I'm going to die if you don't—"

He cut her off by kissing her again, and then she finally got the contact she wanted. Something blunt and hot brushed against her core—and then he shifted, his hand going between them. He knew right where to put himself, and holy shit, she trembled.

Not from fear.

His thumb found the top of her sex and began to rotate in a tight little circle. The orgasm he'd been toying with for however long sprang back to life with a vengeance, and this time he didn't stop. He kept her going until the pleasure snapped free and took her for a joyride even higher and brighter than the one down in the parlor.

And that was when he pushed inside of her.

She was in the throes of the release to such an extent that when he hit a barrier, she felt no pain. Not even as he pulled back and then swept through it. And then he was deep inside—and not moving at all.

As Sissy floated back to reality, she became aware of an incredible sense of fullness, one that was at once foreign and so completely right that she felt tears prick in the corners of her eyes. And then she realized . . . Jim was trembling. From head to foot, his massive body was twitching, the muscles contracting in random jerks and spasms.

"Jim?"

Moving her head to the side, she looked at his face. He was focused on the headboard, his eyes rapt and glassy at the same time, his jaw clenched and grinding, his breathing rough and un-coordinated.

"Jim . . . what's wrong?"

When she shifted under him, he hissed. "Don't move."

"Okay," she said slowly.

"*Fuck*."

"What—"

Just like that he pulled out of her, but he didn't go far. He mashed his head face-first into the mattress next to her shoulders and bowed his arms, the great muscles of his biceps bunching up under his skin. Then his hips ground down hard, his stomach pushing into her pelvis.

Now he contracted. All of him at once. And it was so violent, the bed slammed into the wall behind, clapping hard once, twice . . . three times.

Jim went lax as rope, falling on top of her as he exhaled into the pillow.

Unsure what to do, she tried to wrap her arms around him, but he rolled off and turned away.

All she could do was stare at that tattoo of his, the one of the Grim Reaper that covered his back, the one of the great black-robed figure with its scythe and its bony hand reaching out of his skin.

Clearly, she had done something wrong.

Downstairs in the kitchen, Ad sat at the table and checked the clock again. Ten a.m.

Time to get moving, people, he thought as he glared at the ceiling.

But nope, the lovebirds had apparently tuckered themselves out and were having a lie-in. Meanwhile, he was down here with two bags of ossifying McMuffins and a whole lot of going-cold coffee.

Not that he was bitter.

Okay, he was bitter.

Sex was an easy thing to give up if you weren't around it at all and you were too busy trying to survive to think of the bump-and-grind. But that kind of amnesia was hard to sustain when what you were never going to have again was happening under the same roof as you.

And hell, maybe it all made him miss Eddie even more.

He'd had the best damn time bringing women home for that gameless schlub. Eddie had always been good at everything, the keeper of all knowledge, the perfect fighter, the even-tempered voice of reason in a sea of chaos. Chicks, on the other hand, had been his undoing. One glance from some hot piece and he'd always clammed up like an astrophysicist at an AVN convention. He'd had the sex drive of a lion, however—and that was where Ad had come in.

Lot of the time, he'd felt like a burden on the guy, but when he'd been roping in a volunteer or two? He'd been mission critical and had appreciated the role reversal.

Kind of pathetic that that was all he'd brought to the relationship. Considering everything Eddie was capable of.

Had been capable of.

"Good morning."

Ad jerked to attention. Well, one down, one to go, he thought as Sissy came into the kitchen. Her hair was damp, but brushed, and she smelled like that shampoo-and-conditioner set he'd gotten her during the infamous trip to Target with Devina. Pantene something.

"Hey," he said. "I picked up breakfast 'bout an hour ago. I think it's seen better days—which was probably true the second I bought it."

"Thanks, but I'm not that hungry." She pulled out a chair and parked it. "Coffee will hit the spot."

Going by the way she ducked her eyes and kept checking the doorway to see if her man was coming down, Ad decided that the virginity thing had definitely been dispatched.

Man, Jim was a lucky, lucky sonofabitch. Not that Ad wanted the girl, too. It was just . . . wow. To be with a woman for her first time . . . to treat her right and do her well. What an honor.

He took a draw from his own java. Check him out, getting all sappy.

"Where's Jim?" he asked.

"Upstairs—maybe in the shower. Who knows."

"Oh." Huh. Trouble in paradise? "Listen, I'm going to hit Home Depot and get some plywood—"

"Great." She burst up with her coffee. "Let's go."

Okaaaay, maybe he'd been wrong about what had kept them busy. "All right, lemme go tell Jim. Unless you want to—"

"Nope, you go ahead. You got the keys? I'll start the car."

"Yeah. Sure." He leaned to the side and took out the goods. Tossing the jangle over, he was surprised by how much he wanted to play couples counselor for them. Good ol' Uncle Adrian. But like he had a fucking clue? "I'll go find Jim."

"Good deal."

As Sissy marched out of the kitchen with her head up and her shoulders back, he wondered what exactly had gone down. And then Jim arrived, looking like someone had let a dog take a shit in his boots: grim eyes, drawn brows, whole lot of mean-as-a-snake.

"Breakfast?" Ad asked dryly.

"No, thanks, I'm not hungry. But coffee would be great."

"There's an epidemic of that goin' around."

Jim didn't even glance his way. Probably best. The fucker's stare seemed to have become weaponized.

"So Sissy and I are going to Home Depot."

"Now?"

"No. Next month." Ad got to his feet. "Of course now. You want to stay here and watch the traps—"

"I'm coming, too."

Jim headed for the door at a stalk and let the thing slam behind him. He even left his coffee behind, which was going to improve his mood even more, no doubt.

"Fantastic," Ad muttered. "Soooo lookin' forward to being in an enclosed space with you two. Hashtag 'awesome.'"

Chapter
Nineteen

"Devina, I want to support you in whatever way I can. But it's a challenge when you won't speak."

As Devina sat on her therapist's oatmeal-colored sofa, she figured that the woman had a point. Humans couldn't read minds, after all. But shit, where to start.

"Is it a setback with your job?" the therapist murmured. "I know you said that that colleague of yours was trying to undermine you when it came to the Vice Presidency position. Or is it an issue with the man you've mentioned?"

Ah, yes, a happy reminder of how much she'd had to keep to herself to avoid blowing that little master's-of-social-work-level brain to smithereens: Devina had turned the war into a promotion at a corporation, and Jim into a competing VP. Then, when things between her and the savior had gotten hot and heavy, she'd switched over to something closer to the truth.

That Jim was a love interest that was not going as well as she'd hoped.

"You know, this is the first time I've seen you like this."

Devina cleared her throat. "Silent, huh."

"No, without makeup. You're quite beautiful without all of the so-called enhancements. Have you ever contemplated going without it on a regular basis?"

Devina touched her face. "I guess I forgot to put any on."

"Your hands are bandaged. Did you hurt yourself?"

"Yes."

"I'd like to know how, Devina. I want to help you."

God, the woman's voice was as soothing as a gentle hug, the kind of thing that made you want to pour your heart out, even if it wasn't in your nature.

"I had an accident. All over everything I own."

The woman's eyebrows lifted in her well-padded face. Today she was wearing yet another loose getup, with a skirt that fell to the floor and a blouse that probably had been part of a tent in an earlier life. Everything was in muted shades of brown, just like the office walls, the rug, the couch, the pair of reading glasses around her neck. Even the box of Kleenex was the color of a macaroon.

It was like a sepia photograph.

Although the beach wood pieces were more seventies than suffrage when it came to era.

". . . what happened? Devina?"

Devina refocused on the woman. "You don't know who I really am."

"I don't?" The therapist smiled a little. "You'd be surprised how much I know about you."

Uh-huh. Right. "I don't . . . love people. I'm not built like that."

"But you have love inside of you." As Devina started to argue, the therapist shook her head. "No, you love your things—you care for them, keep them safe, worry about them. It's not healthy, and there's an addiction component to it all, but you do have the capacity to bond. Unfortunately, you choose things because they're safer—that is understandable, though. Inanimate objects don't do unexpected things or break your heart or betray you. Objects are safe. People are complicated."

Well, yeah, Devina thought. But she also wasn't into the hearts-and-flowers shit because she was evil, hello.

"He loves someone else," she blurted.

"This man of yours?"

"The one I'm in love with . . . yes, he loves someone else. But he is *mine*. He's supposed to be mine, not hers."

"The two of you are in a relationship?"

"Very much so."

The therapist nodded. "And you feel that he's been unfaithful?"

"He's now living with someone else. I mean, I was with him when he met her. I just never expected . . ." She pushed her hair back. "Here's the thing, it's like, he and I have this romantic night down at the Freidmont, right? And it's all amazing. The best sex we've ever had." Jim had fucked her so hard from behind that her forehead had left a bald patch on the rug at the foot of the bed. "But the morning after? He goes home to her. Leaves me, and goes home . . . to her. And I'm telling you, it's not like she's attractive. My God, she's built like a Ticonderoga pencil. Flat. So flat, and that hair? Please. I've seen rat fur with better body. It's downright embarrassing that he could actually be attracted to her."

"Did you have an understanding that you were in a monogamous relationship with each other?"

"Of course." How could he want anyone but her? "We're in love."

"But he's seeing this other woman."

"Yes."

"So what happened that prompted you to call? You just said you'd had an 'accident' all over your things?"

Devina fought the urge to break down as she pictured the mess of her basement. "It was bad enough that he was with her after we had our special night. But then I totally put myself on the line for him. I broke some major rules to save his . . . job."

"Are we talking corporate mandates, or state and local laws?"

She guessed the Creator's rules and regs were more like the feds'. "Pretty high-level laws. I saved his job for him—and then I watched as he went to her right in front of me and . . ."

Okay, she totally didn't want to think about Sissy and Jim getting all *reeeeeeeunited and it feeeeeeels so gooooood* after he'd come back from Purgatory.

Fucking hell, she was going to be sick.

"Does she work in this company, too?"

"How can he do this to me?" Devina muttered.

"You know, I think it might be more productive to focus on yourself and where you want to go from here. You can't control him or his choices. All you can do is take care of yourself and put your needs first. At the end of the day, people have to earn the right to be in your life, and it sounds as if he's not doing that. It may be a healthier option to avoid contact with him and reassess the relationship. With distance comes perspective."

"It's going to be impossible not to see him. At least for the next round."

"Round?"

"Week." Depending on how long it took her to win. "Or so."

The therapist leaned forward, her pudgy fingers tightening their hold on her brown-and-gold reading glasses. "Devina, it's important for you to realize that there is no one person for any of us. Relationships come and go out of our lives all the time. Some partings are more painful than others, but that's where the learning comes—learning about ourselves, the world around us, other people."

"Why does it have to hurt like this," she said, letting her head fall to the side. "Why?"

The therapist's face changed subtly, an odd light coming into the woman's eyes. "I'm so sorry you have to go through this, I honestly am. I just don't think there's any other way for us to learn the lessons we're here to learn." The therapist folded and unfolded those glasses. "You know, people really do ask me that all the time, and that's the only answer I have. I wish it could be different, but the more I see, the more I'm convinced that just as children have growing pains as their bodies work to attain maturity, as people's souls deepen and gain resonance it's the same thing. To be challenged, to stretch, to get stronger comes only with the hard stuff—loss, heartache, disappointment. You're doing the work you need to do, Devina. And I'm very proud of you."

Devina stared at the woman for a long time. Funny, at the moment, the therapist didn't seem so doughy as she sat on that puffy couch. She looked . . . regal . . . in her wisdom.

And she was honestly empathizing. Even though Devina was just one of eight, hundred-and-seventy-five-an-hour sessions in the day, the therapist seemed to truly care.

"How do you do it?" Devina asked.

"Do what?"

"Care this much? Doesn't it eat you alive."

Sadness suffused that barely contoured face. "It is my burden to carry. It is my growth and my maturation—my work."

"Glad I don't have your job."

The therapist smiled. "No, Devina, this is not for you."

Devina checked her watch and patted around for her bag. "Time's up. I'll write you a—damn it. Where's my purse?"

"I don't remember seeing you with one when you came in."

"Oh. Can I give you a check for two at the next session? Or do you want to bill me?"

"Actually, I'm putting everything through to your insurance company now. They'll take care of it."

"Oh, great." Devina got to her feet. Hesitated. "I'm not sure where to go with all this."

"Believe it or not, that's part of finding your way. Trust me. And maybe we should keep your regularly scheduled appointment for later this week. What do you think?"

"Yeah, good idea." She'd make sure to do her face for that little tête-à-tête. "See you then."

"Be good to yourself, Devina."

Yeah. Sure.

Over at the door, she paused and glanced over her shoulder. The therapist hadn't moved, didn't move, from her perch on the couch. And yet, between one blink and the next . . . something changed. Something . . .

Okay, she was losing her mind.

No wonder she needed to come here three to four times a week.

"Thank you," Devina murmured. "You know, for . . ."

"I know." The therapist smiled again. "And I want you to keep something in mind. It doesn't sound as if this man truly loves and respects you. I recognize that you believe you love him, but I challenge whether or not you have a good compass on what is right for you in a relationship. I know it's hard to move on when feelings are strong, but sometimes, that is the only way we can nurture ourselves. I'm also willing to bet, if you do the work you're supposed to do, that when the right man does come along, not only will you know it, but you will be able to have a productive, healthy relationship with him."

Devina laughed sharply. "I can't imagine that, but thanks for the vote of confidence."

"I'll see you the day after tomorrow."

"It's a date."

Devina walked out and let the door to the inner office close itself. As she strode through the waiting room, the next client was keeping his head in one of the well-thumbed magazines, like he didn't want anyone to know he needed a shrink.

Just as well he didn't glance up at her. She wasn't looking or feeling her best.

Although at least she did have some direction. The therapist was right. She could bellyache and bitch about all the things that had happened with Jim, and the ways she'd been let down by him, but that was just wasting time with shit she couldn't change. She needed to focus on what to do now in regard to the war, and that was, compared to trying to get over that motherfucker, so very simple.

Besides, considering how lovebird-ish Sissy and Jim were getting? She knew just how she was going to win this.

A little fuck-you to the both of them.

There was just one thing she had to do first: She had to deal with what she'd done to her collections. She had to clean that mess up—scattered house, scattered mind and that crap was definitely true for her. Once that was back in order? She was good to go.

Fuck you very much, Jim Heron.

As she strode out into the lobby of the professional services building, she still felt like death, but at least she was moving.

It was out in the spring sunshine that she paused for a moment and glanced up at the five-story glass-and-steel facade with a frown.

Funny, she didn't have an insurance company.

Up in Heaven, Nigel sat at a table set for four with only two of his fellow archangels. Still, Bertie and Byron were delighted in spite of the critical absence. Then again, for them, at least, a kind of normalcy had returned—and this was good news even in the midst of the war.

As Nigel poured some Earl Grey into his porcelain cup and took a sip, he did not feel similarly, although this repast was a vast improvement over Purgatory's relentless dust.

Was this what humans felt when they survived illness or accident? He was at once totally present amongst his colleagues, feeling the chair beneath him, the weight of his clothes upon his back, the curving handle of the cup in his grasp—and yet he was utterly absent, his mind trying to knit together some kind of link between where he had been and where he sat now.

Thus far, he had not been successful.

In truth, though the body had moved, the consciousness was still on the far side of Heaven, and there was a bumbling, buzzy dizziness associated with the split.

He had the sense that if only he were able to connect with something vivid here, it would help the re-integration process.

But Colin had made his position known on that with a shake of his head back in that parlor—

Off in the distance, across the rolling green lawns, a figure in white appeared and grew closer . . . and Nigel's breath stopped in his throat. Tall and forceful, with a stride like that of the fighter he was, Colin approached with efficiency . . . and brought with his presence a devastation that left Nigel reeling.

When the male sat down, he greeted only Tarquin, the Irish wolfhound, as all others went still and silent.

In the tense quiet that followed, Nigel noticed that that dark hair was wet from a recent washing and that Colin smelled of sandalwood and spices.

"Now that we are all in attendance," Nigel said hoarsely, "I wish to formally apologize for my actions."

Or more accurately: *I am so sorry, Colin. And I would have preferred to do this in private.*

"In an effort to more fully engage the savior, I—"

Colin cut in, "I think we can all agree that given the dire state of the war, the only thing that matters is where one goes from here."

Read: *I am not interested in any kind of explanation or apology, public or private.*

Nigel took a moment to recover from a blow to his gut. "Yes. Of course." He cleared his throat as Byron and Bertie became quite engaged in counting the currants in their scones. "I believe the question is whether or not to tell the savior of his upcoming role in the war."

"You're assuming he wins this round," Colin muttered.

"He will not stand for losing."

"This is an angel who gave a flag away, may I remind you."

"He is changed."

"Because he went to Purgatory and back?" Colin's eyes were level as they finally looked across the tea sandwiches on their stand. "It must be a transformative place, then. Unfortunately, too little, too late and all of that."

" 'Tis not the place, but the nature of mistakes which changes a person's course. The mourning of foolish actions can be a powerful catalyst."

"There are many things that can be catalysts."

Read: *Such as being abandoned and betrayed by one whom you love.*

"Tea?" Bertie asked, as if he wanted to break up the subtextual bickering.

"No, thank you." Colin sat back and stared at the Manse of Souls. "Sustenance is the last thing of interest to me now."

Byron put his cup down in its saucer as if he, too, had lost his appetite—but his eyes gleamed behind his rose-colored glasses. "I am encouraged by your optimism, Nigel. I am of hope that we shall as yet prevail—and although I have always respected your commitment to the rules of this war, I can see why Jim's knowing that he is to be the last soul which is battled for could be beneficial."

"Assuming we do not lose this round," Colin interjected. "As we have lost three others."

"Jim will not be bested." Nigel took a sip from the rim of his porcelain cup. The tea tasted like dishwater, even though it had been conjured in the same manner it had been forever. "Not with who is in play."

"You think that will make a difference?" Colin smiled coldly. "Love is not quite so bankable. At least in my experience."

With that, the archangel got to his feet. "If you all will excuse me, I'm going to do a check of the castle periphery."

"Would you care for company?" Bertie asked.

"No. Thank you."

As Colin stalked off, Bertie and Byron once again busied themselves with ocular endeavors that did not include Nigel.

"Tarquin," Nigel murmured. "Do follow after him, will you?"

The Irish wolfhound let out a chuff and then padded off in Colin's wake, keeping his distance and being as subtle as an animal who weighed ten stone and looked like a floor mop could be.

"I believe I shall retire for some rest," Nigel said as he put his napkin upon his empty plate. "Do excuse me, will you."

He hated getting emotional under any circumstances. Showing sadness or pain in front of others?

In the words of the savior, No fucking way.

Chapter Twenty

"Welcome to Home Depot! What are we looking for today?"

As Jim eyed the source of the noise, he was thinking fondly of knives. Brass knuckles. A tire iron. But come on, the greeter was a seventy-year-old man with more hair in his white beard than on his head—like the poor soul deserved that kind of treatment for no reason at all? Hell, he was like an almost Santa Claus who just needed a course of Rogaine to get there. And a red velvet suit instead of that orange apron. Bib. Whatever it was.

"Plywood," Ad said.

"Oh, that's great!" Yeah, he probably said that in response to every conceivable reply: garden hoses, grills, lightbulbs, flooring. "You want to go alllllllllllllllll—"

He drew out the Ls as he pivoted and pointed past the lineup of twenty-foot-high scaffold'd displays with their packed-in SKU'd merch.

"—llllllllll the way to the back. Ask for Billy. Have you been here before? Because we offer a special checkout for oversize orders."

"Thanks," Ad said as he began to walk off.

"And thank you for your service, young man."

The angel paused. "I'm sorry?"

"Weren't you wounded in the war?"

"Ah, yeah. Guess you could say that."

As Ad gave Almost Santa a nod and limped off, Sissy followed tight on the angel's heels, and Jim lagged behind.

Goddamn, it had been a while since he'd walked through a store like this. Or . . . more accurately, it just seemed like it had been forever.

The shit made him remember back to how out of touch he'd been when he'd finally maneuvered himself free of XOps: He'd known only that he was done with the whole killing-for-the-government thing; he hadn't thought much about being a civilian, or what a simple joy it was to get in your four-year-old car and leave your two-thousand-square-foot ranch and drive three-point-three miles to your local Home Depot or Lowe's and buy a cocktail of lawn fertilizer, a new hammer, and weatherstripping for your back door.

Unfortunately, he hadn't gotten the chance to enjoy much of that.

Not with this whole savior thing coming along and knocking him on his ass.

As his eyes swung around the store's cavernous interior, he intended to check out the lighting kiosk in the middle of the place, with its hanging chandeliers and stand-up units and fake-sunshine glow.

Instead, his peepers locked on Sissy and suffered from a serious case of nope-not-leaving.

In the words of their greeter guy, Goooooooooooooooooooooooo oooooooooooooooooo figure.

Jesus Christ, what a mess. The only thing he'd done right was help her through her first time. Everything else had been a cluster fuck, especially the way it had ended between them with him leaving on some lame-ass statement about having to take a shower. Or something. Fuck, he couldn't even recall what he'd said to her.

The problem was, when they'd been having the sex, he'd been so fucking wound up that all he'd wanted to do was pound into her hard—his body had been a thin inch from totally out of control. Afraid of hurting her, he'd pulled out and come all over the sheets, his hips pistoning into the mattress—which had been better than her. Or so he'd thought.

After that, it had been a case of cue the awkward silence, which had only gotten worse as he'd rolled away from her and tried to get his shit together: Instead of calming things down, the orgasm had only made him hungrier. So much so, he'd been worried about trying to act on it. Which was not what you did when you'd just taken someone's—

"Do we have nails and a hammer?" Sissy asked.

Ad shook his head. "You wanna pick them up while we get the lumber?"

"Yup. Perfect." As if she'd been looking for an excuse to break off.

And go her own way she did, peeling away and dematerializing into the stacks. Naturally, he couldn't let her head off alone—

Ad grabbed onto his arm. "Let her go. We're all under the same roof, and maybe the ride home will be less of a nightmare if you give her a little space."

"The trip over here wasn't that bad."

"Compared to open-heart surgery, sure."

As Ad dragged him along, they passed by more of the helpful types with the orange aprons, and he wondered if he could ask one of them what to do. Man, if only women were like houses, the kind of thing you could fix with some good manual labor and a toolbox.

"What the fuck happened between you two?" Ad paused and

checked out an end cap of Levolors. "And do me a favor and don't say 'nothing.' We could all be wiped off the face of the planet in another day and a half. We don't have a lot of time, but more to the point, this could all be nothing but bullshit very, very soon, so what do you have to lose?"

"No offense, but do you really think you have anything to add to a discussion about women?"

Ad frowned and started walking again. "Good point."

They were turning the corner into big-boy land with the wood when Jim blurted, "She's not a virgin anymore."

Ad coughed into his hand. "Oh. Yeah. Ah, am I supposed to say congratulations?"

"Obviously not. I didn't know what to say afterward. I just . . . up and left. Well, not exactly." Again, he'd managed to choke out something to her about needing a shower. Which in retrospect had suggested he couldn't wait to get clean or something. "I dunno, I was freaking out."

"Because it was a disappointment?"

"No . . . because it was that good. And my brain wasn't working right, so I blew it. By the time I'd gotten my head together, she'd gone downstairs and everything was in the crapper."

And there was another truth in all of it: He'd been worried he was heading back into distraction land—and they all knew how well that had worked for them. Nigel. Purgatory. Busted-up parlor.

Losing.

Guess he'd needed a second to figure out whether or not he was lying to himself when he thought he could do both: fight and be with her. Not that he'd made much of a conscious choice when he'd gone down to her bedroom. That little stroll had been more like a ricochet function, him bouncing off the dire straits of Purgatory into the one thing that he knew would connect him to freedom.

Plus he'd just plain wanted her.

And now things were fucked.

The sad thing? Put him in the wilderness and he could survive for weeks on his own. He could build bombs and dismantle them. He was able to put a bullet in a thimble at three hundred yards—or into a human head.

But he had never suffered from a case of brain jam like he'd had right after that session with Sissy. And meanwhile she was pissed off and hurt—and he wasn't sure what to do to make things better.

Maybe a little breather was good.

As he'd told himself before, he should focus on the war—and worry about having a love life of some kind after they'd crossed the finish line.

Shit.

Sissy found the hammer section and was dumbfounded. To her, a hammer was what her dad had had in his old Sears toolbox—something with a worn wooden handle and a head that was corroded. The stuff for sale here was some kind of glamorous cousin, all about the ultra-deluxe, the titanium, the sure-grip, and the shiny.

It was like a jewelry store for dudes.

She was about to grab one when she realized she'd forgotten that she was invisi—a fact that was made apparent as some woman who looked as lost as she herself felt plowed through her with an orange plastic shopping cart full of venetian blinds.

The sensation it caused was something like a fever breaking through her body, hot and cold vibrations rocking her. And the woman seemed to sense something, too—she yanked her cart to a stop and looked around.

Clearly, Ad and Jim had thought to make themselves apparent or the greeter wouldn't have talked to them.

"Damn it," Sissy whispered.

Then again, did she really want to run the risk of meeting up with someone she knew? Not that any of her friends from college or high school were going to be hanging in a place like this at eleven in the morning on a weekday—but you never knew about friends of her parents'.

And God knew she had enough to worry about already.

She had no frickin' idea what the hell had gone wrong with Jim. And whereas she'd started out hurt and confused, now she'd evolved to a fuck-you phase of things.

That anger of hers to the rescue, she guessed.

The only thing that kept her from going off on him was the reality that they weren't in a relationship. He didn't owe her anything more than what they'd exchanged in her bed. And at least that part of it had gone well. She couldn't imagine anybody treating her any better than he had. But then things had gotten twisted—and stayed that way.

The situation made her think back to all the phone calls and summit talks she and her friends had had as people in school had hooked up, started to date, and then broken up. She'd always been on the periphery of the drama, standing off to the side wondering what the problem with all these otherwise normal types was.

And then this morning had happened.

Yet another ahh-right moment that she would rather not have added to her repertoire. And, boy, it was hard not to think of what that demon and Jim had gotten up to during their night of fun and games.

Which just made her even angrier—

From out of the corner of her eye, she caught sight of a man standing by a display of screwdrivers. He was tall, dark haired, intense-looking . . . and he had a halo. Just like she and Jim did.

"Sissy?"

At the sound of Ad's voice, she looked over her shoulder, then pointed at the guy. "Hey, it's one of us."

Ad's frown tied his brows in a knot. "Yeah. I know him. Um . . . you get what we need?"

"Aren't you going to go talk to him?"

"No." He leaned in and snagged two hammers randomly. "Jim's getting the plywood. Come on—we need some nails and a saw."

Sissy glanced back at the guy, who didn't seem to notice her or Adrian. "How do you know him?"

"It's not important. Come on."

"Who is he?"

"Just a guy."

Giving up, she followed Adrian over an aisle and waited as he scored some boxes of nails. And then it was across into saw land.

Except before Ad made his choice from the two thousand available options, he stopped and stared at her. "How did you know him?"

She pointed to her own head. "He has a halo. Like me and Jim."

Those eyes of his shifted upward. "No offense, but I don't see anything there."

"Little gold circle. Like a floating string of light tied to itself. It's right here."

Ad shook his head. "I got nothing, but whatever. Let's get back and start fixing that room."

By the time they got over to the big-ass-pieces-of-wood section of the store, Jim was pushing a large rolling platform over to a bulk-items checkout—and he must have sensed her presence, because he glanced over his shoulder.

For a split second, she couldn't believe they'd actually had sex. That experience between the sheets seemed as distant as a dream, some kind of hazy hypothetical that maybe she'd just made up.

The delicious soreness between her thighs told her differently, however. So did her anger.

As there was no reason to wait next to Jim, she went over and stood by the automatic doors. People were milling all around, each with things in carts or in their arms, all of them with concentration on their faces like they had mental lists and busy enough lives so that having to come back for something they forgot was going to be a pain in the butt.

Not one of them had any idea what had happened yesterday in that parlor—or that they were being watched by someone who was not like them.

Hard to know whether their ignorance was a good thing or not. Would they be leading their lives differently if they were aware of what was really going on?

Probably. And it made her think of a game she and her sister had played: if you had twenty-four hours left to live, what would you do? She remembered her answers having a lot to do with chocolate. Then again, she'd been twelve the last time she'd—

God, she missed her parents. Her sister. Her friends.

Her life.

For no particular reason, she glanced out into the parking lot—and that was when she saw the car that didn't belong: A big, black Mercedes-Benz was cruising the store at a trolling speed, its sleek lines gleaming in the spring sunlight.

The windows were blacked out so she couldn't see who was driving, but she knew.

She *knew*.

As she stepped out of the store, the sedan eased to a stop in front of her and the passenger-side window went down. Sure enough, the demon was behind the wheel, and the instant Sissy locked eyes with her, the happy fact that they had both been with Jim crashed onto her head.

He had serviced them both. No doubt done the same things to Devina that he'd done to her just over an hour ago.

The kissing. The touching. The licking.

The sex.

Instantly, she was back in that parlor, holding Jim as he returned from the immortal dead, so relieved and a little superior that however much the demon seemed to want his attention, he had eyes only for her. But now? After he'd taken her virginity?

He was as cold to her as he'd been to the demon.

"That fucking bastard," Sissy hissed.

The demon leaned across the empty passenger seat. In a grim voice, she said, "Get in."

Chapter
Twenty-one

"That'll be four hundred ninety-eight dollars and seventy-six cents."

Jim went for his wallet, shoving his hand into his back pocket. Taking out one of his credit cards, he was glad it had been under a month since he'd officially "died." All his accounts were still open.

Come to think of it, he probably needed to liquidate his money before his death became a reality to the banks. Then again, who exactly was going to notify them that he'd died? Long as the monthlies were paid, he could go on forever.

Not that he had forever.

"We gotta find that fucking soul," he said as he swiped the MasterCard down the reader.

"What'd you say?"

He glanced up at the clerk. "Nothing. And no, I don't have one of those savings-card things."

"Well, if you'd like to sign up, you'd save—"

"No. Thanks."

He glanced over at Sissy and lost all train of thought as he saw her: The light was streaming into the open bay, catching the blond streaks in her hair and the glow in her skin. Her body was mostly hidden underneath the baggy sweatshirt, but he knew firsthand exactly how perfect she was built.

As his cock got to throbbing, he glared at his hips. Nope, he told the damn thing. Not the time, not the place, and definitely not with how things were between them.

Closing his eyes for a second, he intended to give himself a pull-it-together-man-whore pep talk—except all he ended up with were snapshots of her naked and spread, her body arching as he worked her out at her breasts.

Not what he needed. Not what was helpful.

Trouble was, his instincts were still to get her horizontal and go NIN on her. Except how was that going to work for them? They weren't speaking, for one thing—for another, she wasn't going to be ready for what he wanted now. Or probably ever.

She wasn't the "fuck you like an animal" type.

"Guess who I just ran into."

Jim glanced over at his wingman. "Who."

"Matthias."

"No . . . shit."

"Yeah. Actually, Sissy pointed him out." Adrian took some initiative and picked up the bag with the hammers and nails from the holders. "Mind if we hit Starbucks on the way home?"

"How the *hell* could she know him?" He frowned and looked to the entrance. "Wait, where is she—"

"Here's your receipt, sir."

She'd been standing by the exit, right by the fucking exit—

"Sir? Your receipt?"

"Where the hell is—"

Ad stepped in front of him. "She's probably just wandering around. Where the fuck would she go? You stay here. I'll find her."

When Jim went to walk off, Ad locked a grip on his arm and yanked him back. "Stay. Here. I'll go get her."

The guy was probably right. Jim was liable to bark at her for disappearing even though she'd no doubt only gone for a stroll down the gardening aisle or something.

Pushing the rolling platform with the plywood off to the side, he waited by the door and patted his pockets for his cigarettes. Damn it, he'd left them back home—but it wasn't like he could have lit up here anyway.

Where was she?

Always a firm believer in not panicking until it was time to, he threw a saddle on his adrenal gland and reined that shit in. Unfortunately, as Adrian came limping back with a frown on his puss and absolutely, positively no Sissy with him, Jim knew that something had gone bad.

"I can't find her," the other angel said. "Maybe she's out at the Explorer."

Jim exhaled in relief and felt like an amateur. Of course she'd go hang there. Take a load off. Blah, blah, blah.

Except when they went out to the SUV, she wasn't anywhere near the thing. Or walking in the parking lot.

Leaving Ad with the stuff, Jim jogged back into the store and made quick work of the twelve million square acres of shelf space. Nothing. No Sissy.

As he ran full tilt from the store and back to Adrian, one last hope that she might have turned up got blown out of the water as he found Ad alone.

"Jesus Christ," Jim demanded, "where is she?"

"He fucked you, didn't he."

As Sissy sat beside the demon in the Mercedes, she was too pissed off to be scared. Too pissed off even to speak.

"Well." Devina glared across the interior of the car. "Didn't he."

She wasn't about to share details with the enemy. But there was a serious satisfaction in slapping the bitch with, "Yes, he did."

There was a long stretch of silence as the demon came to a full stop at a red light and then accelerated in a civilized way when the thing turned green.

Guess she was a law abider in some senses.

Sissy passed the time checking out the interior of the car. She'd never been in a Mercedes before, much less one of the super-fancy models: Everything was sleek lines and high-tech, leather and polished wood—the only thing out of place being the lack of a hood ornament out in front.

Hard to imagine anyone stealing something from the root of all evil and getting away with it.

"How'd he do you?" the demon gritted out. "From behind? He likes me from behind."

Oh, there was a picture. "Not going there. But you know it's true, don't you."

There must have been some way that Devina had known she'd been a virgin in the first place—only logical to assume the demon would be aware when she was no longer one.

"Does he pull your hair?" Devina demanded. "Bite your nipples? He's rough. Was he rough with you?"

No, she thought. He was anything but rough.

Devina looked over again. "We broke the door on the shower at the hotel. The night before last."

Maybe this wasn't a good idea, Sissy thought. 'Cause these little sound bites were making her feel like punching something.

"He didn't sleep when he was with me. Did he sleep when he was with you?"

"Yes," Sissy answered. And then wished she'd kept her mouth shut.

"He was probably tired out from being with me."

"Or the trip to Purgatory." Sissy glanced over at the demon, measuring the stunning beauty that was just an illusion. "Is there a purpose to all this?"

"Yes, yes, there is. I want you to know that he hurt me really badly. Back in that parlor." The demon met Sissy's eyes. "And he's going to do the same to you. You think I'm evil? You think Hell was bad? That is nothing compared to what that man is going to do to you. You're in love with him, I can tell. So am I. And he has treated me with a total lack of respect."

"Maybe he's just not that into you."

"It's his nature, little girl. You don't understand how he got this job. Don't be fooled by anything he says or does—he is half-evil."

"I can't trust a thing you say, you realize."

"Trust me, don't trust me, I don't give a fuck—your opinion about what I'm telling you doesn't change the truth. Back in the beginning, Nigel and I had to both agree on the savior who would be influencing the souls. Jim is fifty-fifty, which is why we each gave our consent." Devina put her directional signal on and made a smooth left turn. "I should have known he'd do this to me. And you might as well know what he's really like."

"No offense, but he refers to you as the enemy."

"Not when he's with me, he doesn't."

Sissy frowned and looked out the front windshield. The spring day was a beacon of summer soon to come, and people in other cars had their windows down.

How she envied them.

The demon shook her head. "Like I said, I don't care whether or not you believe me—because sooner or later, Jim's going to fuck you over."

"I'm not getting involved with him," Sissy heard herself say.

"You two had sex. You're involved. Unless you expect me to

believe a girl who saves it until she's how old suddenly decides to just bang a guy? Personally, I find that prudish bullshit nauseating, but like he has his nature, you have yours."

Well, then hers was changing. She couldn't remember ever having this kind of temper.

"Did he tell you what he did to the men who killed his mother?"

Sissy glanced over again, and found herself staring at the demon's perfect profile as dread nailed her in the chest.

"No. He didn't tell me about her." Matter of fact, she hadn't heard him say one thing about his past. Then again, it wasn't like they'd been on any traditional dates—or had a break in the drama that had lasted long enough for some quiet, reflective conversation.

"He slaughtered them. Hacked them up into little pieces—while they were alive. And don't take my word for it. Do a search under his name."

"Listen, this is none of my business—"

"Look him up." The demon gave her a hard smile. "Iowa. Type his name into Google and it'll all come up. The killings were so violent they made the national news, but he wasn't prosecuted. He supposedly didn't live that long—except that was a lie. The body found in that car crash wasn't really his. The U.S. government covered it all up so they could have him and use him like the weapon he is."

"I'm sorry, what the hell are you saying?"

"Jim Heron, the hero who 'saved' you from me"—the demon had to take both hands off the steering wheel to do the air quotes—"made his living killing people for the country. You think I'm a sick bitch? Ask him how he got paid for over two decades. It wasn't gathering intel. It was putting bullets in people's heads. That tattoo on his back? He has it because he's proud of his work."

The demon hit the brakes at a stop sign and looked over, her black eyes glittering. "The man who took your virginity is no angel. He's a murderer without a conscience. Which is precisely why he and I get along so well."

Sissy opened her mouth to say something. To deny it. To . . .

Except instead of speaking, she just resumed staring out the window.

A little later, the Mercedes came to a halt in front of the old mansion, and all Sissy could do was look up at the window that was across the hall from her bedroom.

Picturing how they'd spent the night, she wanted to vomit.

"That's right," the demon said in a voice that warped. "Know that I speak the truth. And don't be a fucking pussy. Do something about it."

"Like what," she whispered.

"Fight fire with fire."

"I don't understand."

"Your anger is the most powerful weapon against him. Use it. Teach him a lesson. Show him that what he's done to you and to me is a sin for which he must atone."

"Isn't that stuff supposed to be left to God."

"Yes, and God provides us our destinies. Yours is to fight back."

"I can't trust you."

"But you can trust yourself. You'll know what to do. When the time is right, you'll know exactly what to do. Now get the fuck out of my car."

The demon didn't have to ask twice. Sissy popped the handle on the door and slid free of the seat.

The Mercedes took off before she'd shut things, leaving her alone with nothing but all those images of Jim doing things to that other woman's body.

That fucking bastard.

Chapter
Twenty-two

Jim took Angel Airlines to his destination, leaving Ad to drive the Explorer—but whether in flight or on the ground, where he went wasn't that far from Home Depot.

Sissy's parents' house fit in with the tidy neighborhood, the two-story set back on its lot, that pastel Easter flag still by the front door even though the holiday had long passed. No Subaru parked in the driveway, no lights on, but it was a sunny morning.

He walked right in.

And as soon as he was through the front door, he stopped and listened. No sounds of anyone moving, nobody talking on a phone, no TV on. He strode quickly around the first floor, then jogged up to the second. He popped his head into her old room. In her sister's. In her parents'. Went to a window and looked out at the shallow backyard.

Goddamn it.

On his way back to the stairs he stopped at her room again, checking to see if anything was gone or had changed. Having a photographic memory was a bonus.

Nothing was out of place that he could tell.

Downstairs, he stalled in the foyer, putting his hands on his hips and staring at the floor as his brain chewed over the alternatives.

A second later, he took out his phone and called Ad. When the guy answered, Jim muttered, "Not here. I'm rerouting to the cemetery."

Hanging up, he put his palm forward and closed his eyes, envisioning the perimeter of the house marked by a notification spell—so that if she did end up here, he'd know it.

What he really should have done was put some kind of a tracer on her. Too bad Eddie wasn't around. That guy would have been able to tell him how to do it.

When he popped open his lids, a subtle blue glow shimmered on the walls, floors, and windows, like the place had been spray-painted. It was all he could do.

Just as he turned to leave, he caught sight of that armchair in the living room, the one he'd found Sissy's mother in, back before Sissy's body had been discovered in the quarry, back when there had still been some kind of hope for this family that the daughter they were all desperate to have back might still come home.

Before he ducked out, he leaned in and glanced over at the bookcase full of family photos. With a quick jab into his pocket, he snagged his phone and went over, putting the thing up and focusing the lens on his favorite picture of Sissy.

Click.

Then he was off, his wings carrying him over the residential neighborhood and toward the area of town where the Pine Grove Cemetery took up acres and acres of land. He remembered exactly where Sissy's grave was and soared above the treetops and the grave markers, cutting across the Chutes and Ladders lane system that the cars had to stick to.

She wasn't there, either.

Landing next to her granite gravestone, his heart tightened up at the sight of the plastic-wrapped bouquets and green potted flowers that had been placed around where her earthly remains had been buried.

Where the *hell* was she?

Then again, maybe that was the answer. Looking down at his feet, he pictured Devina's Well of Souls and his empty stomach rolled.

He quickly texted an update to Adrian . . . and sent out a beacon to the enemy. If that fucking demon had screwed with his woman?

The last thing Devina was going to have to worry about was whether or not she won the war.

Pacing up and down on the grass, he waited . . . and waited. Just like the bitch to take her sweet time—

As his phone rang, he took it out and answered the damn thing. "Yeah?"

"She's here. At home."

"*What?*"

Ad's voice stayed quiet, like maybe she was in the next room and he didn't want her to hear him. "Yup. Says she got bored and decided to head back."

"Don't let her go anywhere."

"Roger that. She's just going to help me with the plywood—"

Jim cut the other angel off and left Sissy's grave in the blink of an eye.

"No, I've got it." Sissy gave a hard yank and pulled a section of plywood out of the back of the Explorer. "See? No problem."

"Yeah, well, I'm not totally crippled."

"And girls are strong, too."

She and Ad took a break to glare at each other. And then they both grabbed hold of a side of the sheet and walked over the grass, heading for those blown-out windows.

"It was a miracle you got all this in the back of the SUV," she grunted.

"Yup," he strained. "But a couple of bungee cords and that back hatch did just fine being mostly open."

"Have you called the landlords?"

"Not yet."

It was slow going, what with his limp and the fact that her hands kept slipping. Who knew boards weighed this much?

Over at the parlor, they put the plywood down and leaned it against the house. She was glad she wasn't the only one panting—boy, they still had five more left to unload, several of which had to go around the corner of the house on the far side.

"You really should have waited for us," Ad muttered between deep breaths.

"Like I said, I'm sorry."

"Jim's due back any minute."

"Let's get the next sheet."

Back at the Explorer, she reached and locked onto the wood. Giving it another yank, she—

"Shit!" Pulling back her hands, she looked down at her palm. The rough edge had cut into her skin, streaking across and leaving a bloody trail . . . that was silver, not red.

"Are you okay?"

Spinning around, she looked up into Jim's eyes—and promptly forgot what was wrong with her. He was standing on the lawn about three feet away, still in what he'd been wearing when they'd left. But he was totally and completely different.

Rising up behind both of his shoulders were an angel's trademark, the shimmering beauty of what she'd seen on Christmas trees and Christmas cards and on TV suddenly very real. All she could do was blink.

Wings. Iridescent angel wings—

"Why did you leave without saying something?"

It took her a second to figure out he was talking to her. "Ah . . . I just did."

"I'm gonna ask nice. Please . . . don't do that again. You scared the shit out of me."

Overhead, a cloud drifted across the sun, cutting the glare and the warmth. But Jim remained resplendent, somehow creating his own illumination, like he was a kind of destination in and of himself. A place where she wanted to end up—

Like a neon sign that was suddenly plugged in, images of Jim making love to Devina flashed in her mind's eye, popping up and eclipsing the vision before her.

Reigniting her anger.

"Look, can we talk?" he said.

"I've got to take care of my hand."

"I'll come with you."

As she headed into the house, she saw him make a motion to Ad—like he wanted to be sure they had some privacy. Fine. Whatever.

She didn't have anything to hide. Then again, the same wasn't true for him.

Back in the kitchen, she started the water running and got out the dish soap—no reason to get fussy about cleaning things off. Hell, she wasn't even sure she had to bother, but old Neosporin habits died hard.

"You can't do that to me," he said roughly.

"I'm fine," she hissed as she put her palm under the faucet.

"Sissy—"

"You know what I did while you were gone?" She squeezed some Ivory soap out onto the cuts and hissed again. "I looked you up. On the Internet."

She glanced behind herself to find that he was totally still. And his wings were gone now—guess they only appeared when he needed them to travel—and somehow that seemed right.

She refocused on rubbing her hands together until the soap frothed up. "Your computer is pretty fast—and that's a good thing. There's a lot on you. But it made for quick reading."

As he went over and sat down at the kitchen table, she had the sense that his eyes never wavered from her—and it was obvious he was surprised.

"What made you decide to look me up," he said.

"Just a whim." She cut off the water and went for some paper towels to dry things off. "Is it true that they couldn't find all the body parts? Of those men who . . . killed your mother? I mean, I know you murdered them, right?"

"That was a long time ago."

"Some things are never a long time ago."

"So what do you want me to say." When she didn't reply, he shrugged. "You brought this up for a reason."

"What did you do afterward?"

"You read the articles."

"They say you died. Clearly, that wasn't true. So what did you do? I can't believe the military took someone that young in— were you in foster care until you joined? Or were there other arrangements made?"

In the silence that followed, she realized that she was hoping he came clean and told her everything. Which was dumb. Like that was going to change anything?

His stare narrowed. "Where is all this coming from?"

"What do you mean?"

"You just all of a sudden, out of the blue, decide to look me up? Doesn't make sense."

"Kind of like you shutting down after you had sex with me, huh. Doesn't make sense."

He began patting pockets, and then cursed and got up. "Gimme a minute."

When he came back into the kitchen, he had his cigarettes and his lighter—and he waited until he had a live one between his lips and had taken his first drag before he answered her.

"I'm really sorry about upstairs," he said.

"Are you."

"Yes." He exhaled up to the ceiling. "I didn't know how to handle it."

"Oh, really. I'm very sure that I was the only one who lost their virginity."

"I wanted you so bad, so fucking bad—I was scared I was going to hurt you. That's why I pulled out and came into the goddamn mattress. And afterward, I had the worst case of the head-fucks— I know you're disappointed in me, and you have every right to be. I just . . . look I'm not good at this, okay? I don't know how to do . . ." He motioned back and forth between them with his cigarette. ". . . this. You want to know the real me? Well, you've got him right here—I'm tongue-tied and stupid, especially with you, and that is dangerous for you, for everyone. Oh, and yeah, I killed those three men back in Iowa. I came home from school to find my mother bleeding on our kitchen floor. They had done . . ." His voice cracked and he cleared his throat. ". . . bad shit to her. Just so we're clear? I'd do it all over again—and no, they didn't find all the body parts, because some of them were nothing more than mulch after I was done with those bastards."

Sissy looked down at her hand, thinking about how much the wound hurt. Then she imagined what it would be like to have things that were worse get done to her while she was conscious.

"I went into the military afterward. That's where I went, Sissy. I did unspeakable things for this country until I couldn't live with myself anymore and I got out. I was electrocuted at a construction site about three weeks ago—and that's how I ended up here. I got nothing to offer you but honesty—and that's it. This where I'm at."

"I don't . . ." Now she was the one with the head-fuck, as he so aptly put it. "I don't know—"

She cut herself off before she could finish with "who to believe." Instinct told her it was better to keep Devina out of it.

"You sure there wasn't a reason," he murmured.

"For what."

"Looking me up."

"I had sex with a man for the first time and he leaves my bed without a word. I don't need you to hold me afterward and make me feel better, but I—"

"I want to do that." He dragged a hand through his hair. "I am very sorry, Sissy. I handled that really fucking badly."

It was so weird. As she listened to his voice and studied his open, calm affect, she felt like she was straddling a divide, teetering back and forth, shifting her weight from one side to the other. In Devina's car, she'd been so sure that Jim was the enemy. Now, listening to him, she wasn't so sure.

"I had to find out something about you," she blurted.

"I can respect that."

After a moment, her feet moved of their own volition, taking her over to the table. Then her arm extended and she pulled out the chair opposite him. She sat down slowly, her mind flip-flopping between the extremes.

Was he an angel? A devil?

It seemed foolish to believe the source of all evil about anything. But those killings . . .

"They made us get that tattoo."

She looked up, and wondered if maybe he read minds. "They?"

"My branch of the government. Such as it was. We all had the Grim Reaper put on us. It's not a badge of courage to me or something I'm proud of. And God knows, the shit is all over my back, so getting it removed, even if I had the free goddamn time, would hardly be an option."

Straddling, straddling. Images of Jim with Devina warring in her mind with the information he'd just given her so calmly and succinctly . . . like he had no interest in hiding anything from her.

"It hurt," she heard herself say. "When you left like that. I was . . . confused. I thought I'd done something wrong."

He winced. "Last thing I wanted to do. I swear."

"I don't know—"

Jim laid his hand on his heart and stared straight into her soul. "I swear it on my mother."

Chapter
Twenty-three

"Looks like you need some help."

As Ad heard the nasty female voice behind him, he closed his eyes and tried to stop thinking about how much his bad leg hurt. "Not from you."

He turned around. Devina had oiled up to the front of the house in her big black Mercedes, and somehow managed to get out from behind its wheel without making a sound.

Which made him wonder exactly how long she'd been there.

She smiled at him like a raptor as she lounged against the nearest quarter panel. "You know, Adrian, we go well together, you and I. Surely you haven't forgotten how we—"

"I try to forget every day, bitch."

The demon faked a pout and threw some of that heavy brunette hair over her shoulder. "Playing hard to get?"

"Are you here for a reason, or did you just feel like wasting my time." At least the extra protection spell was up and rolling, its red glow separating them. Thank God.

"Jim called me. So I came."

"You sure about that."

"Very."

Adrian turned back to the plywood he'd managed to wedge

into one of the empty sills. Putting three nails between his teeth, he hammered the upper right-hand corner first and then worked his way around. All the while, the demon just stood there, staring at him.

The only reason he didn't push her to get the fuck going was because at least he knew where she was—and it was not with whatever soul was up in this round. But, man, this was like the worst case of the *Jeopardy* theme he'd ever been through.

"I could help you, you know," she drawled as he straightened with some effort.

He smiled with all his teeth and waved his hand around at Jim's spell. "No, you really can't. And I guess my boy ain't coming out to see you, so how 'bout you run along and scare a little kid or something."

"Sissy's an interesting girl, isn't she."

Ad frowned and contemplated hammering something that didn't involve a nail head or any kind of plywood. "You're done with her, remember?"

"Am I." The demon straightened off the sleek sedan. "Tell Jim I'll be back."

"And now you're the Terminator."

"You got that right, Adrian." She high-stepped around the hood like she was on the goddamn catwalk. "Give my regards to Eddie."

"That one's getting old, baby girl."

"Not on my end, it isn't."

"What happened to your hood ornament?"

"Happy accident."

She gave him a wave, and a moment later she was gone, easing on down the road, maybe to Hell . . . maybe to a sale at Neiman's.

"Goddamn bitch."

Ad limped over to one of the other sheets of plywood by the

Explorer and muscled the thing over to the next window. Probably was a bad idea, pulling a DIY on a house like this—what with the whole architectural-integrity/historic-building thing going on. But he had to do something to improve their situation. As it was, all he did nowadays was creep around and complain about the aches and pains he'd taken on.

So this was what eighty felt like for humans, huh.

Shit, he could only hope Matthias was putting the sex drive he'd given the guy to good use—

With a feeling of abject dread, Ad stopped what he was doing and looked through the opening into the parlor. Over on the dusty, bare floor, the book that Devina had supposedly written was right where Sissy had left it.

Oh, God, he thought. What if . . .

Propping the heavy sheet up, he followed a horrible instinct and stepped through the opening with a grunt. His boots crunched on broken glass—not from the windows as they had blown out onto the lawn, but because of the mirrors and lamps that had cracked from the change in pressure before being consumed by the portal.

Bending down, he picked the book up and leafed through it. The sentences were utter nonsense to him, but that wasn't what got him worried. The letters . . . the words . . . didn't look even remotely Latin—and though he wasn't multi-lingual in the slightest, he should have at least recognized some prefixes or suffixes that were common to English words.

Nothing. Hell, it was more symbols than alphabet.

And yet Sissy was reading it just fine.

As he started to wonder how that was possible, warning bells rang in his head.

Stretching his palm out across the kitchen table, Jim knew Sissy was lying to him. Something had happened between their little excursion out and her bolting to come home alone. But whatever it was seemed less important than getting her to believe what he was telling her.

"I'm sorry," he said again. "I wish I were Bryan Reynolds or Stanley Tatum. I'm not."

There was a heartbeat of silence and then she cracked a smile. "You mean Ryan Reynolds or Channing Tatum."

"Yeah, whoever they are."

The lift to her lips didn't last long. "I don't know wh— er, what to believe."

"You don't have to make up your mind now. You don't have to make up your mind at all."

Another long pause. "How did they . . . what happened with your mother?"

His heart skipped a beat and every molecule in his body screamed for him to get up from the chair and walk out of the room. Instead, he took a sharp inhale on his Marlboro and retracted his hand, using the thing to bring the ashtray he was using closer to him.

Even with the TO, he had to clear his throat. "We lived out on a farm. My mom and I worked it, and we made a pretty good living. I was in school, but summers, early mornings, late nights . . . I helped as much as I could. One thing about rural places: not a lot of money around. People tend to scrape by and that's okay, as long as there isn't an external imperative to do otherwise. Like drugs."

Every time he blinked, he saw flashes of that horrible afternoon when he'd walked into the kitchen and found his mother in the process of dying a horrible death. Click—a close-up on her ashen face, her mouth struggling to work. Click—blood on the linoleum. Click—ripped clothes. And the shit came with the worst sound track imaginable, his mother's voice nothing but a weak rasp, her breathing a wheeze. And the smell . . .

Fucking hell, it had been the potato-and-copper smell of fresh meat and blood, like when he'd taken the pigs in for slaughter.

"I didn't stay to watch her die. She told me to run because they were still in the house. I didn't want to leave her . . . she made me go. I ran out to the truck and flew down that fucking dirt road. They came after me, but I got away. Went to the cops. When I finally came back, she was gone. Her body was cold."

"Oh . . . my God."

"The guys who did it went into the court system, but they got out on bail. I figured out who they were—it wasn't hard and I knew what to do to them even though I was young." He shrugged as he tapped his ashes off the tip of his cigarette. "When you live on a farm, you learn about death. How to make it happen. I used her favorite kitchen knife and a saw I'd cut firewood up with. Plus a few other things I found at the three different scenes." He leveled his eyes at her. "I made them suffer just like she did. And I will never be sorry for that. Never."

Jesus Christ, when was the last time he'd spoken about this . . . ?

Interview process for XOps, he thought. When they'd given him the psych screening—to make sure he was a good little sociopath.

"I'm so sorry," she said hoarsely. "I can't imagine what that was like."

"Yeah, you can. I only lost her. You lost your whole family— and you saw them suffer, too. You were at your own grave site." As she ducked her eyes, he cursed. "It's because of what happened with my mother that I just couldn't let you fucking go when I found you in that bathtub. I tried to save you. I tried to . . . get you to breathe . . . they had to peel me off you. I didn't want you to die."

As his eyes actually got teary, he curled up a fist to remind himself that he was a man, goddamn it. And that mostly worked.

"Jim, I—"

"All I want is for you to be safe and stay that way," he said in a tight voice. "That's it. That's why . . . just don't take off on me again, 'kay? You nearly gave me a fucking heart attack."

"Do you still want me?" she blurted.

Okaaaaay, cue the coughing on his side. And not because he'd taken a bad drag. "Sissy, I—"

"Considering everything you just told me, I think you can afford to be honest. And I need . . . I need to know. One way or the other, even if it's no—"

"Yeah, I fucking want you."

Off in the distance, he heard nails being hammered, and sorry, he wasn't feeling guilty at all about not helping his gimp-ass buddy go home-improvement. This had been a real ball-squeezer of a convo, but he was making headway with her. He could feel it.

He didn't want to be at odds with her.

Besides, Ad was right . . . the soul had always come to him. In every single round, the soul had come—

"Prove it," she said. "Prove that you still want me."

Chapter Twenty-four

Across the table, the change in Jim was instantaneous. Even as he stayed right where he was, his big body dwarfing that chair, the smoldering cigarette held in between the fore- and middle fingers of his right hand . . . he was completely different.

And Sissy guessed that was proof enough. But she wanted more. She wanted . . . everything.

"Sissy, I don't think it's a good idea to—"

She shook her head. "It's the only thing I can independently verify. There is so much here . . . that I can't know, and I've got to have something to stand on."

There was a long, tense silence . . . and then he shoved his chair back with such force it landed on the floor with a clatter. He didn't even bother coming around the table. He reached across with his long, powerful arms and grabbed her by the head, yanking her out of her own chair, bringing her mouth to his. The kiss was hard and raw, his lips grinding against hers, his tongue penetrating her like he wanted to be doing that kind of thing with totally different body parts.

When he finally shoved her back, they were both breathing hard. And his eyes . . . his eyes burned through her.

"Happy," he said grimly.

Jesus, and to think she'd assumed he was passionate before.

"You're not going to break me."

"Don't be so sure about that." With his mood clearly in the crapper, he broke away from her, jerked his chair back up and sat in it. Then he shifted with a curse and rearranged something.

He tapped his ash again. Took another drag. Drummed his free fingers.

And then a quick, rhythmic tapping started up under the table.

It was his foot going upanddownandupanddown.

With slow, deliberate movements, she rose to her feet and came around to him. His shoulders were bunched up under his T-shirt, his biceps hard and tight—and as she stood beside him, the twitching started. In his face. His wrist. His jaw.

When he refused to look at her, she almost lost her nerve.

She put her hand on his arm. "Jim."

He shook his head. "Don't ask me, please, don't ask me—I'm not keeping it together here."

"I just want to know—"

She didn't get a chance to finish the sentence.

All at once he was up and at her, taking her body and driving it backward until she landed against the wall. Pinning her with his pelvis, he ripped the tie out of her hair and shoved his free hand into the stuff—but not to smooth it.

He grabbed hold and forced her head to one side. "You want this?" he growled. "You sure you want this?"

"Yes." As he tightened his hold a little harder, she was forced to curve further into his strength, until he was the only reason she wasn't on the floor. "You're not going to scare me."

In fact, he seemed like the one getting rattled as she pushed her hands up under his shirt and onto his smooth back—but the double take didn't last. Lowering his head, he went for her neck, biting his way down to her collarbone.

And then the world spun.

It took her a moment to figure out what he'd done, but as she heard another clatter, she realized he'd picked her up and sat her on the edge of the counter.

"Is this what you want," he growled as he pushed her legs wide.

"Yes," she breathed, pulling him back to her mouth, wrapping her arms around his neck.

"Aw, fuck." He kissed her deeply and worked himself against her core. "Jesus, are we going to do this here . . ."

The sound of a hammer going strong in the other half of the house meant they had time—but not a lot of it.

"Yes, we are." She went for the waistband of his sweats and yanked them down, releasing his . . . "Oh . . . wow."

"Yeah. Oh," he said dryly. Like he'd proved his point.

Except before he could disengage, she gripped his arousal with both hands. Against her palms, he was hot. Hard. Big.

Jim's head fell back, the corded muscles that ran up his neck straining as he cursed. "Sissy—"

"I want to feel you come in my hands."

The groan he let out vibrated through his body—and there was another right on its heels as she started to stroke him, down the shaft, up to the head. Down again. Back up. She had no clue what she was doing, but she knew she was onto something—especially as his hips began to work with her, increasing the friction.

She watched the whole thing, his hips rolling and then pumping, his lower abdominals curling and releasing. It was dizzying, this feeling of power, the sense that she and she alone was doing this to him, bringing him closer and closer to the brink. He was a man, a strong, aggressive man . . . who was at her mercy.

And that was hot.

"Gimme your mouth," he growled as he forced her chin up.

He took without apology, unleashing himself as his lower body rocked faster against her hold. He tasted like fresh tobacco and wildness, and as much as she wanted to stay hyper-aware about everything that was happening, it wasn't long before she was swept up, too.

And then he orgasmed, barking her name as he bit into her lower lip.

Nothing slow and easy this time. Rough and raw, his arousal jabbing into her hold, hot jets coming out of him.

And she loved it.

When he finally fell still, he dropped his head on her shoulder as if he couldn't hold it up. He was breathing like a freight train, his body as hot as his erection still was. And yet he didn't seem finished.

More like this was the appetizer to the meal he wanted.

As Jim lifted his head, his eyes still burned. Especially as he straightened, took hold of the bottom of his shirt, and lifted it up and off of his magnificent chest. Switching his still-lit cigarette to his opposite hand, he pressed the soft cotton into her hands, cleaning things up.

The way he stared at her . . . she felt like prey.

In a good way.

She was not supposed to be like that, Jim thought as he ground his Marlboro out in the ashtray on the kitchen table.

Sissy was supposed to have run out of the room when he pushed things just a little, all come-to-her-senses thanks to him. Instead, she'd had him coming all over her hands. And now, even after that was over, she was sitting back against the cupboards, her hair tangled from his hands, lips red and parted, legs . . . spread.

For him.

He wanted to tell her later. He wanted to tell her no.

He didn't. He tossed his now-dirty shirt on the floor, and went back to her, running his hands up her thighs, going for her core with his thumbs. He wanted to go down on her. Right here in the kitchen. Just get rid of those jeans and put his knees to the floor and let his tongue do whatever it wanted.

But he didn't need Ad finishing shit up and coming back here for a drink.

His next option was to go the true penetration route—God knew he was still hard and raring to go. Again, though, that involved her going pants-off, and the idea of any man seeing her undressed and in mid-orgasm during sex made him want to get a nuclear weapon.

The last option was the conservative one. But it was so much better than stopping—and a big-ass improvement over getting caught red-handed.

"You know what I'm picturing right now," he said into her ear.

"What . . ." So hoarse, her voice was so hoarse and he loved the sound of it.

"You're naked." He started rubbing at her faster. "You're on your back . . ."

She moaned and pushed herself against him, like she was seeking exactly what he intended her to have.

"You're naked and you're on your back and I'm between your legs." He kissed her lips and lingered there. "But I'm doing this"— he circled the top of her sex—"with my mouth."

He thrust his tongue into her as she orgasmed, her nails biting into his back, her breasts arching up. He helped her ride the release out until she went loose in her own skin, her body so pliant and relaxed, he wondered if he could just slip inside of her and . . .

No more hammering, though. So Ad had either taken a breather or was about to.

Easing back, Jim brushed the hair out of her face. Her cheeks were flushed and her eyes dazed and wide. She was in a state of total undone . . . and the most beautiful woman he'd ever seen.

"Do you believe me now?" he whispered as he pressed a kiss to the side of her neck.

"Yes . . ."

"Good."

When she yawned so hard her jaw cracked, he scooped her up into his arms. As he turned around, he recoiled at the mess he'd made: chairs all over the place, crap that had been on the counter now on the floor, his pack of cigarettes spilled across the table.

"We gotta stop trashing this house," he muttered as he walked out.

Chapter
Twenty-five

As Ad came into the kitchen, it didn't take a genius to figure out what had fucked things up—and this time, it wasn't something metaphysical.

Although he was willing to bet there had been some mind blowing going on.

Ad put the ancient book down on the table and arranged the chairs back where they belonged. Then he took a load off and waited. Up on the second floor, he could hear all kinds of movement going on, people walking around, doors closing. After a while, a single pair of heavy footfalls clomped down the stairs.

"I'm in here," he called out.

When Jim sauntered into the kitchen, the savior was all about the no-big-deal and the nothing-special. "You ready for dinner yet?"

"We need to talk," Ad countered.

Jim went over and popped the refrigerator. "About what."

"Your girl."

Three, two one . . . except nope, the guy didn't bother with any kind of denial about that possessive pronoun.

"What about her." Jim closed the ice box door and went to work on the cupboards. "We got any food?"

"Sea salt–and-vinegar potato chips, fresh bag, at your eleven o'clock."

"Fucking perfect."

Ad waited until the guy had sat down across the way and cracked the seal on the chips. "I don't want you to take this the wrong way—"

"So don't say it."

"—but we can't ignore the fact that Sissy might be possessed."

Down went the bag to the table and that heavy jaw stopped chewing. "What."

Ad rubbed the center of his own chest—because even raising the issue was enough to give him the heebs. "I think Sissy brought something out of Hell with her. I think it's inside of her, and the longer it's in there, the more it's going to take root and grow."

Jim shook his head. "No. Absolutely not. She was an innocent when she went in and—"

"There's a reason people like her aren't allowed up in Heaven."

"Excuse me."

"They're contaminated."

Jim got up, his chair squeaking across the bare floorboards. "I'm not hearing—"

"Then explain to me how she can read this." Ad opened the ancient book up to a random page. "This isn't Latin, Jim. It's Devina's language, and I think Sissy can read it because—"

"No!" The savior crushed the bag in his fist. "You're fucking out of your mind."

"It's what her rages are about."

"She's not angry."

Ad got to his feet, and jacked his torso forward. "She nearly burned the fucking house down, Jim. Quit thinking with your dick and get real."

Jim pointed a finger across the table, his hand shaking. "I'm going to forget that you said any of this."

"Then you're going to lose everything. Including her. Devina is a parasite—she gets into people through an injury to the soul, and once she enters, she divides and conquers. It's Vin diPietro all over again—"

"No, no, fuck that. There's nothing wrong with her—I'd sense it like I sense Devina—"

"You didn't sense shit in the last round, did you. Or any of the others when Devina was at work. And that's another reason why I think Sissy's the soul."

Jim stared at him hard. "I don't get it—I thought you were cool with her."

Ad rubbed his tired, aching head. "Goddamn it, Jim—"

"I'm serious. What the fuck is wrong with you?"

He'd been afraid of this. He'd been totally fucking afraid of this. "You need to get real here, Jim. Not fight with me, okay? Of course I'm cool with Sissy, but I'm not going to let that get in the way of my being logical—and you sure as shit can't let that happen." He kept his voice as level and even as he could. "I'll say it again. I think Sissy is the soul in play, and you need to get very clearly here, or we are gonna be in a world of hurt. Especially her."

As Jim stared across at his remaining wingman, he was having a hard time hearing anything over the pounding rush of blood in his ears. Except . . . no, this was wrong, all wrong.

He shook his head back and forth. "No. She's not involved in this. Sissy's not a part of this. I got her out and she's okay and now we move on to the next soul."

"Go talk to Nigel if you don't believe me. Go up there and ask him if she's allowed behind the castle walls. Why the hell do you think she's down here with us? It's because she doesn't belong anywhere anymore." Ad cursed and sat back down. "I'm not saying any of this is her fault—shit happens, and she just got dealt a really fucking lousy hand. But let's not have your emotions get in the way here, k?"

In response, all Jim could do was pace around the kitchen, shaking his head some more and trying to find holes in Ad's dumb-ass, misconstrued, cocksucking idea.

"She can't be the soul," was all he came up with. "She just can't."

Ad took a deep breath, like he was about to re-explain particle physics to a lay person. "Don't be naive, Jim. Every round has had an internal logic to it, a way that you found the soul, a progression from one to another. Sissy's been there from the start—and your reaction to finding her dead way back in the beginning . . . shit, that's like the first clue. It's as if she's been precisely made to trigger shit for you, and you've followed the whole thing through—from meeting her down in Hell, to finding her body, to getting her out. And now she's here with you and you're falling big-time for her—it's all adding up."

"No."

That was all he had. Just . . . no.

"The stakes are getting higher, Jim. Not just for the war and all of us, but for you. That's why it has to be her. This is a big test for you."

His hands shook so badly that when he tried to get his half-empty pack of Reds out of his pocket, he dropped them on the floor.

And like they were trying to point him in the same direction, too, they landed right next to all the shit he'd swept off the counter when he'd started working Sissy out.

So good. She was so fucking good—the way she touched him, the way she felt, everything from her taste to her smooth skin to the way she came for him.

It was the opposite of Devina. Everything about Sissy was the opposite of that devil.

"It's just not possible," he mumbled as he struggled to light up.

"The Creator engineers everything."

"She's not evil."

But . . . she had lied to him. About why she'd looked him up. Although, shit, maybe not. Maybe that was just paranoia talking on his part. Hell, it was entirely possible that she'd left to come home just because . . . and she had looked him up just because. . . .

Stop thinking with your dick.

With a sense of utter dread, he went over to the table and looked down at that horrible fucking book. Ad had opened it in the middle, and as Jim forced his eyes to focus . . . he tried to find Latin in what was written. Tried desperately to see something he recognized.

Except God only knew what the wording was. It seemed like some combination of symbols and the Russian alphabet.

But it was not . . . Latin.

"Let me tell you what the endgame looks like," Ad said grimly. "Sissy's infection gets worse . . . and that's how Devina infects *you*. It's going to be through Sissy that this fucks you up."

The logic of it all started to scare him. "But I'm not one of the souls. And Sissy can't be. She's already dead."

"I didn't see an exemption in the rules for that, did you?"

Well, no. He hadn't. But . . .

"Okay, fine," Ad said, gesturing with his hands. "Say neither one of you can be a soul in the war. You're still supposed to be fifty percent evil, right—that's why Devina agreed to your being the savior. The more angry, the more infected, you are? The better it is for her. And I should know, because I got the cancer, too." The other angel pointed to his own chest. "It's in me . . . too. Eddie was the only one out of the three of us who was pure, because he'd never been with Devina, even after she went for him. That's why she was so afraid of the guy. That's why she took him out."

"I'm not gonna lose Sissy to that bitch again," Jim said numbly.

"I know, and I can't decide whether that works in our favor— or against us. And speaking of the devil, Devina came by just now." Ad said the second half carefully, like the guy knew Jim was two inches from a very steep cliff. "She told me you were looking for her."

Jim ran through the math again, step by step. And he hated the conclusion he came to. There was nothing in the rules that stated someone like Sissy couldn't be the soul . . . and Ad did have a point. The internal logic to the war was undeniable, but only the kind of thing he could recognize in hindsight.

Shit, he thought. He hoped Ad was wrong, he really did.

"Stay here." He put out his cig. "And watch Sissy for me, okay. I'll be back."

"Don't do anything stupid."

"You just worry about her. I'll take care of everything else."

As he strode out of the kitchen, he could hear Ad cursing, but he wasn't going to worry about that crap. He needed to take care of business—and that meant taking a little trip upstairs.

And not to the second floor of this house.

Chapter
Twenty-six

When Jim arrived up in Heaven, he found the place was still lush as Central Park in the summer, the ground green, the sky blue, the castle walls the color of coffee with three creams in it. But the fact that there were only two flags flying up on the parapet was a painful sight.

Jim thought back to the first time he'd woken up with his back flat on the perma-lawn, the sizzle of the electrical shock that had toasted him still coasting through every nerve ending in his body. At least now, he'd made the trip here enough times so that he landed on his feet.

Before he went off looking for the archangels, he turned to the Manse of Souls . . . and imagined his mother in there. Safe. No longer in pain. Nothing to weigh her down or worry her. He hadn't seen her since the day she'd died, and, man, he sure could have used a ten-minute TO in there with her. Even if neither one of them said a thing, it would be good to see her one last time in the event he lost this fucking war—

"I'm sorry. I cannot allow you passage therein."

He pivoted toward Nigel. The guy was like a painting properly restored, nothing dusty or too pale about him now, his limbs apparently having healed up fast and without lingering issues—at least going by the easy way the guy walked over the cropped grass. He was wearing one of his natty 1920s-style suits, the cream of the fine linen glowing like a night-light in the strange, ambient illumination of the place.

"I need you to be honest with me," Jim said.

"Of course. As if I could be anything but."

"I need to know if it's true that a soul that's been released from Hell can't get in there." He jabbed his thumb over his shoulder. "That there's some kind of contamination problem. Or whatever."

Shit. Just . . . shit.

And great. Nigel's face grew sad as he murmured, "This is about Sissy."

"No, the fucking Easter bunny."

"Ah, yes, the mythical rabbit with the basket of pastel eggs. You are correct—that fuzzy little gob, as some would call it, would not be welcomed up here. And unfortunately, you are also right. Any soul who has been down below is not permitted entrance behind the walls or even access to the grounds."

"Discrimination."

"No, you said the word. Contamination."

"She was innocent, Nigel. She didn't ask for any of this."

"And you have my sympathy. Both of you."

"Fucking hell." Abruptly, he pictured what they'd had to do to Vin diPietro in the first round. "What if she was cleansed. What if we . . . took anything that was evil out of her."

Shit, he couldn't imagine doing that violent, deadly procedure on Sissy.

"Do you truly wish to attempt that on her?"

No. "I'm going to fucking kill that demon."

Nigel grabbed his arm in a strong hold. "Please remember this. If you remember . . . only one thing out of it all . . . you must keep this with you." Those incredible eyes bored into Jim's, their odd color imprinting on his mind to such a degree, he felt as though Nigel had implanted a tangible object in his brain. "The kind of anger you feel now is what Devina nurtures. If you give in to it, you give yourself unto her. It is the root of all evil, the balance to the purity of love. This is the expression of her very nature. Whatever you do, do not ride this wave, especially if it takes you to her, and even if you believe it gives you the focus and strength to beat her. Ultimately, it shall be that which undoes you."

Jim looked out over the lush landscape. This was too much, he decided. The whole damn thing was too much, but it wasn't like he could get off this ride. Not until it was over, one way or the other.

"Colin come around yet?" he blurted out.

"I do not know that to which it is you refer."

There was a long silence. And then Jim said, "I need to ask you for a favor."

"And I am prepared to grant it to you."

"You don't know what I'm going to ask for."

"Yes, savior. I do."

Sissy woke up to broad, warm hands traveling over her stomach, her waist, her hip. As they rolled her over gently, she knew who it was. Recognized the scent of him and the way he touched her and arched against her and got in close.

Her eyes opened, but it was too dark to see anything, the sun having set. "How long have I been asleep?"

"A while."

"I didn't even know I was that tired."

"Let me in," Jim said with a kind of desperation she didn't associate with him. "Please let me in."

His lips found hers and it was the most natural thing in the world to split her legs so he could find his place between her thighs. She had taken a shower and gotten between the sheets naked—exactly for this.

She had hoped he would come to her.

His kiss was a drug and she fed off of it, stretching out underneath his great weight as his erection brushed right against her core. She was instantly ready for him, and he seemed to want to check that as one of his hands went between them. He groaned as he felt her heat, and then he repositioned himself.

He joined them with a thrust of his pelvis, that fullness returning to her. And he was careful—up to a point. As his thrusts gained momentum, the bed started to rock, the creaking loud in the dark room. She didn't care if Adrian heard them. Maybe she should have, but it felt so good.

The closer he got to his own orgasm, the harder he pumped, the tighter his hips became. Her release sent her soaring first, her sex contracting around him, gripping his shaft—

"Oh, fuck," he gritted out as he tucked his head and jerked against her.

Their bodies took over, working together, amplifying everything. And when they finally went still, she felt closer to him than she'd ever been to anyone in her life.

He propped his upper body up on his elbows and stared down at her. In the dimness, with the only source of light the little line around the door he'd come through, she could tell he was grim.

"What is it?" she asked.

"I've got to go out and take care of something."

"Okay. Can I help?"

"Yes. By staying here with Adrian until I get back."

"Where are you going?"

"It's nothing to worry about."

Cold seeped in through her skin. "You're going to see her, aren't you." Sissy pushed him off her and pulled the sheets up to her chin. "Aren't you."

"Not for sex."

"So you say." Flashbacks of her conversation with the demon replayed in her mind. "And I'm supposed to just sit around here until you get back?"

"Sissy, I'm telling you. It's not like that."

"You had sex with her forty-eight hours ago."

"And that's never happening again. Why would it?"

Sissy put her hands to her face and rubbed up and down. Maybe this was a dream?

The bed moved as he shifted around, pulling his sweats back into place. And then there was a blue glow. "I want to show something to you."

She looked over at his phone. Then frowned and took the thing from him. The screen was filled with a picture of a picture of her—the one that sat with all the other family photos in the bookcase in her parents' living room.

"I took it today when I was trying to find you. I was scared to fucking death."

God, she'd looked so different back then, Sissy thought as she stared at herself.

"Give me your hand," he said.

Absently, she put her palm out—and found her arm getting stretched up to his neck by him. "Feel this?"

It was a charm. On the end of a necklace.

She frowned. "That's mine."

"I know. Your mother gave it to me."

"When?" she breathed.

"I went to see her after I had to leave you down there. It was before I figured out a way to get you back. I knew how badly she must have been suffering, so I went to your house and found her sitting in that armchair in the living room. She was staying up for you."

As the glowing picture started to get wavy, she brushed at the tears in her eyes. The reality of her mother waiting by the door, not because Sissy was out after curfew . . . but because something terrible had happened . . . was more than she could take.

"I promised your mother I would bring you back," Jim said gruffly. "She gave me this, and I was going to give it to you, but I'd like to keep it. That way you know you're with me. Wherever I go, whatever I do. You're right there with me."

"It barely fits you," she murmured, tracing the way the thin chain had to stretch around his thick neck.

"I'm not going to fuck you over, Sissy. Not going to happen." He leaned in for a kiss and she let him have one. "And you want to know what I want to do?"

"What."

"After this is all over, I want to take you out on a date. A dumb-ass dinner date. Or, shit, I don't know. Walk on a beach— not that there are any around here. I just . . . if I win this war, on the other side of it all, I want you on the back of my bike. Maybe it's only going for a ride. I don't care. Just you and me, nothing else. Promise?"

She didn't know which one of them to believe. The lying demon . . . or the trained killer who seemed the least likely person on the planet to get sentimental—who was nonetheless wearing a tiny dove around his throat and had stopped in the middle of everything to take a picture of a photograph of her.

"That's what you were going to ask," she said.

"I'm sorry?"

"Down in the parlor, right after you came back while we were having dinner. You were going to ask Adrian to take a picture of us, weren't you."

"Yeah."

"Can angels be photographed?"

"You wanna see?"

He took the phone from her and realigned the shooter so that the fuzzy dark shadows that were the two of them came into vague focus.

"Brace yourself for the flash," he said. "Three, two, one . . ."

The bright light blinded her and made her blink, but when her eyesight returned and she looked onto the little screen, there they were, their heads close together, him looking at her, not the camera's eye, her gaze focused myopically straight ahead.

And there, around both of their heads, like some kind of benediction, were the halos.

"You can trust me, Sissy. I'm at war with the bitch, not in love with her."

She thought back to when he'd been down in Hell, tortured by those demons, violated by the masses. How could anybody love or be attracted to someone who could do that to them? Jim was a lot of things, but he didn't strike her as a masochist on that kind of scale.

God, she didn't know who to believe.

But she did like the picture of the two of them together. She really . . . liked the way they looked. If it weren't for those damn halos, she could almost believe they were just a normal couple.

"Can I keep this?"

"Yeah, you can have my phone."

Cradling it to her heart, she scooched down and put her head on the pillow. "When will you be back."

"After I put that cunt in her place."

Well, at least he showed no signs of looking forward to seeing the demon; that was for sure. And the sex the pair of them had just had? Nothing to sneeze at.

"Be safe," she said.

"Always."

She heard him walk for the door—but then he turned and came right back, capturing her face in his hands.

"I'm going to take care of you." His voice had the strangest tone to it. "I swear on my mother's soul. I'm going to make things right."

And then he kissed her and left, closing the door behind himself quietly before striding down the hall. It was a while before she figured out what had been behind that odd inflection, and she shivered.

It was fear.

Jim Heron was terrified, for some reason.

Chapter
Twenty-seven

"May I help you."

Not a question. And the attitude was more along the lines of, What are *you* doing here?

As Jim stopped on the shiny marble floor of the Freidmont Hotel's lobby, he looked across at Mr. Officious, who was manning the front desk. The guy was wearing a discreet black suit with a gold name tag, a bright white shirt, and a black tie—like he was the maître d' of a funeral home.

"The service entrance is around the back," was the tack on.

Annnnnd this was why it was better to be invisi.

"I'm here to see a guest," Jim muttered, and went to head for the elevators.

"Excuse me," the man said as he busybodied his way out from behind the counter.

Jim put his palm out and whammied the little prick into silence. Then with a quick spin and a metaphysical shove, he sent the suit back to his station.

Jim took the elevators, not the stairs.

For one, it was because a set of those ornate doors opened on cue like the damn thing knew he needed a lift. Har-har. And two, the closer he got to the demon, the more worked up he was becoming, and that limited his powers to the likes of the parlor trick he'd pulled on the front-desk guy.

Stepping in, he hit the button marked PH and looked up at the line of numbers over the doors. With a series of discreet dings, the progress up the middle of the old building was slow and steady.

His temper rose as well.

There were mirrors all over the inside of the elevator, and he avoided looking at himself. He didn't want to think about anything other than giving Devina a very clear message—and the sight of his face with the stubble and the exhaustion was too much a reminder of how close to the bone he was.

Shifting his eyes even higher, so he was looking at the ornate wood carvings on the ceiling, he muttered, "Nigel, you'd better come through for me."

With one final ding, things bumped to a halt and the doors opened soundlessly. The hallway beyond was done in the same somber gold-and-maroon stuff as the lobby, the carpet all swirls, the walls striped, the fixtures crystal.

He could give a shit.

Down at the far end, he curled up a fist and banged on the door loudly.

With a click, the thing unlocked and opened on its own. The room beyond with its sleek furniture, built-in bar and view over the river was lit by candles that flickered. R & B bumped through hidden speakers and some kind of sultry, just-out-of-the-bath scent was thick in the air.

And there she was.

The demon was sitting in a chair completely naked, her legs pulling a Sharon Stone as she lounged back and felt up her own breasts.

"Miss me," she drawled.

He kicked the door shut. "What the hell are you doing?"

"Waiting for you to come over here and give me a proper hello. Preferably with some penetration." One of her hands drifted down between her legs. "I'm waiting."

"You need to back the fuck off from Sissy."

The demon exhaled a curse. "Her again. Look, Jim, there's no reason to pretend. It's not like Adrian's here. Or that little idiot girl."

He stalked over to the evil, but didn't get too close. "You don't want to push me on this. Sissy is off-limits."

Devina closed her knees. Then crossed her legs. "Is she. Since when do you set the rules."

"You want to come at me, fine. But leave her alone."

The demon burst up to her feet and paraded over to the bar, her sky-high red pumps clipping across the marble, going silent on the area rugs.

"You are a real asshole, Jim." She made work out of pouring clear liquid from a silver shaker into a martini glass. The olive she tossed in was army green. "You think I'm evil? What do you call a man who's unfaithful right in front of his lover's face, huh?"

He laughed with a hard edge. "Like you and I are fucking dating."

"We *are* in a relationship."

"You're insane. I mean, like, really—you are frickin' crazy."

Devina went quiet and wasted some time taking a long sip off the knife-edge-sharp rim of the glass. Her glittering black eyes stayed on him the whole time.

"I had other plans for us tonight," she murmured, "but I guess we're going to have to do this the hard way."

"If you're talking about sex, that ain't happening."

"You've said that before." Her tone was bored as she put her glass down and came around the bar. "I just want you to know that this is all your fault."

"Excuse me? What the fuck are you talking about?"

"This is all on you." Over at the silk-covered sofa, she bent down and started rifling through a big-ass black handbag. "Ah, yes, here it is."

When she turned around to him, she was holding up . . . a Mercedes hood ornament and a kitchen knife.

"What the fuck are you doing?" he demanded.

"You don't recognize this?" She put the circle with its three-part division forward. "It's from my car."

"So go give it to your mechanic. Why do I care?"

"You are seriously underwhelming right now, you know that." She went back over to the bar and put the thing into an ashtray. "Don't you remember the other night?"

"Sorry. I've been busy trying to forget every second I've spent in your presence."

She closed her eyes as if her chest hurt. But then she seemed to refocus. "You and I had one of our tiffs and I got a little aggressive with my car."

"You tried to mow me over."

"Yes, I did. And as it so happens, you were kind enough to leave me a little souvenir."

Warning bells started ringing in his head as he put two and two together and came up with a whole lot of fuck-him.

But it was too late.

"And this has proved to be really handy already."

Before he could react in any kind of proactive way, she poured some alcohol on top of the silver metal piece and spit a ball of flame at it.

Instantly, he was on fire. Even as his skin remained intact, he felt the burning down to his bones, the pain incapacitating him and sending him down onto the fake Oriental.

"You see, Jim, I'm not the one who made Sissy a part of this. The Creator did. So it's not my fault and it's nothing you can change."

Writhing into a tight ball, he found no relief and so he straightened out, trying to ease the agony. In the end, all he could do was grit his teeth and try not to scream, especially as she came over, those two blood-colored stillies stopping right next to his face.

Kneeling down, she brushed some of her long hair back and put the ashtray on the floor next to him.

If he could only reach—

"Oh, no," she said, pulling the fire out of range. "No, this is my toy. Just as you are."

Like the sick bitch she was, she started to finger herself as she watched him suffer, going so far as to lie out beside him, her perfect breasts heaving, her body undulating as she masturbated on the rug while he grunted and cursed in pain. And then just before she orgasmed, she grabbed for his dick, stroking at him like that was going to turn him on or some shit. Weakened by the agony, dizzy from the pain, he couldn't make his arms and legs coordinated enough to get her off him.

As she came, she said his name at the top of her lungs—almost like she was pissing on a post and hoping Sissy would magically hear her.

And then there was a moment of her just easing on back and staring at him like he was dessert. Whatever, he was about to pass out as she put her arm over her face like she couldn't believe how fucking good that had been.

Shit, it was his only chance, and he jerked in the direction of the ashtray.

"Not for you," she said with a smile. "No, no, that's mine."

Puckering her lips, she leaned down to the flames . . . and blew them out on a oner.

The relief was instantaneous, the burning draining out of his body the second there was nothing but a tendril of smoke over the Mercedes emblem. Except damage had been done. Even though his skin wasn't hanging in ribbons off of him, he was burn-victim out of it, his limbs jerking spastically, his vision going in and out of focus.

"Oh, Jim, I love you."

The tone in her delusional fucking voice was as if he'd just given her a set of pearls and a mink coat—as opposed to having gone third-degree as she YouPorn'd herself.

He was dimly aware as she sat up and fluffed her hair back into place. "So this thing gives me a lot of control over you. It's how I made it into your bed at your house, you know. Such a shame the way that turned out—although I'm not sure I could have kept the lie up as you fucked Sissy's body. Anywho . . ." She picked up the ashtray and then looked around. "This is going to take care of everything."

Stretching an arm out, she pulled a Kleenex free of a box on the coffee table.

"I know better than to think you're going to stand still for this, so I'm just going to take a little precaution here." Bringing the tissue to her mouth, she spoke into the thing, then blew across the fibers once, twice . . . three times. "There we go."

The instant she covered the hood ornament with the Kleenex, a huge weight settled over him, immobilizing his already weak body, keeping him down on the floor—even though ostensibly there was nothing on him.

Devina put the ashtray on the coffee table and looked down at him. "Where's your phone, Jim?"

There was no way of answering the question, as he couldn't open his mouth or use his tongue. The only thing he seemed capable of doing was breathing—that and having a pulse.

"I'll just have to pat you down."

She straddled him in those high heels and bent over him, her

full breasts swaying as she ran her hands down his entire body—
not just around the pockets of the jeans he'd changed into.

"No phone, damn it. But this . . . I think it's best that I take
your little knife. Just in case."

With a flourish, she unsheathed his crystal dagger from where
he'd tucked it into the small of his back. Bringing the weapon up
to his face, she smiled like a shark.

"Were you planning on using this against me? Shit, I should
have kept my bra and panties on and you could have cut them off
me. That would have been hot."

All he could do was blink, but the hatred curling in his gut
must have shown, because she pulled that bullcrap pout routine
of hers. "Oh, come on, Jim—we have to keep things spicy in the
bedroom. It makes couples closer. I read about it in an article that
was forwarded around Facebook."

Jesus fucking Christ, the bitch was—

"Okay, so no phone—any chance you left it with your girl? Because that would be so damned convenient, you have no idea."

Straightening, she went back over to her bag and took out an
iPhone. After dialing, she put the thing up to her ear.

When the call was answered, she said grimly, "Hello, Sissy."

Her eyes locked on his as he tried to fight against the nonex-
istent bars that held him down.

"I think you need to come see me."

Jim gritted his teeth and struggled so hard his bones hurt—
and the only thing that happened was that the Kleenex in the
ashtray moved ever so slightly.

"Penthouse. Freidmont Hotel downtown—I'll let the front-
desk supervisor know you're expected up here. Why?" Her eyes narrowed. "Because Jim's about to arrive here any second, and I figure
enough with the bullshit. You need to see this for yourself. And before you ask, no, it's not a trap. In fact, I'll bet you Jim already told

you he had to go somewhere tonight, didn't he. So get your ass down here—and be the strong female I know you want to be."

Devina terminated the call and shook her head in something close to amazement. "You are so fucking pissed off right now, aren't you. But you can't say a thing, you can't do a thing about it. You know, I should have tried to run you over with my Benz weeks ago. This is *so* good for our relationship."

She tossed her phone back in her purse and looked his body up and down. "And now for a change of clothes."

With a wave of her hand, he was left naked, his threads dematerializing as cleanly as smoke cleared by a draft of fresh air.

And then something utterly horrific happened.

A surge of nausea hit him right in the gut, and it was followed by a strange vertigo, one that seemed to affect his head as well as his body.

"Holy . . . shit," Devina breathed. "I am so fucking *hot*."

It took a second to piece together what she was saying. Oh . . . *fuck* . . .

"We're going to have to allow you a little movement, I don't want me to look dead." She directed a stare at the ashtray . . . and suddenly he could, if he really tried, lift his head about an inch off the carpet. "Besides, I want you to admire my handiwork."

Jesus Christ, *no* . . .

He had become Devina. He had her naked body, with her breasts and her hair, her mile-long legs, those goddamned shoes.

No! he screamed without making a sound.

"And now for my costume."

In the blink of an eye . . . she became him. Everything from his growing-out fade to his broad shoulders to his heavy legs.

"What do you think?" she asked in his voice. "We should totally remember this for Halloween, right?"

Chapter
Twenty-eight

Adrian could not find out she was leaving, Sissy thought as she padded down the creaky stairs, sticking to the far edges where the nail heads were to cut the noise.

On the first floor, she moved through the shadows silently, zeroing in on the kitchen. It was physically painful to see the table and its four chairs, and pass by the counter Jim had cleared off to get at her. But the keys, oh, yes, the keys to the Ford Explorer were right where Ad had put them when he'd emptied his pockets of his wallet, the Home Depot receipt, and his own phone.

She slipped outside and carefully shut the door. When she hit the lawn, she looked up, way up, to the attic. No lights glowing there. Ad had to be asleep.

And he needed to stay that way.

This was something she needed to handle on her own. Because if she got down to that hotel and found Jim hooking up with the demon? She was not going to be responsible for what she did to him. If that was what he was doing, then Jim was pure evil—what the hell else would you call a man who could say what he'd said to her, do what he'd done to her . . . and then go out to some other woman's bed. Some demon's bed.

The SUV had been parked right at the head of the driveway so that they could unload the plywood sheets, and fortunately, Ad had not locked the thing so she didn't have to worry about the chirp of the alarm deactivating. Once she was behind the wheel, she moved the seat up so she could reach the pedals . . . and prayed to God the sound of the engine starting didn't disturb the angel.

The headlights came on automatically, but the engine was relatively quiet—especially as she coasted out into the street, did a slow K-turn, and accelerated cautiously. In the rearview mirror, she double-checked the third floor.

Still no lights. And Ad was not a vampire who could see in the dark.

Thank God.

As she headed off, she knew where she was going. The hotel Devina was at was the super-fancy one downtown where the senior prom had been held. The trouble was, she wasn't sure which exit it was off the highway. There were, like, half a dozen that dumped out into those dense city blocks full of skyscrapers.

But she was going to frickin' find the thing.

Out of the neighborhood. Onto a surface road that took her to the Northway. And then she was speeding in the direction of Caldwell's twin bridges.

Curling her hands on the steering wheel, her head played tennis with itself, batting contradictions back and forth: The way he touched her. What Devina said. The look in his eyes as they'd had sex. What Devina said. The sense of belonging when they were together. What Devina said.

It was like having the Williams sisters on her mental court, the opposite sides slamming balls back and forth, neither giving an inch. On some level, she couldn't believe she was doing this, going downtown in the middle of a war for humanity's future, just to see whether her "boyfriend" or "fuck buddy" or whatever the hell they were to each other was cheating on her with someone else.

Then again, she'd wanted normal and this was it; this precise drama happened to regular people who hadn't done the sacrificial-virgin thing and ended up in Hell and been rescued only to go and watch their own funeral. There were millions of women across the globe who had to deal with this.

It was just . . . for frick's sake . . . why couldn't the "normal" she'd gotten have been more like a good steak dinner, or a night where, instead of worrying about life and death or goddamn portals to Purgatory, she watched reruns of *The Big Bang Theory* and ate Oreo ice cream out of the carton?

She got off I-87 one exit early and became trapped in the maze of one-ways. A few left turns later, however, and she was pulling up to the front of the hotel. Three flags waved above its grand entrance: an American, one for the state of New York, and a third with the place's logo in maroon and gold on it.

There were no valets out front, but, because it was . . . one sixteen in the morning . . . there was a metered space directly across from the revolving doors.

She got out, locked the Explorer, and straightened her clothes. Although, come on, like the sweatshirt and yoga pants were going to look any less schlubby? Or be any closer to the chain mail she wished she were wearing?

It was like she was about to go to war or something.

Jogging across the four-lane street, she took the red-carpeted stairs two at a time and shoved her way into the marble lobby. The first thing she saw was the biggest flower arrangement on the planet. The thing was nearly a full story high, and it was not made of silk: the lilies and roses released a delicate fragrance that reminded her of Eddie.

"Are you Miss Barten?"

Her sneaker let out a squeak as she pivoted toward the marble-topped bays where guests checked in. There was a lone man in a black suit standing behind one of the computer stations, his hair slicked back from his forehead, his shirt so blindingly white it made her think of bleached teeth.

"Yes."

"Please go right up." He smiled at her like he was much, much older than she was—even though he had to be only in his mid-twenties. "The elevators are on the left. You can take any one of them."

"Thanks."

The ride all the way to the penthouse took a while, and she really could have done without the four walls of mirrors. The last thing she wanted to see was her face and wondered whether Jim avoided his reflection when he came here, too. Or had he no conscience? Well, whatever, she certainly wasn't enjoying her own view: She'd been under some delusion, as she'd made it out of the house apparently without waking Ad, and gotten down here okay, that she was in full-on handle-it mode. Instead, even in her peripheral vision, her eyes looked crazed in her pale face, and her hands were shaking so badly, the sleeves of her sweatshirt were vibrating.

Ding!

The doors slid open and she stepped out onto lush carpet. Crystal sconces shed gentle butter-yellow light over walls that had a sheen of wealth to them, and real paintings were hung at intervals in both directions. There were a couple of doors to choose from, and she went over and read one of the plaques. FRAMINGHAM LOUNGE. Another one farther down read, STAFF ONLY.

She found the PENTHOUSE sign all the way at the far end.

There was a little doorbell button under the sign—but before she went to push it, the door opened of its own volition, as if a draft or, more likely, some unseen hand was at work.

And there it was.

Exactly what she had come to see, but hoped not to.

In a seating arrangement in the center of a room with a lot of glass windows, in a chair that faced the view, Devina was buck-ass naked, her long brunette hair spilling down nearly to the floor . . . because her head was thrown back in ecstasy.

Bathed in candlelight, Jim was looming over her, his naked body poised above his bowed arms as he kissed her.

Sissy must have made a noise. A curse. A something—because he suddenly looked up at her. Instantly, the red-hot passion in his face was replaced with shock and then panic.

"Sissy!" he barked. And then he had the colossal nerve to leap back from the woman, demon, whatever she was like he hadn't just been caught red-handed.

He was fully aroused.

Between one blink and the next, the rage inside of her leaped free and she was no longer in control.

As she stepped over the threshold, Jim was holding his hands out like he wanted to stop her from coming into the penthouse. Then he was backing up as if looking for his clothes. The whole time, he was talking to her, his mouth moving.

She didn't hear a thing.

But her sight worked just fine: She saw everything about him and everything about Devina, too. For her part, the demon just sat back in that low-slung chair, her hands lying on the armrests, her hooded eyes following every move that Sissy made.

Then again, what was there to say, really.

There was, however, a knife. On the coffee table by the chair. With an eight-inch blade. Absently, she noted that it was like the fancy one her dad had gotten for Christmas two years ago, the one he treated like it was a work of art. Funny, the Henckels was totally out of place in the room, looking like something that had been left behind by a caterer.

She went for it before she knew what she was doing.

Picking the blade up, she felt its weight in her right hand, and turned to Jim.

"—me get some clothes on, okay?" he was saying. "Sissy? Can you hear me? Let me just get dressed, all right?"

He wheeled around as if looking for a pair of pants.

Something registered in the back of her mind, but she didn't give it even one brain cell of thought. There were none to spare. That rage had taken over everything in her and around her.

"I can't believe you fucking lied," she said. "You bastard."

Jim put those hands in front of himself again and backed up even further—until there was a crash like he'd knocked over a lamp, although she didn't pay any attention to that.

"Sissy, you got this wrong—"

"You fucking bastard!"

All at once, everything that had happened to her since she'd gone out to that Hannaford supermarket came back to her—as she stalked Jim, all of the unjustness of each succeeding horror was made manifest in him. The pain and terror of death. The centuries of quasi-time suffering in Devina's well. The raw mourning of her family and her lost life.

It was the perfect storm that created the super-wave in the ocean.

And that wave was going to come crashing down on Jim Heron. Right now.

As if destiny agreed with her, he took one final step back and came up against the bar. He was still talking to her, and he twisted around as if attempting to judge which side to try to get around.

That Grim Reaper tattoo of his was yet another reminder of why he needed to die.

The rage lifted her arm up, the blade flashing in the candle-light.

She was going to kill him. Even though he was bigger and stronger, she knew that if she made one stabbing motion . . . it was going to be game-over.

Her fury was that great.

Chapter
Twenty-nine

Jim watched through the eyes of another as the end of the war happened right in front of him. And there wasn't a goddamn thing he could do about it.

Trapped in Devina's illusion of herself, frozen to the chair in the position she had arranged him in, he was roaring—but only on the inside. Outwardly, he was imprisoned and mute and unable to move, and as he watched with horror, he knew exactly how this was going to play out. Sissy was going to take that kitchen knife, lift it high over her head, and drive it right into Devina's chest—and that demon was going to make sure there was a good target to hit.

As soon as that blade made contact with the demon? The war was over, and Devina won. After all, it was the choice that counted; it was the intent, not the outcome of actual death that mattered. That knife wasn't going to do shit to the demon, but it was everything that counted: Sissy's crossroads, even though engineered by Devina, was the test she was going to fail. That rage and hatred, the shit Nigel had been talking about, were carved into the tight lines of her face and her body, and she wasn't just going to give in to them.

They had taken her over.

Ad was right; she was possessed.

Nooooooo, he screamed inside his prison of flesh. Sissy, no!

Devina leaned backwards over the bar, like she was scrambling to get out of the way and struck with indecision over which direction to take, but he knew better. She was giving Sissy every single opportunity in the world to score a kill shot.

God, he couldn't believe this was how the demon got everything . . . the quick and the dead, the angels and the archangels, the Manse of Souls and Heaven above . . . all hers.

His vision became wavy from tears as his failure came home to roost. His mother . . . Sissy . . . Adrian and Eddie and the archangels . . .

It was all over.

And Devina knew it. From her contorted position at the bar, she shot him a look out of his own face with a sly, knowing wink.

Abruptly, time slowed down until Sissy all but froze in position, everything becoming hyper-focused—

Except . . . wait.

The slow-mo wasn't a perception issue. Sissy really had stopped with the knife over her head, and her body poised to strike—and she stayed that way.

Devina frowned using Jim's face, like her dance partner had missed a beat and stepped on her foot.

Sissy pivoted, still keeping the weapon up. Her eyes were hollows of what he knew them to be, but they were not completely insane. Especially as they narrowed on him.

"What are you doing?" Devina demanded in his voice.

Sissy lowered the blade and turned fully around—at the very moment one of the tears in his eyes slipped out and traveled down the illusion of Devina's smooth cheek.

"What are you looking at," Devina growled.

Sissy took a step forward toward him. And then another.

All he could do was try to communicate through the pupils that were not his own, begging her to see through the lie.

"What the fuck are you doing?" his voice demanded.

Sissy ignored Devina. Instead, she reached out with her free hand and seemed to touch the air above his head. Then she went down further and he felt her brush against the skin of his neck.

"Sissy," Devina said. "Are you really this stupid?"

Please, God, he thought. Whatever you're seeing, stick with it.

Sissy straightened abruptly and looked at Devina. "How did you do it?"

Jim watched the illusion of himself cross his arms over his chest. He was still naked, but his cock was no longer hard as a rock—apparently, Devina had lost her own arousal.

"I came here," his voice said, "took her clothes off, and got ready to fuck her."

Sissy glanced back and forth between them. And then she countered levelly, "No. You didn't."

As Sissy lowered the knife, she looked over at Jim—who was not, in fact, Jim. She wasn't sure how she could explain the fact that every detail about him was correct, from the cowlick on the left side of his hair by the temple to the flecks in his blue eyes, from the tattoo on his back to the power in his chest—and yet it was *not* him.

Jim, the real one, was sitting in the chair. In spite of the fact that he appeared to be every inch the demon.

There were just two tiny details Devina had gotten wrong. Two things that, however accurate the demon's imitation of him was, she had failed to nail.

The shaking hit Sissy the same way the fury had, rocking her from head to foot, making her feel as if the world were spinning even as she was pretty damn sure the hotel was on solid ground. And it was shortly after the blender routine took over that she realized she had a fucking knife in her hand.

And she'd been about to use it on Devina.

Because, for whatever reason, the demon wanted her to. Devina had set this lie up—for God only knew what reason.

Disgusted with herself, she threw the knife at the coffee table with such force, it knocked off—

"Fucking hell! Fuck you! Fuck you both!"

And just like that, "Jim" disappeared—and "Devina" flew off that chair, the female body exploding up as if released from some kind of hold.

In mid-air, Jim emerged from the lie, everything that looked like the demon replaced by his male body and proper face. He landed like a cat and shot back over to Sissy, throwing his arms around her and holding her so hard she could barely breathe.

She wasn't the only one who was trembling.

"You did it," he said hoarsely. "You did it."

"No, I didn't—I didn't—"

"You saved us."

"What?"

He pulled back and kissed her. "How did you know?"

It took her a moment to hear the words and comprehend what he was asking. "N-n-noo h-h-h—damn it, I c-c-can't talk."

"Breathe, just breathe with me."

"No halo."

He shook his head. "I'm sorry?"

She pointed up to the crown of his head. "N-n-n-no halo. I was about to—" She couldn't even say the words. "I was going to . . . but then I noticed that there was no halo. You—you—you have a halo . . . because you're an angel. And my necklace . . . when I looked over at her—you, I mean—I saw that 'she' was wearing my dove n-n-n-necklace. That's when I knew—but why? Why would she want me to—"

"You're one of the souls."

"What?"

"Lemme explain at home—we've got to get out of here." He looked around on the floor. "How did you get here?"

"E-E-Explorer. Out front."

"Okay, okay, good."

"What are you looking for?"

He bent over and picked up . . . a Mercedes emblem. "This."

"From her car?" Sissy said.

"You got it. Come on."

Jim grabbed her hand and started to hustle her out of the penthouse, but she pulled him to a stop. "You're naked."

"And invisible."

"But won't you get cold—"

"No time, come on."

And that was how they ended up in the hotel's elevator, her in a twenty-eight-dollar outfit from Target, him in the birthday suit the good Lord gave him.

"*I'm* one of the souls?" she said.

He looked down at her, his blue eyes grave. "Yeah. You are."

"So . . . this round is won?"

Jim nodded. "You evened it up for us. You chose wisely—when you stopped. When you didn't act on the rage as you came to your crossroads."

He refocused on the numbers above the elevator doors, the ones that were lighting up sequentially as they descended to the lobby.

"So this is good news," she mumbled.

"Yeah." He gave her hand a squeeze and dropped a quick kiss on her mouth. "The best."

Then why was his jaw clenched like he was still upstairs, fighting with Devina?

No, she thought. There was something he wasn't telling her.

Chapter
Thirty

In Adrian's dream, a spring thunderstorm rolled through Caldwell and settled over the old mansion, flashes of lightning splintering through the attic's opposing circular windows and flickering over his face, waking him up. As was typical, however, there was something wrong, something missing—which was the way you knew that it wasn't real.

No thunder. Just the vivid bursts of sugar-white light.

Which were the kind of thing that could be cured by putting your arm over your eyes. No problem—except then shit got a little more critical. With a massive *pop!*, the transformer tucked under the eaves of the roof was struck, and a shower of golden sparks flowed downward—

Ad jerked up from his makeshift bed.

Wait a minute, he thought, there wasn't a transformer under the damn roof.

So yeah, he pointed out to himself, that was how he knew this was just a dream.

And yet . . .

As he tried to figure out whether shit was real or Memorex, lightning continued to flash around the house, highlighting the old steamer trucks and racks of Victorian clothes and—

The back of Ad's neck went haywire, the hairs prickling so badly he reached up and rubbed them to quiet the irritation down.

The sound of his name being whispered made him freeze.

With a feeling of utter unreality, he slowly turned his head in the direction of the carefully wrapped, sheeted figure that lay next to him like some kind of Boris Karloff movie extra. As another jagged flash ripped through the night sky, the flickering light penetrated the old-fashioned glass and washed over the body . . . making it seem like . . .

"Get a fucking hold of yourself."

Eddie was dead and therefore did not breathe. So there was no up-and-downing of the chest happening—because the guy was *dead*.

Whatever he thought he had just seen was a function of those brilliant and quickly fading bursts of energy. It was not because—

Another flash licked into the attic through the window and . . . the chest was going up and down. Slowly, unevenly . . . but yes, in fact, it was—

"Fuck!" He shoved himself back, slamming into one of the steamer trunks. "What the—"

Instantly he calmed down, because he realized, Oh, right, this was a dream. One of those fucked-up fake scenarios that even the brains of immortals insisted on chucking over the fence of consciousness every once in a while.

"So now what are you going to do?" he muttered at the corpse. "Sit up—oh, yup, there ya go. Fantastic."

The upper body of Eddie's remains lifted off the planks, rising haltingly until it was at a right angle with the wrapped, extended legs.

More lightning flashed, as if on cue. "Annnnd now that we're partially vertical, what's it gonna be?" Ad would have checked his watch if he'd been wearing one. "Freddy Krueger? Or are we going more for a King Tut vibe? It's impossible for you to scare me, FYI."

His own mind had no terrors to offer that could compare to what he'd already lived through. He just wasn't that inventive. And as for this little ditty? In a minute and a half, he was going to wake up in a cold sweat. Not because he'd been frightened, but because anything that had to do with his dear friend was more painful than all the aches he had assumed on Matthias's behalf.

Slowly, the covered head turned to him, the neck straining against the wrapping.

"Really," Ad muttered. "If this is the best you can do, you need to go back to the Nightmare Academy or wherever it is you got your chops. Frankly, you're a total disappointment."

Crossing his arms over his chest, he leaned back against the steamer trunk and looked around, waiting for it all to go away.

One of the mummified hands reached up and began scratching at the wraps around the face, clawing at them as if the layers were preventing the thing from breathing. Ad had to look down at his feet as the first patch of skin began to show at the chin. It was just too fucking painful.

Okay, maybe he hadn't given this bad dream enough credit.

A deep, ragged inhale rattled through the attic, and all he could do was shake his head. This was just too fucking cruel.

Abruptly, the lightning stopped, the storm, or whatever it was, done.

From out of the darkness, he heard, "Ad . . ."

The voice was rough, but as with a person's fingerprints, it was both instantly recognizable and a one-and-only.

Eddie's.

"Ad, where . . . are . . . you . . ."

Ad covered his face with his hands. He was so wrong about his subconscious not going for the jugular: The idea that any kind of Eddie, even a hypothetical one made up by his own brain, could be searching for him made him feel his inadequacies and his why-hadn't-hes all the way to the marrow. He had done so many reckless, stupid things while Eddie had been alive—and capped them off by not being on the ball enough when that harpy came after his buddy.

He should have done something that night. Heard something. Seen something out of the corner of his eye.

So that he could have saved—

"Where are the lights?"

Ad frowned. Then dropped his hands. Leave it to him to ruin an emotional moment even in his sleep—although he couldn't say he wasn't grateful. He'd been on the verge of fourteen-year-old-girling it over here.

"Ad, I can't . . . see . . . lights off or . . . ?"

Right. Now he was back to being bored with the whole goddamned thing. "There's a long string right next to you," he muttered to the mummy.

Unbelievable—

Click!

The mummy thing was still upright, but had managed to get half the wrapping off its face, the perfectly preserved skin possessing that ruddy color that Eddie had always sported. And as the nightmare spoke, that chin moved up and down, the lips moving fluidly.

"Ad, where are you? I . . . can't see. . . ."

"That's because your eyes are covered, dumb-ass."

Time to wakey-wakey, he told himself. Come on, do myself a solid and wake the fuck up, wouldja.

The mummy thing raised its wrapped hand and then, on a oner, peeled off the entire top of the masking. Ad's heart skipped a beat—because the face was so familiar, everything from those red eyes to that dark hair pulled back into that braid exactly right.

"Eddie's" expression turned from confusion to shock. "Dear God . . . what happened to you?"

Ad frowned. Great—clearly, this nightmare thing was taking another turn for the weird. Because come on, like his brain didn't know what he'd done to himself?

Before he could tell the dream to cut the shit, or maybe roll over and hit himself on the head so he'd wake up, the Eddie thing reached out to him with its mittened hands.

"Adrian, what did you do while I was gone?"

Ad blinked once. Twice. And then an ill feeling washed over him. "This is a dream."

"No, it's not. Nigel went to the Creator and begged for my life. Something about Jim calling in a favor for getting the archangel out of Purgatory? What's been happening—and, oh, God, you're hurt. Your eye—"

Adrian opened his mouth and screamed his guts out.

As Jim drove back to the house from downtown, he had to crank the heater on account of all the nakey he had going on. Next to him, Sissy was silent and staring out the windshield like maybe she was in replay mode. He was likewise distracted—although he was doing a brain cramp on what was still ahead of them, as opposed to what had just happened.

Oh, God, he didn't know how he was going to get through it. And he wasn't talking about the next and final round.

Hell, he couldn't even feel the hah-gotcha that should have come with making Devina lose this one. Didn't dwell on the thank-fucking-God that he'd not lost everything to the demon. Wasn't able to even consider strategy for the final/final he was about to go into.

All he could focus on was Sissy and getting her clean: There was no winning this war if she couldn't go to Heaven.

Turning into the old mansion's driveway, he went all the way to the back and parked in front of the detached garage. And when he got out, he did the whole cup-his-manhood thing as he went around and opened Sissy's door for her.

"Sorry about this," he muttered as they walked toward the house together.

"About what?"

He opened the way into the kitchen and held the door for her, standing there like a piker with his bare ass propping the cold wood wide and his hands over his cock and balls.

Someday, he vowed. Someday he was going to give her a piece of normal.

"Everything at this point," he replied. "I'm sorry for fucking everything."

The light fixture over the four-top had been left on and that gave her an awful lot of him to see, unfortunately. Not that she was checking him out or anything—he just felt like it would have been so much better for him to have pants on. A loincloth. A frickin' napkin over his privates.

Head to bed. That was the only thing he was thinking of—

Sissy stopped in the doorway that led into the hall, blocking the way. "What else," she demanded.

"I'm sorry?"

"There's something else here." She motioned back and forth in the air between them. "And whatever it is, you need to be honest with me. 'Cause what's doing me in is the fact that I can feel there's something wrong, and in the absence of knowing what it is, my head is coughing up all kinds of bad things."

Jim cursed and let his head fall back. Ironically, that pointed his eyes toward an old light fixture that had been built in the shape of a three-dimensional star.

"You're scaring me," she said roughly.

"Do you mind if I put some clothes on?"

"Yes, because no offense, I'm enjoying the view even with all this crap going on."

He had to smile at her. He couldn't stop himself.

"You're blushing," she murmured.

"Am I?" He shook his head. "Didn't know I could."

"Now stop deflecting."

"Sissy, I—"

The scream that filtered down from above was like a bomb going off, and Jim sprang into action, beating feet around Sissy and racing for the front of the house. When there was no smell of smoke, and no other sounds, he flew up the stairs, wondering what in the hell was going on.

"Adrian!" he barked. "Ad!"

Shoving open the door to the angel's bedroom, he found no one around, so he hit the attic stairs, tearing up them two at a time.

As he rounded the top of the staircase, he skidded to a halt. Adrian was sprawled on the floorboards, back against a trunk, peepers showing so much white, he looked like he had egg slices for eyeballs. And across from him, Eddie was sitting up, the wrapping off his head, the rest of his body still pulling a mummy.

The two angels looked at him—and both did a double take. Which, considering the Lucy-I'm-home stunt Eddie had just pulled, was really saying something.

"Oh, hey, Eddie," Jim said. And then he remembered he was naked.

As he re-cupped himself, Sissy came up the stairs behind him. "Oh, my God," she whispered.

Eddie's mouth fell open as he saw Sissy. And then he turned back to Adrian and demanded, "What the *fuck* has been going on since I've been gone?"

Chapter
Thirty-one

Eddie Blackhawk was not the kind of angel to get his feathers ruffled very easily. But come on. He'd been stuck in the prison of his dead body, his soul effectively trapped and conscious in a cell with no key—when—surprise!—the Creator decided to grant a rare reprieve. After which he'd gone through something like electric shock therapy to rise to the surface of life once again. Only to find that his best friend had been in a car accident and Jim Heron was evidently getting really fucking naked . . . with the girl from Devina's bathtub.

That'll teach him to die. Yup. Not pulling that shit again, because look what happened.

And not one of the three of them was talking.

"Will somebody here *please* give me a clue," he demanded. "I mean, how long have I been gone? Where are we in the war? And, Jim, what the *hell* were you thinking! You can't go to Purgatory! I never would have let you—"

Abruptly, he realized he hadn't been properly introduced to the lady. He lifted one of his sheet-wrapped paws to the female. "Hi, I'm Eddie, by the way."

"Ah . . . nice to meet you," she said. Then indicated her chest. "I'm Sissy. Sissy Barten. I was—"

"Oh, I know. And I'm so sorry you got mixed up with this stuff."

"Me, too." Except then she glanced over at Jim. "It hasn't been all bad, though—"

"What the fuck is this!" Ad exploded. "I don't dream about you people, okay? Like, ever. Never seen Jim. No Sissy. And no frickin' Eddie. So can I just wake up—"

"Not a dream—"

"—is reality."

"—totally real."

As Ad got three answers, all of which backed each other up, he seemed to lose his train of thought. Then he cursed and choked out, "This is really cruel. This is . . . torture."

Eddie took a deep breath and looked at his oldest, dearest friend. Maybe it was good that there was some chaos to deal with—otherwise, he'd probably be getting really emotional, too. "It is me, Ad. I'm back. I'm right here."

The other angel put his head in his hands again and started to shake all over—and it was impossible not to go to him. Using his arms, Eddie dragged his bound body across the rough floor and all but fell on the guy. Shifting Adrian into his lap, he ducked his own head as his best friend began to weep.

They each said things, things that Eddie wouldn't be able to remember later. But the words didn't matter. They both had the sense that the gears that had been skipping were once again locked in, that life had by some miracle resumed its normal course, that the mountain that had been too high, and the valley that had been too deep, and the river that had been too wide . . . had all been climbed and crossed and swum.

He was vaguely aware of Jim and Sissy ducking out like they wanted to be discreet, and he appreciated that. It wasn't because he was embarrassed to show emotion—more that he knew that Ad would have hated to have any witnesses to this.

Sometimes in life, all you had was your pride—and you were

so far down the hole, you couldn't even safeguard that without a little help.

Besides, Eddie was right there with the guy. It had been agony to be separated, and blind, and mute, immobilized in that body— hell, all he'd been able to do to help was rejuvenate the house, sending energy out to reverse the entropy that had so viciously attacked the place.

But he was back—and he had to know where they stood.

Like Ad read his mind, the guy shoved himself away and wiped his face on the T-shirt he was wearing. "You've never lied to me."

"No, I haven't."

"Are you real? And know that even in my dreams—you wouldn't lie to me."

"I am." Eddie reached up and found a loose tail end of the wrappings. With big loops over his head, he started to unravel what was around his neck and chest. "As far as I know, I am back."

Adrian took a deep breath and sighed it out. "I'm not ready to believe you yet, but, man, that is so the right answer."

Eddie froze in mid-circle. "Matthias. Oh, my God, you took—"

"Whatever. It doesn't matter."

"It's the eye. The bad leg. But Matthias went to Devina—so how did you—"

"He came back. Do-over. The bitch kept the flag, but Jim got another shot at the guy. We won."

"Are we ahead?"

"One behind—unless . . ." Ad glanced over to the head of the stairs. "Unless Jim has good news or something—that isn't tied to his love life."

"Is he . . . are they—"

"Yeah."

"Oh." Eddie cleared his throat. "Oh, okay."

Ad glanced over and smiled a little. "You always were a straight arrow."

"To be fair, the last time I saw her, she was hanging dead upside down over a bathtub."

"True 'nuff."

"How'd Jim get her out of Hell?"

"Long story, but it got ugly. If we lose this? It's because of Sissy—and not because she does anything wrong. Jim's different around her, and not in a way that necessarily helps us."

Eddie continued until his chest was free. "You got a knife?"

"Here." Ad moved to one side and sucked in hard, like the shift of weight hurt. Then he handed over a crystal dagger. "Compliments of the chef."

The weapon was so sharp, Eddie had to be careful or risk cutting his skin, but the good news was that the wrappings just fell off. He left some of the shit around his hips. They already had one flasher in the house; two would be overkill.

"I knew," he said as he offered the dagger back to his buddy.

"Knew what?"

"That you slept up here with me. I could hear you. I really appreciated it—it was the only thing that kept me from losing my mind."

Ad accepted the weapon and cleared his throat. "Yeah, well. Where else would I be?"

Downstairs in the kitchen, Jim watched while Sissy put on some coffee and got out a box of Duncan Hines chocolate cake mix.

"Don't judge," she said as she put the thing on the counter and started grabbing eggs and oil from the fridge and cupboards. "I cook when I'm uptight."

"I got no problem with it." Shoving the long sleeves of his sweatshirt up, he lit a cigarette and blew out a column of smoke.

"Can I just say this? The best thing about being immortal is that I don't have cancer-stick guilt anymore—"

"Can I get pregnant?"

The second her words sank in, Jim embarked on a happy cruise through pulmonary arrest, the coughing fit taking over his entire body. When he finally recovered enough to draw oxygen into his immortal lungs, he . . .

Really didn't know what the fuck to say.

"You finished?" she asked. "Because I think your liver is over here on the floor."

She turned back around, cracked three eggs into the white-and-blue bowl she was using, and then got to filling a measuring cup full of oil.

"Well?" she said as she poured that in and then headed for the sink for some water. "Can I?"

"I have no idea. I wasn't thinking like that—it just never dawned on me."

"Yeah. I wasn't thinking about it either. But is that why you looked so weird on the way home?"

No, he thought. Although now I have an all-new and exciting reason to freak out.

"We don't have to—you know, have sex again," he said. And then took a long drag.

She glanced over her shoulder. "No. Not going to bed with you would be criminal."

Making a fist, he coughed into his hand. "Ah, maybe I'll get some condoms, though."

"Is there anyone who could tell us . . ."

"Tell you what?"

Jim shifted in his chair as Eddie came to a halt in the doorway from the front hall. Dayum, he'd forgotten how big the guy was, how red his eyes were, how long that braid down his back was.

And all he could think of was . . . it was so worth it. Going over there, bringing Nigel back—even with the risks, it was so worth it just to see the favor he'd asked of the archangel up and walking around.

Abruptly, Ad stepped around his buddy and limped over to the table, the expression on his face a tangled, tortured mess.

In the next moment, Jim was in Adrian's arms, the other angel having lifted him out of his chair in a bear hug that was so strong, Jim had to wonder if he was going to end up with a spinal condition afterward.

But he got it. He understood exactly the words that were being said through the contact. "You're welcome," Jim said roughly. "And you'da done the same for me."

Ad stayed there for the longest time, because he was a guy who couldn't express feelings well, especially not ones this big. And then he stepped back, wiped his face on the bottom of his shirt, and cleared his throat.

"Okay," the angel said. Like that was a declaration of Ctrl-Alt-Delete, and he was prepared to reboot and refocus.

As Jim sat back down, he wished he could have given the guy a couple of days off just to recalibrate—after all, you didn't go from your best friend being dead to suddenly standing next to the guy again, without a serious case of the head-fucks. But they couldn't spare that kind of luxury.

"What did you want to know?" Eddie asked Sissy as he went over and opened the fridge.

"Whether or not I can get pregnant?"

Boom! Jim thought. And like an explosion had actually gone off in the kitchen, the other two guys froze; then looked around as if they were doing a damage assessment.

The sad thing? Believe it or not, that issue was not the most pressing one they had.

Chapter
Thirty-two

Devina paced up and down the aisles in her basement, her high heels sounding out and echoing around. Her minions had mostly cleaned up the mess—there was some fine-tuning to be done with the placement of her collection, but for the most part, shit was back where it should be.

She needed the order now more than ever.

How had Sissy known? she thought. What the *fuck* had tipped that girl off?

Fucking hell, it wasn't like Devina had been doing an imitation of Jim like she was some Vegas entertainer pulling an almost-there stage act. When she assumed someone's identity, she was not the halfway Jack Nicholson or Al Pacino, the three-quarters of a George W. Bush or Elvis.

Thanks to that Mercedes emblem, she'd had Jim's DNA to play with—and she had literally pulled him out of her ass, molecule by molecule.

And yet that dumb-ass virgin had somehow figured it out.

Make that just plain dumb-ass, the virgin part having been done away with, fuck you very much, Jim.

Oh, man, she could just fucking imagine Nigel and his three

fruits up there in Heaven, all totes relieved that they had another flag.

How the *hell* had she lost this round?

She should never have made that deal with Jim. If she hadn't released Sissy from her Well of Souls? Then one of the alternates would have been on deck and maybe she could have gotten through to them instead of failing with that girl.

Putting her hands on her hips, she pivoted in a little circle and looked all the way down toward her bed. She still had fantasies of Jim in it with her. Was still committed to winning. But, for fuck's sake . . . this just sucked.

And the worst part? The only person she wanted to share her fears and doubts with was Jim—but he was not only with that little dumb-ass . . . he would probably just use the information against her.

"It is so lonely at the top," she muttered. To, of course, no one.

Evil wasn't supposed to be lonely, she thought. Evil was supposed to be havoc and chaos out having an awesome time fucking shit up. But instead, here she was, all alone and in mourning for some immortal man.

"Love stinks," she muttered. "Yah, yah."

Sure, she could summon some minions and have an orgy—but like any Christmas toy, even the best ones got boring if you played with them enough. Or maybe she should head out to some of the clubs and fuck some random humans—maybe make them do some corrupt things just for shits and giggles.

But God, that seemed like such work.

And meanwhile, she had no friends to call, no girlies to invite over and compare My Boyfriend's the Biggest Shit stories.

Jim was her partner. He should be with her.

Striding down to her bedroom area, she fished around her

purse and got her phone. Keying in her password, she got his number out of the recently dialed call log and . . .

Hovered her thumb over the lineup of black numbers.

She just wanted to hear his voice. Like, he could pick up and say hello, and then she would . . .

What. What would she say? Something like, Did you fuck Sissy when you got home?

As if she wanted to hear the answer to that.

Ugh.

Damn it, why couldn't he just be the man she had in her head? The one who was as unhealthily obsessed with her as she was with him? The one who was ready to drown in a cesspool of Biblical-level fighting followed by epic make-up sex? The one who loved her and only her—and would never, ever be with anyone else.

Unless, of course, they invited another woman to join them. And then bonded over killing her when it was over.

On that note, Hallmark was so missing the mark on its cards. People who were in unconventional relationships, like those involving a demon, were totally shortchanged. Bastards.

"Fuck it," she said, tossing the phone across the duvet.

Her immediate instinct was to reach out, pick the thing back up . . . and double-check to see if he had called and she'd missed it—during the nanosecond the cell was in mid-air.

Closing her eyes, she tried to think back to the latest issue of *Cosmopolitan* magazine. They'd had tips for this "When Your Man Lets You Down" shit. What had they been?

Oh, right.

With the blink of an eye, she banished the silk shirt and leather skirt she'd thrown on after she'd arrived here back to their hangers. Then she blinked again and she was wearing a set of pink flannel pj's with sheep leaping around the legs and a top that read, I Feel Sheepy. Next, she leaned over to her bedside table, turned her TV on, and called up ROKU. Heading into Netflix, she found the part marked "TV Shows," and decided on . . .

Nah, not *Frasier*. She was in the mood for something else. *SATC*.

Yeah, see, actually, she did have girlfriends. Carrie, Samantha, Charlotte, and Miranda. They'd all been through this shit—and they had good wardrobes, too, even if the show was how old now?

From out of thin air, she conjured up a bottle of chardonnay, some Lindt chocolate truffles—dark, of course—and a tub of vanilla ice cream with a sterling-silver spoon.

Tomorrow was another day. And she would rise to fight again.

She was going to have to. Thanks to his win tonight?

Jim was the last soul on deck.

Chapter
Thirty-three

Way to get everybody's attention, Sissy thought as she realized she'd forgotten to check that there was a cake mixer in the house.

As the three men looked back and forth between each other, like everybody was praying someone else would step up to the answer plate, she popped open cupboards and shuffled old pots and pans around. When she finally gave up, the boys were still in the frozen positions she'd left them in.

"So is that a resounding 'I don't know'?" she asked. Yeah, sure, pregnancy was a private subject, but come on, the world could end tomorrow—literally—so normal boundary concepts were out the window. Besides, she really needed the information.

Eddie, the one who was, you know, back from the dead, cleared his throat. Man, he was good-looking, with a strong face and all that hair. Plus he gave off a steady-and-sure vibe that put her at ease.

"No, you cannot carry a child," he said carefully—like he didn't know whether that was good or bad news to her. "The Creator gave that special ability to mortals and mortals only. The instant you crossed over, you—all of us—are no longer capable of creating life. Perhaps it is the exchange for immortality in His eyes? Or maybe it is part of the reason the living must die? But no, in your state, it is not possible."

She frowned and turned back to the bowl. Interesting, she thought. The whole kids/no-kids thing had never dawned on her before. She hadn't been one of those girls who had pre-planned their wedding since before their adult teeth had come in. She also hadn't been guy-crazy, either. And yet the idea that the choice had been made for her?

Really sucked, actually.

"Goddamn Devina," she muttered.

For a split second, she decided she really should have stabbed the bitch when she'd had the chance—and that anger, oh, that anger of hers came back.

Grabbing a wire whisk, she started beating the cake batter so hard, she didn't need help from anything made by Westinghouse.

Someday, she told herself, she was going to reach the bottom of her losses. She just had to believe that at some point, her wrong-place/wrong-time mistake however many weeks ago was going to stop haunting her. Stop changing her life in bad ways. Stop making her want to cry.

"*Sissy*, stop."

As Jim's strong hand landed on her arm, she jumped—and then saw that she'd made a mess, chocolate cake mix splattered all over the counter, herself, the floor.

She'd have had much better luck with a mixer.

"Sorry," she muttered, breaking away and going to the sink.

Washing her hands under too much water, she got stuck in the middle of fight-or-flight—she wanted to run; she wanted to hit something; she needed to cry.

When she cranked off the water, she ducked her eyes and dried her hands on the seat of her yoga pants. "I gotta . . . I gotta get out of here for a minute. 'Scuse me."

She left the kitchen without waiting for a response, her feet going a mile a minute as she gunned for the front door. Opening it wide, she burst out into the cool night and jogged down the shallow steps of the porch. She had no idea where she was going, and picked right at the end of the walkway just because she did.

The good news was that the sidewalk went on forever. Striding forward, she swung her arms and punched her legs into the ground and pretty soon she was going by the house next to theirs. And then the next one. And the next after that.

"Go back, go back, go back," she muttered as she began to pant.

And she wasn't talking about to the kitchen to clean up her epic cake fail. She just wanted to return to that moment when the impulse for some Rocky Road ice cream had hit her while she'd been sitting on the couch at her parents', watching *Pitch Perfect*. It was one of her favorite movies in spite of her not being a big Anna Kendrick fan—too elfin with those little bitty lips and the big teeth and the pointy features. But she'd loved Rebel Wilson and Hana Mae Lee.

It had been right as Rebel was saying, "My real name is Fat Patricia," that the hankering had hit and she'd decided to pause the movie, go for the keys to her mom's Subaru, and head out. The plan had been to get the ice cream, go back to house to finish things up, and start in on either *While You Were Sleeping* or *The Blind Side*.

She'd always had a girl crush on Sandra Bullock—

Sissy stopped dead and realized it was all past tense. Not just the nuances of that evening that had turned her life into a nightmare, but all the things she'd used to like. Do. See.

Be.

Putting a hand on her lower belly, she looked down at her body. "I should have been able to choose."

"I agree."

She gasped and wheeled around, bringing her hands up to throw a punch. But it was just Jim.

"You followed me," she said roughly.

"Yeah. I did."

She dropped her hands. Then crossed them over her chest. Then dropped them again. "I don't want this anymore. I don't . . . want to be here anymore."

With resonant sorrow of his own, he reached up and brushed both of her cheeks—which was how she figured out she was crying.

"I know," he whispered. "I know."

Pacing around him, going on and off the sidewalk, she shook her head. "If you find out who the next soul is, and you win that round—what happens? Am I still stuck here in this netherland? I mean, I've been to Hell and I don't want to go back there. But I'm neither here nor there now—can I go to Heaven? Can you send me there? Please?"

As she stopped and looked up at him, she could see his wings, the shimmering outlines glowing in the dark—and the sight made her feel like she'd gone to the right place with the request maybe. After all, she'd been to Sunday school; she knew that there was a Heaven—or at least, she'd been told there was.

"Jim?" she said in a small voice. "Can you please just let me go somewhere else?"

It was so funny, Jim would later reflect. The heart, as it turned out, could break in a million different ways: It didn't have to be a loss or a death. No, the inability to help someone you loved was shattering.

You'd have thought he'd learned that earlier with his mother.

And maybe he had. Which meant this moment out here with Sissy was one hell of a refresher course.

And there was a selfish part of him that wanted to keep her with him. If she went up to the Manse of Souls, he couldn't get to her; they'd be separated, maybe forever. On the other hand, she was clearly at her breaking point, the stuff about the pregnancy having sent her into a kind of despair he could only guess at.

He'd never wanted kids. Wasn't interested in them, couldn't have cared less.

Although if there had been a chance of having one with her . . .

Shaking himself back into focus, he dragged a hand through his hair and wished he had a cigarette—especially as he remembered the sight of her across the kitchen, beating the ever-loving shit out of that cake batter. Good God, he'd thought he was going to have to surgically remove that wire whisk from her hand.

"What," she said dully. "Just fucking say whatever it is, okay? At this point, there is absolutely no bad news that is going to make me feel worse than I do."

"I think Devina's inside of you."

As she blanched and stopped breathing, his own fury curled in his gut. That fucking demon. If it was the last thing he did, he was going to—

"What do you mean?" she choked out as she wrapped her arms around herself.

"It's a function of your having been to Hell. At least as far as Ad and then Eddie explained it to me. Even after you left there . . . there's something inside of you."

"I think I'm going to be sick."

As she dropped to her knees and braced her hands on the grass, he knelt beside her. "But I think we can do something about it."

Sissy let out a retching sound, her back heaving.

Gritting his teeth, it took every ounce of self-control he had not to find Devina right at that second and murder her with his bare hands.

"Just breathe," he heard himself say as he helped her stay off the ground.

As a car came around the turn in the lane, he stiffened, thinking that if it was a Mercedes without a hood ornament, he was going to—

Nope. It was a Rolls-Royce, believe it or not.

When Sissy stopped coughing in that horrible way, he took her into his arms and held her to his chest. On the one hand, the difference in their sizes made him feel powerful. On the other, it was just a reminder of how impotent he actually was in this situation: Physical brawn wasn't going to do shit for her.

But one of those crystal knives . . .

Playing back what he'd done to Vin diPietro in the first round got him on the nausea train, too, but what choice did he have? And he certainly wasn't going to trust anyone else to do it.

She pulled back. "How long have you known?"

"About you?" He shrugged. "Not very long. I mean, I think you have a right to be pissed off—but there's another edge to your anger."

"What do you have to do?"

"How about we go back to the house?"

"That bad, huh."

"It's nothing we can't manage." Shit, he hated lying to her. "Come on, let's go back. Eddie knows everything and he can explain what's going to happen—if you decide to go that route."

Sissy went still, then looked up at him. "When is it going to end?" she choked out.

Hopefully not tonight, he prayed. "Soon. And it's going to be okay. I'm going to make it okay."

With a prayer he wouldn't violate that vow to her, he helped her to her feet and put his arm around her waist, taking some of her weight as they went along.

"Why are you doing this?" she asked.

"Doing what?"

"Taking care of me. I know I asked before . . . but, I mean, we don't even really know each other, and yet you're always there for me. Ever since the beginning."

He stopped and turned her to face him. As he traced her face with his eyes, he felt like he had never not known her.

Fuck immortality. If he lost her, he was a dead man walking.

"I don't know," he said softly. "It's just the way it is."

"I think you're a really good savior, Jim." She put her hands on his forearms. "You've always been an angel to me—"

"I love you."

Chapter
Thirty-four

Sissy closed her eyes. She couldn't have heard that right. Had he really said—

"I'm sorry," he muttered. "I don't mean to make shit awkward."

"No, no, that's not what I'm . . . how can you?" Her heart pounded. "I . . . if there's something inside of me . . ."

She couldn't go any further than that.

"That's not you, Sissy. It's got jack to do with you. And when we get rid of it?"

"I'm back to normal."

"Exactly."

She wanted to respond to him, wanted to say the words back, once again wanted to be frickin' normal.

Instead, she was obsessed with the fact that she might not be alone in her own skin. Was Devina going to pop out of her at any second? Take her over?

Oh, God, was her head going to spin around as she pea-souped all over everything . . . or was this an *Alien* scenario where something jumped out of her stomach?

Thinking back, she realized that, yes, ever since she'd gotten out of Hell, that anger of hers had been out of control, her emotions all over the place—but like Jim said, she'd just assumed it was because she'd been dealt a tragic hand and wasn't dealing with it well. Now, though, as she reconsidered her happy session with the matches and the sheets in the parlor?

She had actually felt as if that rage were something larger than her. Something out of character and wildly destructive. Something that was an "other."

"Come on," he said roughly. "Let's go."

She followed along beside him, her body moving on its own. "Can I infect you?" she asked in a rush.

"No."

Thank God. Except then . . . "What if it doesn't work? Whatever we have to do?"

"It will. I've done it once before, and Eddie's an expert."

"Okay. All right."

Except she felt completely and totally far from "okay" and "all right." And the walk back home didn't change that.

The smell of a chocolate cake in the oven greeted her as soon as she went through the front door, and when she got to the kitchen, she found Eddie at the sink, doing the dishes she had used. Ad was sprawled in one of the chairs at the table, his eyes locked on the other guy, not in a creepy sexual way, but more like he expected an imminent disappearance and was prepared to follow the example.

"So what are you going to do to me?" she demanded.

Eddie looked over his shoulder, dark brows rising. "Nothing. Why?"

Jim came in behind her and took the seat he usually sat in. "We need to do some de-Devina-ing, if you get my meaning."

The other angel took a deep breath and seemed to forget about the dripping bowl in his hand and the fact that he'd left the water on. "On Sissy."

"Yes, on me," she said, going over and looking into the stove.

There were two cake pans in there side by side, and the batter was in mid-metamorphosis, growing taller and darker.

"Jim, can I talk to you for a minute," Eddie murmured quietly.

"No." She straightened. "You can't. Anything that you can say to him, you'd better say to me. It's my body, my problem."

As she faced off at the men, she didn't give a shit if they felt awkward. Assuming she was cursed, she was damn well going to be on the ground floor of her own salvation.

She was done with having fate serve her bad luck, and taking it like a little bitch.

About twenty minutes later, the timer on the ancient stove gave out a cheerful ring of its bell, and Sissy let someone else take the cake out of the oven. As Eddie obliged, she rubbed her eyes, all kinds of horrific pictures making her head swim.

"Are you sure that's going to work?" she asked numbly.

Eddie, who'd been doing most of the explaining, said, "Yes. That's the way it's done."

She held up her index finger, all hold-it. "You didn't answer the question."

"It will work. The question is whether . . ."

As the guy looked over at Jim, she cursed. "Whether I live through it. Right?"

"The ritual is not without risks."

File that under, Well, duh.

There were some knocking sounds as Eddie freed the cake halves onto cooling racks. Then some water running as he put the pans in the sink to soak. In the meantime, the other two angels were silent and unmoving as statues.

She glanced at Jim. His handsome, hard face was remote, his eyes focused only on her. "What do I do?" she whispered to him.

"It's up to you." His voice was grave. "It's your decision."

Read: *Whatever you decide, I'll back you up, one hundred percent.*

"Eddie," she heard herself say. "You died, right? But you came back."

The red-eyed angel shook his head. "That would not be a backup plan I'd get behind if I were you. Death for immortals isn't what you think it is. It's not an ending—it's an eternal stasis. And the reprieve I got? It was a miracle."

"So I shouldn't do this."

"Well, the concern is that, if you don't, what's inside of you will continue to fester and grow stronger."

"So I have to do it."

Eddie looked at the other two men. "I agree with Jim . . . it's your decision. Unfortunately, however, there are consequences if you choose not to move forward."

All she could do was close her eyes. It was either that or scream at the top of her lungs—and she was suddenly terrified to let out anger of any kind.

Jim spoke up. "Why don't we head upstairs and get some rest. You can think about it until morning. There's no reason to rush this."

"But you have to get back to the war."

"Everything can wait for the morning."

Sissy found herself nodding and getting to her feet. Jim was the one who took her upstairs, not because he carried her, but thanks to his gentle steering.

"Will you stay with me?" she asked as they came up to the second-story foyer.

"Yes, I will."

They went down to her room and both used the en suite bathroom one after the other. And then they were in the bed she slept in, him sitting up against the carved Victorian headboard, her curled in his lap.

"When is this going to stop," she choked out. "I just want it to stop. I'm tired of no-win situations—I feel like I can't . . . I can't do this anymore."

But if she "killed" herself, she ended up in Purgatory.

And that was just another color of nightmare.

Jim stroked her hair, running his fingers down the long lengths as she stared out the big-paned windows across the way. She didn't know what was going to change between now and sunrise. But she just couldn't make her mind up right now.

The only thing she knew for sure was that she was glad Jim was with her.

Chapter
Thirty-five

Jim watched the sun rise up through the budding trees outside of Sissy's window. He'd been sitting in the same position for hours, his back braced against a couple of pillows, his legs stretched out in front of him, Sissy's head in his lap. He couldn't feel his ass, and his feet were tingling, but he didn't give a shit.

The fact that the illumination in the sky was a glorious peach and gold didn't uplift him. Actually, the beauty of the dawn just pissed him off: Instead of wasting a miracle on something so everyday and commonplace, so anonymous, why couldn't the Creator, just once, bless the woman who was lying beside him?

What the hell would it cost Him, really? Just rip some storm clouds out over the horizon and shield the magnificence for this one morning—and give Sissy a miracle.

One right after another, all the bad news and bad breaks Sissy had had hit him as if they were his own tragedies—and with each impact to the chest, all he could think of was . . .

Finding Devina and killing her with his bare hands. Just squeezing the life out of her. Making her suffer and then lighting her corpse on fire—

"Will you do it?"

He shook himself out of his murder fantasies. And reinserted his consciousness back in the real-life nightmare. "Yeah," he said gruffly. "I will."

She lifted her head and looked up at him. "And there's no other way, right?"

"Not that we know of. No."

"Okay. Then we go ahead."

He closed his eyes for a moment, feeling like he'd been hit by a car and was in the process of being dragged across rough pavement. "All right."

When he cracked his lids again, she was still staring at him. "I wouldn't trust anyone but you."

"And I'm not going to let you down."

"Make love to me." Not a question. A statement of desperation—and he felt exactly the way she did.

Moving himself down on the mattress, he took her face between his hands and kissed her as he rolled over on top of her. Their clothes seemed to melt away, any barriers that were between them evaporating until they were skin-to-skin. With every caress and each sigh, with all the arching and the soft moans, he was at once completely with her . . . and somewhere else.

All he could think of was that the two of them were going into the jaws of destiny, and there was no telling what was going to be left of either one of them when it was over. Because if he failed her again?

Insanity wasn't going to be the half of it.

Positioning himself at her core, he pressed in slowly and oh, God, the sensation was so good that it shut even his spinning head down. Letting himself go with the rhythm of retreats and penetrations, he rode her with care, giving her all the time in the world to find her pleasure and go flying.

That he orgasmed eventually wasn't the point, although he

supposed it did bring them even closer together. But his release was secondary. This was all about her.

When he finally went limp, his head falling face-first into a pillow, his body so satiated he couldn't muster the energy to prop himself up and ease free of her—in fact, he wanted to stay there forever. That wasn't where they were at, though.

Forcing himself to shift to the side, he wasn't surprised to find her crying.

But she did shock the shit out of him.

Reaching her hand up, she touched his face and whispered, "I want you to promise me something."

"Name it."

"Don't blame yourself. If this doesn't work, I don't want you to think for one second you did anything wrong. Sometimes . . . sometimes people get dealt a bad hand and that's just luck. There's nothing you or I could do about anything of this."

Not so sure of that, he thought. He was absolutely going to make Devina pay.

In ways even that demon couldn't imagine.

"Promise me," Sissy said.

He nodded his head once and lied. "I promise."

She stared up at him as the sun rose ever further and the birds began to sing and life across this little part of the world got to its feet and stretched its arms, working its own after-sleep kinks out.

"I love you," she said.

His heart stopped. Then began to thud. Except . . . "You don't have to say it just because I—"

"No, I have to. Because I want you to know in case . . . you know, I lose my chance to. I love you, and thank you—thank you for everything you've done for me. I said it once and I'll say it again. You are my angel."

He dropped his head and kissed her—because he wanted to,

but also because he didn't want her to see what was in his expression and she was probably smart enough to recognize what the shit was.

"I love you, too," he murmured against her mouth.

As, meanwhile, he raged inside.

"Can't we just eat this cake? I mean, come on, Eddie."

As Ad shoveled another huge piece of the chocolate with fake vanilla icing into his piehole—or Duncan Hines hole, as the case may be—he prayed that his buddy would just frickin' drop the subject.

No luck. "I want to know."

Ad took a long draw off the rim of his coffee. Eddie had made the java along with the dessert they were having for breakfast, and both were so fucking good—as was sitting across the table from the guy. It was almost like the separation had never occurred.

Almost.

"Ad? I need to know if you can fight in your condition."

"I don't think I'm compromised too much." Ad put his mug down and resumed digging in. Was this his second piece? Or third? "Bit of a limp, that's all."

"And the eye."

"Whatever."

"Can I be honest?"

"Please don't."

Eddie's chair creaked as he leaned back. "I'm really impressed by you."

Ad's brows popped and he lowered his fork. "I, ah . . ."

"Talk about unselfish." Eddie nodded. "Respect, man. Big respect. And I gotta tell you, it's not something I would have thought you'd do."

"Your death changed the rules for me."

"Yeah, I'm sorry about that."

Ad frowned. "What are you saying?"

"I should have heard that harpy. I should have been paying more attention."

"No, it's my fault. I can't tell you how many times I've re-played that whole thing. I let you down." He put up his palm to stop the arguing. "No. I'm supposed to have your back, and I dropped the ball. Matter of fact, that's the way it's always been between you and me. I've dragged you into more dumb-ass shit and dangerous situations—"

"But it's been fun. It's been so fucking fun."

Ad recoiled. "Okay . . . that's not what I thought you'd say. Ever."

Eddie finished his last bite and smiled. "Every straight arrow needs a little chaos in his life. You're mine. We've had some crazy-ass adventures, and yeah, some of it was probably avoidable and very definitely dangerous, but without you? Boring. My immortal life would be very fucking boring."

Ad ducked his eyes and smiled a little. "So this guilt I've been carrying around?"

"Lose it. I make my own choices, too. I could have ditched your ass centuries ago. But the truth is, I'd rather be crashing into some wall with you than going out for a Sunday stroll with any-body else."

"You say the sweetest things."

"Plus, let's face it. With my colossal lack of game, I would never have gotten laid without you."

Ad stiffened. "Yeah, about that. I'm . . . ah, I'm out of commis-sion from now on." As Eddie sucked in a little gasp, Ad shrugged. "But I can still get 'em for you. In fact, you say the word and I'll go on the prowl. Hell, I can live vicariously through you."

"Jesus . . ."

"Come on, it's not like true love was in my picture anyway. Besides, there are only so many ways to pick up a penny, and I've done them all about a hundred and fifty thousand times at this point. Sooner or later, the shit was going to get old, and now I don't ever have to worry about tenting up my pants over some hot piece. So there are advantages."

There was a long silence.

Ad shifted around in his chair, making the thing creak. "Okaaaaay, it would be really great right now if you wouldn't look at me like that. I still have all my arms and legs attached, you know. I'm fully functional, or sufficiently functional, in all other respects."

"Of course." Eddie cleared his throat. "Absolutely."

Ah, hell, he could so have done without the awkwardness, but the guy was going to find out sooner or later. Might as well be now—

Jim and Sissy appeared in the doorway, the pair of them looking like they were on the way to a funeral. Clearly, the decision had been made.

"We're ready to do this," Jim said, putting his arm around the woman and moving her close—like maybe he wished his body were the one that was going to get metaphysically sliced open. "I guess we need a trip out for supplies."

Eddie nodded. "Yeah, we do."

And that was that, Ad thought as he got to his feet. They'd gotten the band back together . . . and now it was time to rock 'n' roll, so to speak.

He just wished it wasn't performing an exorcism. On Sissy.

Chapter
Thirty-six

Of course it was the same damn Hannaford, Sissy thought, as they pulled into a parking lot that was full of average-cost cars and trucks. And yup, everything was the same as she remembered it: the lines for parked vehicles angled toward the store, the cart corrals intersecting them, the constant in and out from the store's automatic entrances creating a bustle of activity.

Eddie put the Explorer in park and cut the engine. All at once three doors opened and the angels got out; she just put her hand on her handle and stayed in her seat.

Jim glanced over his shoulder, like he'd expected her to be right with them. Then he seemed to pale.

Ad and Eddie glanced at him, and their mouths moved like they were asking him something. As he shook his head, he said a couple of words—and abruptly the other angels looked like they'd been kneed in the balls.

Ah, clearly none of them had done the math about where they'd ended up: the very place where she'd been abducted by the demon.

But whatever, she needed to get over herself. It wasn't as if going into the store again was going to change anything. The evil had already happened.

Forcing her door open, she got out and tugged her sweatshirt into place. "I have the list. Let's go."

She pushed her way through all their heavy bodies and strode to the entrance. As she went along, she passed a mother with two kids and three hundred dollars' worth of groceries stuffed into a cart . . . an older man with a single bag and a jug of orange juice . . . two middle-aged women who were talking a mile a minute over each other.

For a second, she mourned the fact that back before all the crap had fallen on her head, she had never noticed the people around her: How beautiful it was to see a young family out buying Popsicles and Hamburger Helper. Or how noble a lonely eighty-year-old could be as he braved a trip out to the supermarket by himself. Or what a special thing it was to see an enduring friendship in its natural habitat.

Humanity was beautiful. In all its different shapes and sizes, from its survival modes to its triumphal strutting, in both its poverty and its wealth.

And most of all in its everyday, moment-to-moment activity.

Funny, the discourse of daily life, before she had had hers forfeited, had been like the breath and the heartbeat in the human body—something that happened automatically, and as such was not seen for the miracle it was. It was only after her death that she recognized the fragile power in mortality . . . and held it in appropriate reverence.

As she walked through the automatic doors and into the lobby-ish part of the store, she faltered. The same Muzak was playing, old Michael Bolton piped in through tinny speakers in the ceiling like they wanted to offend the least number of people possible. The lineup of carts was also just the same, and so were the impulse buys lined up on tables—cookies, bags of chips, garden tools.

She closed her eyes.

The garden tools were new, but the Lay's potato-chip stand and the three different kinds of sugar cookies in their plastic containers were exactly what had been there before.

Amazing, she thought as she went further on and emerged into the florist's section. Standing around the buckets of plastic-wrapped roses and the squat cacti in their little clay pots and the free-standing pastel hyacinths, she felt as invisible as she was: People were passing by her without looking over, and that somehow made the divide she felt seem all the more devastating.

Except then she realized . . . maybe that had always been true.

As she stared back at them, she could remember striding by countless numbers of strangers—and she had rendered them all anonymous because she didn't know their names, faces, families. They had been sort of irrelevant, other than the fact that she hadn't wished any of them ill or wanted to be responsible for hurting them.

But that was reductionist. She didn't know what tragedies had come home or would come home to roost for them. Whether they had had their houses broken into the day before, or were facing an illness, or had lost a child, or had been cheated on.

Joy was worn like a new suit of clothes on people. You could see it on every inch of them, from their step to their stare. But sadness and loss were hidden, kept quiet under composure and the shelter of daily activity.

She had no idea what any of these people were facing in their lives. Any more than they knew she was standing among them, neither dead nor alive.

Invisibility was a two-way street, as it turned out.

Which was sad.

And it gave her a new idea of what she wished Heaven was

like. Before, when the destination had been just a hypothetical and she'd been so very, very much younger on so many levels, the eternal resting place in the stars had been nothing but jelly beans and Jujubes, and endless Sunday sleep-ins, and every movie that John Hughes had made on a loop.

Now . . . she thought it was just love. A forever love that wrapped you up and kept you safe and made sure you were always with your family and your friends.

No separation, even between strangers. No sadness. Nobody leaving or getting left behind.

"Sissy?"

She jumped as Jim's hand landed on her shoulder. "Sorry. Distracted." She held up the list. "I'll go get the salt if you want to handle the lemons?"

"I'm glad you called for another extra appoinment."

Glancing around her therapist's office, Devina smoothed her short skirt down her thighs and forced a smile, thinking maybe she should have just waited for her regular.

"I fixed the damage I did to my things," she blurted. "Well, okay, her minions had done most of that. But she had been the one responsible for telling them to do it. "And I'm . . ."

She frowned as she ran out of words. Thoughts. Impulses.

"Devina?"

Feeling as though she had to keep the session going, she scrambled for something, anything, she could say. Eventually, she murmured, "You know, it was funny how I found you."

"You told me that a friend of yours had recommended me."

"I lied." She glanced over to see if she'd upset the woman, but nope. Her therapist was just sitting like a Buddha on her beige-colored sofa in her beige-colored office, a beige-equivalent expression on her pleasant face. "It was much more . . . it was kind of freaky, actually."

"Tell me more."

"Well, I knew that I was going to . . . see, I'd had the same job forever, and I was really happy in the position. I had a lot of autonomy, I was allowed to do whatever I liked. I mean, it wasn't perfect—but I didn't realize what a situation I had until my boss decided to change everything up. Suddenly, where I'd been was the good old days, you know? And then, from out of the blue, I was working with this new guy, in a race for this promotion thing—and one day . . . one day, I guess I just cracked from the stress. I was getting ready for work, sitting in front of the mirror . . ." She lifted her hands to her face, brushing at her cheeks. "I was putting my makeup on—you know, like I do every day. And I . . ."

"Go on, Devina."

She patted at her jawline, her chin. "I was . . . the problem was the foundation I was using. I couldn't get it right. It wouldn't go over my skin . . . right. It wouldn't cover up the . . ." She blinked fast, memories of the panic coming on strong. "I had to get it right. It needed to be right so I looked right so no one could see . . ."

"Could see what, Devina?"

"What I really am. Who I really am." She stared down at her hands and smoothed her skirt again. And again. And again. "I couldn't get it right. The foundation . . . just . . ." She cleared her throat, pulling herself out of that moment in the past. "I reapplied it. And then put more on, and did it again. And again. It became paralyzing. I went through an entire bottle and opened another one. Even though I knew I was making it worse, I couldn't . . . it was like I was locked in. I was stuck in some kind of loop."

The therapist nodded gravely. "I know exactly what you mean.

The ritual took over to such a degree that you were figuratively imprisoned by it."

"Exactly." She exhaled. "That's exactly what happened. I finally stopped when I just wore myself out. I was covered with the stuff—it had gotten all over my blouse, my hands, my vanity."

"Here," the therapist said, leaning forward with a Kleenex box.

"Oh, I'm not . . ." Except her eyes were watering. "Oh. Thanks."

As she mopped up, the therapist sat back. "That can be truly terrifying."

"It was. I wasn't in control of it—and you know, I'd always been, like, a little OCD-ish. I mean, I like everything perfect, and I like my things where they should be. I like my things, period. I feel . . . safer . . . like, when I have the perfect number of lipsticks with me."

"I remember. It was hard to throw one of them out in our previous sessions."

"Yes." Devina drew her hand through her hair, reassuring herself that it was all still in place, that talking about this hadn't magically revealed her true ugliness. "But that morning was the first time I had the sense that it could cripple me—and that terrified me. It's so fucked-up. It's like your best friend turning on you, you know? Like, the thing that makes you feel better all of a sudden . . . owning you."

"That's very common, Devina. Very, very common."

"So I took a shower. I had to, I was a mess. And I was staying in this loft at the time. I'm not a big TV person, but it had one of those wide-screen things? I came out of the bathroom and the screen was on. I guess I'd turned it on at some point. I was standing over the remnants of those empty foundation bottles, feeling like I was going crazy, when there you were. On the TV. Veronica

Sibling-Crout. Funny, I haven't seen the ad running since. But it was the perfect time for me."

"Sometimes things happen for a reason."

Devina stared at the woman. "You really have helped me. I mean, I still struggle day to day, but you've made me realize I'm not the only person with this . . . problem."

"You know, a lot of my work is just making sure people know they're not alone. That and teaching them structured ways to deal with behaviors they don't want and think they can't change."

"You really have . . . saved me. From myself."

The therapist frowned. "Devina, why does this sound like a good-bye?"

Because it might be. "Things are going to change. Well, for me they're going to change. You might not notice a difference, though."

Although if Devina won, the woman would absolutely know it. And no doubt, if the therapist was aware of what was at stake in the war, she'd pray that Jim won this last round.

"In what way are things going to change for you?"

"The promotion. It's time for the position to be decided. Either I or the other guy will get the vice presidency." Again, the parallel she'd constructed wasn't an exact match, but it was the closest she could get without blowing the woman's mind. "And if I don't get it, I won't be able to come here anymore."

"Why? Are you going to be transferred?"

Almost certainly, and not in a good way. "Yes."

The therapist frowned. "You seem . . . resigned to some kind of fate."

"I guess I am. This can't go on forever."

"Devina, let me ask you something. Do you believe in God?"

Hell, she'd met the guy. "Yes. I do."

"Do you believe He loves all His children?"

"Aren't we getting a little religious?" Not that she minded it, necessarily, it was just a shift in—

"Do you, Devina?"

She thought over her long relationship with the Creator . . . and all the things she'd put Him through. "Yes, I know He does. Even the broken parts of His world . . . He loves even them."

"So be not afraid of any fate that awaits you."

She laughed harshly. "I wish."

"If you believe in the traditional notion of God, then He is all-powerful—so no part of Creation did He not contemplate, and no turn in any destiny is not one He engineers."

"On that theory, He's probably after me. Or should be. I've done a lot of very . . ." Evil. ". . . bad shit."

"But He created you, too."

Devina shifted in her puffy chair, feeling like things were getting a little too real all of a sudden. It was as if . . . "Should we go back to talking about lipsticks?"

"If that makes you feel better, sure."

Devina narrowed her eyes on the woman. Same as she'd always looked, same voice, same Mother Earth body and sixties-holdover clothes.

It seemed impossible that someone like her had made such an impact.

Devina crossed and recrossed her legs. "I don't know. I guess I just want to thank you for everything you've done with me. It's . . . been really helpful."

"That truly touches me."

There was yet another long, long silence. "I don't have much more to say."

"That's okay. We can sit here and just see if anything bubbles up for you."

And that's what they did. Until Devina glanced at the discreetly set clock on the side table. "I guess our time is up."

"So it is."

Getting to her feet, she grabbed her Prada bag and slung it onto her shoulder. She didn't bother to get out her checkbook. If she won the war, she was going to own the woman's soul, so if she needed help, it was going to be free and then some. And if she lost? What was the therapist going to do? Sue her?

Ha.

The therapist used her hands to push herself forward to the edge of the couch and then she heaved her body up off the cushions. With quick efficiency, she pulled her loose clothing into place as if her size made her feel self-conscious and the wardrobe was her way of covering things up.

Devina knew how that felt.

"So, bye, then." Devina lifted her hand. "Yeah. Bye."

Without waiting for a response, she went for the door, but something stopped her from leaving.

Pivoting around, she couldn't fight the absurd conviction that she needed—

As if the therapist knew exactly what she wanted, the woman held her arms out. Devina walked over and bent down . . . and allowed herself to be wrapped in an embrace that seemed to burrow in deep, penetrating her outer lie to her inner case of humpugly—and accepting her nonetheless.

Closing her eyes, she just stood there and accepted the shelter she was offered.

Something told her it might be the only respite she got for a very, very long time.

Chapter Thirty-seven

Well, wasn't this the day for trips down memory lane, Sissy thought as she stared out of the Explorer's back window. Too bad it wasn't in a happy-Christmases-of-the-past kind of way.

As Jim pulled up to one of the many warehouses in the old wharf area of Caldwell, she had to brace herself for going into yet another place she had no interest in ever seeing again.

"Are you sure we have to do it here?" she asked, looking up at the five-story-high, block-wide building.

As a light rain began to fall, it seemed like the cloud cover up above had arrived only because even the sun didn't want any part of what was about to go down.

Eddie leaned around in his seat. "The closer we get to where the infection entry happened, the more successful we're gonna be."

Her eyes flipped to the rearview mirror. Jim was staring at her from behind the wheel, his blue eyes remote—but it was funny. She could read him now. He was viciously angry and trying not to show it . . . and that made her love him even more.

He nodded. Once.

"Okay," she said, pushing open her door.

Her hand went to her stomach. Already, the skin was beginning to burn—and she didn't need to lift her sweatshirt to check to see what it was. She already knew. Those cuts in her skin, the symbols that the demon had carved into her flesh as part of whatever ritual had been performed on her, were back, activated by the proximity to where she'd been killed.

The horrible scars had done this before when Jim had taken her here, in hopes of helping her understand what had happened to her.

Guess this was proof she had something in her still, huh.

The trip up to the demon's former loft was a blur. Or maybe she was deliberately blocking out all the cultivated-rustic, faux-distressed-style decor as well as the fact that those angels were magically getting through any door that was locked.

Good thing, because there were seven dead bolts on the loft entrance they were after.

After those were sprung one by one, she walked into the vast, open space—and that was when she realized they'd all gone invisi: There were no echoes of footsteps, no rustling of those plastic Hannaford bags, not even the sound of Adrian breathing hard from having dragged himself up the stairs.

She stopped dead as she looked over to the far corner and saw the open door to the gray marble bathroom.

Something was pressed into her hand. A blue carton of Morton Salt.

"Come on," Jim said. "Help me."

It was exactly the kind of diversion she needed, and she followed his instructions to the letter, going over to the nearest wall and starting to pour out a thin line of sodium that was supposed to go all the way around the space.

"I'll do the bathroom," he told her after he watched her for a bit.

The hiss of the falling granules sounded like a snake, and no matter how hard she tried, she couldn't get the white rush to fall in a perfectly straight line.

Further, the loft was so large, she needed two whole things of the stuff.

Just as she was finishing up, the scent of something clean and fresh brought her head around. Eddie and Jim had lit up what looked like cigars, and were exhaling pale smoke as they walked around her line. And inside the bathroom, she could hear liquids being poured into the sink and sloshed around.

Heading over to that horrible room and leaning in, she had to rub her stomach as the burning sensation got even more intense. Adrian was pouring witch hazel and hydrogen peroxide into the basin, empty bottles of white vinegar and crushed plastic lemon juice containers littering the sink next to him.

Something glinted on the closed toilet seat and she frowned. "Are those . . ."

"Guns?" He glanced over his shoulder. "Yeah. They are."

Sissy approached slowly, as if the things might decide to think on their own—something that seemed reasonable considering the barrels of both were pointed at her. God, they were unlike any kind of pistol she'd ever seen, the entire grip and body of the weapon made of glass.

They were like the daggers, she thought.

And they had stoppers on them.

"Water pistols?" she asked.

"Special water." Submerging his hand into the brine in the sink, Ad began to stir it slowly in circles. Words left his lips, spoken so quickly and softly they were unintelligible to her.

"What are you saying?"

Abruptly, another scent reached her nose . . . it was that of a fresh field, as bright and clean and vivid as something that could be seen. And that was when he stopped, took both guns, and submerged them, bubbles rising up as their bellies were filled.

"Okay, now we need to get set up in here." Eddie came over to her. "'Scuse me."

As she stepped aside, the angel took out a compass and held the thing up. Walking around the bathroom tile, he stopped and took squat votive candles out of his pockets.

"No," Jim said. "In the tub. We need to do it where she was . . . you know."

"It'll be easier here."

"Tub faces north."

"I need to walk around her."

"I'm doing it."

Eddie gritted his teeth like he was determined not to say the first thing that came to his mind. "Jim. You're too close to all this."

"I'm doing it, and she's getting in that fucking tub."

On that note, Jim popped the top on some more Morton and made a circle around the room, stretching over the tub to make sure a line went around the far edge against the marble wall. The only place he didn't hit was the windowsill.

By the time he was done, Eddie had placed candles at the four compass points along the lip of the tub. He lit them with a Bic lighter that she'd seen Jim use and then he took one of the crystal guns for himself and gave the other to Adrian.

Jim puffed his cigar a couple of more times, the air becoming saturated with the smell of ocean breezes, spring sunshine, fresh rain. And then he dropped the stub to the marble floor and crushed it with his heavy boot.

"Let me help you in there." Putting out a hand for her, he looked at Eddie. "She's not getting naked."

Naked?

Eddie nodded. "That's okay."

Oh, God, it was time, she thought.

Gathering her courage, Sissy accepted Jim's help—needed it, too. As she put one leg and then the other over the high side of the tub, she started shaking all over. But that wasn't the real problem. Her stomach burned so badly, she had to curl in on herself.

"It hurts," she moaned.

"What hurts?" Eddie leaned in. "What's going on?"

Jim just shook his head. "You don't have to tell him—"

"The symbols," the other angel said. "I'm right, aren't I?"

She nodded as Jim looked furious—although not at his comrade.

"It's all right," Eddie said, laying a hand on her shoulder. "We're going to take care of that. Now lie down."

Sissy glanced at Jim, and as he nodded at her, she stretched out on all the hard, cold porcelain. Linking her hands over her stomach, she thought the tub was kind of like her coffin—and decided, if she came out on the other side of this in one piece, she was going to take showers for the rest of her immortal life.

"Do you remember the verses?" Eddie asked.

Jim answered by beginning to speak in a foreign language, slowly and carefully.

"Nice accent," Ad muttered as he stood by the window.

"Close your eyes, Sissy," Eddie said. "Don't look. No matter what happens, don't open your eyes."

For no good reason—other than the fact that she was losing her mind—she had a split-second *Raiders of the Lost Ark* moment, a quick mental snapshot of Harrison Ford and that actress who had played Professor Ravenwood's daughter tied to a stake before the golden box was opened by that French archeologist.

Don't look, Marion. . . .

God, she wished this were a movie. With a happy ending.

Jim was the last thing she saw before she lowered her lids. He was standing over her, staring down from his great height, his lean face grave as a preacher's over somebody's pine box.

Which seemed pretty damned apt.

I love you, she mouthed to him.

He didn't lose his rhythm, but dropped down and caressed her cheek. Which was an *I love you, too*, if she'd ever heard one.

"Not your fault," she whispered.

Instead of waiting to see if he denied that in some way, she closed her eyes. Tried to breathe. Felt her heart pound so hard, she had a headache from the pressure . . . or maybe that was the tub.

The vibration began so subtly, she thought it was just her own case of the trembles. But then it spread out from her torso, growing in reverberation, clearly something other than herself. It was shortly after that that a breeze began to blow across her in spite of the high sides of the tub, her forearms goose-bumping even under the sweatshirt, her nose tickling, her hair ruffling. Had someone cracked that window over—

No, she was turning. Spinning. Slowly.

It didn't stay that way. The speed changed, doubling and redoubling until she was flying around the pivot point of her belly button, centrifugal force lengthening her legs and shoulders, trying to pull her thin, straining her joints as she fought the draw. Nausea twisted her guts like a rope, and the pressure in her head became so great, her skull felt like it was going to break open.

Just as she knew she was going to be torn apart, right at the very moment she was going to lose consciousness . . . all at once, everything stopped.

Abruptly, she was no longer spinning; she was floating, light as a feather on a gentle draft, all the pain gone. And then her eyesight returned—even as her lids remained locked down, she saw a brilliant white light emanating from beneath her, her body cutting a path through the illumination.

Jim's face appeared over her own, a strange warping making him seem right next to her and very far away at the same time. His lips were moving, that unfamiliar language entering her mind not through her ears, but some kind of psychic connection.

Don't move, Sissy, he said to her without interrupting the flow of his verses. *You can't move even an inch.*

All right, she thought back to him.

That was when he raised a crystal dagger above her chest.

Oh . . . shit. This was going to hurt.

Bracing herself, she nonetheless lifted her sternum, offering herself up to whatever was going to happen. She'd rather be some version of dead than live with Devina somewhere inside of her, growing roots like a poisonous weed, choking out the essence of her and leaving her body full of evil.

Do it, she thought at Jim. *Do it hard.*

She could have sworn a sheen of tears licked into both of his eyes. And then he hesitated, as if strung between two impossibles.

Do it, Jim. It's all right . . . I want this to happen. Better to be dead than have her in me.

With his teeth clenching hard, he blinked once and drove down with all his strength.

The pain was so great, she screamed until she had no voice left. And then she nearly blacked out as Jim dragged that blade down her torso as if he were gutting a fish. As a great cavern was created, Jim reached into her with his bare hands, probing, searching.

And she screamed. Screamed . . . because that was all she could do. Screamed . . . even though she couldn't breathe. Screamed in spite of the fact that she could not think or—

Jim pulled on something, and it had to be her spine, she thought, because her battered body strained all over—it was as if he were trying to separate her from herself.

No, it was not her spine. As she lifted her head and stared through her closed eyes . . . she saw that it was some kind of black, oily mess, like part of Devina's wall had somehow ended up inside of her—and the evil was refusing to yield. The harder he yanked, the tougher it adhered, until she began to jerk up out of the tub with every pull.

She was going to die.

As her breathing grew so labored she began to black out, she fought to stay with Jim. Focusing on him, she called on all her strength.

And lost the battle.

Lost . . . herself.

Jim leaned so far into the tub that Adrian and Eddie both latched onto him, as if they were afraid of losing him. Probably a good idea, given the way his back was straining until his shoulders trembled and his thighs burned.

But the evil didn't shift. Didn't budge. Didn't move. God-damn it, it was supposed to—it was supposed to get yanked out like it had in the first round. Eddie had gotten it free of Vin diPietro—

"Let go, Jim!" Ad hollered. "Let it go—we're going to lose you—"

"Fuck you!"

Jim dug his heels in even harder and—

His grip began to slip, and he knew without being told that Sissy would not come through another attempt; they had one shot at this.

And he was failing. Grip slipping, oh, God, the grip, his grip . . .

Someone was screaming. Him. He had gambled and lost—again. He had let her down—again. He was losing another woman he loved . . . again—

Two sets of hands reached down and joined his on the black mass, one from each side of him.

Together, they all pulled. Him and Adrian and Eddie. They all pulled together, the strength brought to the fight not just one plus one plus one, but exponentially more powerful.

The evil began to shift. He felt the give, barely perceptible at first, but then . . . yes, *yes*.

"Harder," he barked. "Fucking harder!"

He could sense the heat rolling off the other angels as they put all the strength they had into the fight, and sweat popped out all over his own face, running down into his eyes. Just a little more . . . if they could just put a little more—

The sound as the darkness ripped free was like the squeal of eighteen wheels across pavement, burning his ears until he cringed. And just as before with Vin, a black seething form ripped away and took flight, screeching around the ceiling like a bat out of a cave.

There wasn't time to dwell on the victory—or even on whether Sissy was alive. Jim flew back as if his torso had been sucked away—or blown away. And as he was in midair, shit went into slow-mo for him: He saw Adrian getting thrown toward the door; Eddie pitched to the window; Sissy's body flopping up and down against the porcelain as if she'd been racked with seizures.

He had to get to her—he had to—

Jim didn't land on his head. He landed on his ass. But when he skidded back further, the base of his skull hit something sharp and hard.

The impact was a grenade going off in his skull, white-hot and obliterating every thought and all senses. The only thing that remained was a diffused panic that what they had released from her was just going to jump back in.

But even that wasn't enough to keep him conscious.

Everything went lights-out.

Chapter Thirty-eight

Down below Devina's old loft, the demon stood in the center of the street, right where the yellow double lines were. She had one pump planted on each side as she angled her head up, up to the fifth floor of the warehouse. The breeze was cold against her body, and the light rain that came down misted her cheeks and weighted down her hair and spotted her silk jacket. Cars passed and sometimes honked—always gawked.

But for once, she didn't pay any attention to all that.

How the *fuck* did they get Eddie back. How the *fuck* did that happen.

Then again, who was she fooling. There was only one way it could have happened.

The Creator.

Up in her former abode, shapes crossed the square-paned window stacks as the four of them moved around while performing the purification ritual and creating a force field to direct the expulsion—and attempt to keep her out. She knew their little tricks by heart: First, they would create the barrier of salt. Then they would smoke the place out. And before they started, they'd have shooters loaded with purifying solution and all the magic Jim could summon—unless, of course, he was the one doing the exorcism, in which case he'd be out of commission for protection spells.

It was impossible not to feel shut out by all the effort—not just because they were working together, but because all of their effort was to fuck her in the ass.

Devina hoped and prayed it killed that little bitch. And there was such a good chance it would. The infection in Sissy had gone deeper than anything those angels had ever tried to remove—

Beeeeeeeeeeeeeeeeeeeeeeep!

As some version of a Honda went by, its horn was a curse made manifest, and she turned around, eyes narrowing.

She let the POS sedan go another block down and then she extended her palm and threw a burst of energy out at it.

Refocusing on the windows up above, she heard a sharp braking, a metallic crunch, a shattering of safety glass, the hiss of a busted radiator. Blah, blah, blah.

She was waiting for another crash.

It came about ten minutes later. Without warning, at least that human eyes and ears could pick up on, the bathroom window blew open and something that looked like a tight-knit swarm of bees sizzled out into the air, hovering as a shower of glass snowflaked down to the sidewalk below.

The part of her she'd so graciously lent Sissy waited for a command from her—and there were a number of directives she could give it. Attack. Reenter Sissy. Expand and join with other minions to create a force capable of overthrowing governments.

She held up her palm and summoned it home, reabsorbing the black energy.

As distant sirens grew louder, and the human cleanup crew's arrival became imminent, she stared at her loft's bathroom, hoping to see a face in the window. Hoping to see Jim, looking out to find her.

He did not.

When nothing but ambulances and a fire truck came toward her, she cursed under her breath and dematerialized.

Even though she was hurt, she tried to stay positive. There was a final endgame still to play out, and Jim was right where he needed to be—in spite of the fact that he was with Sissy, up in that bathroom.

Sacrifices must be made in order to win.

Besides, his time with that bitch was coming to an end. Devina was going to make sure of it.

Sissy came awake to the sound of dripping.

Her first instinct was to open her eyes and sit up. She wasn't sure where she was or why her head hurt or why she was so very, very cold and she was scared. Something had happened—

Okaaaaay. She couldn't move and her lids refused to budge.

And that dripping . . .

. . . was gone now. She didn't hear it anymore. Had she lost consciousness again?

Time to get over herself.

Putting her hands out from her body, she felt something smooth and cool and followed whatever it was up—

A *tub*.

All at once, her brain came on like a laptop that had had a re-boot. Images of the ritual flickered through her mind, snapshots taken and internalized, everything from pouring the salt to the whispered verses to the light coming up from underneath her.

To that moment when the evil had left her body.

Jerking upright in a scramble, she sucked in a breath and dragged up her sweatshirt. Gone. The runes or symbols or whatever the heck they were? Not with her anymore. Except even as tears of relief made her eyes sting, there was no time for a victory dance.

She tried to twist around and look to see how Jim and the angels were, but her body was too stiff. From her torso to her neck, her muscles were locked so tight she had to force herself onto her knees and shove herself around.

Eddie was the first one she saw sprawled on the gray marble floor, his big body relaxed as if he were just having a quick lie-down, his feet lolling to the sides in his boots. Ad was over by the door, in a similar slump. Where was—

"Oh, God, Jim!"

Gripping the edge of the tub, she pulled herself up and over, and fell down on the far side. Jim was across the room, lying partially under the pedestal sink, his head cocked at a wrong angle, his body twitching unnaturally.

Her knees cracked against the hard floor as she crabbed over to him. "Jim?" She put her hand on his chest—his body was still warm, but she didn't know if that meant anything. "Jim—wake up!"

Silver blood had pooled around the base of his skull.

"Jim!" She wanted to slap him or shake him, but God forbid if he'd broken his neck? "Jim—"

Groans rose up from behind her, and there was a rustling, as if Eddie and Adrian were coming to. "Help me," she barked without looking back. "Jim . . . wake up, Jim. . . ."

This was not supposed to be the tragedy at the end of it—she was the one who was supposed to have "died." Not Jim.

"Easy there," Eddie murmured as he restrained her, easing her back.

Good thing—she was all but jumping on Jim's chest. Hardly a help.

"Lemme get a look at him." Eddie reached across and thumbed Jim's eyelids up, one by one. "Shit."

Adrian shuffled himself over. "What we got?"

"One hell of a concussion—or worse. I don't know—I'm not a healer like this." Eddie looked at Sissy. "First things first. Get some salt and put it across that windowsill. Ad, light up, will you." Then the angel glanced around. "Fucking hell, one of the guns broke."

Which explained the dripping: Over where Eddie had been thrown, crystal shards gleamed in the light from the frosted window, a puddle of the solution Ad had prepared on the floor in front of the busted-up barrel.

Sissy went vertical stiffly and hit the Morton bag, grabbing one of the remaining containers. She was more concerned about Jim than anything else, but that didn't mean she wanted Devina in here while they figured out exactly what was wrong and how to fix it. With hands that shook, she peeled off the little paper square over the spout, and then there was that hiss again as she closed the loop around the bathroom.

"Can you take care of this?" Ad said to Eddie.

"It's outside of what I can heal."

Sissy shut her eyes and thought, No, no, this is not how this ends. It just can't be.

"Is he dead?" she heard herself ask as she went back and crouched down. "Is he?"

Eddie didn't meet her eyes. "No. But he's gonna be soon."

Chapter
Thirty-nine

As the archangel Nigel stared up at the Manse of Souls' great walls, his eyes were focused on the new victory flag that waved next to the other two. But he wasn't thinking about Jim's victory or dwelling on the fact that although it was customary for the savior to come up and mark the occasion with a visit, the angel had not, in fact, made an appearance.

No, Nigel was tied up in his head. He was well aware of what had transpired and was transpiring down below—Jim was on the verge of passing away, and given that they were heading into the final round, Nigel should be taking initiative and interceding. After all, the Creator did allow interaction with the savior by him, and curing a head wound, one could argue, was a sort of "interaction."

Instead, he waited for the summoning. And was rather unimpressed by his apparent willingness to use this dire situation for his own, personal, means.

Indeed, desperation changed one, didn't it—

"Ah, yes," he whispered. "Welcome, Edward. . . ."

With permission from him, the angel materialized on the lawn beside him . . . and it was rather good to see the chap. So tall and strong, Edward was, but what made the male even more useful was his calm stare—even with Jim gravely injured on earth, all the necessary faculties were intact.

Nigel smiled, and not in a politely dismissive manner. He was honestly pleased to have this fighter back. "How nice to see you."

Edward's bow was reverent. Appropriate. Considerate.

And it was like a cool glass of water in a hot, dry place: oh, so very appreciated.

"I have missed you, my old friend." Nigel offered his hand and the two shook. "And I shan't waste time. I am aware of why you come."

"Can you help?"

"No," he lied. "I am still recovering from my ill-advised holiday. But let us go and conscript another, shall we?"

He led the way across the lawn, striding by the table that was already set for afternoon tea, though that repast was as yet hours away. Predictably, the closer they got to the meandering river and the tent of his former lover, the more Nigel's immortal heart pounded. Colin had been avoiding him with such studious and concerted effort, that there had been neither hide nor hair of him.

Beneath Nigel's calm mask, he was on the verge of breaking down, and the energy required to affect the lie of pragmatic reasonableness created a pain at both of his temples.

He was terrified that the other archangel would not be there, but alas, Colin was reclining upon his cot, an old leather-bound book cradled in his palms—and he looked up at Edward as they approached. Immediately, he put the Tennyson aside. Walked over and embraced the angel. Clapped him hard upon the stout back.

"I am glad you have returned, mate." Colin's eyes, those lovely, intense eyes, roamed around Edward's face as if checking to see that the features were all in the right place. "And you look no worse for the wear."

Oh, how one longed for that kind of welcome home.

The two exchanged brief pleasantries, none of which Nigel heard or cared about.

"Your assistance is required," Nigel interrupted. "There has been an accident down below."

Edward glanced in his direction as if he were surprised at the show of tension. Meanwhile, Colin stared out of the entrance to the tent, no doubt wishing that the visit from Edward had been a solitary affair.

Nigel felt compelled to tack on, "There is healing to be done and I am not capable of it."

"Then lead on, mate," Colin said to Edward. "And I shall—"

"Let us all go together."

That got him the attention he had been seeking, those eyes swinging over and narrowing on him with a dislike the archangel had previously reserved for Devina, yellow-jacket wasps, and television evangelists down on earth.

Nigel cocked a brow. "I know that you would never let personal enmity stand in the way of doing your duties."

Colin's jaw ground hard, the hollows under his cheeks standing out in sharp relief. But he didn't disagree.

It wasn't much of an easing to the conflict, but at least the two of them were going to be in an enclosed space together for however long it took to get Jim back and in action—and, of course, that had to be the outcome with the savior. Whatever the troubles between him and Colin, they truly did have to work together to ensure Jim was not lost.

And if there was a chance to broach a discussion? In the midst of it?

Nigel was prepared to be an opportunist.

In her old life, Sissy had seen a couple of head injuries—mostly on playing fields. She'd been in the football stands three years ago when a left offensive tackle had pulled a pile drive into one of the opposing team's guys, popping off his helmet, knocking him out cold. She'd never forget how everyone in the crowd had fallen quiet and barely breathed as paramedics had rushed onto the field and stabilized the poor kid. He'd been so far gone that he'd had to be carried out on a stretcher and he'd not even acknowledged the standing ovation he'd gotten. Later, she'd read in the newspaper that they'd had to teach him how to walk all over again.

Then there had been that catcher on the girls' softball team who'd been hit by a ball. The kid on the hockey team who'd ended in the goal. One drunk guy at a house party who had decided he could fly and learned the hard way he could not.

Each one of them had gone to a medical center.

"Can't we just call nine-one-one?" she heard herself ask.

Jim had been admitted into a hospital in the last round, not that it had helped him much—and that had been when she'd learned that she could step into the skin of people. If she could do that now? With him? She'd put herself in his position in a heartbeat. He was needed and important. She was not.

Especially with one more round to go.

"It's better to wait here," Ad ground out.

"Is he still breathing?"

"Yeah. He is—"

There was a flash of light, as if someone had turned a lamp on and off real quick. And then suddenly there were three more people in the bathroom: Eddie and the archangels, Colin and Nigel, had materialized out of thin air. But they didn't have little doctor bags with them. Or a stretcher. Hadn't come in an ambulance, either.

Hard to decide whether the arrivals were good news or not.

Both of the archangels narrowed their eyes on her.

"Good," Nigel said. "This is well-done."

"Not if he's dead, it isn't," she muttered, getting out of the way so they could do whatever it was they had to.

When Nigel gestured forward, Colin gave the other archangel a nasty look—then he stepped over and crouched down next to Jim. Leaning this way and that, he checked out the angle of the head, and the pool of silver blood that was getting larger.

And then he ignored Jim. Rising up, he inspected the corner of the sink, making the *mm-hmm* noises she'd assume would be associated with—hello—the assessment of the nonresponsive semi-corpse on the floor.

Just as she was about to say something, Ad took her elbow and whispered, "The way humans get treated for injuries like this is different from how we need to deal with Jim."

"What do you mean?" she asked in a hushed voice.

"It's an accident. So there's no will attached—he didn't have it done to him by someone else, and he didn't choose it for himself and that's what makes the difference. Without malice or will involved, Colin can try to erase the impact—but it gets done where he hit his head, not on his body."

Without making any contact, Colin cupped his hands around the silver smudge that had been left behind on the sink, then moved his palms upward and around in a slow, deliberate motion. At first she didn't think anything was happening, but then there was a subtle sound that rose up—

Cracking. The porcelain was cracking as if being subjected to some kind of pressure or heat even though there was nothing that she could see between those hands and the surface. And the spiderweb pattern grew more intense and spread wider as Colin kept up whatever it was he was doing.

"Oh, my God," she hissed as she looked at Jim. "It's working."

Like magic, the blood on the marble floor was retracting, that puddle growing smaller and smaller . . . until it disappeared under his hair.

Meanwhile, Colin began to shake, a gritted string of curses coming out of his mouth, the muscles in his forearms standing out in sharp relief like he was pulling at a rope. And Jim shook, too, his arms and legs twitching, his head going back and forth in a series of jerks.

Then the strangest thing happened. A warping emanated from Colin's hands and suddenly, the sounds of someone falling, hitting his head, and slumping to the ground were played in reverse: shambling fall of arms and legs under the sink; sharp, nasty impact; and then whoosh! as if somebody had flown through the air in front of her.

Abruptly, Colin slumped to the side as if the effort had taken all his strength—and Nigel was the one who caught him before he hit the ground, the other archangel rolling Colin over onto his back and then easing him carefully onto the marble.

"Is it done?" she asked as Nigel moved away.

But she knew the answer to that as she rushed over to Jim: His lids flipped open and he took a deep breath, his mouth gaping, his eyes popping wide. And then he all but jumped up off the floor, focusing on the tub—

"Sissy!" he screamed.

"I'm right here, hey—I'm right here. Jim?"

Jim turned his head so fast, it was a wonder it didn't snap off his neck. And then he froze—like he couldn't figure out if he were seeing things right.

"Jim, I'm okay. I'm all right."

He grabbed her face with both hands and kissed her. Then he patted her down. "Are you sure?" he asked hoarsely. "Fucking hell, tell me you're—"

She pulled up her sweatshirt and flashed her smooth, un-marked belly.

Jim sagged with such relief, she actually reached out to make sure he didn't land on his face. And in response, he wrapped her up tight and held her against him.

"It's over," she said. "It's over and we're all okay . . ."

As he trembled against her, she offered up a prayer of thanks, and took a deep breath of relief. She had no idea how long this precious slice of peace was going to last, but she sure as hell was going to enjoy it.

Especially because she was, once again, alone in her own skin.

Chapter Forty

As Nigel sat on the hard marble floor across from Colin, he kept stock-still. Although ordinarily he was not one for long periods of inaction, it had felt like an eternity since he had been allowed an unimpeded view of the male, and he was going to damn well take advantage of the good fortune—especially as the others departed and the two of them were left alone.

It was a long while before Colin stirred from exhaustion, and as those lids slowly opened, Nigel jumped into the silence, seizing what was no doubt going to be his only opportunity to say his piece.

"I am so very sorry, Colin. I should never have left you as I did. I should have spoken unto you my fears, and come to a solution with you. My thinking . . ." He motioned toward his head. ". . . was faulty. I blame none but myself, and do not expect you to forgive. The explanation, however, is necessary."

Colin grabbed the edge of the sink and pulled his torso upright. Then he rubbed his face. Took a deep breath. Scrubbed his short, dark hair.

"And yes," Nigel said, "it is unfair of me to accost you here when you are not at your best. But how else am I going to say this."

Colin arranged his legs such that they crossed at the ankle, and he put his palms upon his thighs. His hands moved slowly up and down.

Nigel cleared his throat. "I regret this. . . ." His voice cracked. "More than you can know. But in asking Jim to give up Sissy, I felt it was unfair of me not to offer a sacrifice of similar impact in this war. A true leader expects no more of others than they do of themselves. You are the basis of Heaven to me. There is no greater pledge unto the fight than leaving you—and that is why I acted alone." He wanted to reach out and try to take the archangel's hand, but he knew that would be folly. "Whilst I was over in Purgatory, the pain at losing you was more unbearable than the torment that was upon me from that place. I was . . . bereft at the loss of you, and what I had done in favor to the battle against Devina was cold, cold comfort. I would choose another path, if I had to do it all over again. I would . . ."

As his voice drifted off, there were so many more words clogging his throat, jamming up his mouth, twisting his mind, but they were simply variations on what he had just spoken. Still, there was a temptation to give in to the torment, to keep talking and talking in hopes that something would change the position he had put them both in.

But Colin hated wasted time, and the justification, such as it was, had been made.

Dropping his eyes, Nigel got to his feet and found that he was unsteady and fairly well close to fainting. Especially as he turned away and began to walk out of the water closet and across the vast emptiness of the loft Devina had once inhabited.

The barren expanse seemed such an apt metaphor.

"I do not believe you understand what it was like."

At the sound of Colin's voice, he turned so fast he had to

throw his arms out into the thin air. With a thundering heart, he said, "Tell me."

Even though this was going to kill him.

As he stood in the loo's doorway, Colin's face was drawn in lines of anger. "I stood over your body. I cried . . . over your body. I picked you up and carried you to the river's edge and I sat beside the fire that consumed you. It burned for hours."

Nigel closed his eyes and put his hands up to his face.

"No," Colin snapped. "You do not get to do that. You do not get to shield yourself from your actions. There was naught that I could do with your aftermath—you left me to deal with that alone, without knowing . . . goddamn it, without knowing why you had done what you had. So you can damn well be present in this moment."

Nigel lowered his arms and refused his eyes the permission to go anywhere else—even though his chest was so tight he could not draw breath. "I am so sorry. I am so very sorry. . . ."

Colin's dark brows drew tightly together. "Do you think I do not know you."

"No, you know me better than all."

"And that is why I am offended anew." Colin crossed his arms over his chest. "Did you think . . . dearest God, Nigel, did you think I did not know what was ahead of us at that moment in the war? What you were facing and what choices you would believe you had? With Jim in failure as he was, tied up within the destiny of that innocent, Sissy, giving wins away, do you think I did not recognize all of that and . . ."

When Colin did not finish, Nigel cleared his throat. "And what?"

"Do you think, no matter how much it destroyed me, that I would not have let you go?"

Nigel returned his hands unto his face, and this time Colin said naught about the veil of palms over his eyes.

"I would have let you go," Colin said roughly, "because that was the best thing to do, the only pathway that we had in this forsaken war. Someone else needed to be the savior at that point, and the only way to get Jim out of the role . . . was to do exactly what you did."

It all seemed so freshly devastating, Nigel thought in the silence that followed.

Colin exhaled a curse. "I would have made the sacrifice, too. But you either didn't trust me enough to do that or worse, mayhap, you do not really know me that well, after all. I am a soldier, and as such, I do not forgo logic to feeling. Even if the emotions are . . . overwhelming."

Nigel was aware the moment the other archangel left, even though there was not a sound or further movement taken. Instead of following Colin back up to Heaven, however, he found himself sinking unto his knees in the middle of the emptiness.

He had no practice with regrets. He had hitherto lived his immortal life with deliberation and self-control—and had curried no small amount of superiority because of it.

Now, though, he felt connected unto humanity at a whole new level.

Compassion was easier to proffer if one had suffered.

Chapter Forty-one

"Did you get enough to eat?"

As Jim sat beside her on the front steps of the old mansion, Sissy took yet another deep breath. She'd been doing it a lot since they'd all come back here, eaten five large pepperoni pizzas between the four of them, and gone their separate ways.

Which was to say, Ad and Eddie had headed up to the attic.

And Jim had come out here with her.

After a day of on-and-off rain, the night was cool and damp and smelled of good earth and growing things. Smelled of Jim's aftershave, too, she thought as she pulled his leather jacket closer around her.

"Sissy?"

"What—oh, sorry. Yes. God, yes. I don't think I'll ever eat again."

Shoot. Maybe she shouldn't phrase it like that.

Down at the far end of the lane, a car turned onto their street and proceeded carefully toward them. For a moment, her whole body stiffened—except it was not a big black Mercedes-Benz that was missing a hood ornament.

She relaxed the instant she recognized it as a Lexus.

"It's so weird," she murmured. "I feel the absence more than I noticed the presence."

"Of what—oh, that." He cleared his throat like he didn't want to give the thing a name. "What'd gotten taken out, you mean."

"Yeah." She put her hands over her pizza-filled stomach and rubbed back and forth. "I had no idea it was there and controlling me. But now that it's gone, I feel . . . myself. Which doesn't mean that I've, like, forgotten everything that was done to me or what I lost. I still feel the same things I felt before. It's just . . . the foundation is different. More solid. More . . . me, I guess? I'm babbling, aren't I."

"Not in the slightest. Makes perfect sense to me."

She looked over at him as he took a drag on his cigarette and the tip burned bright orange. "I swear, that is one of the things I like most about you."

His brows popped. "What is?"

"You always understand me."

"You're pretty reasonable. Pretty damned smart, too."

He leaned in and put a kiss on her mouth—and it seemed like the most natural thing: the soft brush, the giving and receiving, the warm thrill that came with the contact. And when she didn't want him to move away so fast, all she had to do was put her hand on his massive arm and he stayed right with her.

As if he once again knew what she needed.

Laying her head on his upper arm, she stared up at his face as he resumed looking out ahead of them both. And sadly, the preoccupation that bled into his features was a reminder that this moment between them was the exception, not the rule.

The war was still ongoing.

"What happens now?" she asked roughly.

"With you? Nothing. You're clean."

"I mean with Devina."

Those brows went down hard and stayed there, and the coldness that gleamed in his eyes was a reminder that he was a soldier, not just a lover.

"You don't have to worry about that." He leaned in and kissed her again. "You're safe. You're free."

Not as long as you're still fighting, she thought.

It felt like a crime to contaminate this quiet time between them with talk about the last round. But she figured that was where he was in his head, too. Had to be. He had to be thinking about where the next soul was going to be found, and what Devina was going to—

"I really wish you'd met my mother," he said roughly.

As Sissy jerked back, he looked over at her. "Did my smoke get in your face? Shit, I'm sorry—lemme put this out."

"No, no, not at all." She stopped him. "Honestly, it's okay. I'm getting used to it now, and it's funny, it kind of smells nice to me."

Probably because the scent of tobacco was coming to remind her of him.

"You just surprised me," she murmured.

"About my mother."

"Well, yes. And I would have loved to have met her, too." God, the more she thought about it, the more . . . "I really would have liked to meet her."

"She would have loved you."

Sissy blinked a couple of times. Coming from a man like him? That was the best compliment she had ever received.

"What was she like?"

Jim took a long inhale and made smoke rings that drifted up into the light that bled out of the house.

The night was so much less dark when you were not alone, she thought. And there was never a more connected feeling than talking with him like this.

Well, except for the sex part.

And they were going to get to that later on.

"She wasn't super-tall," he said eventually. "But she was strong. Oh, fuck, she was strong. Most farms out there, the women labor in the house, you know—and that's a lot of work. Farmers are going from before sunup to after sundown, and they need food . . . need someone holding down the fort with the kids and the bills and the other stuff, too. My mom, she did both sides of it. I once saw her chop up a hundred-year-old oak tree. Tornado knocked it down in the front yard. Took her two school days to do it—but we had firewood all winter just from that beast alone."

"Do you miss her? I guess that's a dumb—"

"I miss all of it. I miss the life and the land, and her." He rubbed his eyebrow with his thumb like he was trying to hide a weakness from her. "I thought that was where I was headed. You know, after I got out of the military. I was going to work here in Caldwell only long enough to make sure Matthias wasn't going to be a problem." He glanced over at her. "I was not going to bring that shit out west. No way. A farm in Iowa was going to be my slide into middle age. My final resting place."

"I guess your life didn't turn out as you thought, either."

"No, it didn't." He stared at her. "I met you, though."

She smiled and kissed the curve of his triceps. "There you go again, making me blush."

"Did I?"

"Yes."

He made a sound that was somewhere between "Mmmm" and "Wait'll I get you upstairs, woman—then we'll see about blushing."

But soon enough, he was back to staring out in front of him.

"Jim?"

"Yeah?"

God, she hated to ask this. "What happens next."

Apparently, Jim was a Neanderthal. Not a surprise, really, considering how brutal he could get. But it didn't exactly make him a contemporary hero. The reality was, however, that as Sissy put that question out there, all he could think of, as he tried out various gloss-shit-over explanations in his head, was that he didn't want her anywhere near any of this.

It made him remember something he'd heard about parachutists, the guys who jumped out of planes into war zones. The military commissioned a psych study on them, and one of the interesting things that had come out of it was that a huge majority of them never felt any fear at all in the regular course of their work. None. An issue of self-selection? Probably—after all, you didn't get into that kind of work unless you had an adrenal gland that was asleep on the job.

But that hadn't been the data point that had struck him: Nearly one hundred percent of the men said that the only time they did get scared? Their last jump. It was as if they knew they'd rolled the dice and come out on top too many times—and they expected the odds to regulate on their finale, like the universe was going to reach out and grab them at that point because it was its last shot.

And that was exactly how he felt now.

Sissy had squeaked by not just once, but twice. He didn't want to gamble on a third try.

And as he considered the danger she'd been in? Naturally, he had to think about Devina—and all at once, an unholy anger coiled in his gut, one that was so powerful, it wiped out even any thoughts of Sissy. Fuck the war. Fuck the souls. Fuck everybody and everything.

Devina was going to go down—and not just because she lost the Creator's little game.

The bottom line was that for him, watching Sissy in that bathroom today had been the final nail in the coffin. She had suffered yet again, been tortured . . . yet again. And something inside of him had snapped: Even as he sat beside her here, and smoked like he was normal, and was ready to take her upstairs and make love to her like he was normal, he was a beast.

Inside his skin, he was an unhinged, vicious sonofabitch on the knife edge of insanity.

And until he brutalized Devina? He wasn't going to be able to concentrate on anything else.

"Jim? What happens next?"

He cleared his throat and twisted away from her—ostensibly to stab his cigarette out in the ashtray he'd brought with him, but also because he hated that he was lying to her.

"Same as always."

"What does that mean?" she pressed.

"I find the soul, somehow, and go to work."

"Are you worried about the last round?"

"No, not at all." At least this was the truth, and he turned back around toward her. "I feel great. I feel strong. I'm ready to shut this game down in the right way."

And that was also the God's honest. The rage in his bones was a great clarifier, a figurative Windex wash of the filter he had on the world and the war and himself. With it around? He could see everything clearly, what he needed to do, where he needed to go. His target set, he was able to tune out all background noise and movement, zeroing in solely on discharging a kill shot.

"Jim?"

"Yeah?"

"Are you all right?"

He tucked her in tighter against him and kissed the top of her head. "Never better. I've never been better."

The shiver that went through her made him frown. "It's cold out here," he said. "Let's go in."

"Okay."

He helped her to her feet and held her close as he led them over to the front door. Inside, he shut things up and locked them, even though his protection spells were better than anything Schlage ever made.

Looking down at her, he lowered his lids to half-mast. "We going to bed?"

"Yes."

Right answer. So the right answer.

Hitting the stairs, they stayed side by side, even on the landing. Which was good. What sucked? When they passed by the grandfather clock, the one that no one set and nobody cranked, the goddamn thing let out a gong. And another. And a third.

Jim ground his jaw and glared over his shoulder. In a series of quick inspirations, he imagined himself going after the cocksucker with a chain saw . . . an ax . . . a flamethrower.

Fourth . . . fifth . . . sixth . . .

"What is it?" Sissy asked as they came up to the second-story sitting area.

. . . seventh . . . eighth . . .

He knew she'd asked him a question, but he was too busy counting, even though he knew damn well what the total was going to be.

"Jim?"

. . . ninth . . . tenth . . . eleventh . . . twelfth . . .

"Jim."

. . . thirteenth.

"Motherfucker," he muttered under his breath before snapping himself back to attention. He was not going to let that nasty piece of shit ruin what little time he had with his woman.

Refocusing, he eyed the doorway to the bathroom he used, and was struck by an urge to reroute from the destination of her bedroom. Especially as he pictured her breasts hot-water-slick with soap suds dripping off the tips of her nipples.

Tugging at Sissy's hand, he drew her over. "Come in here with me."

Chapter
Forty-two

Like she was going to say no to him when he looked at her like that?

As Jim drew her over to the bathroom, Sissy followed, because her body wanted exactly what was in his eyes. Her mind, though . . . her instincts? They were popping red flags all over the place—something was off about him, that hard glint in his eyes the kind of thing she hated to see.

But what could she do? It was late and everyone had had an exhausting day and there was always tomorrow morning. She'd talk to Eddie and Ad then—maybe they could help.

Jim let her go in first, and then he shut and locked the door behind them while she blinked and winced. The crane-arm light fixture over the old-fashioned sink was on, the clinically bright illumination on all the white tile about as romantic as an eye exam—but he took care of that. Reaching up, he unscrewed two out of the three bulbs and then draped a towel over the remaining one, careful not to get the terry cloth too close to the heat.

"Better?" he said.

As she nodded, for some reason she felt shy—although, come on, it wasn't like they hadn't gotten down with it before. This felt different, however . . . maybe because it seemed so planned and intentional. Or, no, maybe it was the fact that with the evil out of her, she felt as though she was about to be with him for the first time. Before? Even though everything had been intense and amazing, that contamination had clouded her—

Holy . . . shit, she thought as Jim lifted his T-shirt up over his abs, his pecs, his thick neck, his head. Even in the now-diffused lighting, his muscles stood out in sharp relief, carved rather than born, powerful even though he wasn't fighting anyone at the moment.

Leaning to the side, he started the shower, his body flexing in a coordinated series of movements while he twisted the knobs to get the right combination of hot and cold.

As far as she was concerned? He could futz around with the temperature for the next twenty hours.

Except then it was time for him to work on her. Straightening, he came at her with a burning look on his face—like not only did he want her, but he needed the connection they were about to have.

"You're beautiful, you know that." Not a question. A statement—and how great was that? "But you have way too many clothes on."

"Are you going to fix that problem?" Check her out with the come-ons. "Or make me do it myself."

"I'm going to take care of it."

She put her hands over her head as he pulled her sweatshirt off, and then his touch was all over her skin, running up from her waist to her simple white bra. Dropping his head, he nuzzled the white cotton out of the way and latched onto her nipple—

With a hiss, she went lax, her body curving against the hard bar of his arm at the small of her back. As he continued to work her, her clothes disappeared, pants and panties gone, bra off, nothing but naked skin left for his eyes, his hands, his mouth.

She was up and over the edge of the huge Victorian claw-foot tub a moment later, and he joined her under the hot spray, his body already primed and raring to go as he pulled the curtain around them. But instead of lifting her up around his waist, or pulling one of her legs high and going in? He went for the soap, rubbing that bar over and over in his hands until the sudsy froth fell in fragrant lots into the swirl around the drain at their feet. His hands were slow and thorough, and she wished she were lying down so that the only thing she had to concentrate on was the way he caressed her, lingering over her neck and her collarbones, her breasts and her stomach, her thighs and her backside.

And when he finished going over every single square inch of skin she had? He got the shampoo and went for her hair—which of course meant she had to get flush with him, the soap making her slip and slide against his hard body.

Naturally, she had to amuse herself as he worked at the long lengths.

She went for his erection, taking it into her palms, making him curse and lose his rhythm.

"You sure you wanna do that?" he asked in a guttural way.

"Oh, yeah. Yup. Very sure."

As she worked her hands up and down his length, the soap was the perfect lubricant, and, God, she loved how he felt. Hard and hot, with that ridge and the blunt head. It wasn't long before his body slammed against the wall, his great weight pulling the shower curtain out of its graceful fall of folds.

His eyes were stoned and hyper-alert at the same time as he stared not at what she was doing, but right at her face—as if the physical friction was nice and all, but what really turned him on was the fact that she was the one doing it to him. And then he closed his lids and gritted his teeth, his breath going short as he got closer and closer. . . .

He came all over the front of her and she loved it.

But he didn't recover for long.

He kissed her deep and traded places with her, shifting her under the spray, the rush hitting her hair and drawing her head back. When there was a squeak from the tub, she looked down and saw that he was on his knees in front of her.

His hands were like the warm water, all over her body—his mouth, too, his lips traveling to her hip bones, the tops of her thighs—

The top of her sex.

And then he licked her, his tongue extending, tasting.

Thank God he took control, lifting one of her legs over his shoulder as he went in further, his hands locking on her pelvis to keep her from falling. Now she was the one tangling the shower curtain, grabbing onto the folds, using them to hold herself upright.

She orgasmed against his lips and his face, the sight of where he was and what he was doing pitching her right over the edge within moments. And he didn't stop.

She didn't want him to.

Warm and wet—everything was warm and wet, from the heat in the air around them to the shower down her back to the way he made love to her core—

The crash was a shocker, not just bursting the bubble of sex, but blowing it the hell up.

With a quick surge he was up on his feet, ready to fight—but there was no enemy in the bathroom with them.

Sissy lifted her hands, and the soggy, soaked shower curtain came up with them. "Oh . . . crap. I ripped . . ."

Glancing up, she saw a whole lot of eye hooks with bits of fabric hanging off them still attached to the metal ring that hung from the ceiling.

"Never mind," he growled as he picked her up and got out of the tub.

He left the water still running as he backed her against the door, put her legs around his hips, and went into her with a strong thrust. Gripping his shoulders with her nails, she gave herself up to the sex, and oh, man, if what had happened in the tub had been good, this was even better.

And it was what she needed right now.

Joined like this? She could pretend that they were going to be together . . . forever.

Chapter
Forty-three

An hour and one more shower later, Sissy was downstairs in the kitchen, helping herself to the last slice of Eddie's perfectly cooked chocolate cake. Jim had passed out cold in his bedroom— because that was as far as they'd made it. Even though hers was just four or five more doors down the hall, they'd been too greedy and impatient to make the trip.

Funny, there had been a new and different satisfaction in leaving him in tangled sheets, his fighter's body all used up because of how much he wanted her.

Before she'd left, she'd stood over him and watched him . . . even carefully touched the gold dove pendant of hers that he wore around his neck. He'd stirred at that point and that was why she left.

For some reason, she couldn't shake the conception that something bad was about to happen.

"So, yup, chocolate is perfect," she muttered as she sat down at the table and took the first bite.

Oh, God, it was amazing: All the endorphins in her body from those orgasms, coupled with the chocolate cake and the fake vanilla icing? High-octane euphoria, even with that spiking fear in the center of her chest.

There was a copy of the *Caldwell Courier Journal* on the far side of the table, and she pulled it over so her eyes had something to do. The top half of the front page was all about international stuff. The bottom had a picture of some real estate tycoon who had apparently decided to sell off all his holdings and was creating a stir in town—

Sissy frowned and leaned closer to the black-and-white photograph. Then decided she was seeing things.

Except no . . . that man had a halo: Even with the grainy nature of the image, she could see a faint circle over the businessman's head.

Vincent diPietro. And the photo had been taken the day before, as he'd walked into his lawyer's office downtown to sign papers.

Strange, that he had one, as well. But considering everything else that was going on? Not something she was going to give much thought to.

After she finished her midnight snack, she had a skim-milk chaser, and put her dishes in the sink. Then she was all about the upstairs, ready to cozy up to Jim and have him throw an arm over her—because God only knew what the morning was going to bring.

Except she didn't make it to even the first landing of the staircase.

She ended up in the trashed parlor.

The plywood sheets over the busted-out windows did a fairly good job of keeping the rain out, but they weren't a tight lock, so the room felt colder and even more damp than the rest of the house. And even with the drafts, the piney smell of the fresh-cut plywood permeated the air, like someone had hung evergreen air fresheners off all the sconces.

As her bare feet went silently over the chilly, bare floorboards, there were no lamps to turn on, because they'd all been sucked away along with the tables they'd been sitting on. There was, however, enough illumination to see by: Thanks to the exterior fixtures mounted on the corner of the house, artificial light bled through the loose seals around the window wells, looking as if maybe the plywood panels were doors you could pass through to other planes of existence.

She found what she was looking for on the mantelpiece over the marble fireplace.

Devina's book barely fit on the ledge, its ragged leather cover hanging off nearly to the point of falling. She figured Adrian must have put it there while he'd been working on the room. Or maybe the thing had climbed up the moldings and taken a seat by itself.

She hated the weight of the tome in her hands, and the old-man-flesh feel of its cover. Hated being near it at all. Before, it had been nothing more than some book; now it felt like she was carrying a severed arm over to the light.

It was two deep breaths before she could open the thing. Two more before she could actually look down and—

"What the hell?"

Frowning, she flipped through the pages, going back and forth and . . . nope, she recognized nothing. The writing now seemed like something utterly foreign, a hodgepodge of symbols and strange letters that was unreadable as far as she was concerned.

Closing the volume up, she returned it to its place on the mantel.

The relief was so great, she was dizzy.

Hitting the stairs, she was halfway up before something Jim said came back to her. It had been when they'd sat outside and she'd asked him, What happens now?

With you? Nothing.

At the time, she'd been talking about the war, not her future, but his answer had been about her and her alone.

Assuming he won the war—and she had to believe he would, because the alternative of her, and everyone else, going into Devina's possession was too horrifying to contemplate—what then? She had to think that if she'd been welcome in Heaven, she would have ended up there after the ritual in that tub at the loft. But no, she was still here.

Guess eternity on a cloud wasn't in her future.

So what did that leave her? Endless years roaming the earth as some disembodied soul? Because halo aside, that was what she was, for all intents and purposes.

Resuming her ascent, she went to Jim's room, slipped through the doorway, and took off her sweats before getting in between the sheets. As strong arms scooped her up and pulled her into a tight embrace, she needed the warmth and the grounding.

They'd figure it out, she told herself. If they could get Devina out of her, they'd be able to make something work.

As long as they had each other, Heaven was wherever they were.

Jim waited until Sissy's breathing was slow and even—and then he stayed in bed a good twenty minutes past that. When he finally did urge her over onto her back and remove his arms from her, she murmured something, but stayed asleep.

Getting out of bed and dressed without making a sound wasn't a problem. Belting his dagger holster around his waist and tucking a crystal knife into the thing was easy in the dark. Snagging a conventional SIG Sauer and tucking it into the small of his back was a piece of cake.

But leaving her was hard.

As he paused with his hand on the doorknob, he stared at the bed. There wasn't a ton of light in the room, but he knew where she was, heard her sigh as she burrowed into the pillows, pictured her rubbing her face in her sleep.

Instead of giving him pause to reconsider, it only sharpened his resolve.

Before he left, however, he had an impulse that had to do with her safety, and he gave in to it quickly and efficiently. Then he was out into the night, passing through the glass of the circular window that overlooked the sitting area, Angel Airlines taking him through the air. It was not until he was well away from the house that he dropped out of the sky and sent the summons.

For once, it was answered immediately. As if the demon had been waiting for him.

Proceeding downtown, he didn't fuck around with the hotel lobby's judgmental busybody. He just landed on the terrace of the penthouse and walked over to the French doors. When he tried the brass handles, they were locked.

Of course she was going to make him knock.

As he curled up a fist and put his knuckles to the glass, he kept his cool. The only thing he cared about was getting into the demon's space. Whatever he had to say, to do, to make that happen? He was going to rock that shit.

Now Devina took her own sweet time. With the cold wind blowing hard up this high, he might have gotten chilled to the bone, but he was too pissed off to care whether or not he was in the damned arctic—

Devina finally turned a corner and came into the living room, posing by the bar like she was at a photo shoot for *Vogue*—or maybe *Hustler* was more like it. She was in a bra and panties that were more black lace than satin, a gossamer-thin "robe" falling from her shoulders to the floor. Her hair was loose and curled into big fat ringlets, and her makeup was film noir, all smoky eyes and blood-red lips. And to top it off? Her skin-colored heels were a

mile high, and made out of something that shimmered like diamonds—plus, yeah, there was some kind of garter belt involved.

To him, she was about as sexually attractive as a ninety-year-
old woman with her teeth out.

But clearly she didn't know that: Apparently deciding that
he'd seen enough, she came forward, her hips swaying, that hair
bouncing along with those double-Ds of hers, her tongue licking
her lips. As she opened things up and he stepped through, she ran
her hand over his chest and shoulders.

And he let her do it.

"To what do I owe this pleasure," she drawled as she shut them
in.

He kept his voice casual as he scanned around the living area,
cataloging objects. "We need to talk."

"Finally," she muttered as she went over and positioned herself
on one of the leather armchairs. "I thought you'd never come
back."

Jim wandered around, putting his hands out and letting them
float over the side table, the back of another chair, a lamp. "I've
been doing some thinking."

"Yes?"

He could hear the hope in her voice. "And I've decided you're
right."

"Yes . . . ?"

Okay, now she was downright breathless.

He stopped. Pivoted to face her. "Yeah. I think we should
quit."

Chapter
Forty-four

Goddamn it, Devina thought.

As she sat in her chair, with her Heidi Klum legs crossed, her hair glossy as varnish, and her breasts looking like a million bucks in La Perla, she'd been so ready to hear something else come out of him.

Something like, *I made a mistake and I need only you.* Or, *Sissy's so fucking boring, I want to slit my own throat when I have sex with her.* Maybe even, *Marry me.*

Instead, he wanted to quit.

"You were the one who suggested it," he said as he continued to stroll around her living room. "You brought it up as an option. And I think you're right. I think that's what we need to do."

Excuse me while I readjust the settings on my monitor, she thought bitterly.

He stepped over to the bar. "You want a drink?"

No, I'd like you to be romantic. For once. You heartless motherfucker.

"No, thank you."

She narrowed her eyes on him as he leaned over and took . . . ugh, a beer out of the little refrigerator under the countertop.

"Do you mind drinking that out of a glass?" she muttered.

"Bottle's fine for me."

"Of course it is."

There was a pop and a hiss as he cracked the top and then a glug as he swallowed. Standing in the midst of the penthouse's luxury, he was like a groundskeeper in the main house, nothing but a T-shirt and jeans covering his body, those boots on his feet something you'd find at an Army/Navy surplus store instead of Saks Fifth Avenue.

Even Macy's didn't carry shit that cheap.

And yet here she was, sitting across from him, heart in her throat, ears pricked to hear some nuance, any nuance, that authenticated her romantic fantasies.

Bringing her manicured hands up to her face, she rubbed her temples, being careful not to smudge any of her foundation.

"I really need to end this," she heard herself say.

"Yeah, and that's my point. We both have way too much to lose. We're even, going into this last round. Why should you give up your collections if I win? Why should I be the one who fucks Heaven in the ass if you win? This is all bullshit."

As he threw his head back and sucked down a third of the beer in there, she watched his Adam's apple go up and down.

Then she had to shift her eyes elsewhere, because he was just a total suck zone for her. In spite of all the reasons she should not just find him unattractive, but hate him . . . she was utterly enamored.

Which made what he was suggesting all the more compelling.

Especially because he was the soul.

If he *did* win, she was going to lose him. She was also going to lose herself—as well as her children down below. But if they quit? Then it was back to status quo.

Well . . . status quo provided the Creator decided not to blow up the world, after all. And somehow, she didn't think He was going to do that. While she'd been going back and forth with Him after she'd copped the blame for the whole portal-to-Purgatory thing, she'd had the sense that He had reconnected to His creation in a way He hadn't been when he'd set up this final endgame.

Jim finished the beer on his fourth "sip" and left the empty on the bar. For her to clean up, naturally.

Men, she thought.

"I gotta go. But think about it and let me know before the next round gets started—"

"Wait," she snapped. "This is it? You're leaving?"

He went over to the door he'd come through. "Yeah."

She hopped up from the armchair and marched over. "I put on my new Louboutins for you."

His brows went up. "I'm sorry? You mean the"—he motioned around her chest—"this stuff?"

"No!" She stamped her foot. "No! That's La Perla, you dumbass! My shoes, motherfucker—would it kill you to notice one goddamn thing about me for once!"

Jim put his hands out like he was warding off a crazy woman. "Listen, I don't—"

She jabbed a finger in his face. "You are the most egotistical man I have ever met. You never call me unless you want something, you are never there when I need you, and you're not even monogamous! I'm beautiful and I'm worth it!"

Oh, my Christ, she thought, he had her so fucked in the head she was quoting a L'Oréal ad.

Jim stared at her for the longest time.

And then he shocked her for real: "I'm sorry."

All she could do was blink. "What . . . what did you say?"

"You heard me, I'm sorry. I . . . look, this war? It's not good for either one of us. It's coming between us, you know?" As Devina opened her mouth, he shook his head like he knew exactly what she was going to say. "No, no, leave Sissy out of it—forget about her. This is between you and me right now. Let's just end all this so we can put aside the fucking bickering, 'kay?"

Devina put her hands up to her face and blinked some more. Every line in his face was open, his body relaxed, his eyes level and unmoving from hers.

But he'd lied to her once already, hadn't he.

Narrowing her stare, she bit out, "If you are playing me, I will never forgive you."

"Fair enough."

And that was it. He just stood there by the door, sincere, calm, and ready to stop fighting.

"I can't get hold of the Creator," Jim said. "Only you can do that. So if you agree with me and you want to end this, you're going to have to get Him to come to both of us."

OMG, that would be awesome, she thought. Kind of like introducing your new boyfriend to your parents, which, hello, was yet another human fantasy she'd never been able to live out.

Until now, a part of her squee'd.

"I'd better go." He opened the door, and a cold breeze shot into the warm interior. "I don't want to cloud your thinking—you need to decide this on your own. But if you're up for it, get the Creator and bring Him to me. The sooner, the better, okay?"

He paused as a gust blew her hair back, as if maybe he were captivated by her. "Yeah," he murmured as he seemed to shake himself. "You think about it."

As she followed him out onto the terrace, she watched as his wings, his incredible wings, formed over his shoulders. A moment later, he was off, soaring into the night sky.

Like something out of Shakespeare, she clasped her hands to her heart, and ran to the railing, leaning against it so she could see the shimmering presence of him disappear into the face of the revealed moon.

The only thing that could have made it better . . . was if they'd been in Paris.

Sissy woke up with a start. Everything was dark in Jim's bedroom; there were no sounds disturbing the peace; nothing seemed missing—

No, wait. There was no Jim.

Sitting up, she clicked on a brass lamp and looked around, although, come on—a man as big as he was? You were going to hear that moving around. Maybe he'd gone to the bathroom? Forcing herself to lie back down against the pillows, she waited to hear footsteps. Flushing. Running water.

Nothing.

Maybe she should just go and check . . . ?

Except, jeez, it seemed waaaaay too early in their relationship to become so possessive that the guy couldn't even take a leak on his own. Folding the sheets carefully up to her chest, she told herself to calm—

Cranking her head to his side of the bed, she felt the blood drain out of her skull.

Lying on the pillow where he had been sleeping . . . was her necklace, the one with the little gold dove on a chain.

Grabbing the thing, she brought it right up to her face—like maybe she'd gotten it wrong or . . . no, it had not broken. The clasp had been reengaged.

After he had taken the thing off.

"Shit!" Scrambling out of the sheets, she threw some clothes on and shot out the door. "Jim!"

She ran for the stairs and took them two at a time on the way down. Halting in the front hall, she froze and listened—prayed for the sound of him moving around in the kitchen, the smell of cigarette smoke, the creak of some floorboards somewhere, any-where.

"Jim!" she hollered.

The front door was locked, although it wasn't like he was go-ing to leave that open if he'd gone out that way—and when she shot back to the kitchen, she found the back exit was the same.

"What's going on?"

As Eddie appeared in nothing but a pair of pajama bottoms, she wheeled around and held out the necklace.

Yeah, like that explained everything.

"I'm sorry?" he said. "What is that?"

"He's gone. Jim's gone."

"What?"

"I woke up and he was gone—and he left this behind."

Eddie's red eyes narrowed. "And that is . . ."

"My necklace." She waited for the OMG! Of course! When it didn't come, she said, "You don't understand—"

Adrian came in, having been slower on the descent. "What's—"

"—my mother gave it to him. He told me he never took it off—and now he's gone and he left it behind."

"Shit," Adrian muttered, heading over to the table and falling into a chair.

"And he's not anywhere in the house?" Eddie said. "You've—"

"Come on," Ad cut in. "You know exactly where he is."

"Damn it." Eddie shook his head. "He needs to work on the next soul. Now is *not* the time to go after Devina."

The two angels started talking back and forth at each other, but Sissy suddenly couldn't hear a word they said.

The newspaper.

Drawn by something she couldn't explain, she went across and flipped the CCJ over so that the bottom half of the front page showed. That picture, of that man . . .

"Hey," she cut in. "Hey! Who is this?"

She flashed the paper to the pair of them and they looked at her as if she'd lost her mind. "Who is this?" she demanded, pointing to the man. "This is one of the souls, isn't it."

As alarm bells rang in her head, she focused through her fear.

"Yeah." Ad shrugged. "So what, we got bigger problems than where Vin diPietro is holding a garage sale of all his—"

"Do you see this?" She jabbed her forefinger at the picture. "Do you see what's over his head?"

The two of them leaned in as if they both knew damned well they either checked it out or she was going to shove the newspaper in their faces until they answered her.

"No," Eddie said. "I don't see anything."

"You?" she said to Ad.

"Nope. *Nada*. No offense, but if you need your eyes checked—"

"Jim's the last soul." As they stared over at her with all kinds of WTF, she jogged the newspaper and spoke with crystal clarity. "Jim is the final one in play."

Chapter
Forty-five

As Adrian narrowed his eyes on Sissy, his heart skipped a beat and seemed to consider taking a lunch break altogether. Except then he thought, as smart as Sissy was, she had this wrong. Somehow she had to have this wrong.

Eddie clearly felt the same way. "Listen, Sissy, I'm not sure—"

"This man has a halo." She pointed at the grainy picture of Vin. "Was he one of the souls in the war?"

When neither one of them replied, she nodded grimly. "He was. Wasn't he. And the man I saw in Home Depot, the one I pointed out to you, Ad. He was also a soul, right? And then there was a guy at my funeral who had a halo, a musician here in town—and I read that he had died in the paper . . . right after Jim told me we'd lost the round before mine." She pointed to her own head. "I have a halo."

Now, an electrical shock went through Ad's nervous system, the kind of thing that he imagined happened when humans saw what they thought were ghosts, or maybe when you were driving down the highway and an SUV swerved into your lane.

It was the response of an adrenal gland that had just up and wakey-wakey'd.

"Jim also has a halo." She tossed the newspaper down onto the table. "So I have to be right about this."

With a curse, Ad closed his eyes and prayed that Eddie jumped in and came up with the ironclad reason this was not true. Eddie would know. He knew everything—

"Let me make sure I understand you," the other angel murmured. "You see these things?"

"As soon as I got out of Hell, I noticed that Jim had one, and I asked why you two didn't. He didn't see it. Doesn't see mine."

"Well, I have to tell you, I don't see anything over your head."

She shrugged. "Fine, but that doesn't mean I'm wrong. Is there anyone else who was a soul? Let me see a picture of them, and I'll tell you. Come on—let me prove this to you."

"Okay, okay . . . lemme see what I can find," Ad muttered, taking out his phone. "How the fuck do you spell DelVecchio— never mind. His father was that serial killer, both of them are all over the Net."

When he'd found what he was looking for, he turned his phone around and flashed the screen at Sissy. As she bent down and her brows came together, he measured every nuance of her face, from the clarity of her eyes to the tightness of her mouth.

She exhaled with frustration. "Well, I guess I'm wrong. He doesn't have—"

"That was his father," Ad said, taking his phone back. Another touch or two and he flashed her a second picture. "How about him."

But he knew what she was going to say.

"Yes," she breathed, pointing down. "Right here. It's right here."

Ad glanced across at his best buddy. "I thought Jim was supposed to be the fucking savior."

Eddie's shell-shocked peepers were not good news. "I, ah, I would not have seen this coming. But I guess . . . it's the Creator's game, right? He made all the rules, and there's certainly nothing in them that suggests Jim couldn't also be in play."

"Mother . . . fucker." As Ad leaned back, his bad leg ached so badly he had to sit forward again. "You know, just when I thought things couldn't get worse."

"He went after Devina," Sissy said in a dead tone. "Because of what that demon did to me. Is that his crossroads?"

Eddie whistled under his breath. "Yeah. If he tries to destroy her—"

"Even if it's for the right reasons," Ad chimed in as he got to his feet. "Shit."

"—then, yeah, I could see how it could be a loss for us. Even though Devina is evil and has done a lot of shit, the target isn't the point. It's the soul's decision at the time, it's the intent that is the measure."

"We have to stop him," Sissy said in a small voice.

"Assuming we can."

Ad rubbed the back of his neck. "Look, regardless of whether or not he's in play, we gotta go get him. We can't let him try to take her out on his own. He's powerful, but Devina? That bitch is capable of things even he can't make happen."

"Can she be killed?" Sissy asked.

Eddie shrugged. "Only under the most extreme circumstances. But again, it wouldn't matter in terms of the war because it's about his intent."

Sissy kicked up her chin and glared at the both of them. "I'm coming, too. I don't care what you say, I'm not—"

"Of course you're coming," Ad gritted out. "You're probably the only one who can get through to him. More to the point, you're going to find him for us. He could be anywhere in this city."

Jim landed in a park down by the river, the one close to the boat-house that he'd been in during Matthias's second round. He stayed away from the lights on the walking lanes out of habit, not necessity: He was deep invisi, undetectable not only by the human eye, but the demon one.

The bene of a little spell he'd been working on in his spare time.

Putting his hand forward, he stared at the knife he'd managed to lift from the penthouse. It was the one Sissy had almost used against Devina, the one that had come from the demon's precious collection of kitchen cutters. And how did he know its origins? The instant he'd snagged it off the bar while they'd been talking, a vibration had traveled up his arm and nailed him in the chest.

It was her. It was Devina's very essence.

Getting the thing out of there had also been easier than he'd expected—all he'd had to do was slip it into his waistband and make sure his T-shirt stayed down.

Turning the weight over in his palms, he pictured Devina not just from memory, but as if he were creating a 3-D sculpture of her out of thin air. Every nuance, from the arch of her eyebrows to the curve of her breasts, from the length of her torso and dip of her waist to those long legs and the narrow feet, became totally front and center. And even when he figured he'd gone far enough, he made sure he added the black gleam of her evil eyes and those cherry-red lips . . . as well as the glow that was always above her and the vicious aura that surrounded her—

The knife began to vibrate.

Like the point of a compass fighting to find true north.

He put one hand over the other and squeezed hard to make sure the thing didn't get stripped away from him . . . and then he followed where it took him. Traveling at a jog, he followed the pull sure as if there were a rope around the metal parts and some-one was drawing them home.

Passing out of the park, he went by skyscrapers, jogged down streets that paralleled the warehouse district, continued onward to the seedy part of downtown with its clubs and strip joints. And then the knife started to veer to the right, leading him by the apartment building complexes and toward the suburban strip malls and the—

The building it eventually brought him to was low-slung and gray, a nondescript box of functionality with a sign that read, IN-TEGRATED HUMAN RESOURCES, on the front facade.

Against his palms, the Henckels grew hot, as if it were excited at being so close to their mutual goal.

"Let's get inside," he hissed, walking around to the back.

Chapter
Forty-six

Sissy walked out of the old mansion's front door, following Ad and Eddie into the night. As she zipped up Jim's leather jacket, she breathed in the scent he'd left behind on it . . . and wondered how in the hell she was going to find him. The two angels seemed convinced she'd be able to, but damned if she knew how.

"Did you know that Devina is a hoarder?" Eddie asked as he held up the necklace Jim had left behind.

She struggled to track what he was saying. "Ah, no."

Ad sheathed a crystal knife at his hip. "Yeah, she puts the 'demon' in OCD."

"The reason she collects things," Eddie said, handing the chain with its dangling dove over, "is because ownership is transmitted and collected in metal. The purer the metal, the stronger the tie, but that's not the only determinant. Strong emotion, physical pain, bloodshed—these strengthen the bond between the animate and the inanimate."

"It's why he left that necklace behind," Ad muttered. "He didn't want any tie to you to fall into Devina's hands. Too dangerous."

"But it's also going to be how we find her." Eddie nodded. "That's gold, for one thing. Very powerful. Add to that the fact that your mother gave it to him and it was yours? And he wore it during times when he was searching for you? Lot of emotion. He's bonded to that thing as much as you are."

She stared at the fragile links, the sweet charm. "Okay, so what do I do?"

"Close your eyes. Picture Jim standing in front of you, and re-call every detail of him that you can think of. Imagine him in three-D, feel his presence, the weight of him—make eye contact with him. The stronger and more clearly you see him, the better the direction will be. Then when you get the link and it begins to guide you, we'll drive to wherever he is."

Sissy nodded, thinking that of all the things she'd done in the last couple of days, this made the most sense and was the least scary. Shutting her lids, she thought about Jim and visualized him before her, noting everything from his dark blond hair to the shadow of beard on his jaw, from the cigarette in his hand to his combat boots, from the jeans and the perennial white T-shirt to the muscular chest. And then she even imagined the necklace it-self was on him . . .

He became so clear to her, her eyes started to water.

"Do you have him with you?" Eddie asked softly.

"Yes . . ."

"Okay."

In the silence that followed, she waited for the little gold dove on the thin gold chain to talk to her in some way.

And waited.

Waited some more.

"What is it supposed to do?" she murmured.

"Concentrate harder," Eddie replied.

Frowning, she went into even greater detail, seeing things like the blue flecks in his eyes, and the way his front teeth were slightly off center, and the scars from old wounds on his body. She imagined that horrible tattoo under the clothes she'd put on him. She pictured him talking to her, hearing the sound of his voice and his rare laugh. She saw him smiling. Then not.

In her hands, the gold of the necklace warmed . . . except it seemed to be only from her own palms, not anything supernatural or paranormal.

Come on, she thought. *Come on.*

Anxiety threatened the clarity of what she was visualizing. And the longer she went without any kind of response from the necklace, the more she worried about him locking heads with Devina and bad, bad things happening.

"I don't think this is working," she whispered.

"Goddamn it," Ad said. "What the hell are we going to do now?"

"Give it a little more time." Eddie cleared his throat. "Let's just relax."

Except no amount of relaxing helped. Eventually, she opened her lids and shook her head. "I'm so sorry. I can't . . . oh, God, I can't feel anything."

"He's gotta be really fucking invisi." Ad cursed again. "I mean, for Sis not to get a fucking thing?"

"There has to be another way, right?" Sissy grabbed Eddie's arm. "There's got to be something else we can do."

The angel's eyes narrowed, like he was playing file-cabinet with every single piece of information that he'd ever learned about anything, going through the headings and subheadings, searching, searching.

"Did he take his phone?" Ad asked.

Sissy shook her head. "It's upstairs."

"So much for GPS. Man, too bad they didn't chip him when he was in XOps. Unless they did?"

Eddie slowly turned and looked toward the plywood-covered

windows over on the house's left flank. "Where's her book," he said in a grim voice.

"Devina's? In the parlor." Sissy put her necklace on, stretching her arms behind her head to work the clasp. "But I can't read it anymore."

And to think she'd assumed that was good news.

"Follow me," Eddie said before striding back into the house. "I've got an idea."

As Jim picked the lock on the back door of the nondescript office building, he wasn't sure how much time he had once he infiltrated the interior. Assuming Devina had bought his bullshit, there was a good chance she'd go to the Creator right away—he just didn't know how long that convo was going to last. He was also banking that her protective virgin-sacrifice signal system wasn't going to work when she was talking to God Himself. This was based on nothing but a hunch, however—although when he'd been in the Big Guy's presence himself, the experience had been so completely overwhelming, he'd nearly lost consciousness. With any luck, Devina would have a similar response.

If he was wrong about all of that, though?

Then he had only a matter of seconds to find the bitch's mirror and steal it—

Click. The stainless-steel locking mechanism retracted on cue, and he quickly put his pick kit away before grabbing the handle. He was doing this B and E the old-fashioned way on the theory that the more magic he used, the more he was going to compromise his invisi. Again, he didn't know that for sure, but it didn't cost him shit to be conservative.

In his mind, he counted it down, three . . . two . . .

No intel on the layout of the facility. Nothing but the knife to guide him. Probable ambush at any moment.

No backup.

. . . one.

Jim slipped inside and let the door close on its own. The hall beyond was lit dimly by after-hours energy-savers, and the fact that nothing motion-activated came on proved he was rocking the not-there. But he had to assume that the penetration had triggered her protective spell, and he got a move on, jogging down the brushed-nap wall-to-wall carpet with the knife once again out in front of himself. He passed by empty offices and low-level debris like pieces of paper scattered on the floor, an office phone or two, electrical cords. He was pretty sure that Devina had created an illusion over the "business" to hide herself and her things from prying eyes, but the shit was clearly not working on him.

Either that or the lie rolled out only when she cued it to.

The good news? At least the knife in his hands was talking to him big-time, growing hotter and hotter, vibrating so much it was in danger of slipping out of his hold.

The elevators. It took him to the elevators in the front lobby.

And that was a big no. He was not going to get trapped in one of them if she came back in the middle of him going wherever he had to in the building—

Oh, God, there was the sacrifice.

Even though there was no time, he still approached the naked body that was strung upside down over a tin tub by the main entrance.

He couldn't leave the young man there.

Moving fast, he got the body down while still hanging onto the knife, and then he dragged the poor battered soul over to the first office he came to and hid it in case Devina came back.

After he was done with her? He was going to take care of the guy somehow.

It was just too much like his Sissy to walk away from.

Refocusing, he looked over at the glowing red exit sign in the far corner the lobby. Racing over, he found that the door had a passcode pad installed by its jamb, but he'd anticipated that. Reaching for his back pocket, he took out a leather sheath and opened the wallet-like fold-up. Inside, there were all kinds of goodies that he'd used in his old XOps trade, and he took out a square piece of plastic that was the size and shape of a credit card—just with added tricks: A set of wires came off one end and he plugged them into a tiny CPU that was no bigger than a driver's license. Drawing the card through, he froze it in the middle of the reader, initiated a sequence, and watched the red numbers on the readout scan so fast his eye couldn't track the discrete numerals.

Bingo. The door unlocked itself.

He put his kit back together, popped the door, and entered a concrete-and-steel stairwell that had mood lighting and smelled like clay—

With a sudden burst of enthusiasm, the knife leaped away from him and clattered down the steps, making the turns around the landings in a sloppy way, banging into the walls, rattling over the straightaways. He followed at a dead run, keeping up the pace.

They didn't have far to go.

The basement.

Of course.

Chapter
Forty-seven

As Sissy led the angels into the parlor, her heart was going a mile a minute. The idea that Jim was out there and maybe fighting with Devina already was enough to give her palpitations. That they didn't know where he was?

It was enough to make her nauseous.

"The book's over there," she said, pointing to the mantel.

Eddie crossed the bare floor and took the book into his hands, flipping through the pages. For some reason, he apparently could read it and not be evil—at least, she assumed that was the case.

"These words," he said, "were written using the semen of her minions. And if I remember—yeah, there we are. The list from Hell, literally."

"What does this have to do with finding Jim?" Sissy asked.

"He's going to go after her mirror first before he attacks her. If he takes the mirror, Devina won't be able to escape down to Hell and hide. He'll have a better chance of killing her without it. Ad, gimme your knife?"

Ad was front and center with the crystal weapon, and Eddie took it and put the book down on the floor. Closing the cover, he dug the sharp tip into the old leather, making a circular hole that went into the pages themselves; then with a quick slice and a hiss, he cut his own palm. Making a fist, he held the thing over the hole that he'd made, the silver blood dripping down into the pages, but not pooling.

Each drop was absorbed into the ancient tome, disappearing.

In a soft voice, the angel began to speak words that ran together, the language nothing that Sissy understood.

"What's he doing?" she whispered as she crouched down.

Ad nodded in approval. "He's using his will to turn the book into a locator."

"The inventory list," she breathed.

"That's right. Devina keeps her collection and her mirror together. This goes right, we'll find the latter because the book will help us find the former. I'll be right back."

It was a powerful sight, she thought as she was left alone with Eddie. And something she'd like to paint: the fallen angel with his thick braid hanging over his shoulder and his massive body curled above the ancient book, his fist extended with a shimmering path flowing down, linking the two together.

Ad had just returned as Eddie stopped and seemed to need a moment to reconnect with reality.

Eddie cleared his throat. Shook his head. "Do we have a—"

"Right here," Ad said, holding something out.

"You read my mind."

It was a compass, one of those old-fashioned Swiss Army jobs, and Eddie took the green and silver dial and fit it into the circle he'd dug in the book. Then all three of them leaned in. The red arrow went haywire, spinning all around before falling into a series of seizures, flipping this way and that.

Until it finally settled on a northeast direction.

"Looks like we got it," Ad muttered. "Assuming the damn thing doesn't just want to go to a Barnes and Noble."

Sissy jumped up. "Let's go."

Except Eddie stayed where he was, staring down at the compass.

"What's wrong?" Sissy asked.

The angel's red eyes lifted, focusing on her, but also on Ad—like he wanted to be sure that both of them heard him. "Nobody breaks the mirror. Do you understand? If you shatter that glass, you end up in a million pieces, too."

Sissy frowned. "Does Jim know this?"

"Yes, but I'm not sure he'll remember. And that's why we have to get to him first."

Holy Mary, mother of OCD.

As Jim stepped from the stairwell into the basement proper, and his knife buddy went clattering off to join its friends, he was momentarily stunned even though he'd seen Devina's collection before: In a dimly lit, vaguely musty space that seemed big as a football field, hundreds of bureaus were scattered around, facing in all directions. There was no order to them, no rhyme or reason to their placement, their style, their age.

So Devina didn't know he was in here yet.

Where were the clocks and the knives? he wondered, searching out the vast space. Had to be here somewhere or Fido the Ginsu wouldn't have run off like that.

Mirror, mirror, on the wall . . . where the fuck are you.

He started forward, heading away from the elevators, because if he were Devina, he'd put his most precious thing as far away from the egress/ingress as he could get it.

He'd gone about ten yards when he pivoted around and decided to give himself a little backup.

Working fast, he started pulling out drawers, and dumping their contents on the floor, creating piles of metal buttons and earrings and watches and signet rings. Glasses with metal rims and the locks to suitcases and car keys and coins and all manner of metal ephemera hit the bare concrete and danced a little, like they were happy to be freed.

Then he turned back and—

Ding!

Ninety-nine percent of his body froze in place. The one percent that didn't unsheathed one of his two crystal daggers as the elevator doors opened.

Whoever it was couldn't be Devina, unless she—

"What the *fuck*!" he barked.

Eddie came out first. Adrian was last. Sissy was in the motherfucking middle.

Jim's rage went mushroom-cloud. "What the fuck are you bringing her—"

Sissy put her hands up as she walked forward. "Jim, you can't do this."

He ignored her, his grip tightening on the weapon as part of him wanted nothing more than to kill the two criminal idiots who'd apparently thought it was a great idea to bring his woman along for the ride. The only thing that stopped him from attacking? The SOBs were the ones who were going to have to take her the fuck out of here.

"Jim, listen to me." Sissy got up in his face, throwing her body in the way. "You're the soul. Do you hear me? You're the soul—and you can't do this. This is your crossroads, if you try to kill her—"

He pushed her out of the way and went for Eddie, grabbing onto the guy's jacket with his free hand and angling the blade right to that thick neck. "You get her out of here. *Now*."

But the motherfucker didn't say a thing. He just focused off into the distance like he knew—he *knew*—that anything he uttered was just going to lead to a fight, and that was not going to be a distraction he allowed to happen.

Sissy grabbed onto Jim's arm. "That's the reason for the halos. You have one. I have one. Vincent diPietro. Detective DelVecchio. That man at my funeral. Nobody else does."

"Don't you cheat me of this," he growled at Eddie. "Don't you—"

"I'm not leaving here without you," Sissy yelled at him. "And we're not going to let you do this—"

"Take her—"

"—because you're not only going to lose the war, you're going to lose yourself!"

"—out of here—"

The rattling started up all around them, the bureaus vibrating on the concrete and then shifting positions, pushing the drawers and the things he'd ripped out of a few of them across the floor, ordering themselves of their own volition into whatever rows and lineups were proper.

"Jesus Christ!" Jim shoved Eddie away and paced in a tight circle. "Fucking hell! This is just—"

Sissy got right up on him again, blocking his way even as he put his hands over his head so she couldn't grab onto his arms.

"You don't have to do this—"

"She hurt you!" he screamed. "She fucking—"

"Don't do this for me. Don't you dare do this for me like some kind—"

"How can I not! She hurt you! She cut your body! She made it so I had to nearly kill you to get you clean! You think I can let this shit go?!"

Sissy recoiled as if he'd struck her. But she didn't back down. "You're not right in the head."

"I'm very fucking right!"

"You're infected. Just like I was."

That stopped him dead for a split second. But then he shook

his head. "No, I'm not. And I'm not one of the souls, Sissy—I don't know what you think you're seeing—"

"Your anger is her inside of you, Jim. Listen to me." She reached up and took his face in her hands. "Listen to me—she's inside—"

"No, she's not! Do you think I wouldn't know that?"

"I didn't know it until she was gone, remember? Jim, this anger is going to take us all down."

"This is for you!"

"Bullshit! If it was, you wouldn't be trying to ruin yourself and lose this war! I want you safe more than I care about Devina getting what she deserves! Christ, Jim, *please* listen to me!"

He gave up reasoning with her and pegged Ad and Eddie with a hard stare. "This is on the both of you. If anything happens to her, I'll kill you, too—"

And then it was too late.

The bureaus stilled, the elevator dinged again, and Devina's voice said in a nasty tone, "Guess I wasn't invited to my own party, huh."

For a split second, Jim wanted to explode at everything: The fact that Eddie and Adrian had put Sissy in such danger. That she was talking bullshit. That Devina had arrived.

Instead, he picked up Sissy and all but threw her at the idiot angels. "Run," he hissed at them. "Fucking *run*!"

Chapter
Forty-eight

As the demon stepped out of the elevator, Sissy felt herself go airborne and then it was a case of an Olympic sprint she was allowed to have little or no independent opinion of—Eddie grabbed one of her arms and one of Ad's and the three of them hustled like they were being chased through row after row after row of antique bureaus.

She tried to look over her shoulder, but couldn't manage even a glance thanks to Eddie's death grip.

And then the collection changed. Moments later, she had a vague impression of clothes, countless clothes hanging on racks like they were in some kind of department store. And shoes. Handbags. Then a bed the size of a living room, and a vanity with enough makeup on it to do a hundred thousand faces.

Eddie yanked them to a halt in front of a tall, freestanding three-part mirror that was encased in all kinds of fancy French swirls.

"Is . . . that . . . it?" she asked between heaving breaths.

"Not even close." Eddie panted as he looked around. "We've got to take cover."

"No," Ad countered. "We gotta find that mirror and hide it. That'll destabilize Devina and maybe give us some time with Jim."

"So where the hell would she put it?" Eddie muttered.

"Not where it's light," Sissy heard herself say. "It would be in the darkness. Although . . . I have no idea why I know that."

On cue, all three of them looked over to a far corner. Now that the demon had arrived, the overhead lighting had come on, illuminating everything . . . except for that one place.

Back to the dead run.

The three of them raced over into the blackness, and Sissy felt a chill that seeped down past her skin and into her bones.

"It's here," Eddie said in a low voice.

As Sissy's eyes adjusted, she could only make out the dimensions of the thing first. Then the details were gradually revealed to her, everything from the decrepit glass that didn't seem to actually reflect anything that was in front of it to the rotted frame and the twisted, contorted bodies that seemed to ornament all four sides of it.

"Man, that bitch is twelve kinds of ugly. And for once, I'm not talking about the demon," Ad muttered.

Eddie cursed under his breath. "She'll know we're moving it."

"But maybe it'll give us some leverage against her." Ad stepped over to the mirror, and braced himself, before grabbing hold. "Come on. Let's do this."

Eddie went to the opposite side and made a grimace of distaste as he put his hands on the frame. "On three. One, two . . . *three*."

Both angels groaned as they inched the tremendous weight off the concrete floor, their big bodies straining. When they were finally fully straightened, it was obvious Adrian was struggling because of his injuries.

"I'm helping," Sissy said, ducking under Ad's arms and expecting an argument.

Except none came—which told her how dire things were.

"Oh, that's nasty," she gasped as she locked onto the frame and joined the lift. "It's like . . . the flu."

Her entire body reacted to the connection, her stomach rolling, a cold sweat breaking out all over her skin, her head pounding.

"Let's go," she snapped. "I already can't wait to put this down."

×———————×

It was Devina's worst nightmare made manifest: Every time she entered one of her protected places, her fear was always that something was gone, missing, out of place—and what did she find now? Someone—probably that cocksucker Jim—had ripped drawers out of bureaus and thrown her shit on the floor.

And to top it off? She had to deal with the sight of that now non-virgin and those two fallen angel motherfuckers standing like the fucking tools they were in the middle of her goddamn, motherfucking shit.

It was enough to make her say to hell with everything and kill all four of them.

Jim deserved nothing less for lying to her.

Again.

Tears flooded her eyes as everyone but her lover started running away, going deeper into her basement. Her first instinct was to call her minions and send the crew after them, but she held off. This was the kind of thing she wanted to settle on her own. Besides, that trio weren't the ones who mattered; Jim was. And after this all played out? She was going to own Sissy, Adrian, and Eddie—along with everyone else on the planet—so they were more than welcome to try to hide where there was nowhere to hide.

Besides, she wanted Jim alone without distractions.

Brushing at her cheeks, she wiped her hands on the seat of her leather pants. She'd changed out of her negligee to go see the Creator, but had kept on her beautiful, sparkling Loubous.

Man, she'd been so damned pleased with the audience she'd been granted and happy that He had been willing to see them both. So cocksucking excited about the turn of events.

Except as soon as she'd gotten back, she hadn't made it farther than a makeup check at the hotel's penthouse.

She'd known the instant her space had been violated.

The instant her *trust* had been violated.

She had to wipe her eyes again—which was a bitch, because she didn't want to smudge her makeup. "Jim . . . goddamn it. Am I never going to learn with you."

The bastard kept looking over his shoulder, checking to see if his precious Sissy and his douchebag besties had gotten away.

It was enough to make her violent. But she needed—

As he refocused on her, the hatred on his face was so deep, so pervasive, so overwhelming, it twisted his features out of place.

Which was kind of touching, really. Also a sign that the infection in him had reached an all-new level.

"You got something to say to me," she drawled, looking forward to the fight they were about to have.

Except all he did was take a step back. And another.

And then tear off at a dead run.

It took a split second for her brain to do the math. And then she screamed—and went airborne.

Her mirror!

Fuck! They were going after her mirror—

Traveling in a scramble of molecules, she gunned for the back corner of the basement—and didn't make it. Somehow Jim was able to pluck her right out of midflight, and the instant the contact was made, she reformed against her will, her body becoming solid and corporeal. And he took advantage of that. With a powerful yank, he pulled her down to the hard, cold floor, and rolled around with her as his hands locked on her shoulders, then her neck.

Her instinct was to fight back—but then she thought, no . . . this was the perfect setup for his endgame, the chance for him to make the decision to "kill" her and follow through on the impulse—his crossroads made manifest, his choice resulting in her winning the game.

Except, *fuck*, she couldn't lose that mirror.

On a tremendous shove, she flashed out from under him, and things were too urgent for her to try to dematerialize, so she ran in her high heels, streaking toward her wardrobe and her bed—

Jim pulled some kind of flying tackle, taking her down again, knocking her over into her shoe collection, the racks falling down, high heels, pumps, boots going everywhere. But fuck that. Throwing his heavy weight off of her, she sprang up once more, losing her footing and then finding it again even in the stillies, her eyes seeking out that far corner of darkness—

Jim was on her again.

It was as if he had endless reserves of energy—and this time he wasn't going to let her go. His vicious hands tightened around her throat and he shoved her body into the vanity and then her regular mirror, glass shattering all around them as they fought each other, him to take her down, her to get free.

And suddenly, there was a glint of crystal over his head.

He'd unsheathed his dagger.

Now was the time.

Even though it went against the terror of losing her portal to Hell, she forced herself to go lax. The angels and that little bitch weren't incented to destroy the thing, she reminded herself. If they did, they'd just kill themselves in the process.

Let him stab you, she told herself as she focused on his crazed, hate-filled blue eyes. Then they're all yours and you can save the mirror that way.

"Do it," she said, bracing herself.

Unlike the mere kitchen knife she'd been prepared to have Sissy use against her, this was going to hurt like a nightmare.

Ultimately, though . . . it was going to get her everything she had ever wanted.

Chapter
Forty-nine

Jim was going to fucking do it. With the dagger over his head and hatred screaming in his soul, he was going to fucking stab Devina—and not just once. He was going to Hannibal Lecter her into pieces, hack at her until there was nothing left but a pool of her evil blood and shit that looked like the inside of a fucking sausage.

With her locked in his grip, everything came back to him, and it was a slide show of gruesome and sad—starting with his mother on that farmhouse kitchen floor and ending with him and Adrian and Eddie fighting to rip something out of Sissy's pure body. And everything, all of it, could be traced back to this evil of this demon, all the bloodshed and the suffering, even some of his own—

From out of nowhere, the image of Sissy's face appeared and blocked out everything else. He saw her walking over to him from that elevator, getting up in his grille, yelling back at him.

There hadn't been anger in her eyes.

It had been terror.

Jim shook his head like that would clear it and tried to get back to business. But that mind's eye picture of her wouldn't fade, almost as if it had been placed there by some other source.

And oh, God, her lips were moving. She was talking to him, telling him things that made no fucking sense, that went against everything he knew about the way the war worked and what his job was.

"Do it," Devina growled. "Just fucking get this over with, will you! You fucking pussy!"

Jim recommitted to the program, rearing his shoulder back—

I want you safe more than I care about Devina getting what she deserves!

Gritting his teeth, Jim fought against Sissy's voice in his head, trying to get around it and do what was right, what was proper—

"Stab me, you sonofabitch!"

Jim snapped. With every ounce of strength he had, he . . .

. . . spun Devina around once, twice . . . three times, and slung her away from him, sending her careening across the concrete floors, her high heels catching the light and flashing, the clattering of her footfalls echoing all around.

"You can't have me!" he screamed at her. "You can't have them!"

And then shit went slow-mo.

In a series of events that he no doubt was going to remember for the rest of his immortal life, Devina lost her balance and this time couldn't recover, her body falling backward, arms pinwheeling, brunette hair waving around as she traveled across the concrete floor on the verge of landing on her ass.

Except that wasn't where she ended up.

From the one dark corner in the basement, like they were thieves smuggling a painting out of a museum, Eddie, Adrian, and Sissy came into view. They were all on a hustle, the three of them racing across the floor with Devina's mirror hefted up in their communal hold.

It was the hole in one that saved all of humanity.

In spite of the fact that there were acres of floor space for Devina to yard-sale on, whole great stretches of no-big-deal, she tap-danced backward right into the ugly, pitted glass of the mirror, her body shattering the surface, the impact blowing open a suck zone that put that portal the bunch of them had opened up in the parlor in the shade.

He would never forget Devina's expression as she realized what had happened. The shock and horror were the kind of payback he would have been overjoyed with—except for the fact that the instant she was pulled in, something inside of him lurched . . . then got its own pull on.

The center of his chest was yanked forward from his spine, and he felt as though his rib cage were going to blow open. And yet the mirror didn't want him.

Only that part of Devina that was in him.

His torso bowed back so hard, he was sure he was going to snap in half, and he levitated off the ground. Just as he was about to pass out from the pain—

Snap!

Like a rubber band, the foreign substance shot free of him and hit the air, the black cloud of bees exactly what had come out of Sissy's metaphysical incision. And he wasn't the only one who lost something.

As he fell to his knees, he was terrified about Sissy or the angels getting sucked in, but the mirror wanted to claim only Devina—and that was why Ad jerked and spasmed, grimacing in pain, his body twitching as he lost his grip and levitated and—

The evil left him as well, the cloud forming in front of his chest and then breaking free to enter the swirling black vacuum.

As Jim struggled to stay conscious, he became aware of a strange sound over and above the howling of the broken mirror— and that was when he realized that the bureaus had begun to move, doing an about-face on a oner.

"Stand behind the mirror," Jim yelled at them. "Get out of the way!"

Eddie disappeared and then came back into view as he grabbed Ad from where the guy had fallen, and Sissy, too. Then Jim couldn't see them anymore.

All he could do was pray.

And his prayers were answered.

Everything in the basement got dragged into the void, all the clocks and the knives, the collection of metal pieces, the clothes and shoes and makeup, the bed . . . every object that Devina had bought or taken went along with her, her essence having tainted everything that was around her. Weakened by the fight, all Jim could do was watch in awe at a sight too monumental to comprehend or explain, like something out of a dream where what you witnessed was possible only because it wasn't real.

Except this was actually happening.

With each object consumed, black flames licked out of the suck zone like the mirror was enjoying a good meal, wood and fabric and metal disappearing. The last thing to go was the frame of the mirror. And as with all of the things that went before it, the four sides disappeared into the vortex and then there was a sonic boom.

A cosmic burp, as it were.

And that was how, in the last round of the Creator's war . . . Jim saved the world.

As Sissy's ears popped with twin bursts of pain, the enormous *boom!* that ripped through the basement shocked her stupid for a moment. But then that cleared and she opened her eyes and . . .

It was empty.

The whole basement was nothing but floor space, the concrete floor bare of even a covering of dust. Except for Jim.

He was a mile away, it seemed, slumped on his knees, one hand planted as if he could barely hold himself up.

"Jim!" She scrambled to her feet. "Jim . . ."

He held his free arm out to her, and when she got to him, she didn't know who was holding on harder.

"You saved me," he said into her hair. "You saved me."

"No, I—"

"It was you, all you. I saw you and you were talking to me and . . ." Like there were too many words stuck in his throat, too many things to say, he just kissed her deeply, and—

"Holy shit!"

Both of them jerked back and looked over at Eddie and Adrian. Ad was getting to his feet slowly, both hands out like he expected to have to catch himself from falling over at any moment.

"Holy . . . mother*fucker*."

He began to move his body all around, arms and legs going this way and that—and for a moment, she had no idea what he was doing. Then she realized . . . he was hitting the Running Man?

"Oh, my God, he's lost his mind," she whispered, thinking three exorcisms in as many days was a little bit much. Even by their standards.

"I'm cured! I'm cured!"

With a quick shift, Ad bolted across the floor, did some cartwheels, pulled some kung fu moves, looked like he was going to try a split—only to think better of that one.

"I can see!" He ran over to them, jabbing his own finger toward his now-clear eye. "I can see! It took what I took from Matthias—the injuries went with the Devina shit!"

"Oh, my God," Jim breathed. "That's . . . awesome!"

"I know, right? And you know what thiiiiiiiis meeeeeeans! Hellllllllo, ladies."

Sissy had to duck her head into Jim's pec as Ad's hips rolled up and back and then he broke away and ran around again.

"Unbelievable," Jim said with a laugh. "We win the war, and all he cares about is the fact that he gets his love life back."

Sissy tilted in her man's arms and looked over his head. "Your halo's gone."

"Really?" He patted at the airspace above his skull. "Guess this really is over."

"You did it."

"No, we did it. I was going to kill her, I really was . . . but all I could see was you. All I could hear was your voice. Without that? God only knows what would have happened."

Eddie came over and smiled. Then offered his palm to Jim. "Well done. I'm proud of you."

Jim grunted and got to his feet, taking her with him. And then he accepted what was offered. "I couldn't have done it alone."

"You got that right," Ad said as he cha-cha'd over, one hand on his flat belly, the other held up at a right angle. "But I gotta say . . . it ain't been no pleasure."

Ad didn't offer a palm. Instead, he grabbed Jim and hugged him hard. "But I wouldn't have wanted to do this with anyone else."

Sissy's eyes got watery as Jim clapped his friend on the back. "That's a two-way street, buddy."

As they separated, Ad cleared his throat like he was flushing the emotion out of himself. Then he pointed both his thumbs to his chest and said, "Who's got two thumbs and is about to be laid? *This guy.*"

Eddie rolled his eyes. "You know, we don't have to—"

Ad's stare got shrewd. "I can find you a redhead. You knooooow how much you like a good ginger."

Eddie's brows went up into his forehead and he gave the waistband of his jeans a tug. "I, ah . . ."

"Don't tell me you wouldn't want some if you could get it."

There was some shuffling. A little throat clearing. And then Eddie's libido apparently made up his mind. Glancing over at Jim, the angel said, "Well, here are the car keys. You guys okay to go home?"

"I think I can handle it," Jim said dryly.

"Good. That's good."

There was a long moment between the three men, as if there were too much to say even if they had all night to talk.

"Go," Jim whispered roughly. "Enjoy yourselves. You deserve it."

"Don't leave without saying good-bye," Ad said.

"You have my word."

And then the angels were gone, disappearing into thin air.

Jim put his arm around her waist, and the two of them fell into a stroll across the emptiness, their footfalls echoing all around. "You hungry?"

She had to laugh. "I don't know. I can't . . . everything is almost too much."

"I have an idea."

"And what might that be?" She craned her neck to look up at his face. "Something along the lines of what Adrian is so excited about?"

"Well, yeah." Her man blushed. "But, ah, something else first."

"Pizza."

"No. I was thinking . . . how 'bout you get on the back of my bike and we, ah, go riding?"

Sissy leaned into his strength and laughed. "That's a line from a Prince song, you know that?"

"Is it?"

"Yes. And my answer . . . is yes."

Over by the elevators, he pushed the *up* button, and she had to frown.

"What is it?" he asked.

"There was someone like me here, wasn't there. Someone sacrificed to protect her mirror."

"Yes, there was."

"I didn't see them."

"I took care of the remains as I came in. And I'm going to make sure that he's taken care of."

Part of her felt like she should help that process. The other half . . . she wasn't sure she could handle seeing what she herself had looked like.

But she wasn't a wimp. Damn it, she needed to help whoever it—

"Sissy." Jim took her hands and put them on his chest. "Let me deal with him, all right. You don't need to see that. Besides, I have to believe he's free now."

"Can you find that out for sure?"

"Yes, I promise. But we won the war so I'd imagine that anyone righteous goes to Heaven. It's the only thing that's fair."

"Just . . . find out for sure."

"I give you my word."

Sissy exhaled as the doors opened and the two of them stepped in together. There was a mirror mounted on the wall, encased in a stainless-steel frame. Leaning into the glass, she saw . . . no halo.

It truly was over.

"Will you stay with me?" she heard herself ask roughly. "Will you . . . I mean, I can't go to Heaven, right, and I don't want to be here alone."

As they began to rise, Jim turned her in his arms and stared down at her, brushing her hair back from her face.

"I love you," he said. "So where else would I be than with you for eternity?"

Putting her arms around his neck, she smiled and teared up at the same time. "That . . . sounds like Heaven to me."

Chapter Fifty

It was the fall that lasted forever.

At first, Devina thought she was stuck in a suck zone, but as the walls of her Well of Souls appeared on all sides of her, she realized she was actually descending into Hell on a dead drop.

This was going to hurt.

And she was right.

The impact was soul-shattering, the kind of thing that made her lose breath, sight, heartbeat . . . as well as the illusion of beauty that required her conscious support. But she didn't die. Even as all the pain receptors she had screamed in agony and her rotted flesh contorted and twisted against the onslaught, she was still "alive."

So when the flickering began high above her, she was able to witness it.

At first, she assumed that it was stars dancing in front of her eyes from a head injury, but then she realized . . . no.

It was a kind of shimmering snow.

Except . . . no.

It was her collection. Filtering down through the stagnant air of the well, all the pieces of metal she'd collected over the millennia drifted in a descent, as if they sought to stay with her even though she was in some kind of eternal prison now.

Sitting up, she held out her arms, ready to catch the beautiful shower as it rained—

None of the objects reached her.

From out of the viscous walls of the prison that was now her jail as well, the tortured hands of the damned reached out and retook whatever was theirs, claiming the objects, grabbing them back, reestablishing ownership.

Stealing from her.

That was when the loss of the war hit home. And the demon wept tears that became black diamonds that skipped and jumped on the ragged stone floor by her worktable.

She let the emotion have its way with her because she had no choice. She had lost her shot at domination. She had been cheated of an eternity that was rightfully hers. Her collection was gone. God only knew if she had any minions left to listen to her.

Cupping her skull in her hands of bone, she wept so hard she thought she would shatter all over again, just as her beloved mirror had.

But she did not.

Eventually, the heaving and the tears stopped, and she sniffled and tried to mop herself up—although that was hard to do with the raw bones of her arm.

Marshaling up some strength, she called on the illusion she had been relying on to make herself beautiful, thinking that at least that would cheer her up.

Nothing happened. Her flesh did not reknit and rekindle its color and warmth. Her luxurious brunette hair did not sprout from her bald skull. Her legs did not magically appear smooth and luscious.

She cried again at that point.

Except then the sound of something clattering next to her brought her head up. It was a shoe. It was . . . one of her sparkling—

The other half of the pair of Louboutins dropped right beside her.

Sniffling, she reached out and brought them close, wiping off black smudges from the creamy-colored crystals . . . all of which were in metal settings.

Proof positive that if you buy quality, it'll last through everything. Including the portal into Hell.

Looking them over, watching as the ambient light caught on those minute facets and reflected back to her, she prized them all the more because they were the last of her life up above, the final dredges of her precious collection. As it was now? All she had was that stained worktable of hers and this busted, rotting body.

She stretched out and put one on, then the other. The fact that they were a size too small worked well now that there was little to no meat on her feet.

As she turned her ankles this way and that, the shoes gleamed in spite of how ugly she was, the red soles still vibrant because she'd barely worn them.

But soon she lost interest in admiring them.

It turned out that therapist—who she was now convinced hadn't been a human female at all, but rather the Creator Himself—was right. The stilettos were just objects. And anything that had truly mattered was out of reach now: her work doing evil, her love for Jim, her freedom to roam where and when she wanted.

Just shoes.

The Creator had been trying to get her to see a truth she had learned too late.

The things? Were not the thing.

But come on, she was evil. What else was a girl to do?

Leaning her head back, she stared up, up, up . . . and wondered what Jim was doing. Probably celebrating with that Sissy.

God, she hated him; she really did.

Maybe someday, if she ever got out of this place . . . she could find herself a real man, someone who appreciated her for who and what she was. Someone who was sick and twisted, but had good traditional values, a nice bank account, and a sense of humor.

And could go for hours in the sack.

Probably nobody like that existed. But considering she had nothing else to do for . . . well, shit, maybe forever . . . she might as well live in fantasy.

Memories and her mind were all she had now.

Chapter
Fifty-one

The following afternoon . . .

Up in Heaven, Nigel rolled the tea cart over to the knoll by the walls of the Manse of Souls. Typically, the table was willed into being, but with naught to occupy himself, he wanted to do things more manually.

He was the one who flipped free the damask tablecloth from its careful folds, and he set the plates out, and the cups and saucers. He arranged the teapot and the caddies of sugar and cream and also the rounder that held the assortment of scones and biscuits.

All right, fine, he had conjured the edibles—but he was no baker.

Leaning down, Nigel lined up the silverware precisely along with the napkins. Adjusted things so they were perfect. Fiddled with the flowers—

"That for me?"

He hid a small smile as he turned around and saw Jim. "You are welcome to join us, savior."

The angel seemed awkward, as if he didn't know how to handle having done his job well. "You don't have to call me that anymore."

Nigel inhaled deeply. Straightened his white suit. And walked around the table.

Without preamble or artifice, he hugged Jim and said roughly, "I do believe we shall call you that forevermore."

Jim returned the embrace and they stayed there for a moment. Then they both stepped back. By that time, the other archangels had appeared with Tarquin—who bounded up to Jim and nearly knocked him down.

As the group spoke of victory and praise, Nigel stood on the periphery and witnessed the exchange of congratulations: Byron and Bertie threw their arms about the savior as much as their dog did, and even Colin joined in, the warrior archangel going so far as to pop a smile that reached his beautiful eyes.

Unable to bear the sight of that, Nigel glanced up to the parapet. There were seven flags waving in the breeze, Jim's final win laying claim to all the rounds, even the ones Devina had prevailed in. The colors were varied and looked as a rainbow up in the sky.

"—Nigel?"

"I'm terribly sorry," he said, shaking himself back into focus. "What was that?"

"Mind if I ask you something in private?" Jim repeated.

Nigel glanced over his table. The three archangels had sat down, Byron and Bertie chatting like songbirds in a spring tree, their innate energy boosted by the fact that the fear was gone, the stress was gone, and all that remained was the place and the job they loved best.

"There is no need," Nigel murmured. "Your answer is yes."

Jim's eyes closed and he weaved in his boots.

"You okay, mate?" Colin asked.

The savior nodded and rubbed his face. Then he looked at Nigel. "You sure?"

"Do you think I would do aught to jeopardize the souls of the righteous?"

"Okay, then. Thank you."

"Not my doing, but your own." Then he relented. "But I am . . . so happy for you. So very happy for you both."

"Thanks." Jim hesitated. "One last thing . . . the souls like Sissy? The innocents who've been slaughtered over the centuries by Devina to protect that mirror of hers—"

"They have joined the righteous herein. The Creator saw to it immediately after Devina was banished to her Well of Souls."

"So that's where she is."

"And that is where she shall stay."

"Good deal. That's . . . good."

The savior left a moment later, and Nigel stared at the spot where he had stood. There was so much to be grateful for, so much to rejoice in . . . and yet he was sad to the point of despair.

"If you will excuse me," he said without meeting anyone in the eye. "I shall retire to my quarters."

Byron smiled. "But of course. There is much to recover from."

Bertie nodded as he slipped Tarquin a bit of a biscuit. "By all means, we shall watch o'er it all for you."

Nigel nodded and turned away. There was no reason to wait for any response from Colin, even though the archangel was the only one he truly cared about having one from.

As he made his way across the grass, he thought of the humans down below, living, dying, falling in love, getting their hearts broken. They were stronger than he had ever known, he realized— for all these millennia he had wrongly pitied them their mortal coil.

Now he viewed them as triumphant.

They had to not just fear loss, but live through the reality of it . . . and the victory that had transpired was not going to change that. With evil gone out of the world, they still had death to contend with, and how he respected them for their resilience.

When he reached his tent, he pulled back the flap and stepped inside to the luxury he had once found so intrinsic to his well-being. Now, it was all simply trappings of a colorful sort.

His eyes went over to the chaise longue where he had done his terrible act, and although he hated the thing, he'd kept it for a reason. The reminder of his arrogance and his faulty thinking was necessary to—

"Do you know what I am?"

Nigel wheeled around. Colin was standing just inside the tent, his eyes remote, his body filling the entrance.

"I-I-I . . ." Nigel required a moment to contend with his surprise. "I'm sorry, whatever do you mean?"

Colin entered and did a little turn, holding his strong arms out from his body. "Do you know what I am?"

You are the love of my existence, Nigel thought.

"You are Colin," he said instead.

The other archangel made a non-committal sound in his throat—such that there was no telling whether the inquiry had been answered correctly. "There is a saying, down upon the earth about one such as myself. I'm certain you have heard of it?"

"I'm afraid I am not a mind reader." Nigel touched his own head. "This does not work as well as it used to."

Colin came a little closer, and closer still. And then he did the most miraculous thing. He reached out and touched Nigel's face, brushing down his cheek. "The saying that is so often tossed about among the souls down below is . . . 'To err is human, to forgive is divine.'"

Nigel's heart began to pound. And then his head became dizzy. "Yes, yes, I have heard this."

Please do not break my heart, he thought. Even though I broke yours.

"And what am I," Colin prompted.

"You are . . ." Tears made things go wavy. "You are an archangel. You are God's favored warrior, protector of Heaven and earth. You are . . ."

He couldn't get the last word out. So Colin finished for him. "I am divine." Colin leaned in and kissed him. "I am divine. And I forgive you."

Nigel was not gallant at all as he threw himself into his lover's arms. He knew not to question the gift of this reunion. He did not care what conclusions Colin had wrestled over and come to terms with. He didn't dwell on what precise realization had changed everything.

In the past, he would have insisted on knowing the particulars.

Now? He took what he was offered and held on for dear life.

There were other human sayings that came to mind, ones involving gifts and horses and mouths, even one involving "happily" and "ever" and "after."

But as he eased back in Colin's arms, he went with the most powerful human saying of them all.

"I love you," he said softly. "I love you . . . forever."

As Adrian let himself into the back of the old house, he had about thirty-five thousand calories of Dunkin' Donuts between the three bags and the box of twenty-four assorted that he'd just bought. It was around four in the afternoon, and even though some might have considered the load breakfast material only, he was far less judgmental—and because he was a good guy, he'd even tested the lot for poison, eating two jellies and a chocolate-covered on the way home. Talk about whetting the appetite. He was so looking forward to noshing a dozen more, drinking his coffee, and so then crashing with Eddie to recover from the night before.

"You got my java?" he said over his shoulder.

Eddie looked at him stupidly for a second. And then got with the program. "Yeah, um . . . yeah. Yeah, I do."

Yup, Eddie had had his brains fucked out.

Ad smiled and headed right for the table. They'd done a trio of women throughout the course of the evening—or had it been four? It was the good ol' days back again—made all the more intense because of the almost-lost-it's that had happened.

Now? For once in their immortal lives, he and his buddy were going to take a vacay. Maybe head somewhere warm, where the ladies wore thongs and nothing else, the beer was cold, and the fishing was spectacular—

The sound of something scratching at the back door brought his head around. Eddie opened things back up and the little scruffy dog that limped in was a welcome sight.

Dog had disappeared during this last round.

But now the little guy had returned, running in circles around Eddie's ankles, jumping up into Ad's lap.

"Hey, you wanna share?" Ad asked. When he got a bark in return, he popped the top of the box and hunted around for something that didn't have nuts. Although considering that Dog was not actually a dog, it probably didn't matter—

"What's that smell?" he said, recoiling.

And that was when he saw the smoke rising from the surface of the table. Dog had jumped up and out of his lap and was putting a paw down . . . under which a pattern was burning.

Ad slumped in his chair. "No. Uh-uh. No way. We need a break—"

"Oh, fuck me," Eddie breathed.

When Dog finished with his little picture, the "animal" shuffled back and barked twice. Then planted his paw down again like he was pointing.

Ad leaned over and felt all the blood leave his head. "No. Anyone but him."

"Where is he?" Eddie asked. "I thought he was in Purgatory—"

Dog cut that off with a bark.

"Well, shit," Ad said, putting the lid on the box down. "No doughnuts for you."

Crossing his arms over his chest, he pouted and didn't give a fuck if that made him an asshole.

"Please," Eddie implored. "Not Lassiter. Anybody but Lassiter—he could be anywhere on the planet, doing anything."

Dog just leveled his eyes at the two of them.

"Can we take the weekend off, at least?" Ad muttered.

"As opposed to what?" Jim said from the doorway.

As the savior came into the room, he was freshly showered and for once didn't have massive black circles under his eyes. In fact, he actually looked about a quarter of a century younger than he had the night before—but that was what twelve hours of good loving could do for a guy.

Ad should know.

Dog leaped off the table and into Jim's arms, tail going a mile a minute, tongue licking, looking every bit the canine showing adoration. And Jim returned the shit, ducking his head, talking softly, petting.

When Jim put him down, the two stared at each other for the longest time, and then Dog let out a soft whine . . . before turning around and heading for the door as if he'd said a difficult good-bye.

On his way past, the SOB glanced at him and Eddie as if to say, Chop, chop, boys . . . go get me that fool I just burned into the table.

With Dog gone, Ad traced the face. The lines that had been made were still hot.

"Who is that?" Jim asked.

"A nightmare," Ad muttered.

"Our next assignment," Eddie cut in.

"That fast? Really? Don't you get some vacation or shit?"

Ad nodded to the box he'd closed. "We get doughnuts. Yay."

There was a moment of silence. And then Eddie said softly, "You're leaving, aren't you."

Ad looked up in time to see Jim's eyes go to the window over the sink. He seemed to be picturing things as he stared out there, things that were not actually in the backyard.

"It was all about her to begin with," the guy said. "And I don't mean Sissy."

"Yeah." Eddie nodded. "I know, but what about—"

"All taken care of." The savior's stare swung around to the two of them, and he was quiet for a time. Then he said, "You know, when this whole thing started, I didn't want the pair of you involved. I'd always been a solo operator"—he glanced at Ad—"and your singing really fucking got on my nerves."

"Annnnd my job is done," he replied with a nod.

"But you know, when we were trying to get the evil out of Sissy, and I couldn't do it alone . . . you two were there. If you hadn't been? I'd have lost her. You two . . . saved her with me."

Okay, now Ad was the one ducking his eyes. It was just too much, and he did *not* do misty. He just . . . did. Not. Do—

Fuck, his eyes were watering.

Jim was still talking, mentioning things like sacrifice and putting the common good first, all of which in his opinion, Eddie and Ad had apparently done.

Oh, man, the motherfucker had to stop. He really had—

Ad went into one of the bags and took out some paper napkins—and at least Eddie had to snag one to mop up as well, so he didn't feel like he was the only pussy in the room.

"So thank you," Jim said roughly. "I owe you my life."

Ad burst up from the table and enjoyed the total lack of pain that came with the sharp movement. "Enough with the talk. You keep this up and I'll end up growing a set of ovaries or some shit."

Ad hugged Jim hard, so hard. And then stepped back so Eddie could do the same.

"Hey, what's going on?" Sissy said as she came in. "Everything okay?"

Ad stared down at the woman. She was glowing from head to foot even though she was dressed in the simple clothes he'd gotten her from Target. She was just . . . such a beauty with her no-makeup and her straight, no-fuss hair.

"It's time to say good-bye, Sis," he heard himself say.

"You're going somewhere?"

No, he thought sadly. You are.

Chapter Fifty-two

For some strange reason, watching Sissy embrace each of the angels was hard.

Then again, Jim didn't like to see his woman get teary, and it was clear she really loved the guys, even though she hadn't known them all that long. War, however, had a way of bonding people tight and quick.

"Will I ever see you again?" she asked as she took one of the napkins that Ad offered her.

"I don't know. Maybe," Ad murmured as she patted her eyes.

"Never say never," Eddie said with a sad smile.

There was a long pause, and Jim knew he had to get the fuck out of here before he lost it, too. "Come on," he said roughly as he tugged on her arm.

"Where are we going?"

"Just . . . come with me."

He led her out toward the front of the house, pausing only to offer one last wave at Eddie and Adrian as they stood in that kitchen with all those doughnuts.

"Jim? I'm kind of freaking out here."

As they emerged into the foyer, the grandfather clock started to chime, and he closed his eyes. Don't count . . . it doesn't matter . . . don't count . . .

One, two, three . . .

"Jim, are you okay?"

. . . four, five, six . . .

"Jim?"

. . . seven, eight, nine . . .

"Okay, it's official," she said. "I'm totally freaking out."

He held up his forefinger.

. . . ten, eleven . . .

"Jim . . . ?"

. . . twelve.

After a moment of nothing but pure, beautiful silence, he popped his eyes back open and saw only her. "Oh, thank God."

"What?"

"I'll tell you later."

Drawing her out in the warm spring sunlight, he took her over to the steps and sat her down, exactly where they'd been before. God, he thought, what a long distance they'd traveled, just so they could be here side by side again.

"Jim?"

"You remember when we went by your house last night on my bike?"

She nodded, and brushed her hair back. Her eyes were a complicated mix of sadness and peace. "Yes. And thank you for that. Did I tell you thank you?"

"Yeah, you did."

"It was good to see my family sleeping so soundly, you know? It gives me a little hope that maybe as time passes—"

"I want you to spend eternity with me."

The smile he got in return was wide and instantaneous. "Are you asking me to marry you in the immortal sense? Because if you are, my answer is yes." She leaned in and kissed him on the lips once. Twice. "Very much yes."

"Even if it means . . . maybe you don't see your family?"

"You mean, like, go out west with you?" Sissy took a deep breath. "Well, the truth is, I can't really see them now, can I. It's not like I can . . . be with them. In fact, it's almost more painful to stick around Caldwell. So yes, even though I can't believe I'm saying this . . . yes, I think I would like to get out of town."

"You sure?"

She fell silent for a while. Then looked at him. "I can get through anything as long as I'm with you."

For a long moment, he memorized her face, from the way the afternoon light fell across her forehead and her cheeks, to the beauty of her blue stare, to the curve of the mouth he had kissed for hours.

"Okay," he murmured. "Close your eyes and hold my hand. . . ."

A big spin, and a second later he said to her, "Now open them up."

Her lids slowly rose and she recoiled as if the fact that the landscape had completely changed was a shocker. "Where are . . . is that a *castle?*"

"Yeah, it is. Come on."

He pulled her to her feet and led her across the bright green grass of Heaven, steadying her as she craned her neck to look up at the brilliant blue sky.

"This is the most beautiful place I've ever seen."

Funny, he hadn't really noticed that . . . until he'd come here with her.

They came to a stop at the moat that ran all around the ancient fortification, its water so clear that you could see the koi fish that lolled around, their butterfly fins waving back and forth in the invisible currents.

There was a resounding *ker-chuck* up above and then the rattling of great chain links going through a pulley system.

The bridge across the water came down slowly, as if it were giving them time to reconsider. And he figured he should let her know what they were about to do—except when he glanced over at her, she had tears rolling down her cheeks.

"This is Heaven, isn't it," she choked out.

"Yes. Once we cross over . . . there's no going back. You'll have to wait for your family to come to you."

She brushed her hands over her cheeks. "But I thought I wasn't allowed."

"Nigel said you were welcome. You're pure now—we got the evil out of you. Out of me, too."

Sissy started to laugh through the crying. "Are you serious? Are you . . ."

"Yeah." He smiled down at her. "So what do you say? You want to take the plunge with me?"

She looked up at him. "I love you."

"I'll take that as a 'yes.'" As the bridge landed with a thunk of heavy weight, he indicated the way over with a gallant hand. "Ladies first."

Sissy hesitated for a moment. And then all but exploded in laughter and dance, her spirit soaring as she skipped across the ancient, well-worn planks with such joy, she lit him up from the inside, too.

Jim shook his head and had to smile as he took his first step. His second. A third.

This was so not how he had pictured any of it ending, but, man, he'd take this over whatever he could have dreamed up.

Walking steadily a couple of yards behind his woman, he discovered that the farther you went across the bridge, the farther the destination seemed to become, like a funhouse kind of distortion was at work. Except all of a sudden, he looked back and the green grass and the blue sky and the trees seemed a hundred miles away.

Turning around, he—

Stopped dead.

Sissy had slowed . . . and then halted, too, some kind of lighted fog threatening to eclipse her. With a sudden burst of sheer terror, Jim bolted over the planks to catch up. . . .

Except she wasn't in any danger.

And in fact, she'd stopped because there was a figure standing in the swirling, thick air in front of her.

A woman.

And Jim knew exactly . . . who . . . it . . . was.

Shutting his eyes, he sagged in his own skin, his bones all but caving in. When he opened his lids again and discovered that the presence was still there, he felt as though he couldn't walk. And yet he did.

He had to slap his palm over his mouth to keep himself from weeping.

Finally, he, too, was in front of the figure.

Dropping his hand, he said in a choked breath, "*Momma.*"

His mother was not crying. She was smiling bright as the sun that he and Sissy had left behind . . . she was smiling, and she was whole and healthy, her body repaired, her hair gleaming, her eyes sparkling.

"I've been waiting for you, Jimmy." With that, she wrapped her arms around him and held him tight, even though his was the bigger body. "Oh, son . . . it's all right. You're okay . . . everything is okay."

He totally. Fucking. Lost. It.

But she held him up off the ground, and Sissy was there as well, stroking his back, supporting him.

And then the most miraculous thing happened.

All at once, all the suffering was gone, all the sadness and the pain was taken from him, and he became light and buoyant as the mist around them.

Easing back, he touched his mother's face, her shoulders, her hands . . . just to make sure she was real. And she was.

Then he turned to Sissy and pulled her in against him. "Ah, Momma, this is my Sissy."

"Hi," Sissy said offering her hand. "I'm so—"

His mother was just the same as she always had been, pulling Sissy in close and hugging her. "I know you're separated from your kin, but when you realize this is waiting for them? It makes the distance so much easier to bear."

For the first time in about thirty years, Jim took a deep, easing breath.

"Come on, you two," his mom said, falling in on his other side. "Let's get you settled. You're going to *love* it here."

At his mom's urging, he and Sissy walked forward into the mist. And as they went along, he glanced over at his woman, giving her a squeeze before kissing her on the mouth—and when she smiled back at him?

Well, now, as they said back home, that was just proof that God truly existed.

"It's all about love," his momma was saying. "No matter what side you're on, it's all about love."

Amen, he thought as he entered Heaven with the two people who mattered most to him.

Amen to that.

Do you love fiction with a supernatural twist?

Want the chance to hear news about your favourite authors (and the chance to win free books)?

Keri Arthur
Kristen Callihan
P.C. Cast
Christine Feehan
Jacquelyn Frank
Larissa Ione
Darynda Jones
Sherrilyn Kenyon
Jayne Ann Krentz and Jayne Castle
Lucy March
Martin Millar
Tim O'Rourke
Lindsey Piper
Christopher Rice
J.R. Ward
Laura Wright

Then visit the Piatkus website and blog
www.piatkus.co.uk | www.piatkusbooks.net

And follow us on Facebook and Twitter
www.facebook.com/piatkusfiction | www.twitter.com/piatkusbooks

piatkus